Crown of the World

Book I
Knight of the Temple

Crown
of the
World

Book I:
Knight of the Temple

Nathan Sadasivan

Arx Publishing
Merchantville, New Jersey

Arx Publishing
Merchantville, New Jersey

First Edition

ISBN: 978-1-889758-92-3

Library of Congress Cataloging-in-Publication Data

Sadasivan, Nathan, 1989-
  Crown of the world / Nathan Sadasivan. -- 1st ed.
     p. cm. -- (Knight of the temple ; bk. 1)
  ISBN 978-1-889758-92-3
  1. Knights and knighthood--Fiction. 2. Jerusalem--History--
Siege, 70 A.D.--Fiction. 3. Sieges--Fiction. I. Title.
  PS3619.A325C76 2009
  813'.6--dc22
                                        2009020279

To my mother, to whom I owe everything,
and to Our Lord, to Whom I owe my mother.

☩ ☩ ☩

To Hannah DeRocher and Ben Idoni, who encouraged and criticized Godfrey and Malik even as they came into existence, many thanks. To Andrew Woodworth, for his help ordering the book, thanks as well. And finally, thanks to Meghan Cheyne for her beautiful map of the Land Beyond the Sea.

Non nobis, Domine, non nobis, sed tuo nomini da gloriam.
[Not to us, Lord, not to us, but to your name give glory.]
Psalm 115, Motto of the Knights Templar

*"...and they plaited a crown of thorns, and put it on His head,
and arrayed him in a purple robe; and they came to him
and said, "Hail, King of the Jews!"*
—The Gospel of St. John, 19:2–3

*"I will not wear a crown of gold where
my Master wore a Crown of Thorns..."*
—attributed to Godfrey de Bouillion,
upon being offered the Crown of Jerusalem

Author's Note

This is a story of the Outremer—the Land Beyond the Sea—which men called the Kingdom of Jerusalem. It is a tale of its fading years, and of the men who lived and died around it. There are two in particular who stand at the center of the tale: one Godfrey de Montferrat and the other Malik al-Harawi.

But there are many others besides: a princess and a great lady, a king and a king's son, a sultan and an assassin, a scholar and a wanderer, one who became a famous knight and one who became a famous lover. And there are the countless men and women, nobles and commons, Christian and Muslim, false and true, good and bad, whose lives were all swept up in the maelstrom of events that culminated in the Fall of Jerusalem.

The first book, Knight of the Temple, *tells the story of Godfrey de Montferrat.*

Prologue

Spring, AD 1164

Asharp wind blew through the desert, sending sand spinning into the air. It sifted through flat and unchanging lands where sand was all that could be seen for miles around. The wind blew on towards the Red Sea, towards Jerusalem where the Knights of the Temple were training, and towards Damascus with its rich palaces and golden domes. Beyond lay distant Cathay, with its strange gardens and twisted spires, protected by its Great Wall from the savage Tatars that roamed the wastes of Mongolia.

As the sand settled down in the wind's wake, two horsemen came riding along a dusty path that cut through the desert. Both the horses and the riders were coated in dust from long travel, but the red crosses on their long white tunics were clearly visible. Every so often they cast curious, anxious glances about them—the land of Egypt was new and strange to them.

"Jacques," said one of the travelers, "I think we've gone too far to the south."

Jacques de Maille gave a tug on the reins and brought his palfrey to a halt. He considered, scratching his head and rubbing dust out of his yellow hair and beard. A few paces ahead of him the other horseman came to a halt and glanced back at him.

"We should have found Amalric's camp by midday, and now it's close on dusk," continued the first speaker. Godfrey de Montferrat was shorter and scrawnier than his companion. Moreover—and this was unusual among Templars—Godfrey was dark-skinned and swarthy of complexion. He was what the Franks of Jerusalem called a *poulain*: his father was a Christian, come from Italy on Crusade, who had married an Arabic woman in Jerusalem. Where Jacques's eyes were a bright blue, Godfrey's were brown and quiet.

"Yes," said Jacques slowly. "This path leads too far to the south."

"I think it will take us to Cairo, if we follow it far enough," said Godfrey.

1

His companion grunted ruefully. "Well," he said, "I guess there's nothing for it but to go back."

"Or," said Godfrey, "we could leave the path and cut north. We're close to the Nile floodplain, so there'll be plenty of streams and oases on the way. The camp can't be more than a day's journey to the north."

Jacques considered again, and then gave a nod. "I don't want to spend one day more than I have to in this stinking sandpit. We'll cut north."

The two Templars turned their horses from the path and set them at a trot across the sea of sand. To their left the sun was sinking below the horizon, and the cool of an Egyptian night was settling over them. Godfrey glanced across at his comrade and old friend.

"Do you really hate Egypt so much? You think it's just a stinking sandpit?"

Jacques looked surprised at the question. "Yes. I do."

"Why?"

Jacques shrugged. "There's nothing but sand and rocks and ruins, and I doubt that the cities will be much better. I want to get back to Jerusalem." He glanced at Godfrey for a moment, and added in a low voice, "And sometimes I want to get back to Italy."

Godfrey smiled. "I can see that. For myself...for myself, my head is too full of stories. Egypt is where the adventure is. This is where the giants and the genii still lurk behind the corners. A place where a hero can prove himself."

Jacques nodded carelessly. "Still looking to be a hero, Godfrey? Just like the old days?"

A shadow passed over Godfrey's face. "In the old days, you wanted to be a hero too," he sighed.

"It's only been a year," said Jacques.

"Yes," agreed Godfrey. "But it's been a long year."

☩ ☩ ☩

Soon after the two Templars left the path, a larger column of horsemen came riding along the other way, not more than thirty in number. The horsemen were Arabic, coming from Cairo, whither they had borne a message to the vizier. At their head was a young man, an Arab, with a neatly trimmed dark goatee and a turban on his head. He rode with the easy air of one who commands men. A young warrior, around the same age as the captain, was speaking carelessly to him.

"I don't like this land, Yusef," he muttered. "Nothing like Damascus.

Here there's too much...*sand.*"

Yusef, the leader, nodded quietly. His expression was serious—as it always was.

"I want to get back to Damascus as much as you, Malik," he said. "But it won't be long now. The war's almost over."

Since the past autumn, Egypt had been a marching ground for Arabic and Frankish armies. The Christian king of Jerusalem, Amalric, had squabbled with the Egyptians and launched an invasion of the Nile floodplain. The Egyptians called for help from their fellow Muslims, and the sultan of Damascus sent an army to stop Amalric. For months the Christian and Saracen armies had maneuvered and counter-marched, each grasping for position. Both were thoroughly sick of it now, as spring was fast turning into summer.

"You say the war is almost over," replied Malik, "but that's what they've said ever since winter."

Yusef laughed, but Malik only scowled. Yusef knew what it was that made Malik uneasy. Both Frankish and Saracen tradition made Egypt a land of myth; a land where fantastic creatures filled the land, sea, and air. Genii, demons, leviathans, any of these might lurk in the holes or the riverbeds or the trees. Creatures that normally belonged in the emerald depths of the sea walked before men's eyes in Egypt.

Yusef shook his head. "You're afraid, I think."

Malik bristled. "I do not fear this place."

Yusef smiled. "Well then, neither do I."

Malik opened his mouth to respond, but he stopped suddenly, his eyes narrowing.

"What is it?" asked Yusef, after a pause.

"Up there," said Malik, "do you see? There are hoofprints leading off the path to the north. Recent ones too—the wind died down less than half an hour ago. Someone was riding our way...but here they turned off the path and rode north. Maybe they heard us coming and tried to get out of the way."

"It could be," said Yusef. "But I doubt it. We need to find Shirkuh's camp—no time to go chasing shadows."

Malik frowned. "I don't like it. Let me ride after them a few miles. It's nearly sundown, and we'll be setting up camp before long. I'll find you there."

Yusef sighed and followed the hoofprints with his eyes as far as he could. "Follow the tracks, Malik, but no more than five miles. Then turn back and find the camp."

Smiling, Malik threw a salute. He turned his horse and rode off across the sands. Behind him, Yusef ordered his men to look for a place to camp.

Malik rode northeast, careless and glad to be out on his own for a few short hours. He had no fear of what he might encounter. He was a swordsman of no little talent, and he knew it. A few weeks ago there had been a small skirmish with a Frankish scouting party, and Malik had slain two Hospitallers. He could fight. And he could kill if he had to. Possessed with the cocksureness of a young warrior certain that he could slay whatever he encountered or escape unharmed, Malik lost sight of the camp and soon was gone in the endless sea of sand.

The sun set in the far west, plunging the desert into blackness.

✠ ✠ ✠

Half an hour past midnight, the two knights Templar stopped by a little oasis close to the Nile. Jacques scrambled down from his horse, glancing up at Godfrey.

"Let's camp here," he said. "We'll say the Office and then sleep. We've still got a ways to go before we reach the Frankish camp. We'll find it tomorrow."

Godfrey de Montferrat gazed longingly at the water just ahead of them, and nodded. He dismounted and tied his palfrey to a tree. The two were in the shadow of a hill, with a small patch of grass and a little stream running around the other side. And they were on their own, in the middle of the Egyptian desert.

But that concern was secondary compared to the one that had been on Godfrey's mind for the past hour. He pulled out his waterskin, dumped out the last drops of turgid liquid, and refilled it with water from the stream. It tasted sweeter than wine. The two Templars led their horses to the stream and let them drink their fill.

The sky was dark, but clear; and the light of moon and star shone brightly on the Templars as they tied up their horses.

Godfrey sat down and breathed a sigh of relief, glad to be done riding for the day.

"Come on, Godfrey," said Jacques, "let's say the Office and get to sleep."

Reluctantly, Godfrey de Montferrat stumbled over and knelt on the sands next to his friend and fellow Templar. His eyes flickered up to the clear night sky and the stars, then he closed them and began to pray.

As the two Templars prayed, they didn't notice the dark Arabian horse trot up the dune overlooking them. Malik looked down on the two crusaders, surprised but silent. He considered for a moment that he could shout a challenge and fight them both now—he had no fear of fighting two foes at once. But he reconsidered; if he brought Yusef and the others, they might be able to take one of the Templars prisoner.

Malik turned his horse and cantered off into the night.

✠ ✠ ✠

Yusef and his men had just finished setting up camp when Malik's black charger galloped into their midst.

"Yusef! There are some Templars camped a few miles from here. If we move quickly we can capture them!"

All turned to stare up at Malik, sitting erect on the black steed. Yusef hesitated for a moment.

"How many, Malik?"

"Two."

Yusef glanced around at his men.

"It is a good plan," he said. "Soldiers, we mount!"

Reluctantly the soldiers, who had been hoping for a good night's sleep, began strapping weapons on. With scimitars, bows, and lances in hand they scrambled onto their light, fast-moving little horses. Malik strapped his scimitar to his side and grabbed a long lance. The column of Arabic horses galloped off, leaving the empty sand behind them.

✠ ✠ ✠

At the back of Godfrey de Montferrat's mind, he could sense something out of the ordinary. He tried to focus on his prayers, but something was tickling the edge of his senses. His eyes were shut, but he could feel it and hear it. He turned his mind away from prayer for a second, and listened intently. The sounds became distinct: dozens of hoofbeats coming near them.

Jacques had heard it too. He leapt to his feet, shouting to Godfrey as he strapped his sword on. Godfrey stumbled to his feet and reached down to draw his sword. Jacques grabbed his shoulder with a heavy fist.

"Put up your sword," he said in an urgent voice. "Ride!"

Godfrey obeyed and ran for his palfrey, wildly ripping loose the rope with which he had tied it.

Three horses came flying over the top of the hill above them, their riders flailing wildly with their scimitars even while in the air. More lancers spurred around the hill, the long metal-tipped lances held in the crook of their arms. Godfrey and Jacques scrambled into their saddles.

"Split up! Head northeast!" shouted Jacques as he spurred his horse forward. "Look for the camp—I'll meet you there." Jacques's palfrey shot out across the sand, carrying its white-clad load with it.

Sweat slicked Godfrey's palms underneath his gloves as he took a firm hold on the reins. He glanced back at the Saracens spurring towards him.

"Hyah!" he shouted as he dug his spurs in. His horse also sped out into the night. The wind whipped Godfrey's face and hair as his horse picked up speed.

✠ ✠ ✠

Malik cursed angrily as the two palfreys sped away. "What happened? We were supposed to trap them!"

"Mehmed was too slow!" shouted someone.

"Where's Mehmed now? I'm going to—"

"Stop squabbling," shouted Yusef. "Keep after them!"

Malik repositioned his lance and rode swiftly after the Templars, followed by a dozen of the Kurdish lancers.

✠ ✠ ✠

Godfrey spurred his horse again to pick up speed. He followed the little stream eastward, looking for any cover it might afford or hiding place it might provide. Far behind him he could hear shouting. The Saracens were still after him, though he had a good lead. If only there were some cover…

One of the riders was gaining on him. Godfrey hazarded a glance back. It was a tall rider with a lance, helmetless, with long dark hair blowing in the wind. Godfrey kept a tight hold on the reins. Light Arabian chargers could outrun a palfrey like his at a short distance, but they couldn't match his mount's endurance. If Godfrey kept ahead long enough, he might escape.

✠ ✠ ✠

Jacques had vanished somewhere to the north. Eventually, most of the Saracen riders dropped off from the chase and returned to the little hill where Yusef waited. Only Malik al-Harawi kept on going. Malik was gaining on Godfrey, and was not about to let him go. The other Saracens did not worry about Malik—rather, they pitied the poor Templar who had to face their young blademaster alone.

Godfrey knew that his palfrey was tiring and couldn't keep the chase up much longer. He looked ahead and saw another stream flowing down from a little wooded berm. He looked behind and saw that only one Saracen still followed him.

As his horse approached the berm, Godfrey pulled on the reins and turned around to face the Arab. He drew his sword, and sat up in the saddle, ready to strike. His shield and helmet had been left behind when the Arabs had attacked, but he could do without them.

As Malik drew within ten feet of the crusader, he made a swift, unexpected, and unorthodox maneuver. He veered sharply to the right, and, letting go of the reins, took the lance in both hands. Then he struck Godfrey with the lance's butt. Godfrey was knocked from the saddle to the sand, his sword falling out of reach. His horse panicked and bolted.

Godfrey rolled over in the dirt, weaponless, and looked up to see the black Arabian charger riding down on him, the tall rider bringing his lance to bear. Godfrey rolled aside, just escaping a trampling. He scrambled to his feet and began searching frantically for his sword.

Malik wheeled his horse around and charged again. Godfrey felt through the dirt and grass desperately as the rider thundered towards him. The Saracen was about to ride him down. Still swordless, Godfrey leaped to the side, and as the horse rode by, he caught the Arab's stirrup. The horse galloped on, with Godfrey hanging on desperately. For a second he was airborne. Then he caught on to the back of the saddle and grabbed Malik from behind.

The horse ran wild as the Saracen and the crusader wrestled. Finally, Malik brought the butt of his lance into Godfrey's stomach, sending the young Templar toppling into the sand.

Godfrey lay dazed as Malik once again wheeled his horse around and thundered towards him. He felt around—and gripped the hilt of his sword. Godfrey stood up as the Arabian steed charged him. The Arab brought his lance to bear on Godfrey but just as he stabbed, Godfrey sidestepped the lance and struck, splitting it in two. The horse sped on, unable to stop its momentum.

Malik dropped the shattered lance and drew a long, sharp scimitar as his horse slowed and turned back towards Godfrey. Once again the Saracen charged at a gallop.

Godfrey stepped back as the horse thundered past him. The rider struck out with the scimitar, and Godfrey parried. Then he struck at the horse, tearing its neck open. The horse reared up, thrashing in its death agony as blood spurted from the wound. The Saracen was thrown from its back.

Malik avoided his steed and landed on all fours, his scimitar still in hand. His horse stopped writhing and collapsed on the sand, dead. Godfrey stood on the other side of the dead animal, gripping his sword tightly, his face dirty and bruised.

"You fight well, Templar," said Malik in poor Frankish.

Godfrey said nothing, but stepped over the horse's body and struck quickly, a high blow, with both hands gripping the hilt.

The moonlight reflected off the Arab scimitar and the Frankish sword as the two blades crossed. They fought across the sand and the sound of their blades clashing echoed through the desert night. Godfrey fought dutifully and strongly, but he could not match Malik's speed and grace. Malik spun and slashed, ducked and wove, his dark robes whirling about. Godfrey gave ground, step by step.

Malik seized the broken butt of his lance in his left hand, using it as a second weapon. He drove Godfrey back, up the berm, until they fought on the steep edge, with the stream running fifteen feet below them.

With a mighty blow of the lance-butt, Malik knocked Godfrey off the edge of the berm, into the stream. Godfrey landed on his hands and knees in the shallow stream, bloody and battered.

Malik leapt down after him and raised his scimitar. Godfrey forced himself to move. He rolled over and kicked up, smashing Malik's knees. Malik stumbled back and dropped the lance-butt. Godfrey struggled up, finding his balance on the slippery stones in the streambed.

Then Godfrey rushed the Arab, raining down blows on him. Malik parried each one easily with his scimitar, but was borne backwards by the very force of Godfrey's attack until he found himself trapped against the berm.

At that moment Godfrey brought his sword down in a two-handed blow. Malik raised his scimitar to parry, and it snapped. The broken hilt fell from the Arab's hand. Malik looked around, but he was caught between the hill and the crusader. Godfrey swung round to deal the killing blow, but even as he did, he slowed and then stopped himself, a bewildered look on his face.

For a second they stared at each other in silence.

"Well, Frank," said Malik proudly, "you have beaten me. Kill me."

Godfrey did not move. "God's beard," he said, "I can't kill an unarmed man."

Malik gave a hollow laugh. "Then you are at an impasse. I pity you your plight."

Godfrey de Montferrat stared at the Arab, bewildered, for, as he had remarked earlier that day, his head was too full of stories. Long ago he had taken to heart and head all the high-flung ideals of a knight; and particularly the stories of chivalry. He sought after the ideals of fortitude and courage, but also after the idea of mercy.

Fool that I am, he told himself, *I want to be Roland and Oliver at the same time.*

But this isn't how it's like in the stories! he thought desperately. *If I spare him, he will only fight against us another day…but I can't just cut him down like that! To spare him is folly, but to murder him wicked. So I will choose folly.*

Godfrey shook his head. "I can't take you prisoner. I've only got the one horse, and I don't know where she is."

"Your forebears had no objection to cutting down unarmed Muslims when they conquered Jerusalem," Malik sneered. "One cannot expect mercy from a Frank. Kill me."

Godfrey's anger flared up. "God's bones! Whatever Tancred and the maddened, starving army of crusaders did, Godfrey de Bouillion murdered no innocents when he took Jerusalem. He was a true knight, and so long as there are true knights left in Jerusalem, you and all enemies will have cause to shudder."

Malik did not reply. On the edge of his hearing, Godfrey sensed his palfrey approaching, returning to her master, having recovered her courage. Godfrey called her name, and she came running towards him.

"No," he said to Malik. "I'm not going to kill you. I'm going to let you go free."

He reached out his hand, and caught onto his horse's bridle. Keeping his eyes on the Arab, he pulled himself up into the saddle, sheathing his sword.

"Go in peace, Saracen. You are free to do what you will, even to take up arms against us again. But remember: a Christian spared your life this day."

Now it was Malik who stared at him, confused, even frightened. "What do you mean, Templar? You cannot do this!"

"Would you rather I opened your throat?"

Malik could say nothing. Godfrey smiled. "I must go now, Saracen."

"What is your name, Templar?" Malik blurted out.

"My name is Godfrey de Montferrat."

For a long moment, Malik stared up at Godfrey, his bewilderment etched on his face. Finally he spoke.

"You fought well, Godfrey de Montferrat. My name is Malik al-Harawi. You have my gratitude…and my admiration. You are the noblest Christian I have ever met. May you prosper, and perhaps we shall meet again."

"Perhaps," said Godfrey. "Hyah!" He dug his heels in, and his destrier took off, heading northeast until he vanished into the darkness.

Chapter 1

THE KNIGHT OF THE TEMPLE
Godfrey

Alone horseman trotted across the sea of sand, the sun beating down hard on his uncovered head. Godfrey de Montferrat rode on towards the rising sun.

Jacques had thought the Frankish camp lay to the northeast. But the camp was small compared to the desert—Godfrey could miss it by miles and never know it. He rode on across the dunes, consuming his water sparingly. The sun rose higher in the sky, and his palfrey slowed, tired both by the heat and by the previous night's wild ride.

Seeking to turn his thought from the heat and the exhaustion, Godfrey tried to lose himself in memory. As always, he thought first of Italy and the Piedmont where he had been raised.

Godfrey was still young, barely twenty-two years of age. He had been born in Jerusalem itself; born into the large clan of Montferrats, one of the richest and oldest families in Christian Europe, a family known for its crusaders. He had been named after Godfrey de Bouillion, one of the Lords of the West in the First Crusade.

When Godfrey was eight, his father, a younger son of House Montferrat, had sent him to be raised in the household of Godfrey's uncle William, who lived far across the sea in Italy. There Godfrey had been raised with his cousins Will, Conrad, Boniface, Adelaise, and Renier. Along with Will and Conrad he had been taught to ride and to fight like a knight, while his Uncle William had lured his brother-in-law, the churchman Otto of Freising, to Montferrat to educate the boys. So Godfrey had learned Latin and bits of Greek, read the Scriptures and the Fathers, been given a smattering of mathematics, and even read pieces of Peter the Venerable's translation of the Qur'an.

Above all, though, Otto of Freising had taught them the histories. The old man's passion was for stories and for histories. He had himself written a chronicle of the history of the world. Otto tried to impart all this love to his nephews. Will had yawned and daydreamed through it, more often than not, but Conrad and Godfrey had passionately absorbed everything Otto told them.

Indeed, as they grew older, Godfrey had turned more and more to history for comfort, for he was scrawny, clumsy, and ill-at-ease on horseback—poorly qualified to be a knight. So he consoled himself by trying to become as learned as old Otto the churchman. Even Conrad's fascination for study waned as he grew strong and handsome, while Godfrey remained weak but learned.

Scrawny or not, Godfrey had been expected to make a fine lord once William de Montferrat married him off to some nobleman's daughter. His uncle had just begun the search for a bride when Godfrey announced to the family that he would not marry…but instead he would go across the sea to Jerusalem and become a Knight of the Temple.

Ironic, thought Godfrey, *that after all I was the one who went off to become a knight, to fight in battles and defend the Holy City, while Conrad lives as a lordling in Montferrat.*

That decision of Godfrey's, however, was not one he wanted to think on now, with the sun beating upon his coat and mail, and the sweat rolling down his face. Thoughts about the past could distract him only so long. Now Godfrey tried to divert his attention from the heat by talking to his horse, by praying, and as a last resort by singing. He had a thin, broken singing voice, but there was no one for miles to hear, and he was desperate to take his mind off the heat.

For half an hour he sang: hymns, ballads of knights-errant, the bawdy marching songs sung by the soldiers, anything that came to mind. Finally, he heard a shout from somewhere behind him.

"God's bones, Godfrey, *will you stop singing*!?"

Godfrey tugged on the reins to stop his horse, and turned his head about to look behind him. Jacques de Maille came riding down the sand dune, calling to him as he rode. "I thought you learned long ago that you can't sing!"

Godfrey smiled in relief. "What else could I have done? I was miles away from humanity, completely lost. So I started singing, lest I go mad with silence."

"Yes," growled Jacques, "I heard singing a ways off, and I decided that only Godfrey de Montferrat has a voice that bad." Jacques's blond hair and bearded face were even more saturated with dust and sand than they had been the day before. Both Jacques and Godfrey sported scraggly beards, for the Templars were forbidden to shave their faces.

"Any of the Mussulmen catch up to you?" asked Godfrey.

Jacques shook his head. "They chased me a while, but they never stood a chance. You?"

Godfrey paused a moment, then shook his head. "No. I left them in the dust."

Jacques nodded. "Come on, we must be close to the Christian camp. If we keep north, we'll find it."

✢ ✚ ✢

As Godfrey and Jacques crested a little hill, they were accosted by a band of armed men. Two knights who had been waiting on the other side of the dune spurred their horses forward, and a group of Frankish men-at-arms and bowmen hiding in the brush emerged, the bowmen pulling arrows from their quivers, the men-at-arms reaching for their swords.

One of the knights, a tall man whose device was an argent hawk on a blue field, pulled to the lead.

"Who are you, and what business have you near Bilbeis?" asked the knight in a deep, growling voice muffled by his helmet.

Jacques rode forward a few paces, peering through the slit in the knight's helmet. Then he laughed. "Humphrey? Humphrey de Vinsauf? You're supposed to be in some God-forsaken northern province; Antioch, or Tripoli, or something like that."

The knight of the argent hawk stared at Jacques for a few moments. Then he took off his helmet and his face brightened with recognition. He roared in a still-gruff but more friendly voice.

"Jacques de Maille! God's hands, I didn't recognize you through all the dust! Templars all look alike to me, anyway."

Humphrey de Vinsauf was a young man, though he was older than Jacques and Godfrey; he looked around thirty. His brown hair fell sloppily across his grizzled face. He clapped Jacques on the shoulder, laughing.

"You should have entered the king's service, De Maille, or taken up with one of these lordlings. You could have had your own coat of arms. Make it a lot bloody easier for me to recognize you. And, more importantly, you wouldn't have to avoid women and wine like you Templars do."

Jacques smiled. "And what about you? You're in the service of Raymond of Tripoli, if I remember aright. Is Tripoli with the army?"

Humphrey nodded. "That bloody beardless fool? He's here, but by the Mass, he doesn't know what he's doing. Never fought before, and doesn't

13

know how to lead men either. He's almost as young as you, and five times less competent. Good thing Amalric's here, else we'd all be carcasses for Egyptian dogs to chew on."

Jacques snorted, and muttered quietly, "I put little more trust in the king than I would in Tripoli. He isn't half the captain his brother was."

Humphrey sighed. "Yes, it would be like you to think that, De Maille. You and all your fellow monks. Anyway, I thought the Templars weren't supposed to be taking part in this war. Not holy enough for them."

"Yes," said Jacques. "The Templars will not fight this war. The master of the Temple sent us merely to observe the campaign."

"Oh," growled Humphrey. "In that case, better not take you to Amalric. He won't be happy to see Templars. He never liked them much anyway."

"No," murmured Godfrey, half under his breath. "Lechers never like men sworn to celibacy."

"No," said Jacques, speaking over Godfrey. "I was hoping we could avoid the king. Word reached Jerusalem that the war was going badly, so we were sent to make sure of it."

"Come with me, then," said Humphrey. "You can camp with Raymond of Tripoli's knights. I'll bring you to Tripoli. He doesn't mind Templars; not as much as Amalric does, at least. Oh, by the way, who's this other lad?"

"Godfrey," spoke Godfrey quickly. "Godfrey de Montferrat."

"Godfrey," muttered Humphrey gruffly. He laughed. "You look like Godfrey de Bouillion." All the men stared at Humphrey.

"Oh, no," said Humphrey, waving his burly arm as if to push their questions aside. "I never met Godfrey de Bouillion, of course. He died before I was born." Humphrey continued to stare curiously at Godfrey. "You just look the way *he* must have looked like."

Humphrey laughed again; his deep, growling laugh. Then he spun his horse about, and trotted down the dune towards the Christian camp. The other knights and footsoldiers went back to their posts. Godfrey and Jacques exchanged glances.

"Strange thing to say," murmured Godfrey. Jacques shrugged, and they rode after Humphrey.

Humphrey led the two Templars through the camp, taking a roundabout route in order to steer clear of the king's men. All around, men were packing supplies and taking down pavilions. Humphrey gestured towards the hasty work going on.

"You heard right back at home. Amalric has lost his nerve; he's packing up and leaving. Gave orders that we're to march tomorrow. It looks like he's fleeing Egypt for good."

✠ ✠ ✠

Count Raymond III of Tripoli sat by a campfire with a few of his knights, roasting meat. Humphrey had called his liege lord a 'bloody beardless fool', and he was beardless to be sure. For the rest, Godfrey withheld judgment.

"Count Raymond," bellowed Humphrey, loud as always. "May I introduce you to an old friend of mine and his companion. This is Jacques de Maille," he said, gesturing to Jacques. Tripoli looked up and nodded at Jacques, a slow, deliberate movement. It was so deliberate, in fact, as to look forced, but Godfrey could sense some good will behind it. The count was a small man with a tuft of sandy brown hair falling about his face and ears. "And this," continued Humphrey, "is Godfrey de Montferrat."

Humphrey took a step closer to the count and spoke to Raymond of Tripoli in a low voice. "I had to bring them here; couldn't let the king get his hands on them …" Humphrey and Tripoli stood up and began to walk a little ways away, Humphrey speaking quietly as they did. When Humphrey was done, Tripoli turned back to Godfrey and Jacques.

"Templars," announced the count. "The two of you are welcome to stay in my encampment."

"Thank you, m'lord," said Jacques. The two Templars bowed before the count. Tripoli received their bows with a grave nod and sat back down. The meat was ready. The knights began tearing away at it.

"God's beard," growled Humphrey impatiently to the two Templars. "Eat, fool monks! Help yourselves to the meat. Tomorrow we're on the march again."

Chapter 2

CROWN OF GOLD
Amalric

malric, king of Jerusalem, was alone again.

He sat in his pavilion, letting the night chill sink into his bones. Outside, the darkness was lit up with a thousand campfires, but within the tent, Amalric had not so much as lit a candle. He clutched a horn of ale in his hand, but he had held it like that for a long time without drinking.

Outside, a loud burst of laughter came from one of the campfires. The horn of ale slipped from the king's hand. Amalric started when the ale splashed against his foot.

Swearing angrily to himself, he stood.

It is done, he thought. *It has been a year. You should have forgotten about her by now.*

But thoughts of Agnes pressed into his head. Angrily, Amalric kicked the camp table that stood upright in his tent. It fell against the tent wall, papers scattering. He turned and stormed out of the tent. The two guards saluted as he passed. Amalric ignored them and walked out into the night.

A few of his knights were sitting about a campfire, their voices ringing with ribald laughter. The king stood at the edge of the firelight and listened for a few moments, but he could not find it in him to laugh along with them. Worry and discontent plagued him as he moved away; this had never been a problem before.

Amalric was loved by his knights and his footmen, loved like few rulers ever were. He was one of them; he laughed with them, suffered with them, ate with them, shivered with them, bled with them, drank with them, and wenched with them; he was a man of the people. Whatever his adversaries said about him, they could not accuse him of being cold or remote.

This day, however, a strange melancholy was on him.

I think you have taken your revenge, Agnes, without even trying.

Amalric moved on through the camp, brooding quietly, until he suddenly caught sight of a man sitting by one of the fires.

"Joscelin!"

Amalric strode over to the campfire.

A blond knight, almost as big as Amalric himself, was sitting on a rock next to his young squire, drinking red wine. He was Joscelin de Courtenay, count of Edessa. Amalric sat down next to Joscelin, taking a flask of wine and drinking deeply. For a few moments the king, the count, and the squire sat in silence.

"Tristan," said Joscelin to his squire, "you had better go to the horselines to see to your mount."

The squire, who was still a child, got up, looking nervously at the king.

"Yes, lord Joscelin." He hurried off into the darkness.

Amalric and Joscelin looked at each other, then went back to drinking. Amalric fumbled in his mind for the words he had meant to say, but none came. Instead he could only fight down the memory of old days, when he and Joscelin had not been so awkward.

It was Joscelin who spoke first. "It has been a long time, Amalric. Almost a year."

"I know," said Amalric. "But I have need of all my friends now, Joscelin. *All* of them."

Joscelin said nothing, only looked down into his wine. Amalric remained intent.

"Well, Joscelin?"

Joscelin spat into the flames. "We've lost the war, haven't we?"

Amalric nodded. Joscelin glanced up at him.

"You aren't going to say anything in your defense?"

Amalric shrugged. "What is there to say? I beat off every attack the infidels made, captured a few cities, and lost a war. We are out of grain now, and the army must eat. It was a mistake to come in the first place."

"It was," agreed Joscelin unsympathetically.

Amalric sighed. "Joscelin, don't be an ass. I never did anything to wrong *you*."

"Haven't you?" asked Joscelin. "Ever since you... since you became king, you have taken out your anger not just on her, but on both of us."

"How, Joscelin? I have done nothing to you for a year."

"Exactly, Your Grace. You have ignored me. Once, I would have considered you the best friend I ever had, but you have changed that, *Your Grace.*"

Amalric bowed his head. "Very well, Joscelin. I will not appeal to you as a friend. Perhaps I have done things I should not have, but whatever may be, it is too late now. I ask you then as your king. Will you help me?"

Joscelin looked up. "As the king?" There was a long pause. "Yes," he said at last. "I will serve the king, but only the king."

"That is all I require."

"I have always wanted to serve the king, Amalric, but know this: your brother should be king, not you. There are some things that cannot be, but Baldwin is the king who should have been."

Amalric shrugged. "You are right. There are some things that cannot be."

Joscelin drank deeply from his cup. "What, then, does my king ask of me?" he said bitterly.

"I need knowledge, Joscelin. What do the men think? They laugh and joke when I'm there, but what do they *really* think? What do *you* think, Joscelin?"

Joscelin sighed and took a deep draught from his beaker.

"The men want to return to Jerusalem. They're sick of this war; we had no business coming here in the first place. We've had little plunder, no victories, nothing but sand and food that kills a man's stomach."

"The food isn't all that bad," muttered Amalric. Joscelin sat in silence. After a few seconds, Amalric spoke again.

"Will they fight one more battle for me?"

Joscelin shrugged. "It depends. If you can get plunder quickly, they'll be happy. Otherwise...you'd better get the army back to Jerusalem soon, or you'll have a mutiny on your hands. The plunder from Bilbeis was good, but most of the men have squandered it already and are looking for more."

Amalric spat into the flames. "Why?" he growled. "Must I let my men burn, pillage and rape to keep them happy? Is there no other way?"

Joscelin glanced sideways at the king. Amalric, despite all his faults, had a softer heart than many rulers. *A soft heart...but he never acts on his better impulses.* He shrugged.

"What do *you* think, Joscelin?"

"What do I think? I told you, a year ago, when your brother died. I think we should go back to Jerusalem, and we should *stay* in Jerusalem. I think we should have peace. The only hope for your kingdom now is to build a lasting peace with the Saracens."

Amalric scratched at the stubble on his chin. "There are some," he said, "who would call that treason."

"There are some," said Joscelin icily, "who would call you a lecher."

Amalric snorted. "God's bones, Joscelin, must you bring *that* up? Just because your blood is frozen cold in your veins doesn't mean mine is."

Joscelin said nothing, only stared into the flames.

Amalric found that he was feeling warmer, feeling happier, at least in contrast to Joscelin. What Joscelin had said was true; once, they had been the best of friends, but now that had been replaced by a sort of hatred that made the one happier when the other was in an ill-temper.

"Well, Joscelin," said Amalric, "I will see what I can do about your peace. Is there anything else?"

"One last thing, Your Grace," added Joscelin. "There are two Templars in the camp. They are trying to stay hidden, but one of my men noticed them. I suspect that Blanchefort is using them as agents; more than that I do not know. Be wary, your Grace: Blanchefort is a dangerous man, and the Templars have always been brutal."

Their discussion was brought to an abrupt end when Tristan, the squire, came back, having fed and brushed his steed.

Amalric stood up, thumping Joscelin on the back and laughing as though nothing had happened.

"Well, Joscelin, I have more campfires to visit. Enjoy the wine. You know we march tomorrow."

Joscelin de Courtenay, count of Edessa, looked up at the king.

"But do we march home, Your Grace?"

"Home? Not yet. We have one last adventure to try."

"I thought you said we had lost the war!"

"Not if this venture succeeds."

Still laughing, the king of Jerusalem strode off into the darkness. Joscelin sat immobile for a minute or two, staring into the depths of the flames.

Chapter 3

THE GREAT RIVER
Joscelin

The next day, around noon, Joscelin found himself regretting the sleep he had lost. He yawned as his horse trundled slowly up the hillside. Their old campsite lay miles behind—they had been marching west all day. A few feet ahead of him, the king's horse had reached the top of the hill. Amalric paused at the crest, looking down at whatever lay beyond.

"There!" he cried to Joscelin. "Tinnis! That is our destination—by tonight we will have sacked the city."

Joscelin's horse crested the hill, and he stopped next to the king. A few hundred yards before them, the scattered Frankish outriders were trotting down the hill. Aside from this, there was nothing between the king and any ambush the enemy might lay.

He was always brash as a count, thought Joscelin. *Now he is brasher as a king.*

Joscelin followed the king's gaze. Far out across the plain was the city of Tinnis. They knew little of Egypt, but the rumors Amalric had of Tinnis told him that it was full of grain and unprotected by walls—the perfect place to attack.

It was a few moments before Joscelin noticed something much bigger spread out on the plain below them.

"Your Grace," he said. "The Nile!"

A long, wide ribbon of muddy blue ran from one end of the horizon to the other. The plain, Joscelin realized, was the Nile Floodplain. Joscelin could not help but be awed by the sight. To him, as to all Franks, Egypt was a land of mystery. He had looked at maps, all of them grossly inaccurate, but it was something else seeing them come to life. All these places, Pelusium, Cairo, Bilbeis, Tinnis, the Nile itself, had not been seen by Latin Christian eyes for centuries.

Joscelin drank in the sight of the Great River, of the floodplain, and the tiny dot in the distance that was Tinnis. As he did, he noticed something troubling. The Nile curved out there to meet the city. It was impossible to be sure from here, but it seemed that it flowed around both sides of the city...

An island! Can that be possible? If Tinnis is on an island, it would explain why there are no walls. The river will stop an invading army better than any walls could.

Joscelin pushed the worries from his mind.

Have faith in your king. He will pull the army through. He did it before as count of Ascalon, now he will do it again as king. Have faith in Amalric.

He broke faith with me last time, why should I have faith in him now?

Because you have no other choice.

More knights crested the hill. They stopped to gape at what lay below them. The sky was blue and clear, and below it lay the Great River, the object that the ancient Egyptians had worshipped as Osiris. It was wide, and muddy, stretching along from horizon to horizon, the longest river in the world.

The hill was filling up with knights and with footmen, men born in the villages of France and Germany or the slums of Jerusalem; they had never seen anything like this.

Amalric spurred his horse forward. "Keep the men moving, Joscelin!" he shouted. "By nightfall we'll have reached Tinnis, and by tomorrow morning, we'll have stormed the place."

If only it were true, thought Joscelin. *Now is the time to speak, so that we might salvage something at least.* General Shirkuh, the commander of the Arabic army, would not be far off. If there was trouble in Tinnis, and Shirkuh appeared with his army, things would go badly.

"Your Grace!" shouted Joscelin.

Amalric pulled on the reins and turned his head to stare back at Joscelin.

"Yes, Count Edessa?" he said icily.

"Your Grace, look! I think...I think it's on an island."

"What is?"

"The city, Your Grace. Tinnis. The river runs on both sides of it. We will not be able to take it by direct assault, Your Grace."

Amalric squinted out towards Tinnis. "I see no island."

"But Your Grace," said Joscelin. "What if it's on the other side of the river? There is too much chance involved, Your Grace. We should have taken the time to scout out the city properly. As it is, we're marching blind.

And you know, Your Grace, if the city is *not* on this side of the river, we will not be able to simply turn around and march off."

"Do not contradict me!" roared Amalric.

"I am sorry, Your Grace, but it is the truth. Shirkuh will know of your movements by now. As far as we know, he may be lurking in those hills just to the south. If we rush blindly into the floodplain, Shirkuh will fall upon our baggage train. Then, should Tinnis prove impregnable, we will be caught in the flood valley, without food, with the river on one side and Shirkuh on the other."

"What would you suggest then, Count?" snapped the king.

"Your Grace, I would merely ask that you send outriders to the south and east, to warn us if Shirkuh comes. Then let the outriders to the west get farther ahead, so we will have advance warning if Tinnis is really an island."

Amalric frowned. "Very well. Grenier!"

"Yes, Your Grace!" Hugh Grenier, Lord of Caesarea, rode forward.

"Take your knights to the south and east. Fan out and form a screen about a mile from the army. I want to know well in advance if Shirkuh comes."

"Yes, Your Grace."

Amalric turned back to Joscelin. "Now, Count Edessa, it would please me greatly if you remain silent until we reach Tinnis."

"Yes, Your Grace."

Joscelin grimaced as Amalric turned and went galloping down the hill into the Nile floodplain. With a sigh, he dug his spurs in and rode after him.

Behind him, more knights began cresting the top of the hill. He heard shouts of surprise as men beheld the Nile for the first time. But the river had lost any fascination for Joscelin de Courtenay, and it was in a black mood that he rode down towards the Nile.

Chapter 4

odfrey de Montferrat watched as a rider came speeding across the dunes and headed towards the head of the army.

"Do you think they've sighted the Saracen host?" asked Jacques.

At that thought, Godfrey looked up. "Jacques, I've been thinking…if there is a battle, what do we do? Do we fight? Or do we cower in the rear? The Temple does not approve of this war, and the Master made it clear when he sent us that we were only to observe. Would it be right for us to fight? But would it be right for us to cower?" Godfrey had battled the strange Saracen two nights before, but that had been in self-defense. Now there was a pitched-battle to be fought.

"Of course we fight," said Jacques. "Are you suggesting we cower in the back like cravens?"

Godfrey tried to work out a solution in his mind. "But it's an unjust war…we cannot fight in it. Even if it means appearing to be craven."

Jacques snorted impatiently, but before he could answer, another rider rode up beside them. He was a knight in full mail and a surcoat of red with three black foxes. His hair was a tangle of golden curls, and his face was a little too pretty. For no good reason, other than perhaps a natural distrust of any man who looked like that, Godfrey felt an instant dislike for him.

"Templars," said the knight, with a cherubic smile. His eyes were somehow distant: scornful and aloof. Godfrey and Jacques stared back at him, unsure how to answer.

"I always wondered," continued the knight of the three foxes, "how the Temple could field an army of celibate men."

Godfrey stared back, nonplussed.

"But seeing you," sneered the knight, "I realize that it's because they only accept eunuchs and effeminates." Then he tossed his golden curls, laughed, and rode on.

Godfrey and Jacques exchanged glances.

"Who do you think that was?" he asked Jacques.

"That," said someone from behind him, "was Gerard de Ridford."

Godfrey and Jacques turned to see who was speaking. It was Humphrey de Vinsauf.

"Humphrey!" said Jacques, looking relieved. "Ride with us a while. Godfrey is a good enough friend, but he seems to abhor normal conversation."

Godfrey snorted. Humphrey slowed his pace to ride with them.

"Who is this De Ridford?" asked Godfrey, still glaring at the back of the knight's golden head.

"He is a knight," said Humphrey, "who is, sad to say, also in the service of Raymond of Tripoli. I have known him for a few years. God's beard, a day is too long to know that one! But he is very popular in Tripoli. That's the damnable thing about it. The men admire him. The women...they think him charming. They love that pretty face of his, and he loves them back."

Jacques snorted, but Godfrey gave a mirthless laugh.

"One day," continued Humphrey, "he found his lady love, and at last stopped chasing the girls of Tripoli. This love of his is a ward of the count, a bloody noble-born girl. Since he met her it's been all courtly love and gallantry and tokens of a lady's favor. After some haggling, Tripoli agreed to betroth her to De Ridford. There was, however, a condition. Tripoli promised De Ridford that if he served him faithfully, he would get the girl. But Tripoli never said how long he would have to serve. He could wait fifty years until De Ridford's pretty curls turn grey and his pretty face grows wrinkled, and still De Ridford would serve him faithfully. It's been a great source of comfort to me of late—when I want to put a dent in that smug face of his—that one day De Ridford's going to realize that Tripoli tricked him, and that by then it'll be too late."

Humphrey glared ahead at where Gerard de Ridford was talking with Raymond of Tripoli. Before long, however, Humphrey fell into conversation with a soldier on his other side. Godfrey and Jacques rode on ahead. Godfrey glanced at Jacques and laughed a little.

"Amused?" asked Jacques. "Humphrey has a wife in Tripoli. Children too. He loves them all, and is a better husband and father than most. He's a good man. I met him in Jerusalem a few months ago. He sometimes takes an instinctive liking to those he meets, like he did with both of us. But when he dislikes someone...he despises them passionately."

"I can tell," said Godfrey. He smiled, shaking his head. At the back of his mind, though, he had not forgotten De Ridford's words.

"Eunuchs," he said slowly. "Is that what we are, Jacques? Less than men?"

Jacques shrugged. "We're told somewhere that 'some are eunuchs for the sake of the Kingdom of Heaven…'"

"Yes," said Godfrey, "but that shouldn't be taken literally. Origen tried it: the Church was not pleased."

Jacques sighed. "God's beard, Godfrey, I'm not a philosopher or a theologian. I became a Templar to serve God, not to make myself happy. I don't know."

"Neither do I," said Godfrey. "But I think I despise this De Ridford as much as Humphrey does."

After that, there was nothing more either of them could say. They rode in silence for a while, though Godfrey was thinking on Jacques words. Jacques claimed that he had become a Templar to serve God. Godfrey thought that he himself had entered the Temple for the same reason. He had told it to himself night after night for the past year, and now he began to suspect that Jacques had done the same. For a moment his memory flickered back to those desperate nights, alone on his pallet, dejected and afraid, searching for an answer.

Jacques had been raised with Godfrey as a squire in the household of William de Montferrat. He had been Godfrey's closest friend as a child… besides perhaps his cousin Conrad. Jacques had entered the Temple just a week after Godfrey, and they had taken the vows of Poverty, Chastity and Obedience together.

Why did you follow me, Jacques? he wondered. *Why did you not marry her? What happened after I left Italy?*

"Templars," said Humphrey suddenly, interrupting Godfrey's thoughts. "Has anyone heard news from home, lately?"

It took Godfrey a few seconds for the question to register; he had been born in Jerusalem and had always thought of it as home, even during his years in Italy. The kingdom of Jerusalem beckoned to him, the kingdom that the people of Europe called *Outremer*, the Land Beyond the Sea. That Land Beyond the Sea had always held a magic and a wonder for Godfrey de Montferrat.

But Humphrey had been born in Languedoc, in France, and though he had been many years in the Holy Land, home for Humphrey still meant southern France with her fields and her troubadours, her cold winters and her ripe summers that were so different from the lands and seasons of Outremer.

Jacques understood and answered immediately, his head bobbing up and down with the jolt of the horse.

"Yes, I have heard news from home, Humphrey. A month ago, some of the Templars who serve as bankers in Italy came to Jerusalem. Master Blanchefort sent me to collect the list of sums. They brought news of the continent. Catharism is rampant in your homeland, Humphrey. They say it's tearing the Church apart. Even the king is getting worried."

Humphrey spat. "Bloody heretics! Let them live for a year in the Holy Land and they'd forget their stupid quarrels with other Christians. It's hard enough keeping the Saracen at bay without them creating trouble at home. God's death! Can't they just live like Christians without their lies about food and weapons and sex?"

"*Oportet haereses esse,*" murmured Godfrey. "For there must be heresies among us, that those with true mettle may be shown."

Jacques and Humphrey stared at him.

"Saint Paul," said Godfrey. "It's Scripture."

Humphrey snorted. "You *are* a Templar, aren't you?"

He spurred his horse forward and rode ahead to the count of Tripoli, leaving Godfrey and Jacques behind.

"Any other news from the continent?" asked Godfrey.

Jacques nodded slowly.

"There's trouble in England; King Henry is fighting with the archbishop of Canterbury, one Thomas à Becket, over the rights of the Church. Monarchs in the continent are always squabbling with the Church. I think Humphrey had something; if the people of Europe would live for a year out here they'd forget their quarrels with each other; it's hard enough fending off the Saracen. The Italians and the Germans are fighting each other, and the Church is mixed up in that mess as well: the emperor is fighting with the pope, who took the Lombards' side. The emperor set up an anti-pope who styles himself Victor IV. War has started; the Normans and Lombards against the Germans; Welf against Imperialist, with the pope calling for a holy war on the empire. It's a bloody mess up there."

"I wonder which side William de Montferrat will take," mused Godfrey.

Jacques snorted. "Whichever side seems most powerful."

"True," said Godfrey, and he sighed. "War in the North, just as we need help in the South."

"Help will come," said Jacques. "It always does. They'll call a new crusade."

"No," said Godfrey. "They haven't forgotten the failure of the German emperor and the French king twenty years ago. Men are wary of Crusade now—it might be thirty years before they take the Cross again."

Jacques laughed. "They will call a Crusade sooner than that, I think."

Godfrey shrugged. "I hope. But for now we must fend for ourselves... and you and I must come to a decision: if the Saracens come, and there's a battle, do we fight?"

Jacques sighed. "You have the right of it this time, Godfrey. We cannot fight in this war."

Suddenly they heard the sound of bugles blowing, calling the halt. Humphrey de Vinsauf came riding back down the line, his face flush with excitement.

"Better get into line, Templars! Shirkuh's coming and bringing his whole bloody army with him. The Ishmaelites are going to try to crush us here and now!"

Chapter 5

BEFORE THE STORM
Joscelin

oscelin felt his pulse pounding faster as the Frankish trumpets sounded the alarm, sending high, proud trills echoing about the floodplain. Shirkuh had come to fight. Joscelin started to reach for his sword, but he hesitated, and then turned his horse to look for Amalric—the king might make a foolish move in the heat of the moment, if there was no one more prudent to restrain him.

Joscelin could remember a time when Amalric was the best captain in the Kingdom of Jerusalem, a better commander even than his brother, Baldwin.

He could also remember a time when Amalric had been his friend, a time when Amalric was married to his sister.

Baldwin, he thought, speaking in his mind to Amalric's dead older brother, *why did you leave us? Things would have been so different if you had lived, or if you had at least fathered a son with that pretty Greek wife of yours.*

But it was fruitless to wish the impossible. Theodora Comnena, once the blushing bride of King Baldwin, now wore widow's black, and Agnes de Courtenay brooded alone in some tower in Tyre.

Joscelin rode off towards the banner of the kingdom, where he knew Amalric would be. The banner bore a white field with a gold cross, and a little box at the top with a piece of the True Cross. As Joscelin rode towards that flag, he passed by the ranks of the Hospitallers. They wore black surcoats emblazoned with white crosses. Joscelin reflected briefly with amusement that the Hospitallers would do anything to oppose their rival religious order the Templars—right down to wearing black to contrast the Templars' white. But Joscelin did not ride too close to the warrior monks. He was none too fond of either the Templars or the Hospitallers.

The Templars do make the Hospitallers seem tame by comparison, though.

Then Joscelin saw Gilbert d'Aissailly, the Master of the Hospital, conferring with a Hospitaller officer in front of the line. At this Joscelin did ride closer, for there were questions he must ask D'Aissailly. He did not begin asking what he should have, though, for he was in an irritable mood and could not resist the urge to make trouble.

"Master d'Aissailly! I expected to find you fawning over the king!"

D'Aissailly looked up to glare at him. "Hold your tongue, Edessa! You like to call yourself a count, but where is your county? Win it back before you speak so insolently."

Joscelin felt his blood rising. He knew he should take the Hospitaller's counsel and move on to civil conversation, but his anger got the better of him. "And tell me, Monk," he retorted, "where is *your* fief? For one who has sworn a vow of poverty, you hold landholders in high esteem."

"At least I do not cower in another's court while the infidels ravage my lands. You think to find *me* fawning over the king? You, the king's toady? Go back to the north and retake your lands. Then come here and insult me."

D'Aissailly turned to ride off. Joscelin sighed and spoke more respectfully.

"I apologize for the jape, Master d'Aissailly. It was ill spoken. I wish to speak with you in earnest."

D'Aissailly turned, his face still dark with mistrust. "You may have japed, *Count Edessa*, but I did not. Speak what you will, but I will not listen with a friendly ear."

"Be that as it may...why aren't you with the king, sir? I do not mean it ill in any way, but you usually are at his side. Have you incurred his displeasure?"

D'Aissailly's face grew darker. "Incurred his displeasure? He has incurred *my* displeasure. But why should it seem odd for me to speak to my own men? Is not my place with the knights of the Hospital?"

Joscelin smiled. "It is, but... you are not often found there."

The Hospitaller scowled. "The king sent you here to nose around, did he not?"

"No," said Joscelin. "The king and I are not on the best of terms."

D'Aissailly's scowled lessened. "So you say...do you mean it? I should take you to speak to Tripoli...but no, we cannot trust a craven such as you. Run along to your king."

Joscelin was frowning. "It is just as well you will not have me in your councils. You misunderstand. Whether Amalric and I quarrel or no, I am the king's man, to the death. Never forget that, when next thoughts of treason cross your mind."

Joscelin turned and rode off quickly, followed by D'Aissailly's curses.

That man is a fool. It was no secret that Gilbert D'Aissailly had become Master of the Hospital merely by pouring wealth into the electors when the last grand master died. As a monk, he owned no worldly possessions, but his family was one of the richer houses in the kingdom.

For a monk, he lives in comfort. And for a Master of the Hospital, he has neither shrewdness nor piety. His conversation revealed that much. A sad state we are in if such a man is Master of the Hospital. When I talk with fools like that, even Bertrand de Blanchefort seems preferable, if only by comparison.

Joscelin sighed and proceeded to reproach himself mentally for his own folly. However arrogant and unpleasant D'Aissailly was, he ought not to antagonize him unnecessarily.

As Joscelin rode on towards the banner of the kingdom, he thought back over D'Aissailly's words. The Hospitaller had revealed much that even the simplest of peasants should have known better than to say.

Take me 'to speak with Tripoli'...I wonder what Tripoli is doing.

Raymond, count of Tripoli, was the lord of the northernmost reaches of the Crusader Kingdom of Jerusalem. Tripoli's relation to the Crown of Jerusalem had always been vague—the counts of Tripoli wanted to assert their independence; the kings of Jerusalem to bring Tripoli under their dominion. Joscelin was, as he had said, a king's man, but he cared little about the mastery of Tripoli so long as the barons cooperated with the king during time of war. But Raymond was young and impetuous, and if he was plotting with D'Aissailly, it boded ill.

☩ ☩ ☩

When Joscelin found Amalric, he also found the large group of knights and nobles that was always crowding about the king, flattering him and fawning over him. D'Aissailly was notably absent, but Joscelin had already known that. Tripoli was not there either, though Joscelin had guessed at that. Lord Barisan d'Ibelin was absent too, and that surprised Joscelin.

It could mean nothing. He does have his own men to see to.

All the same...if Ibelin, Tripoli, and the Hospital hold council together separate from the king, it could mean trouble. I should warn Amalric...once this crowd of fools has dispersed.

"Joscelin!" called Amalric. "There you are! Lord Grenier's riders have found Shirkuh. It seems your warning was timely—Shirkuh is racing north through the hills with his army to catch us. I've drawn up our army in preparation for battle. Shirkuh may give us the chance we need: if we can crush him here, we will have all the time we need to conquer Tinnis."

No, we won't, thought Joscelin. *We don't have enough food to wait around long.*

"Well thought out, Your Grace," he said, suppressing the accusation his conscience made of flattery.

"Now," said Amalric, "my plan is simple. We will lure Shirkuh into the floodplain and crush him with a well placed cavalry charge. Shirkuh is known for his elaborate battle plans, and has outwitted some of the finest generals ever to take the field. The best way to defeat one such as him will be to use an uncomplicated plan. Let Shirkuh wonder what hidden trap lies behind our movements, let him delay and hesitate, and stumble into a simple defeat."

God help us, thought Joscelin, *He's trying to be clever. It always led to trouble when we were children. Now a kingdom is at stake. I have to find some way to stop him from destroying the army.*

"Your Grace," said Joscelin, "may I offer a suggestion? Our primary concern right now is not winning battles. We need food before ought else. If Tinnis is well protected, it would be fruitless to stay here any longer. We are close enough. I propose that we march on to Tinnis, and take it if we can. Then we can pull up defensive positions in Tinnis and outwait Shirkuh. If we cannot take Tinnis, we should try to force a way out without engaging in pitched battle."

Amalric laughed. "Would you have us hide or run like cravens, Edessa? We *did* come here to win battles, not sit on our arses in some river town. No, we will not cower, and you know already that we have come too far to run. I am going to show Shirkuh that he is not invincible! If we send him back to Damascus with his tail between his legs, it will cow the infidels from Iconium to Minya."

The nobles gathered around them shouted their agreement. Joscelin sighed. The army would be destroyed after all.

"We will draw up our battle line so," said Amalric, dismounting to draw lines in the dirt. "Lord Grenier, your outriders will fall back like this, drawing Shirkuh into the floodplain like this, so that they come out toward the southern end of our line. When Shirkuh comes over the last hills, he will find our army drawn up like it is now, with Tripoli on the southern flank, then Jaffa, then Ibelin…"

Joscelin listened as Amalric outlined his plan. It was sound enough, a simple ploy in which Shirkuh would be drawn to the south. The southern flank, guarded by Tripoli's knights, would appear to collapse before Shirkuh's onslaught. The knights of Tripoli would flee until they were clear of the battle. Shirkuh would throw all his weight on the south side, but even as he did, the north end of the Frankish line would be swinging down in a cavalry charge. The whole Frankish line would swing about almost to right angles with its previous position, crushing Shirkuh.

When Amalric was done, he looked up, appearing pleased with himself. He mounted again.

Joscelin glanced down at the drawings in the dirt.

It is a sound plan. Better than I expected…but for such a simple plan, it requires too much precision and too much coordination. Battle plans never go off exactly as they were intended, and with Amalric's plan, even a slight change could mean disaster. But I should not be pessimistic. Perhaps it will work.

"Well, my lords, what do you think?"

The lords and barons cheered their assent. Joscelin remained silent.

"Go then, and prepare for battle. God wills it!" The barons rode off to their men. "De Milly," said the king to one of his knights, "go find Ibelin and Tripoli and inform them of the plan of battle. Oh, and the Master of the Hospital too."

Joscelin grimaced at the king's careless manner—the count of Edessa hated leaving anything to chance. But he sighed and shrugged it off.

"Joscelin," said Amalric. Joscelin looked up. "Ride with me. I require your company."

"Yes, Your Grace."

✟ ✟ ✟

Half an hour later, Joscelin looked out on an army drawn up just as Amalric had drawn the lines in the dirt. He sat his horse with the knights of the king's household, stationed on a little hillock on the northern end of the line.

He had sent his squire, Tristan de Monglane, to the rear after Tristan had finished helping him with his armor. Joscelin had his hauberk of chainmail covered by a green surcoat. The hauberk was long and heavy, but Joscelin had been fighting in heavier ones for years. On his left arm was his heavy oaken shield, painted with the colors of House Courtenay. His left hand held the reins, keeping the horse at bay. He carried his helmet in his right arm, for he would not put that on until he absolutely had to. It was a full helm—a metal box that encased his entire head, with only a thin slit for the eyes and a few holes to breathe.

Every few minutes another rider came to report to the king. Shirkuh's advance guard was sweeping down from the north, overrunning Hugh Grenier's outriders. Saracen horsebowmen were racing up from the south, but at such an angle they would come out in front of the Frankish line rather than behind it. Shirkuh's center would be coming out of the hills in less than half an hour.

"Joscelin," came a voice from behind him. Joscelin turned to see Amalric sitting on his horse, looking anxiously towards the hills.

"Yes, Your Grace?"

Joscelin looked at the king's worried face, and saw a kind of openness there he had not seen for a year.

He is more like the Amalric who was brother to a king, not Amalric the king.

"Joscelin, I need to know something. I saw your face when I proposed the battle plan. You thought it folly. Tell me what you think, Joscelin. Perhaps it is too late for me to be the friend I should have been, but now, as your king, I need you to tell me everything."

"Yes, Your Grace." Joscelin hesitated. *Will he take offense if I speak all my mind? No...he has just commanded me to speak it.* "Amalric, do you remember, when we were children, and we would play chess?"

"Yes, Joscelin. All too well."

"With all due respect, Your Grace, if my memory serves me right...I seemed to win most of those games."

Amalric laughed. "You did at that."

"Well, Amalric, I remember once, when you were getting frustrated at always losing, you tried doing what you are doing now. You had read in books of brilliant generals who foiled the shrewdest of opponents by using the simplest scheme possible. So you tried using this against me in chess... I seem to recall that I only crushed you even more easily. You tried it again and again, but all that it did was to make the game's end quicker."

Amalric shook his head. "This is not chess, Joscelin. And you only won those games because you knew me too well. Shirkuh has not played me at chess, nor has he fought me. He will be deceived."

"With all due respect, Your Grace, I think that Shirkuh has a very... low opinion of your intellect. He will find nothing strange with you using a simple strategy."

Amalric laughed. "Joscelin, why are you switching back and forth between my title and my name?"

Joscelin frowned. "What should I do, Your Gra...Amalric? I think that they are two different men, Your Grace and Amalric. I use the name of the one I am speaking to."

Amalric sighed. "Joscelin, spare me your attempts at being clever."

"Yes, Your Grace."

"You know, Joscelin, Agnes always beat both of us. At chess, I mean."

"I know," Joscelin said, very quietly. "I had not forgotten."

Amalric shook his head vigorously. "God's bones, Joscelin. We have to put your sister behind us. I would still have you as a friend, whatever you may say."

Before now, Joscelin had thought that he would find it easy to forgive Amalric everything if he only heard these words from him. Now, though, he found his anger only waxing stronger.

This is all I have hoped for from Amalric...why am I still wroth with him?

"Amalric, how can we put my sister behind us? She is your wife."

Amalric's face darkened. "God's blood, Joscelin, she is not! The Church has spoken!"

Joscelin smiled bitterly. "The bishop was well paid to make his decision."

"God speaks through the Church, Joscelin. It is final!"

"Through the Church, yes. Not through corrupt bishops. Why did you cast her off, Amalric? You loved her! You should have loved her more than you loved power!"

Amalric's face was red with anger. He seemed about to bite off another angry reply when they heard the trumpets sounding again. Both of them turned towards the hills.

There, just cresting the top of the ridge, was the first of the Saracen riders. He sat his horse, poised on the top, holding aloft the great banner with verses from the Qur'an written across it. For a moment he stood alone, then the ridge was outlined with hundreds of horsemen.

"They're here," said Amalric. The red in his face was gone, and it now appeared almost pale. "Joscelin, I need your help."

"Of course, Your Grace...Amalric."

Joscelin clapped his helmet on, and his vision became a narrow slit. They drew their swords and turned to ride down to where the knights of the king's household were waiting. Joscelin glanced back towards the southern end of the line.

"Tripoli should start falling back now," he said. The knights of Tripoli were showing no signs of retreating.

Amalric had turned too to watch the line. "Bloody fool Tripoli. If he's too slow, I'll go down there and prod him with a burning pair of tongs just to get him moving."

Then the knights of Tripoli began to move. They did not fall back. They charged.

Joscelin stared at them, unable to formulate thoughts, much less words.

Amalric's face had turned even whiter, but it was with rage now.

The whole southern flank began to ride forward. The knights of Tripoli surged forward first, then the knights of Ibelin followed. Between them, the knights of Jaffa remained where they were, but farther up the line, the Hospitallers joined the charge.

Tripoli and Ibelin and D'Aissailly...I knew I should have warned Amalric before it was too late!

Now Joscelin felt the anger coming—anger and hatred for these traitors.

None of them has as great a cause to hate the king as I do, yet I remain loyal while they commit treason! That traitor D'Aissailly...if I had known this morning, I would have struck him down instead of speaking to him.

Amalric had finally found words. "What in hell is he doing? If we charge into the hills, we'll be trapped and unable to charge. Shirkuh will have us like fish in a net."

"Your Grace," said Joscelin, the anger still red. "They mean to make you seem a craven by charging when you gave orders to retreat. They think to force you to charge, and thus follow their lead. D'Aissailly and Tripoli see this as just another game of politics—Tripoli wants to assert his beloved autonomy, and D'Aissailly to remind you that the Hospitallers are not under your rule. And they are willing to throw away the battle, throw away thousands of lives, for that."

Amalric cursed violently. He looked out angrily at the knights streaming up the hill to attack the Saracens. "Well," he said at last, "they seem to have succeeded in forcing my hand. If I do not charge with them, we will be destroyed in halves."

"No, Your Grace!" shouted Joscelin. He could picture D'Aissailly's stupid face, and young Tripoli's irritatingly cheerful grin, and Barisan d'Ibelin's airs of false chivalry. He wanted nothing more than to take those three heads and smash them. But letting the Saracens do it would serve just as well. "Amalric...they have done treason, but in the same move they have given you the weapon with which to punish them. Send out riders to the rest of the line and order them to remain in position. We will leave these traitors to die on the infidel spears."

Amalric stared at him, aghast. "That would mean the destruction of a third of my army!"

"It would mean justice for these traitors. You will return to Jerusalem a defeated man, but you will return the master of your own kingdom. Leave Egypt to the Ishmaelites. Return to Jerusalem, and leave these traitors here to rot." Joscelin was so angry he was shaking.

Amalric looked out towards the knights charging up the ridge. They had almost reached the Saracens. Joscelin could see him struggling with the decision.

"Amalric," said Joscelin, "you sacrificed Agnes to become king. Now claim your kingship, or you will have given her up for nothing."

Slowly, Amalric's face resolved itself into a wrathful glare. "Very well. De Milly!" he roared for his aide. Sir Stephen de Milly came riding up. "De Milly, send riders out to all the other barons. Tell them to remain in the battle line. They are not to attack under any circumstances."

"Your Grace?"

"My orders, De Milly."

"Yes, Your Grace."

Amalric looked vaguely satisfied as De Milly rode off to send out the riders.

"I suppose these are the first traitors I will execute as king."

"But not the last," murmured Joscelin bitterly. "Now you truly are a king."

Even as he spoke, his words were drowned out in a roar of steel and shouts as the knights of Tripoli joined battle with the Saracens. The Arabic cavalry came rushing downhill to meet the Christian knights, and the neatly formed lines came apart in the chaos of battle. Joscelin could make out little of the battle's detail from where he sat his horse, but he sincerely hoped that Gilbert D'Aissailly met with a painful death.

The main part of the army was still waiting, immobile, at the bottom of the hill. Joscelin glanced down at them, knowing that they must be wondering why they were not being ordered to attack.

Let them wonder. Wonder...and watch three traitors pay the price for treason.

As he looked down towards the far end of the line, something caught Joscelin's eye. It was a rider, some lone knight, breaking away from the mass of troops at the bottom of the hill and riding on his own up the ridge to join the battle. Joscelin frowned, but his heart was hard with anger and a writhing resentment.

Let him go and die then, paying the traitor's price with the rest of them.

For a few minutes the knight rode alone. Then three or four others broke away from the battle line to join him. Then there were ten riding towards the battle.

A moment later a huge piece of the line broke away, like a piece of wet parchment. A sheet of knights rode away towards the fight. Roaring a battlecry, the Jaffa contingent charged with them.

Joscelin watched in dismay as the whole line went riding to their deaths.

They are traitors, all of them! he told himself desperately.

But Amalric's face had taken on a look almost of relief.

"There is no choice now, Joscelin. We must charge. I have told the knights of my household…told them that you would be leading them into battle."

Joscelin looked bitterly at the king. "Yes, Your Grace."

Sword in hand, he rode down to where the knights of the king's household were waiting.

"Knights of Jerusalem!" he roared. "It is time to charge! For the king!"

"For the king!" the knights roared after him.

"For the king!" he shouted again. "*Usque ad mortem!* Unto death!"

"*Usque ad mortem!*" roared the knights.

Then Joscelin spurred forward. Behind him he heard the thunder of a thousand hooves as the knights of Jerusalem charged.

Chapter 6

BLOOD AND STEEL
Malik

The leather felt cold to the touch, and Malik's hand was soaked with sweat.

Taking a deep breath, he let go of the hilt of his sword and clenched it tightly into a fist. His pulse only beat the harder.

Yusef was next to him, and a few feet in front of them was Lord Shirkuh, commander of the Saracen army and Yusef's uncle. The general and a handful of his officers were waiting in a little hollow beneath the long ridge. Malik glanced up towards the top. On the other side was the Nile floodplain, and the Army of Jerusalem.

Malik glanced at Yusef. His friend did not show the least sign of sweat, or of fear. Yusef radiated calm anticipation—a happy anticipation that scared Malik.

For his own part, Malik should have been up at the top of the ridge with the cavalry. But at the last moment his nerve had failed him. He had not hesitated because he feared to fight, to die, or to kill—he had fought and killed before, and was willing to risk death. Rather he was held back by the phantom fear that when he plunged into battle he would find himself face to face with Godfrey de Montferrat. The Templar's face had haunted him for the past two days, and Malik could not bring himself to draw sword against a foe who had spared his life.

Malik had been saved at the last moment when Yusef saw his uneasiness, and had told Shirkuh that Malik was down with the falling sickness that afflicted many in Egypt. Shirkuh had consented for Malik to stay back this day. So now Malik sat his horse shamefacedly, hating himself for cowardice and weakness.

The Frankish trumpets sounded again, shrill and clear from the other side of the ridge, sharp and proud in the morning.

"General Shirkuh!" Three horsemen approached Shirkuh, his chief officers: Hassan al-Athir, the captain of horse, Ali Nu'man, the captain of Mamelukes, and Musa al-Tafiq, Shirkuh's bannerman and bodyguard. Hassan wore the white and brown robes best suited to the desert. He rode a light Arabian charger, which was a few hands shorter than the other two horses. Ali wore the shining armor of the mamelukes, the slave-soldiers of Damascus. Musa wore black, and sat silent and foreboding on his great black horse. In one hand was Shirkuh's banner, in the other, a scimitar of giant size. He never spoke, for his tongue had been cut out years ago.

The three of them were riding down the ridge to where Shirkuh was waiting. "General!" said Hassan. "The Franks are there in the floodplain. I think they knew we were coming. They're in battle formation."

"That's the strange part," said Ali. "They're just waiting there. They've formed a long line facing us, and they're just sitting there, cooking in their steel armor. It's not like anything they usually do. I expected them to charge as soon as they saw us. I don't understand it, but the Franks must think they have some advantage over us if they can afford to wait down there, leaving us the high ground."

Shirkuh laughed. "Like as not, they're just displaying their ignorance of warcraft." Then he sighed. "I will have to ride closer and see for myself."

Ali gave a shout, and ten mamelukes formed up around Shirkuh, Malik, and Yusef. Musa al-Tafiq remained by his side, still silent. Shirkuh began riding up the ridge, the mamelukes and Musa staying in formation around him. Malik and Yusef followed.

Shirkuh stopped at the top of the ridge, looking down on the Frankish war host. As Hassan had said, the crusaders were arrayed in the floodplain, sitting there staring up at them.

Yusef frowned. "Could this be a trap, Uncle?"

Shirkuh laughed. "No trap, boy. Amalric is just too used to commanding his own little handful of knights. Now he's got the whole bloody army, he doesn't know what to do. He thinks to lure us down there so that he can crush us with whatever little plan he has in mind."

"But what will *we* do?" asked Hassan.

"It seems," said Shirkuh, "that the new king of Jerusalem has little knowledge of warcraft. We will have to teach him. Hassan, have your horseman fix arrows."

Hassan glanced down at the crusaders waiting in the plain below, and he smiled. Normally, arrows were little use against an armored knight. Knights could ride through clouds of arrows with only a few suffering harm. However, if the knights merely remained in place while the arrows continued to fall on them...

Hassan raised him arm, and the horsebowmen drew out their bows.

Suddenly, the Frankish trumpets began sounding again. Shirkuh's head whipped back around towards the crusaders.

The southern end of the Frankish line had broken away and was charging uphill. More groups of Frankish knights were coming away in organized fashion, riding to charge the Saracen line.

"Bows away!" shouted Shirkuh, no hint of anxiousness touching the calm in his voice. "Scimitars out!"

"My lord," said Ali Nu'man, riding up beside them, "you and your nephew must get back from the battle."

"Not yet," said Shirkuh, irritably. "Hassan, you know what to do. Wait until they are fifty yards away, then charge. Send your best swordsmen around the flanks, roll them from both sides at once. Ali, I don't know what it is this fool king is trying to do, attacking us in pieces, but you need to be ready for whatever he does. Keep an eye on the flanks, but sooner or later, I think the rest of that army will be coming up this hill. I need you to have your mamelukes ready to meet them."

"Yes, my lord."

"Now," said Shirkuh, "I will move back."

He turned his horse around and began riding back down the ridge. Yusef followed. Malik hesitated a moment, looking down at that mass of steel that was the army of Jerusalem. There were long blocks of red and blue and gold and silver and a thousand different sigils, but nowhere did he see the long block of white that would mark the knights of the Temple.

Malik breathed a sigh of relief. *No Templars here.* He turned and rode after Shirkuh and Yusef.

Shirkuh stopped at the bottom of the hill and looked up at Hassan's cavalry. They could hear the pounding of hooves as the Frankish destriers rode up the ridge. Malik was sweating again, a cold sweat that made him shake slightly. He felt dizzy. He reached again for the hilt of his sword, but the handle still felt too cold, and he shook even more as he tried to draw it.

Shirkuh was listening hard to the pounding of hooves. He looked up at Hassan's riders.

"If Hassan doesn't time it right..." Shirkuh clenched his fists, his eyes searching the ridge for Hassan. The sound of the crusaders grew louder. "He should make the countercharge...Now! Now Hassan!" Shirkuh roared as loud as he could, though he knew that Hassan could not hear.

A few seconds later, Hassan's riders sounded their horns and went charging down to meet the Franks.

"Bloody fool," muttered Shirkuh. "He always did hesitate too long." He began riding back and forth, craning his neck to try to watch the battle, but the top of the ridge hid it from their view.

Malik tried to shut the sound out, but could not. His mind was torn between fear and excitement, both fighting with such intensity that it seemed to Malik he was feeling physical pain inside his skull.

O Allah, let it end!

But it did not.

A Frankish horseman broke over the crest of the ridge and went riding down, followed by another, and then three more, and ten.

"Franks!" growled Shirkuh. "Where's Ali?"

Even as he spoke, the mamelukes came charging up from the south, arrayed in their shining armor, wielding their heavy axes and greatswords.

Malik felt his panic lessen at the sight of the mamelukes breaking upon the Frankish knights. But the heavy destriers of the Christians trampled down their shining armor and stout shields.

Shirkuh turned to Musa al-Tafiq. "Now, Musa!"

Musa sheathed his scimitar and drew a great horn from his saddle. He put it to his lips and blew a blast that echoed through the hills.

aHOOOOOOOOOOOOOOOOOOooooooooooooooo!

Musa blew until his face began purpling. Then he lowered the horn, breathing hard. He slung it from the saddle again and drew his scimitar.

From behind them, the Bedouin which Shirkuh had held in reserve came charging out from their cover, swarming over the rocks and rises.

Then all was chaos. Malik could no longer see any clear picture of the battle, only a swirling view of Bedouin and mamelukes and Franks hacking at each other, of steel and blood and bone.

There was no sense to it, no time to it. One moment seemed no different than the next, and yet always there was movement. Movement and noise.

Suddenly a Frankish horseman reared up before them, making for Shirkuh. Malik reached for the hilt of his sword, but his mind seemed to freeze and his hand shook violently. The Frank bore straight towards Shirkuh…until Musa severed his head with a great blow of his scimitar.

Even as he did, though, a Frankish knight put a lance through his back.

Musa al-Tafiq fell from his saddle, three feet of steel and wood protruding from his chest.

Yusef shrank back as the knight drew his sword and turned on them.

And in that moment, all fear fell from Malik. He drew his sword and swung it in a great glittering arc. The knight saw him at the last moment and parried. Malik swung again, his blow biting into the knight's oaken shield.

From that moment on, it was too easy. It was no different from training in the practice yard, except that the knight was less skilled than most of the men Malik had trained against. All the Franks knew of swordplay was bashing and more bashing. Malik played around the knight's blade like he would with a child.

The armor was harder; three times Malik's sword rang off the chain mail, leaving the knight unharmed, before he sliced through the knight's forearm on his fourth hit.

The sword fell from the knight's hand. He shouted something in Frankish, something that sounded like 'yield', but Malik was poor at Frankish, and at that moment, he didn't care. His next blow shattered the knight's helmet and his skull.

Malik wrenched the blade out as the knight fell from his frightened destrier. It was spattered with blood and bone and brain, but it was undented.

A good sword indeed.

Then there was more chaos, more of the swirling hell that was a battle. Time meant nothing, Malik only marked its passing by the knowledge that he had slain two more Franks by the time a frightened Saracen horseman came riding up to Shirkuh, shouting that Hassan was dead and the cavalry was collapsing.

Shirkuh looked around calmly at the maelstrom that surrounded them. "Malik!" he shouted. "It's time to prove your worth, boy!"

Malik frowned, feeling the panic return.

"Go out there, and gather as many of the horsemen as you can. Bring them around the back, and charge."

"Me, my lord?"

"*Move!*" roared Shirkuh.

Malik hesitated, glancing at Yusef. Yusef smiled uncertainly. Then Malik plunged into the battle. He cut down a Frankish crossbowman and an unhorsed yeoman before he found a clear spot. He rode on, finding groups of Hassan's riders, broken and fleeing. He shouted out to them, not really sure what it was he was saying. His mind was racing. Some of them kept on fleeing, but some followed him.

Another eternity later, he found himself on the south side of the battle, with a group of riders gathered behind him. He tried to count how many, but his head was spinning too much. It could have been any number from ten to a thousand.

Malik looked out over the battle. He could not make out any battle lines any more, only death and chaos. He glanced back at his riders again, and then he shouted with all the breath left in his lungs.

"Charge!"

One of the riders must have had a horn, for he started blowing on it.

aHOOOOOOooooooooo! aHOOOOOOOOooooooooo!

From before them, they heard the Frankish trumpets blowing, still proud and defiant, shrill and high compared to the deep tone of the Saracen horn.

Malik spurred forward, heedless now of whether anyone followed him or not. He plunged again into the battle, hacking out wildly, hoping that he was striking at Franks and not at Saracens. He could sense and hear the riders coming behind him, a long line of them, trampling down everything in their path.

Once again, time slid away into chaos. Malik found that his sword was slick with the innards of his foes.

How did it get like that? Last I remember, it was clear and shining.

Then Malik caught sight of something, far ahead. A great Frankish helmet, still gleaming in the sun, topped by a bright golden crown.

Malik tried to look around, but could make no sense of the chaos around him. All he saw was that crown.

"It's the king!" he shouted. "It's Amalric! Take him!" He plunged into the sea of men between him and that golden crown, unaware that only a few of the riders were still following him.

Yet as he charged, the wall of steel gave way before him.

Why is that? he thought idly.

Far ahead, though, the golden crown was moving further away. Moving north.

DA-DAA! DA-DAA! The Frankish trumpets sounded again. They were calling something else now…

It finally dawned on Malik. *They're retreating. The Franks are retreating!*

DA-DAA! DA-DAA! The horns sounded sorry and forlorn as the Saracen horns answered, deep and strong.

AHOOOOOOOOOOOOO! AHOOOOOOOOOOO!

Malik looked around wildly, caught glimpses of fleeing Christians. He caught sight of the crown once more.

"The king!" he shouted again, and rode after it.

"Malik!" someone shouted from behind. Malik cast one more longing look at that golden crown, then he reined in.

"Malik!" It was Yusef. His sword and clothes were also stained in blood, but Yusef looked happy. Malik looked around, saw that only live Arabs and corpses remained on the field. He looked north to see the Frankish host fleeing. "Malik, are you mad? You were about to charge the Frankish army on your own."

Malik felt the battle frenzy draining away. He looked around helplessly.

"Where...where are my...my riders? They were with me...with me right here."

"Mostly," said Yusef, "they're dead. You did a brilliant job. Broke in their rear. It was bloody suicidal, but it worked." Yusef glanced at his scimitar, saw the blood. His eyes widened in surprise, as though he had just noticed it. Grimacing, he climbed down from his horse and wiped it off on a patch of dead grass.

Malik glanced at his sword. It was stained from the tip to the handle. He sighed, and climbed down from his horse to follow Yusef's example.

Malik sat down in the dirt, feeling dazed.

"Yusef, I hope I never fight another battle again."

Yusef sat down next to him. He glanced around, then whispered, "So do I."

Chapter 7

Like a Troubadour's Tale
Godfrey

odfrey de Montferrat rode on through the darkness. The night seemed pitch black now. *As though all the light had died.*

He had left the pickets somewhere behind him. That seemed ages ago. They had said the camp was just ahead, but it seemed he had ridden for miles since then.

Everything was blurred together in his mind, the charge, the battle, his escape, the long ride back through the day and into the night. He was bone weary, but he had to find... *What is it I have to find?*

Godfrey looked up at the sky, but there was no light there, no stars. *What do stars look like?* Godfrey's tired hand slipped from the reins. His horse continued to trot on, into the night. The burden slung across the saddle behind him shifted. Godfrey reached out instinctively to grab it. *It is important that it doesn't fall off.*

But what is it? Godfrey's limp brain could not recall what it was he was carrying.

Suddenly a pillar of flame loomed up before him out of the night. The horse began trotting more quickly towards it. Godfrey stared at it in alarm.

What is it?

Godfrey could feel his fear fighting his exhaustion. Slowly, he began to slide sideways. He did not even try to right himself. Suddenly the dark ground came rushing up at him and he landed hard on some dead grass and dirt.

That jolted some awareness back into him. He looked up at the flame, no longer a pillar of fire, merely a campfire. He heard voices.

"It's the Templar," someone said. "He looks more dead than alive."

"What's that on the horse's back?"

Slowly, Godfrey stood up on unsteady legs. He grabbed his horse's stirrup for support, but slipped again as the horse continued to trot forward. Now he remembered what the burden on the back of his horse was. He reached up and pulled Humphrey de Vinsauf's unconscious body off the back of his horse. Godfrey smiled groggily at the knight's battered face.

"You look even worse than I must look."

Humphrey did not respond. Godfrey tried to turn around to face the campfire, and his legs gave out again. A sharp pain lanced through his left thigh. He collapsed on the dirt and dead grass, the world spinning about him.

He felt himself lifted up by many pairs of arms. It hurt to see, so he closed his eyes. He could feel the warmth growing.

They must be carrying me to the campfire.

✠ ✠ ✠

Some time later, Godfrey awoke. He had no memory of going to sleep, but his mind was much clearer. Clearer...except for an image and a thought on the edge of his memory. He had been dreaming, dreaming very vividly, and he had dreamt something about...

Godfrey tried to call the images into his mind:

Conrad and Adelaise...and me. Jacques was there too, but not with the rest of us. And old Otto of Freising. He was telling something to Adelaise and me...

Godfrey's heart ached, but he could recall no more. The dream faded, and Godfrey let it go wearily.

How long has it been?

It was still dark, still night. He was lying on some torn piece of cloth next to the fire. Someone was sitting next to him. His vision was a little blurry, but he stared for a few seconds and it cleared. It was Humphrey. Humphrey still looked battered and wounded, but there was a broad grin on his face.

"I was bloody right, Templar."

Godfrey frowned, but quickly went back to staring. Frowning hurt.

"About...what?" he managed.

"You do have some of Godfrey de Bouillion in you."

Godfrey smiled weakly. "I'm not a saint...only crazy."

"It seems to me," said Humphrey, "most of the saints had a touch of madness in them. I think it's a sign that God loves them."

Godfrey tried to laugh, but it came out as a weak gurgle.

"If you are mad," continued Humphrey, "we need more madmen. A few more fools like you and we'd have had the Ishmaelites running."

Godfrey could remember now what had happened. *You fool,* he thought with a sinking heart, *You've gotten yourself too deep in for even Blanchefort to get you out.*

He had been waiting with the knights of Tripoli. He had at last convinced Jacques that it would be wrong to fight, so the two of them were waiting at the rear. Godfrey had seen the infidels come, and had watched, shocked, as Tripoli began riding up and down, shouting out to his men.

'Knights of Tripoli, do you know what the king wants us to do?' Tripoli had roared, visibly angry. *'He wants us to run! He wants us to flee, to try to deceive the infidels. Then his knights will crush the Ishmaelites and return to Jerusalem with tales of the cowardice of the men of Tripoli. What do you say to that?'*

The knights of Tripoli had not approved of the king's orders. Their uproar had drowned out Tripoli's voice for a while, and Godfrey had caught only snatches of his speech. He caught words like 'glory' and 'honor' often. Finally the noise subsided, and Tripoli had ridden to the head of the line. All the men of Tripoli had waited in silence as Tripoli faced the infidels. Then the count had given the order to charge.

Godfrey had sat there on his horse, still not fully believing what he was seeing. The knights of Tripoli had surged forward towards the Saracens, leaving the rest of the army behind. A few minutes later, the knights of the Hospital had broken formation to charge, and then the knights of Ibelin. Jacques had made some insulting comment about the Hospitallers, but Godfrey had been too surprised to really notice.

So Godfrey had watched as a third of the kingdom's knights charged up the hill, while the rest of the army sat and watched. He had kept looking up towards the king's banner, to see if Amalric were going to come to their aid.

It was then that he had realized what was happening. To Amalric, this battle was no more than his bloody game of thrones. Tripoli and D'Aissailly and Ibelin had committed treason, so those three must die. If two thousand others must die with them, so be it.

Godfrey had grown angry at that, and in his anger had thrown caution to the winds. He still felt dizzy remembering it. He had spurred forward, drawing his sword and shouting incoherently. Then he began riding up to join the knights of Tripoli, forgetting any past resolution to stay out of the battle. As he rode up the hill, Godfrey had thought he was leaving them all behind, the king and the Army and Jacques, but to his surprise he had heard the sound behind him as others followed. By the time he had reached the top a dozen others had joined him, and most of the army was behind him.

A sudden thought jerked Godfrey back to the present. He frowned again. It hurt less this time.

"Humphrey," he said, his voice anxious. "Where is Jacques? Is he… alive?"

"He's alive," said Humphrey. "He was in camp when I woke up. He'll be somewhere nearby."

Godfrey breathed a sigh of relief. "I think I can stand now," he said. Slowly he pushed himself up onto his elbows, then he began to struggle up.

As soon as he did, he felt the pain lancing through his thigh again. Wincing, he reached down and felt where the pain was. His hand came away slick with blood. Vaguely he remembered a Saracen spear piercing him there.

How much blood have I lost?

Godfrey tried again, putting as little weight on his left as possible. Slowly he struggled to his feet.

"Sir Templar!" came another voice from behind him. Godfrey did not try to turn around; he would have fallen again if he had. Instead, Tripoli came around to face him.

"Well done, Templar," he said. "I was told about your valiant charge. It is quite possible you saved us all."

Saved you all, maybe, but I have won the enmity of the king. If Tripoli knows of this, so will Amalric…

"He saved me, that much I know," said Humphrey. He laughed. "I should have been dead there. I had lost my shield, and I was cut in my left arm and my right leg. All alone, with Saracens coming from all sides. Then Godfrey comes riding down, trampling through the infidels. His face was a fearsome thing to see, and him all arrayed in white like some hero from a troubadour's tale."

"All Templars wear white," murmured Godfrey, but no one heard him.

"He was shouting for me to grab on," Humphrey continued. "So I reached up to catch on, but it never occurred to Godfrey to stop. I dropped my axe and caught his stirrup, and we went bouncing along like that for a good hundred yards. Just when I thought my arm was going to come off, Godfrey reins in sharply, and I clambered up behind him. By then, all the other Franks were gone. No one but us and the bloody Ishmaelites. So we rode like hellfire was at our backs."

Godfrey smiled slightly. "I got lost," he said, a little louder. "It's only luck that I found the camp when I did."

"Godfrey?" Jacques seemed to materialize out of the darkness. "You're alive!"

"Barely," murmured Godfrey.

From a campfire a little ways away, there came an uproar. Humphrey stared out in that direction.

"Mass," he spat. "It's the king himself."

Tripoli stiffened. "Amalric? Humphrey, I want you to go gather as many of my knights as you can. Bring them here."

"As for you," said Tripoli to Jacques and Godfrey, "you'd better get moving. If I found out about your insubordination, so will Amalric, and I don't think he'll find it half as amusing as I did. The horselines are a few hundred paces to the left. Get two horses and *ride*. Make for Jerusalem and the Temple. Once you're there, your names will fade back into obscurity and Amalric will forget about you. But if he catches either of you here in the camp....Anyway, there is something more important: when you reach Jerusalem, tell the master of the Temple to prepare the defenses. Shirkuh may not realize it, but the way to Jerusalem is open. If the Saracen moves fast, he can smash through the southern principalities and besiege Jerusalem."

"Thank you, Lord Tripoli, for your hospitality," said Jacques. "I will inform Grand Master Blanchefort of your aid to us."

"You shouldn't have made the charge, Lord Tripoli." Everyone turned to stare at Godfrey, who had spoken. "You shouldn't have charged," Godfrey repeated. "I shouldn't have charged either. It was an act of pride, sacrificing a piece of the army to humiliate Amalric."

Everyone turned to stare at Godfrey. Tripoli's face darkened. "I have aided you and given you hospitality, and protected you from the king. Is this your only gratitude?"

Humphrey, who had been lingering a few moments to listen, burst out laughing. "Leave it, my lord. He's sincere, and that's something you rarely find. Save it for the Ishmaelites. You're dealing with a hero here; that or a madman; and you must make allowances for either."

Godfrey bowed his head. "I beg pardon, my lord. I did not speak to offend, merely to admit my...mistake."

"Apparently to admit my mistake as well," said Tripoli. "Nonetheless, I will let it pass. We part in friendship then?"

"If my lord so wishes." Godfrey made as best a bow as he could.

The noise was growing closer.

"Go now," said Tripoli. "The king draws nearer. Humphrey, you too. Hurry."

Humphrey rushed off into the darkness. Godfrey took a few stumbling steps and winced, doubling over. Each step sent pain lancing up his thigh.

Tripoli looked at his limp, alarmed.

"I will have one of my knights help you. De Ridford!"

Godfrey's face darkened at the name. "My lord Tripoli, we will be—"

"Caught in Amalric's iron fist unless you accept some help. De Ridford!"

De Ridford appeared by the campfire, his face cherubic as it had been that morning.

"De Ridford," said Tripoli, "help this Templar to the horselines. Help him mount and see them off."

De Ridford smiled, angelic as ever. "Yes, my lord." He moved over to Godfrey, who scowled at him.

"I don't need—"

"I'm sure you do," said De Ridford calmly. He took Godfrey's arm and put it around his neck. "Walk," De Ridford commanded.

Reluctantly, Godfrey hobbled forward, supported by Gerard de Ridford. Jacques ran ahead to get the horses. As soon as they had passed out of earshot of the count of Tripoli, De Ridford began to talk quietly.

"You need not be ashamed, Templar. I am told that true men would not accept help of this kind, but I do not think that applies to eunuchs."

Godfrey made a move to throw De Ridford off him, but the pain shot up again, and he bit his tongue to keep from howling.

You are a Templar, he thought. *You do not have enemies. Well, maybe you do, but you must love them.*

But with each step, Godfrey found himself loathing De Ridford all the more.

It was a great relief when Jacques appeared again, leading their horses. He nodded to De Ridford.

"I can help him from here. You'd better get back to help your count."

De Ridford smiled knowingly and left without saying a word. With a little help from Jacques, Godfrey scrambled up into the saddle. Silently, the two turned and rode off into the darkness.

For a few minutes they rode in silence, though Jacques kept glancing over at Godfrey. Finally he spoke.

"What was that about?"

"What?"

"You had no right to reprimand the count of Tripoli. He, at least, has authority over his men. The men you led on a charge were not even yours to command."

Godfrey nodded. "As I said; I should not have charged either. I was more in the wrong than he was."

Jacques laughed. "Godfrey, you are the one person I know who always puts into practice anything he believes to be right. I think it scares me. You defied the king of Jerusalem to save Tripoli, and then you angered Tripoli by declaring that both you and he had done wrong. If you go on much longer, you'll make enemies of everyone in the kingdom. I hope you aren't planning to rise high in the ranks of the Temple. It's going to take a good deal more diplomacy than you have."

"No," said Godfrey, "I'm happy as I am; I wouldn't make a good seneschal or marshal, and certainly not a good grand master."

"But," said Jacques, "you really believe that Tripoli did wrong in disobeying the king? The king has never been the absolute ruler of the kingdom; Tripoli was within his rights."

"Legally, yes," said Godfrey stubbornly. "But to do as he did, forcing the battle on Amalric by threatening to destroy half the army? That was pride."

Jacques only laughed. Neither of them spoke again that night. They fell into pensive silence as they rode on through the desert. Godfrey's leg throbbed a little with each heave of the horse's flanks, but the pain was not overmuch. Soon Godfrey's thoughts were turning to Jerusalem, the city which had always been home for him, even during his long years in Italy. The Outer City, the noisy, crowded city streets, filled with people: Arabs, Jews, Syrians, Greeks, Franks, a hodgepodge of nationalities; the Inner City, the peace and quiet of Jerusalem Temple. Jerusalem was home.

There would be work to do there, too, but that was the work he was used to, the work he loved. He and Jacques de Maille's first task, when they got back, would be to report to the master of the Temple, Bertrand de Blanchefort, for Jacques and Godfrey had been entrusted more than the ordinary tasks of a Templar.

A year ago, shortly after the two of them had become Templars, the master of the Temple had picked them out. Neither Jacques nor Godfrey knew why they had been picked, but Master Bertrand de Blanchefort must have seen something in them, for he immediately began training them to be his agents, his eyes and ears in hostile places. The hundreds of factions all vying for the Holy Land, Latin, Greek, Shi'ite and Sunni all had their spies scattered throughout Palestine, Arabia, Syria and Egypt. The Fatimids, the Assassins, Nur ad-Din, Amalric, Tripoli, the Greek empire, all had their agents. Even the Master of the Hospital had his network spread through the Holy Land. So the master of the Temple could not afford to be left blind and deaf. There were many others who reported to Blanchefort, but Jacques and Godfrey were the only Templars, so far as they knew, who were used as the Master's agents. Since they had been chosen, they had traveled all about the Holy Land, going wherever the Master of Jerusalem Temple required them.

Suddenly, Godfrey felt himself slipping. He flailed out wildly and caught on the reins. He had fallen asleep even as he rode. He shook himself fully awake and glanced around at the endless wastes of sand. The young Templar prayed fervently that he would never have to return to Egypt again.

Chapter 8

A Reckoning
Joscelin

The last light of the sun had left the sky by the time Joscelin de Courtenay found the Frankish camp.

He trudged along the browning grass that grew in the floodplain, bloodied and soaked with dirty Nile-water. Next to him his squire Tristan stumbled along, careful at every moment to see if his master needed support, even though he himself looked ready to collapse.

Sweat and blood still trickled down the count of Edessa's face when the first campfires came in sight. The gash along his cheek was not deep, but like any face wound, it bled profusely. The wound in his shoulder was worse.

And I am growing too fat for all this walking, thought Joscelin dryly. *I am too used to riding a horse.*

He glanced sidelong at Tristan—the boy looked so helpless and pathetic, yet so ready to come to his aid. Joscelin felt his pity go out to the child.

More campfires appeared through the darkness. Joscelin and Tristan stumbled towards them, and soon were apprehended by the sentries and brought into the camp. Joscelin glanced about despondently at the haphazard organization and the bloodied, beaten men who sat listlessly about the campfires.

A sentry led Joscelin to the king. Amalric sat before an unlit heap of wood, still in his chain mail, gazing blankly at the stars.

"Amalric," said Joscelin, "I am here."

The king almost jumped at his voice, but when he saw Joscelin, a look of genuine relief passed over his face. But only for a moment. Then his face resumed its blank look.

"It is finished," he murmured. "We must flee now. Flee in defeat."

Joscelin sat down across from him. Tristan stood dutifully behind him, unwilling to follow.

"Is Shirkuh following us?" asked Joscelin.

"Not tonight," said Amalric. "We hurt him that badly, at least. But in the morning, when he has rested, I think he will give chase."

"Should we begin marching now?" Joscelin replied.

Amalric gave him a look of tired irritation. "Did you see the men, Joscelin? They will not budge. If I tell them to move now, the army will disintegrate and we will all be picked off in little groups by Shirkuh's lancers. No, we too must wait for morning."

Joscelin nodded wearily. "As you say, Your Grace." In spite of his weariness, his thoughts began to turn to anger as he remembered the battle. Anger at the senseless defeat, anger at Shirkuh, anger at…

"Your Grace," said Joscelin suddenly. "We cannot march tonight, but there is something that we can do."

Amalric looked questioningly at him.

"The traitors," he said. "D'Aissailly and Ibelin, but especially Tripoli. I think he is behind it all."

The king stared at Joscelin a few moments, and then his face began to purple. He, too, had forgotten.

"Yes," he said. "This is where their treachery has got them. What can I do? I cannot arrest Tripoli—not here, in the middle of Egypt…"

"Confront him, at least," growled Joscelin, angrily. "Humiliate him."

Amalric rose. "Call my knights, Joscelin." His fist clenched.

✝ ✝ ✝

The king strode through the press of men who were gathered about the count of Tripoli. The footmen and knights rose to greet him as he passed. He was still in his battle-stained armor, his sword at his side and his golden crown atop his helmet. Behind him came Joscelin de Courtenay and a handful of the knights of his house. Joscelin wore a bloody bandage now across his cheek and his shoulder, but his step was steady and his face a mask of anger.

Abruptly the men parted, and nothing but an open space of fifteen feet stood between him and Raymond of Tripoli.

The count of Tripoli and the king of Jerusalem glared at each other for a moment, each waiting for the other to speak.

"You disobeyed my orders!" growled Amalric, his hand on his sword hilt.

"As a Christian, I am bound to obey only those put in lawful authority over me," replied Tripoli.

It took Amalric a few seconds to figure out what his words meant. Joscelin caught its intent immediately.

"Count Raymond," said Joscelin, "Tripoli has always been recognized as subordinate to Jerusalem. For as long as Outremer has been in Christian hands, it has been this way. You are obliged by law and by custom to do the will of your sovereign. Do not forget that you swore fealty to him when he came to the throne."

"It was foolish and blameworthy of me to swear," said the count of Tripoli. "But the oath was not valid." There was a murmur of assent from his men. "Tripoli's sovereignty has always been equal to Jerusalem's; it has been so since the First Crusade. In the past, the counts of Tripoli may have subordinated themselves because it was necessary. Now it is no longer needed. The county of Tripoli is legally autonomous, and always has been."

"And you saw today where Tripoli's autonomy got us," said the king. "Because of that autonomy, we are fleeing toward Jerusalem, leaving the field of battle to Shirkuh."

Tripoli laughed scornfully. "My charge saved some part of our army at least. Your battle plan was worthy of an infant, Amalric, not of a veteran knight."

Amalric's face purpled. "Because of your disobedience, your men will form the rearguard tomorrow as we retreat."

"That," said Tripoli, "we will not. Knights of Tripoli!" he shouted. "We are leaving. Now!"

Tripoli now smiled smugly at the king of Jerusalem. "Farewell, your Majesty. I pray that no disaster may befall your men on the way back to Jerusalem; it would be most unfortunate, considering that you will not have the Tripoli contingent with your army."

Joscelin had watched in growing chagrin as Tripoli got the better of the confrontation. "Your Majesty," he murmured quietly, "it would be best to return to your tent."

Amalric kept his eyes fixed on Tripoli. "I will make you suffer for this."

Tripoli smiled serenely.

"Your Grace," murmured Joscelin again. "*Now.*" His anger was gone, and now there was only resentment and disappointment. Even the satisfaction of humiliating Tripoli had been lost.

Amalric shoved Joscelin out of his way, turned on his heel, and strode off into the darkness, followed by Joscelin and his knights.

✛ ✛ ✛

Joscelin let Amalric return to his tent to fume and to curse in vain his rebellious vassals. He made for his own campfire with his knights.

Tristan de Monglane was waiting by the campfire outside his tent, turning a haunch of meat over the fire. Joscelin sighed wearily as he sat down next to the boy squire. He could smell the juices in the meat, and he realized that he hadn't eaten all day.

"Lord, Tristan, that smells good," he said, pulling off his surcoat and working off his hauberk.

"Yes, my lord," said the squire, who kept his eyes on the meat.

Tristan was fourteen years of age. He was the son of a poor, landless knight named Fulke who had gone with Joscelin's father, Joscelin II, on one last hopeless expedition to retake the county of Edessa—for Joscelin de Courtenay was the lord of a city that had been lost to the infidels when he was young. Joscelin II had spent his life trying to regain Edessa, but had been captured and died in Nur ad-Din's dungeons, leaving his son Joscelin III in exile. Tristan's father Fulke had been slain defending Joscelin II, leaving behind a pregnant wife.

A few months later, the son had been born. Joscelin had done his best to support both mother and child. When Tristan grew older, he had taken the boy as his squire out of pity, for otherwise Tristan would have been fated for the slums of Jerusalem.

Tristan was quieter than any boy had a right to be. He was dutiful to a fault, but he never spoke a word more than he needed to. He worked at the lists and the training yard for hours every day, but he was still a scrawny boy, and clumsy. Joscelin worried that he would never make a knight, but he kept him as a squire, if nothing else so that he would remember both of their fathers.

But earlier that day during the battle, Joscelin had been separated from Amalric in a desperate rearguard action and been knocked into the Nile, wounded and bleeding. He had floated half conscious amongst the reeds until his squire dragged him onto the sands. Tristan helped him to a hollow in the hills, where they rested and hid a few hours from the Saracen horsemen, until Joscelin was able to walk. He owed his life to the scrawny boy.

The knights crowded around the fire, sniffing at the meat. Joscelin leaned back, resting his back against a log. He nursed his shoulder gently, and found that the pain was subsiding already. His surcoat and ringmail lay next to him, leaving only his woolen shirt, which felt as light as silk after a day of wearing armor. His stomach gave a growl as he smelled the meat again.

Joscelin shut his eyes and let all the worries of the day roll off him. For the moment, at least, life was good.

Chapter 9

MEN OF IRON
Godfrey

Some days later, at the laziest part of the afternoon, Sir Aimery de Milly looked down from the ramparts of Jerusalem to see two horsemen pounding down the road toward the gate. He glared down at them for a moment, then gave a command.

"Open the gate!" he shouted. "Open the gate!"

Below him, the heavy bolts were thrown aside and the postern gate flung open. Aimery rushed down the stairs to get information from the horsemen.

The two men were Templars. They clattered through the doorway and made for the inner city.

"Halt!" shouted Aimery, standing in their way. He leapt aside as the horses rode past him, and caught the reins of one of the horses.

"What news do you bring?" shouted Aimery to the Templar, who was glaring down angrily at him. The other Templar reined in, his hand going to his sword hilt. "I have orders to question everyone who passes through the gate," said Aimery. "Do you have any news of Egypt?"

"Let go of my reins," said the Templar, impatiently. He wrenched them from the startled knight's hands. "Amalric has been defeated. He will be here by tomorrow. We fear that he may be pursued by Nur ad-Din's armies. I must see the master of the Temple."

The Templars spurred forward again and galloped through the crowded streets of the Outer City.

✠ ✠ ✠

Jerusalem, the Holy City, was divided into two parts: the Inner and Outer cities. The Outer City was where the common people lived. Men of all nationalities and faiths lived here, Moors, Syrians, Jews, Greeks, Franks,

Armenians, all crowded into the dirty alleys and byways of this outer ring. Here the muezzin could be heard ringing next to the church bells; here the Jews, Christians and Muslims held their peace and celebrated their feasts and sold their wares.

Only Christians lived in the Inner City. This was the Old City of Jerusalem, the city in which Christ had come to worship at the Temple. Solomon's Temple, destroyed long ago in antiquity, had been rebuilt fifteen hundred long years ago by Ezra and Nehemiah, and that Temple too had been destroyed by the Romans. Traces and ruins of that second Temple remained where it had stood, and the headquarters of the Knights Templar was built over these ruins, from which they derived their name.

Godfrey and Jacques plunged through the crowded streets towards the Inner City, forcing vendors and peasants to leap out of the way. The two Templars could not afford to be delayed; if Shirkuh's army was coming to Jerusalem, the master of the Temple must be warned.

Men thronged around them, asking what news they brought. Syrian shopkeepers hemmed them in, offering to sell them food and goods. Godfrey and Jacques ignored them, pressing on through the mass of men. They had no fear of the mob; this was their city, they had grown up here, and they lived among these people.

They passed through the portal to the Inner City. Here the crowds were much thinner, and they made better progress. At last, dusty and tired, they arrived at the gate to the Temple. The porter, recognizing them by sight, let them in without question. As they passed through, Jacques turned to look up at the portal.

"De Torroga! Where is the Master?"

"He is in the refectory. You had better wash yourself off before you go to see him. Blanchefort will not be happy if two unkempt vagabonds tramp into the Temple."

Jacques shook his head. "This is urgent. Nur ad-Din's army could be here by tomorrow evening. We have no time to waste with baths."

Godfrey and Jacques rode to the stable, a cave carved out in the base of the Temple Rock. As Godfrey dismounted, his wounded leg gave a sharp twinge of pain. He took a slow step, and another, and another. It was slow going, but Godfrey found to his relief that he could at least walk now. The two Templars handed their horses to the grooms and hurried towards the refectory.

Bertrand de Blanchefort was a big man, his body lithe and muscled. His hair and beard were both golden-brown, just starting to turn white. He had a commanding presence—a born leader of men.

Blanchefort stood at the head of the long tables in the refectory, intoning the daily psalm before the two hundred or so Templars that made up the Order of the Temple. The men stood, their heads bowed, as they listened to the grand master.

Right there, in that room, was gathered the most powerful military force in the kingdom. The Templars were not great in numbers, never more than three hundred. Nor were they chosen because they were exceptional men. Rather, they were a handful of souls doing penance for some sin, or monkish men giving their life in defense of Outremer. Yet the Order of the Temple was a force to be reckoned with.

But if the Templars were not chosen as exceptional men, the Order of the Temple made them so. They fasted constantly, and while they were in Jerusalem they spent an hour each day at the barracks, training with their swords. They lived with little food or sleep, so they had no trouble adjusting to campaigns. The Order made monks into hard men, and hard men into monks, ready to fight or die at a moment's notice.

They lived as monks in that they took vows of poverty, chastity and obedience. Though they did not always succeed in living up to these vows, they spent their lives trying. Many of the men were little more than outlaws come from Europe to escape punishment, men used to murdering and raping indiscriminately, but the Temple broke them in to the monastic life, and turned their fighting spirit to the defense of the kingdom.

The knights of the Temple were the most fearsome warriors in the East. A handful of Templars, mounted and armored, could smash through an enemy five times their number. But time and again the Saracens brought up more than that, and so each year, Templars died in droves. But, like a pruned fig tree, each year the Order grew back to fight the Saracens again.

Seeing the master of the Temple intoning the psalm, Godfrey and Jacques stopped and bowed their heads with the rest of the Templars, no matter that they had just ridden at breakneck speed to get here. When Blanchefort prayed, every Templar bowed his head and prayed with him, or dire consequences followed.

"I will lift mine eyes up to the hills. From whence does my help come? My help comes from the LORD, who made heaven and earth."

It was the hundred and twenty-first psalm, one of Blanchefort's favorites. *I will lift up mine eyes to the hills.* A song of ascents, it was called in Scripture. Blanchefort went on in his deep, stentorian voice, to the end of the psalm.

"The LORD will keep you from all evil; he will keep your life. The LORD will keep your going out and your coming in from this time forth and for evermore."

Blanchefort looked up, and so did all the Templars. The master's gaze stretched over the table, and then fell on the two Templars standing in the entrance, covered in dust from head to toe.

"Ah, De Montferrat, De Maille. You have a reason for trooping in here looking like a pair of common criminals? Perhaps I should hang you, like I would the criminals?"

"Grand Master," said Jacques, "the king's army has been defeated. They are fleeing towards Jerusalem, and the Saracens may give pursuit. Nur ad-Din's army could be here by tomorrow night."

All faces turned towards Jacques and Godfrey.

Blanchefort was silent for a moment.

"You are sure of this?" he asked.

"We are sure that Amalric has been defeated and is fleeing towards Jerusalem," said Godfrey. "General Shirkuh might not have pursued him, but if he did, he will be here soon."

Blanchefort gritted his teeth together, his brows knitted into a frown. He looked out over the table again.

"We can take them," said a voice next to Blanchefort. Godfrey looked up to see Odo de Sant'Amand standing at the master's left side. Odo was the marshal of the Temple, the chief military officer below the master. At thirty, he was young for a marshal. Odo was noble-born, and would never let any man forget it. He lived by the code of chivalry, and would never avoid a fight.

"We should send out for reinforcements," said the man on Blanchefort's right. "We could rally a thousand men from Antioch and the northern principalities."

This man was Phillip de Milly. He was also a powerful knight in the Temple. More prudent than Odo, but perhaps a touch overcautious, he had run against Odo in the election for marshal, and had been defeated by a narrow margin. But Bertrand de Blanchefort liked to keep both Odo and Phillip by him and play one against the other.

"No time to send for reinforcements," said Odo.

Blanchefort held up a hand for silence.

"How much of Amalric's army is left?"

Godfrey grimaced. "I don't know for sure, but I would guess at two thirds of the army that left Jerusalem. They're in bad order, not fully armed."

Blanchefort nodded. "Nonetheless, there will be enough there to hold Jerusalem. Let Shirkuh come. The Temple will be ready. Jerusalem will not fall this time. If Shirkuh comes, he'll be walking into a trap. Jerusalem will hold, and the southern principalities will rally against him. His army will be torn apart."

Blanchefort looked out over the crowd of Templars.

"Arm yourselves, all of you!"

The Templars broke into a ragged cheer and they stood, boasting and chattering in high spirits, and tramped towards the entrance.

Jacques and Godfrey looked at each other. Then they turned and led the way out.

In the courtyard outside, a man was waiting, dressed in a black clerical frock. Godfrey smiled when he saw him. Jacques, who did not know the man, passed on, but Godfrey stopped to speak with him.

"William! What are you doing here? Aren't you supposed to be in Tyre, or some other God-forsaken place?" Godfrey clapped him on the shoulder as he spoke, and the man smiled back at him.

"I was, but the archbishop of Tyre sent me to Jerusalem on an errand to the patriarch of Jerusalem. Right now I have a message for the master of the Temple."

"Did the patriarch send you?"

The man shook his head. "I have come of my own accord."

Godfrey raised his eyebrows. "Blanchefort may not have time to listen to any priest picked off the streets."

The man smiled. "Perhaps not, Godfrey, but you see, they've made me an archdeacon. And my message today is urgent."

Godfrey laughed. "Archdeacon William of Tyre. I like the sound of it. Come with me and I'll take you to the master."

In the refectory, Bertrand de Blanchefort was sharpening his sword while discussing the defenses with Odo de Sant'Amand and Phillip de Milly. He looked up as the two men entered the room.

"Master," said Godfrey, bowing. "Archdeacon William of Tyre has a message for you."

"Master Blanchefort," said William, bowing also. "I came to warn you: the patriarch of Jerusalem has just caused panic in the streets. He announced to the people that Nur ad-Din's army was coming. He told them that there was no one to defend Jerusalem, and that the best thing to do would be to pray for their salvation. You can imagine the reaction, sir."

"Curse that doddering old fool, the patriarch," muttered Blanchefort. "When this affair is over, I'll have a word with him. He has very noble sentiments but perhaps a little *ill-advised*. Prayer is needed, but panic is not. Thank you, Archdeacon. You're a man of good sense. They ought to make you the patriarch."

William laughed. "Thank you, Master Blanchefort. Sadly, it takes more than good sense or even holiness to be made the patriarch. It takes good money, given in the right amounts to the right people."

"Sad it is," said Godfrey, "that the kingdom has sunk so low."

Blanchefort laughed. "That's the way the world works, my young and inexperienced Templar. Now, I'm sure that when my soul is gone to rest, these two honorable knights will not resort to bribery?" He motioned to Odo and Phillip. They both nodded vigorously. Blanchefort laughed again.

"Look at them, the pair of jackals, just waiting for me to die so that they can both pounce. They'll start bribing the electors before I'm in my grave."

"You misjudge me, Master," said Odo. "I would not stoop to such a tactic worthy of a knave."

"No," said Phillip. "You would never do anything serflike, would you? What he means is that he will bribe them like a king, with bribes that he can promise but never pay. Now, as for me, I am a man of my word. When I promise a bribe, I pay it."

"Be quiet, all of you," said Blanchefort. "I want to think now. How did the patriarch find out that Shirkuh might be coming?"

There was silence for a moment. Then a possibility struck Godfrey.

"At Jerusalem gate the guards tried to stop me and get information. I blurted out something about Nur ad-Din coming to Jerusalem, so that they would let me pass. I would hazard a guess that that doddering old fool isn't as foolish as he appears. He probably has the guards bribed to tell him any useful information."

Blanchefort laughed uproariously. "The clever old whoreson."

Then the master of the Temple stood, buckling his sword on.

"Once again, thank you, Archdeacon. You may return to your duties. As for the Templars, we will see to the defense of the city."

Chapter 10

THE CROWN OF THE WORLD
Godfrey

During the late watches of the night, Godfrey de Montferrat looked out from the walls of Jerusalem. The Master of the Temple had roused the whole city to prepare for the possibility of a Saracen onslaught. Peasants and old knights were rushing about the walls, carrying makeshift weapons and shields. Scattered throughout the defenses were the Templars, metal bulwarks in the hodgepodge defense.

To Godfrey's left, the rising sun was getting in his eyes. He squinted, and saw, far to the south, a cloud of dust rise along the sky.

"Master Blanchefort!" he called.

Blanchefort came hurrying down the ramparts, with Phillip de Milly and the marshal of the Temple lapping at his heels, like two dogs following their master.

"What is it, Godfrey?"

"There's a column coming up from the south. It looks like a mounted party. It could be a handful of our knights...or Shirkuh's advance guard of Kurdish lancers."

Blanchefort squinted off towards the dust cloud.

"You have good eyes. Marshal, call in all the outriders."

Odo de Sant'Amand hurried down the ramparts. Bertrand de Blanchefort moved on down the wall. Philip de Milly stayed, scanning the horizon with Godfrey.

"You know, Godfrey," he said at last, "both you and De Maille neglected to explain what you were doing in Egypt. We thought you were in Gaza."

Godfrey said nothing. He had thought that one so high in the master's favor might know about his assignment, but if Bertrand de Blanchefort did not see fit to reveal it to Phillip de Milly, then Godfrey would not either. He ignored the question.

"Well, De Montferrat? I expect an answer."

Godfrey still did not respond.

"It would be wise—" began De Milly, before he was interrupted.

"Get back to your position, Knight of the Temple," growled Odo de Sant'Amand, returning on his rounds.

Phillip de Milly glared back at the marshal of the Temple and did not move.

"As Marshal, I command you to return to your post."

Glowering, De Milly turned and strode down the ramparts, not looking back. Odo smiled. "Look at him," he sneered at Phillip de Milly's back. "Acting as though he were master."

Odo laughed and was silent for a while. Then he turned to Godfrey, who was still eyeing the dust cloud, which by now was beginning to materialize into a party of horsemen.

"De Milly did have a point..." began Odo slowly. "I was told you were in *Tyre*, not Egypt. What were you doing in that Godforsaken place?"

With his back towards the marshal, Godfrey smiled.

Does Odo really think that because he stopped De Milly from finding out, I will tell him?

But Godfrey was saved by yet another arrival: the master himself.

"Marshal!" shouted Blanchefort as he hastened along the walls. "Come with me. One of the outriders has caught sight of the cavalry; they're Christians. It appears to be the men of Tripoli."

With a parting glance at Godfrey, Odo de Sant'Amand turned and followed the master.

After Blanchefort and the marshal had vanished, Jacques sidled down from his position until he stood next to Godfrey. They looked at each other.

"Godfrey de Montferrat," said Jacques, "you will never make a politician."

"Did I say that I wanted to?"

Jacques shuddered. "I don't want you to. You'd cause too much havoc with your honesty.

"Tripoli," said Godfrey, looking toward the column of horse.

"What?"

"Tripoli. Those men down there are Tripoli's knights. I wonder why they're not with the main army. You don't think that Amalric got ambushed and Tripoli abandoned him?"

Jacques frowned. "Tripoli? No, he seemed a noble enough knight. He wouldn't sacrifice a comrade-in-arms."

Godfrey chuckled mirthlessly. "I may not make a politician, but I at least know enough not to trust one. I would not trust any noble, least of all a lord like Tripoli."

"Well," said Jacques, "you were born a noble yourself."

Godfrey smiled. "Perhaps you shouldn't trust me," he said lightly. Then he sighed and said more gravely, "No, Jacques, when I entered the Temple, I gave up any rank."

"I know," said Jacques. "I meant it as a jest."

"Perhaps," said Godfrey, "I would trust my cousins, William and Conrad and Renier...but no, I am only saying that because they are safely across the sea in Italy. If I met them again, I would be wary, if nothing else. I think the power and high birth twists them all, sooner or later."

What of Adelaise? the quiet, insinuating voice in Godfrey's head asked. Angrily, Godfrey fought down the tormenting thought.

"You think it twists them all?" asked Jacques. He frowned, and said almost petulantly, "Not all. There are some. There must be some..."

"Some? Who, then? Give me one."

Jacques stuttered for a moment before Godfrey cut in.

"Dukes, counts, kings, popes—yes, even popes. All of them find themselves unable to live up to their old standards, as soon as the crown or the tiara is on their head."

"But not all of them," said Jacques, more sure now. "There are the saints."

"Yes," said Godfrey, slowly. "The saints...perhaps. Perhaps they alone were able to keep their heads when the world bowed before them."

"But," said Jacques, "is there any *ruler* who can measure up to your standard? Charlemagne perhaps?"

Godfrey grunted dismissively. "If there were any, it would not be Charlemagne. But," he added, "perhaps there is one. Sixty years ago, when Godfrey de Bouillion conquered Jerusalem, they offered him the crown of the kingdom. And he turned it down, saying that he would not wear a crown of gold where his Master wore a Crown of Thorns.

"He was a true knight," continued Godfrey. "A true captain of men. He lived the life of a saint, even when his comrades betrayed him and undercut him and undid all the good that he did: even when they slaughtered innocents and divvied up the Holy Places like so many fiefs and dominions. He was the hero, not Bohemund or Raymond or Baldwin or Tancred."

Jacques snorted. "Godfrey, you know well enough that he wasn't everything the legends make him to be."

"Wasn't he?" asked Godfrey sharply. Jacques snorted but did not answer.

Godfrey had been fascinated by his namesake, Godfrey de Bouillion, ever since he was a boy. Time after time, he had gone over the stories and tales, committing them to memory. He had recited it to himself over and over, until it became like Scripture to him. As he grew older, their tutor Otto had tried to explain gently that the legends were exaggerated, but Godfrey refused to believe that the stories which he had loved as a boy were all fictions.

Godfrey de Bouillion had been the first man over the walls of Jerusalem; he had stood atop the ramparts of the Holy City hewing at the Saracens who attacked him. Then, having forced a way through the Mussulmen, he had rushed to the Holy Sepulchre to pray. And while he prayed, the crusaders sacked the city, murdering, burning, raping and looting, until the city was nearly empty. When Godfrey de Bouillion at last came out of the Holy Sepulchre, he looked upon what his men had done. The crusaders, jubilant in their triumph, had come to their leader and offered him the crown of Jerusalem, lifting up their bloody hands and begging him to rule over them. He had looked out in sadness and dismay at the men who would make him king, much as another Man in the same country had looked in sadness and dismay on the crowd that wished to crown Him because He had filled their bellies with bread. Then he rejected the crown of gold.

At least, that was how the story went in Godfrey's mind, and he maintained that story against all skeptics. Whenever he pictured Godfrey de Bouillion refusing the golden crown, his hero's face was like the icons of Christ that Godfrey saw so often in churches.

Godfrey and Jacques stood a while in silence as Godfrey lost himself in thoughts of his hero. Suddenly, Jacques spoke again.

"What became of him after the Crusade? What became of Godfrey de Bouillion after he refused the crown of gold?"

"He lived the life of a knight errant," said Godfrey, firm and certain. "They crowned his brother, Baldwin, in his stead, and forced on Godfrey some title—the Advocate of the Holy Sepulchre, or something of the sort. Godfrey lived as a knight, fighting in defense of truth and justice and mercy, just as the troubadours sing of in the ballads. And he died, eventually, a poor and landless knight."

Jacques nodded quietly. There was another silence, as the two Templars looked out at the swiftly approaching column of horsemen. It was Jacques again who broke the silence.

"Do you still want to be a hero, Godfrey?"

"Yes," Godfrey answered. "That is why I joined the Temple—to be a hero like Godfrey de Bouillion. And we'll need a hero, soon. That is how the Kingdom of Jerusalem has survived since Godfrey de Bouillion founded it: every few years a new threat arises, a new champion among the

Saracens, a new warlord among the Egyptians, and then a hero must appear to save the kingdom. I want to be the next hero, Jacques—and to be that hero I would make any sacrifice."

"Even wear the Crown of Thorns?"

"Well," said Godfrey, but then he stopped, for there was no answer to that.

Instead the Templars stopped and listened to the noises around them. The men on the walls were talking in low murmurs along the ramparts. The knights of Tripoli were nearing the gate, a mass of silver and gold and bright vivid crests and sharp swords and bright shields flashing in the rising sun. Behind them the city of Jerusalem was silent. Normally she would have been abuzz with vendors in the streets and traders in their shops and caravans passing in and out, but word had spread that Shirkuh was coming to the city with an army, and so this morning she was silent with fear.

"Godfrey," said Jacques at last, "do you really believe all the tales about Godfrey de Bouillion? All the stories you just told about him?"

Godfrey smiled. "As fervently as when my aunt Julitta told them to me, when I was a little boy sitting on her lap."

Jacques sighed. "Godfrey, you know that many of those stories are legends. Have you ever thought that the real Godfrey de Bouillion would have been far more human, more flawed, than the stories your aunt told you?"

Godfrey glanced over at Jacques. "Yes," he admitted quietly. "Yes, I know that Godfrey's Crusade didn't go exactly as the stories would have it. I know he was more human, and more flawed, but still...I can't shake the feeling that there's something to the stories. Something deeper."

But Godfrey never had a chance to finish, nor Jacques a chance to answer, for they were interrupted by a clamor from below.

"Open the gate!" shouted Odo, as he came pounding up the stairs. "Open the bloody gate! Tripoli's coming, and Shirkuh might well be right behind him. Open it!"

There was a creak of chains and bolts as the great southern gate of Jerusalem was unlocked. The two heavy doors were swung open and the knights of Tripoli came pouring in.

Godfrey took a step toward the stairs, but Jacques stopped him.

"We have orders to stay on the walls, Godfrey."

Reluctantly, Godfrey stayed on the ramparts, though he itched to go down and speak to Tripoli.

"De Montferrat, De Maille," came Blanchefort's deep voice as the master of the Temple hurried down the ramparts, Phillip de Milly and the marshal in his wake. "Come with me. I may need you when I speak to Tripoli."

Godfrey smiled as they followed the master down the steps.

In the street below, the knights of Tripoli had halted. Some had dismounted and were opening their saddlebags. The count of Tripoli sat on his horse, watching the proceedings impatiently. A ways behind him sat the man with the angelic face and golden hair: Sir Gerard de Ridford. Humphrey de Vinsauf was next to the count, swearing blasphemously about the sand and the weather and whatever else there was to curse about.

"Tripoli!" roared Bertrand de Blanchefort over the commotion. "What is the meaning of this? Where is the king?"

Tripoli swiveled in his saddle and looked down imperiously at the master of the Temple.

"The king," said Tripoli, "could be anywhere between Tinnis and hell, and I really don't care which."

"God's bones! You understood what I meant the first time," growled the master. "Why are you not with the rest of the army? Are you turned deserter?"

"Don't impugn my honor, Blanchefort. I fought for as long as the king did. We merely got separated during the retreat."

"Separated!" roared Blanchefort. "You abandoned the army! Was it because Shirkuh was on your tail?"

"I don't know whether or not Shirkuh was pursuing us, but I hope that Amalric is rotting in hell as we speak."

The master and the count went on shouting at each other, but Godfrey and Jacques were distracted by something else. Humphrey de Vinsauf had caught sight of the two young Templars, and addressed them with an outburst of cheerful profanity.

"God's bones, I didn't expect to see you so soon, De Maille! You too, De Montferrat. See any bloody Ishmaelites on the way back?"

Jacques shook his head. "Not a soul. Where *is* the king?"

Humphrey laughed. "I can only repeat what the count said already: somewhere between Tinnis and hell. We left his camp shortly after you did; Tripoli and Amalric quarreled. Lucky for you that you were gone; things got pretty nasty. I thought I might have to bury my axe in a few royalist skulls that night."

Gerard de Ridford was eyeing the three of them with his cherubic gaze, which seemed to put a damper on the conversation.

"How long will it be," asked Godfrey in a low voice, "before Tripoli marries off his ward and gets rid of De Ridford?"

Humphrey shrugged. "Could be weeks, could be years. De Ridford would serve him faithfully for a decade, as long as Tripoli keeps dangling the girl before his eyes."

Godfrey wasn't sure whether De Ridford heard; and he wasn't sure that he cared.

A young Templar named Arnold de Torroga, the Temple Gatekeeper, came running down the stairs.

"Master!" he shouted. "There's another rider outside the gate! Shall we open it for him?"

Blanchefort broke off from cursing the count of Tripoli and frowned. "Yes, open the gate."

The heavy gate swung open, and a lone knight rode in. He was greeted with silence, as every man turned to stare up at him.

The knight was young, scarcely older than Godfrey. He had a pleasant face, clean-shaven and fair. He surveyed his audience, the trace of a smile at the corners of his mouth.

"Who are you, lad? Where are you from?" asked the master, still frowning.

"I bring tidings from the king," said the knight. "He sends this message to Jerusalem: he has been defeated, but the army is in good order and will be in Jerusalem by nightfall. He also sends word that Shirkuh has broken off the pursuit and turned west, probably to Cairo. The people of Outremer need not fear an attack."

For a moment, none spoke. Then a spontaneous burst of cheering arose. The knight's horse was taken off to be stabled while the knight was given a dozen simultaneous offers of drink and food and asked his name by a score of men. He introduced himself as Balian d'Ibelin, and accepted all the offers in good cheer.

Tripoli eyed the cheering crowds angrily. "Knights of Tripoli!" he bellowed over the commotion. "Remount! We cannot stay here; we must return to Tripoli. Nur ad-Din may try to strike in the north while we are away."

Humphrey growled something profane. "The count," he explained to Godfrey and Jacques, "doesn't want to be here when Amalric arrives. Ah well, I will see you again when chance allows. De Maille, De Montferrat."

Humphrey nodded farewell and turned to mount his horse. The knights of Tripoli were fighting through the press of men to reach their horses. Tripoli began bellowing for the people in front of him to clear a path. The crowd began backing up to make way for the knights of Tripoli.

Arnold de Torroga and a handful of Templars raced up the stairs to open the gate again. Tripoli swore impatiently as the Templars worked the chains and bolts. The gate was flung open, and Tripoli galloped out into the daylight. Humphrey nodded again to Godfrey and Jacques as he passed through the gate. Gerard de Ridford glanced at them again with silent, searching eyes that made Godfrey flinch.

The dust rose up in the wake of the knights, and the crowd drew back some more, coughing and covering their faces. The last of the knights of Tripoli passed out the gate, and the dust settled. Arnold de Torroga closed the gate behind them. Word was spreading like wildfire through the city that Jerusalem was not under attack after all. Godfrey turned and made for the Temple. There would be celebrations in the streets.

Chapter 11

A Quest
Godfrey

It was with relief that Godfrey de Montferrat passed out of the crowd and into the inner city. He looked back at the celebrations that choked the city streets and smiled. The people of Jerusalem wasted no opportunity to celebrate. Jerusalem had been saved, and the fact that she had never really been in danger was irrelevant.

Jacques emerged from the crowd and stepped up his pace to catch Godfrey. Together they entered the Temple court. As they passed into it, a knight hailed them from outside. Godfrey turned his head to see.

Immediately he stiffened. It was Balian d'Ibelin, the knight whom Amalric had sent ahead to calm the city. Hanging at his sides, Godfrey's fists clenched unconsciously. A Templar was supposed to put aside any temporal prejudices, but the houses of Montferrat and Ibelin had long been rivals, and it was in their blood to quarrel with each other.

"You there, Templar ... Godfrey is it?"

Godfrey nodded slowly.

"You were at the battle by Tinnis?"

Godfrey nodded again, even more cautiously.

Balian paused, as if working up the nerve to speak.

"I heard that you...led a charge to come to our rescue. You...did well. Even if we did lose. It took courage."

Godfrey nodded a third time, not knowing anything better to do. Balian gathered himself up. "God be with you, Templar. You're a Montferrat, are you not?"

"I am," said Godfrey. "And you, an Ibelin?"

"Yes," said Balian. "Perhaps not all Montferrats are swine."

Godfrey smiled. "God be with you, Balian of Ibelin. Perhaps there's a good Ibelin or two, however much you hide it." Godfrey bowed and crossed the threshold of the *Templum Domini*.

Before them lay the Temple Court, an open stone court built upon countless other layers of stone that marked the centuries that Jerusalem had been inhabited by men. And they were many; Jerusalem was an ancient city, measuring among the oldest.

Godfrey and Jacques walked into the Court. When he was sure Balian was gone, Jacques spoke to Godfrey.

"What was that all about?"

Godfrey shrugged. "I don't know."

The sun shone down on the Temple, illuminating the ruins of what had once been the *Templum Domini*. When Godfrey had first come to the Temple, he had been fascinated, both by the stones and the memories that they seemed to hold, of the last prophets, of the Maccabees and the High Priests, and of Christ and the final destruction of the Temple forty years after His death.

Arnold de Torroga was waiting outside the chapel. "The master wishes to see you," he said. "He is in the refectory."

With a sigh, Godfrey and Jacques turned and made their way across the sun-warmed stones.

Inside the refectory it was dark; the windows were few and poorly arranged. Bertrand de Blanchefort sat upon his chair, looking imperiously at the two young Templars who entered. Jacques and Godfrey bowed quickly as they saw him, then stood at attention. There was something commanding about the master of the Temple that always made Godfrey's first instinct on seeing him be to genuflect, an instinct which was hard to repress.

Bertrand de Blanchefort made no move to tell the two to sit. He was not one to let a man below him forget his place.

"Ah, De Maille, De Montferrat. I hope you have enjoyed a restful stay in Jerusalem, because you're about to leave again."

That they had gotten no sleep that night or the night before, Godfrey dared not mention. The master was not in a mood for it. Bertrand de Blanchefort was a man to obeyed.

"Where?" asked Jacques.

"To Antioch," replied the master of the Temple. Blanchefort's face remained steely and emotionless, waiting to see their reaction.

Antioch. The name meant little to Godfrey, save what he knew from the histories and the legends. He had never in his life been farther north than Acre, and he knew next to nothing of the strange city at the corner of the Mediterranean where the Levant met Asia Minor. As always, his first thought went to the history of the place. It had been one of the first wholly Christian cities, and it was there that the term Christian had first been applied to followers of the Nazarene. During the First Crusade, a great battle had been fought there. It was before its gates that Yagi Syan had died and Kerboga's armies been smashed.

"Antioch, Master?" asked Jacques. "Is Nur ad-Din making trouble in the north?"

"No," said Blanchefort, placidly. "In fact, the north is more tranquil than it has been in thirty years. I doubt you will so much as glimpse a Saracen or a Turk."

"Then for what reason, Master, are we going there?"

Blanchefort remained silent for a moment, before he answered Jacques de Maille with a question of his own.

"Have either of you ever dealt with a Greek before?"

Jacques shook his head.

"Yes, Master," said Godfrey. "I had a friend among the serving men at my uncle's castle. He was a Greek Christian. Skinny little man, a head shorter than any other I knew. He always said that a clever tongue served him better than a strong arm, but apparently it didn't. He got his throat cut by bandits a year before I entered the Temple."

Blanchefort smiled, slightly amused.

"I am sure, though," he continued, "that you both have heard tales of the Greeks—or the Romans as they style themselves."

Both Templars nodded. Every Frank in Outremer knew of the perfidious and effeminate Greeks who placed their hope in silver tongues and silver coins, rather than in strength of arms, as the Franks did. The two peoples were almost as different as the Franks were from Islam; the Empire of Byzantium—formerly the eastern half of the Roman Empire of old—had almost a thousand years of civilization behind it, while the Franks were the newly (and sometimes only partially) Christianized barbarians of the west, men who lived for battle. The Byzantines met scorn with scorn, looking down on the barbarous westerners, but even a scholarly Frank like Godfrey despised the Greeks as spineless cowards.

"Greek politics," continued Blanchefort, "are centered around the city of Constantinople. Any man who hopes to rise high must be there. No man, be he a golden-tongued Demosthenes or a conquering Belisarius can hope to achieve rank unless he goes to the city of Constantine. And so, as a security measure, Emperor Manuel Comnenus has dispatched most of his relatives and political rivals to cities far out in the empire, unimportant border cities. Or, better yet, he sends them outside of the empire."

To Antioch, thought Godfrey, though he dared not say it. No Templar dared try to hurry the master along.

"Are either of you aware," asked Blanchefort, "that the empire claims Antioch to be her city, and has done so for a century?"

Jacques and Godfrey shook their heads, looking slightly bemused. Antioch had been held by the Franks ever since it had been taken by Bohemund a hundred years ago.

"You see," began Blanchefort, "when the Lords of the West passed through Constantinople, the Emperor Alexius Comnenus made Bohemund the Norman and Raymond of Toulouse swear an oath that any cities they conquered which had once belonged to Byzantium would be returned to her. However, when Bohemund and Raymond swore this oath, they believed that the emperor's troops would accompany them on the Crusade. When they learned that the emperor planned to send them on alone, to conquer cities for him while he remained safe in his city, the lords of the West denounced the oath, saying that it had been taken under false premises."

"At first," continued Blanchefort, "it did not matter. The cities they captured did not interest them, and they were only too glad to turn them over to the Greeks. Antioch, however, was different. The crusaders were nearly destroyed outside Antioch. Several times their army was on the verge of starvation, or of breaking apart. All the while, their time was running out, for Kerboga was coming with two hundred thousand men and they had to get inside fast. They took the city and got inside just as Kerboga's army appeared across the Orontes plain."

Godfrey knew this history, had heard or read it a thousand times in a thousand different ways, but the master of the Temple was enjoying himself.

"When at last Antioch was secure, Alexius demanded it be turned over to him. But the crusaders refused, saying that he had forfeited it by not accompanying them. At the time, Alexius had few troops to fight for him save the crusaders themselves, so he dared not go against them. All the same, he maintained a legal claim to Antioch."

"Five years ago, Manuel was on the verge of negotiating the peaceful transfer of Antioch into Greek hands. He was planning to seal it with the marriage of his cousin, Andronicus Comnenus, to the young queen-regent of Antioch, Constance. Manuel was hoping to simultaneously get Antioch and rid himself of Andronicus, for his cousin was popular and well-liked in the court, making him a potential rival."

"Andronicus, however, was delayed on the way by Turks, and in his absence, Constance decided to marry for love. She chose a penniless adventurer from France, a knight errant by the name of Reynald de Chatillon."

"When Andronicus arrived at Antioch, he found his bride-to-be already taken. Having once got rid of him, Manuel forbade Andronicus to return to Constantinople. So Andronicus Comnenus has sat in Antioch these five years, twiddling his thumbs and looking for some way to make trouble."

"He has failed, however, to make any serious stir…until now. A week ago I received a letter from him. That letter contains an offer that I dare not refuse."

"Jacques," said Blanchefort, his tone changing suddenly to a more urgent note. "Check the door. Make sure we are quite alone."

Jacques stepped outside and looked around, squinting slightly in the sun. There were guards at the far end of the Temple Court, and Templars praying in the chapel, but the Court itself stood silent under the sun. On the far side lay the ruins of the *Templum Domini*, but these were too far off for a man hidden in them to eavesdrop.

Jacques stepped back into the dark refectory. "No one, Master."

Blanchefort stroked his long beard. He waited in silence. Godfrey got up to a slow count of twelve before the master of the Temple spoke.

"Andronicus Comnenus has made an overture regarding the reconciliation of the East and West. He has offered to discuss terms for the reunification of the Greek and Latin Churches, should he ever become emperor."

Godfrey looked as though he had just received a blow on the head. He tried to sit down, but remembered simultaneously that he had no chair and was not permitted to sit.

Jacques was not so overwhelmed. "But why us, Master? Why the Templars? Even the master of the Temple has no place in the hierarchical authority of the Church."

"I know that," said Blanchefort. "And so does Andronicus. But we're not the ones he's is interested in. He wants to get through to the pope."

Jacques frowned, not drawing the connection.

"The Templars owe allegiance to no king, only to the pope," continued Blanchefort. "So outsiders see us as the pope's soldiers, his guards. We aren't really his guards, of course—the pope has no army—but to a Greek noble wanting to negotiate a treaty with the bishop of Rome, we seem the logical choice."

"The pope's soldiers," said Jacques. "I like that."

Godfrey, however, frowned. "I don't. As you already said, Master, the pope has no army, so we have no right to negotiate anything on behalf of the pope. Just because we obey the Holy Father does not give us the right to usurp his authority. We should send to Rome for a Papal Legate to properly negotiate a peace."

"Send to Rome?" growled Blanchefort. "And have some corrupt cardinal come to bungle the whole reconciliation? No, this has been brought to the Templars, and it will stay with the Templars. I want to see the unification of the two churches as much as you do, De Montferrat, and I trust no man but myself to do it."

"Master," said Godfrey, and there was real anger in his voice now. "Would you usurp the Holy Father's authority merely to keep this matter under the Templars' control? If such is the case, I *will not* obey."

If Godfrey's voice had been passionately angry, it was nothing to the anger in the master of the Temple's voice when he replied.

"You *will* obey. You swore an oath—poverty, chastity, and *obedience!* Fool boy, you'll do what I say. I am the master of the Temple."

"My obedience," said Godfrey, more calmly now, "is to the pope before the master of the Temple. You can expel me from the Order, or take off my head, but I will have no hand in any schismatic negotiations. Send another man."

After swearing several very profane and blasphemous oaths, none of which befitted a man of God, Blanchefort shut his eyes. His fists clenched until they turned white, but when he opened his eyes, he was slightly calmer.

"There is no other man, you fool. I picked you two as my eyes and ears, my agents and my messengers, because I know that you two are innocent enough to be trusted, something I could not say for any other man in the Temple, not Philip de Milly nor Odo de Sant'Amand, not the oldest veteran or the newest accepted."

"Very well, boy," continued the master. "Let me put this to you in a different light. These are not official negotiations. We are merely making contact with a Greek noble who may never be the emperor. It is not a matter that the pope should be troubled with; it's not a matter that the pope *could* be troubled with. All you are being ordered to do is go and make contact with a foreign nobleman, and you have no moral grounds on which to refuse *that.*"

Godfrey was taken aback, he had not expected the master of the Temple to change his tack so quickly. The ground had been knocked out from under his feet. He should have known that only a master politician would ever rule the Temple.

"But Master," he said, "how do I know that when it does get to that stage, a papal legate will be sent, and you will not just keep the matter in your hands?"

"You do not know!" roared Blanchefort, his face red. "You have no assurance, and no one owes you one. You are nothing but a beardless boy who has sworn to obey."

Godfrey fingered his scraggly beard. *Not completely true.*

"I have given you an order," continued the master, still bellowing. "And you have no grounds to object. You will obey, or it is *you* who will be in the wrong. Now keep your bloody mouth shut, unless it is to beg forgiveness for your insolence."

"Yes, Master," said Godfrey, bowing his head.

Blanchefort took a deep breath. "Then you both are ready to leave?"

"Yes, Master," replied Jacques and a much-cowed Godfrey.

Blanchefort nodded, looking relieved.

The master of the Temple, thought Godfrey, *is relieved that a beardless boy did not contest his orders. That is something new. Though not something to be proud of.*

"You will leave tomorrow morning. The Archdeacon William of Tyre has agreed to ride there with you and introduce you to the city. I have informed him of the scheme, and he has agreed to help as much as possible. He will tell you all the minor details, as well as advise on the political situation in Antioch. After you are set up in Antioch, he will return to Tyre."

"For now, remember this: you two have no political experience, so you will not be carrying out any negotiations yourselves; you will instead be my agents in Antioch: observers and contacts for any negotiators I send to Andronicus Comnenus. You are to keep me constantly informed by way of letter."

"How long will we be doing this?" asked Godfrey.

"As long as I need you to," said Blanchefort. "It could be years. All the same, you are to adhere to the Rule as best you can. I realize, however, that you may need to take certain liberties with the Rule, so I am granting you a dispensation to do what you must. Do not to abuse my trust. If you do... I shall hear of it. Any questions?"

"No, Master."

"Good. The archdeacon is waiting in the chapel. You have fresh horses ready, along with supplies, in the stable. I expect you gone by tomorrow morning."

The two Templars bowed.

"Oh," added Blanchefort. "Remember: even though you will not actually be negotiating, Andronicus is arranging several meetings with you as my agents. Make a good impression on him. And learn. With the right knowledge and experience, both of you could rise high. Watch and learn. Dismissed."

Jacques headed for the door, but Godfrey stayed, looking anxious. Jacques glanced back at his friend questioningly, but, seeing the look on his face, he left and headed for the chapel.

Blanchefort looked up at the young Templar.

"What is it now?" he growled. "More objections?"

"No, Master. Will you shrive me?"

Bertrand de Blanchefort's face softened just a touch at that. A smile crossed his face, though it did not quite reach his eyes.

"Yes, my son. Come forward and kneel."

Godfrey came before the master's chair and knelt, using his hand to screen his face.

"Bless me father, for I have sinned."

The men of the Temple were flesh and blood, just like any others, and so Bertrand de Blanchefort was used to hearing his men's confessions of lust and hate and avarice. Godfrey de Montferrat, however, was the only man whose confession made him want to laugh, for it was at once foolish and innocent, worried and over scrupulous.

Godfrey himself knew well that most of his innocence was not so much a result of holiness but of habit and inexperience. He suspected that some of it might even be a cowardice of sorts—for he doubted that he could ever work up the nerve to visit a whore or strike down a man in cold blood. It was not a matter of purity or love or holiness, just timidity.

Virtue itself is simply a good habit. Does that make it holiness, though?

When Godfrey was done, the master of the Temple's eyes followed him as he got up and turned to leave.

"Godfrey," he said in a firm voice that immediately turned the young Templar around.

"Yes, Master?"

"You did right to question my action this day. Go on as you have. Fear no man, no power, no principality, but fear only God. One day you will make a saint. It may be a lonely road, and there will be suffering, but it will not be too lonely as long as you love God, nor too painful as long as you remember the Savior's Passion."

Godfrey bowed, his face coloring. He had not expected such a blessing from Bertrand de Blanchefort; for all his vows, the master was a worldly man. "Thank you, Master."

"But I must give you this warning, a warning that every man who tries to be a saint must know: never forget why you do it. You do it for Him, you do it for love. Never be holy merely for its own sake, or worse: for your own sake, or you will fall as nothing since Lucifer has fallen."

"Yes, Master."

"Now, get out of here."

✠ ✠ ✠

As Godfrey walked out into the sunlight of the Temple Court, he felt ready to fight even the Archenemy himself.

"O God," he prayed, feeling his heart soar, "let me be a hero."

It was a rash prayer; a prayer made only because Godfrey felt full of life and love and happiness at the moment. Had Godfrey seen a little farther into the future, he might not have prayed so—it is always a painful process, being shaped into a hero. But it was a heartfelt prayer. Such prayers do not go unheard, and they are answered in ways far beyond the supplicant's expectations.

"Lord," begged Godfrey, continuing his prayer, "I want to do something great—for You, of course." It had been his dream ever since he was a boy.

Chapter 12

A SON AND A DAUGHTER
Joscelin

Dust and old wood fell from the long table as Joscelin brushed his hand across it. Amalric looked up from where he sat at the end of the banquet hall. The room was empty and silent; it had been unused while the king was away in Egypt. The high roof and wide walls seemed forlorn and sad—Joscelin was used to the sounds of raucous laughter, crackling fires, and cheerful talk. Now the only two in the usually crowded room were the king and the count of Edessa.

"Joscelin," said Amalric gruffly. "I didn't hear you enter."

"No, Your Grace. You were lost in your own thoughts."

"I was," admitted the king.

There was a short pause, before Joscelin spoke impatiently. "Amalric, you can't indulge in self-pity. You have no time for it; *you are the king.*"

Amalric looked up, annoyed. "Self-pity?"

Joscelin sighed. "Forget I said anything, Your Grace." He started to turn. "Your children are waiting for you."

"Why did you come, Joscelin?" asked Amalric.

"To see if you needed help," he answered, his back turned to the king. "It seems that you do, but you won't accept it."

Amalric laughed mirthlessly. "I know you too well, Joscelin. You have something to say, but are too proud to say it. Well, I'll help you this time. I have something to say to you, and perhaps what you had to say will come out as we talk."

Joscelin stopped in his tracks. Hate welled up in him, and it was all the stronger because Amalric was right: he knew Joscelin too well.

"In Egypt," began the king, not waiting for a response, "just before the last battle with Shirkuh, you were angry at me—as you always are these days—and you asked me why I repudiated Agnes."

Joscelin ground his teeth together. "Are you trying to find some

85

consolation, Amalric, now that you have failed in Egypt? Trying to vindicate yourself for your own conscience?"

"I'm not trying to vindicate myself," said Amalric. "I just want *you* to understand. I've been thinking about your question—thinking about why I gave up a wife for a crown."

"Maybe you should have spent more time thinking about winning the battle," said Joscelin angrily, but he turned around to face the king again.

Amalric ignored Joscelin's words and continued. "Joscelin, do you really think I gave up love for power? Is any man really that cold? There are many things we will sacrifice for power, but a loving wife is not one of them."

"Oh," said Joscelin, "I think that is exactly what you did, whatever words you try to hide it with."

"You wouldn't know," said Amalric fiercely. "You couldn't know. Tell me, Joscelin, do you love Jerusalem?"

Joscelin started at the question. "Yes, Your Grace—as my own heart and soul."

"And," said Amalric, "if she were in danger, you'd give up anything to save her?"

Joscelin frowned suspiciously.

"Anything, Your Grace."

"Joscelin, the kingdom is in danger. Ever since Godfrey de Bouillion and Raymond of Toulouse forged this kingdom, ever since they wrested it from the infidels' hands, it has been in danger. The Saracens and the Turks and the Egyptians, they all want to close in on it, all want to swallow it up. Every few years there is another attempt. And we have always escaped, but only barely. I was count of Ascalon before I was king, and I would know. They always attacked from Egypt back then, and I had to fight them off."

"When Baldwin died," continued Amalric, "there were many who hoped I would refuse the crown. There was no appointed heir after me, and I did not have authority to appoint an heir myself. They were all waiting hungrily to make a grab for the throne—Tripoli and Ibelin and the lords of Tyre and Sidon, with the Hospital and the Temple ready to join in the struggle. I knew then that if I refused the Crown, they would tear this Kingdom of Jerusalem apart. I could keep Agnes and abandon the kingdom, or I could choose the kingdom and leave my wife."

"So," said Joscelin, "you claim that you gave up Agnes to save the kingdom?"

"Yes," said Amalric. "That is why I gave her up. You wanted to know... now you do."

Joscelin gazed at the man who had once been his best friend, disgust and affection warring in his heart.

"You're a fool," he said, not sure whether he spoke out of hate or out of fondness. "Keep telling yourself what you just told me. But it won't heal Agnes's grief, nor it will unite your children's parents. The very children that are waiting for you right now."

Joscelin turned again. "I'm going to send your children in." He strode purposefully towards the door, and opened it. An old tutor was waiting with the king's children by Agnes, a son and a daughter.

Sybilla, the girl, sprang forward first, rushing across the dirty floor towards her father, her arms open to embrace him. She was six, and tall for her age, her black hair already long and beautiful.

The son, Baldwin, hung back a moment shyly. Baldwin, a scrawny boy, four years old, had been named for his paternal uncle—he had been born in a happier day when King Baldwin III ruled in Jerusalem. But that uncle was gone now; his only living uncle stood right in front of him. Joscelin gently pulled his nephew into the room, patting his mop of blond hair.

"Go on, Baldwin," he murmured tenderly. "Your father's back. Go embrace him, just like Sybilla." Joscelin smiled fiercely, and Baldwin smiled back uncertainly. Joscelin gave the boy a little push, and he stumbled across the floor towards Amalric.

The count of Edessa paused a moment in the doorway, next to the old tutor. He watched as Amalric laughed with his children, setting Sybilla on his lap. Joscelin shut his eyes, fighting back tears as he remembered happier days.

"Defend Jerusalem," he murmured, too quietly for any but himself to hear. "If you really gave up Agnes to save the city, to save the kingdom, you had better defend it, Amalric. That is all I ask. Defend Jerusalem."

Chapter 13

RES QUONDAM RESQUE FUTURAE
Godfrey

The red rim of the sun was just peeking above the horizon the next morning as three horsemen rode out the north gate of Jerusalem.

Godfrey's breath misted in the morning chill, and he laughed for the joy of it. He was back in Outremer. They rode northwest, making for Jaffa, so the sun was to his back, but after the relentless heat of Egypt, he reveled in the chill on his face. Ahead of him, Archdeacon William was wrapped tight in his cloak. It had been years since he had left Outremer, so he did not appreciate the chill half as much. Jacques shivered every now and then, but said nothing.

As the hours passed, the sun rose higher, and the riders loosened their cloaks and jackets. Outremer was not as hot as Egypt, but summer was coming on, and before long beads of sweat were dripping down their faces.

Past noon they stopped to eat. William of Tyre, silent all morning, now began to speak, while Jacques and Godfrey fetched salted pork and water from the saddlebags.

"We're going to ride northeast to Jaffa, then ride north along the coast until we reach Antioch. Jaffa we can reach tomorrow night, but it will be a week's ride at the least from there to Antioch."

"Do you know Andronicus Comnenus?" asked Godfrey as he sat down with his pork and water.

"Know him? Not well. The archbishop of Tyre knows him, and I have spoken with him several times on errands that the archbishop gave me. Bertrand de Blanchefort doesn't know it, but I was already under instructions from the archbishop of Tyre to assist with these negotiations. That is why I was in Jerusalem in the first place."

Godfrey doused his thirst in a long draught of water. The pork was tough and stringy, but he had expected no less.

"What about the lord of the city, Reynald de Chatillon?" asked Jacques. "Andronicus Comnenus was supposed to marry his wife. How does he deal with the Greek now?"

"Reynald de Chatillon," said William, a faint smile on his lips, "does not like Andronicus Comnenus in his city, but Reynald does not control matters as firmly as he wishes. He was initially just an adventurer from France who came with the French king on crusade twenty years ago—they still call him 'The Hawk,' the name that he went by as a soldier of fortune in Europe. He charmed his way into the inner circles of Antioch, and married the princess just before Andronicus Comnenus came to collect her. The Hawk is not a man to be intimidated by anything, or a man to allow a rival to stay in the same city as himself, but he is only a lowborn who won his way into high places, and at the current moment he has to endure Andronicus as a sort of…penance…set upon him by the emperor in Constantinople."

"Penance?" Jacques frowned.

"Yes," continued William. "A few years ago, just after the Hawk had married Constance of Antioch, he found that his treasury was empty. To remedy this, he captured the Greek patriarch of Antioch, and tried to force him to turn over the church treasury. He accomplished this by smearing the patriarch's bald head with honey and tying him to the dome of the Greek church in Antioch. For a day the patriarch lay up there, with the sun burning him and bees stinging him and flies buzzing about his head, unable to ward any of them off, for his hands were bound. After that, the patriarch decided that perhaps the Hawk could use the funds reserved for the church. Reynald de Chatillon stripped the treasury bare. It was, however, still not enough. The Hawk has a keen mind, and he struck upon a way to make his money grow. He used the money from the treasury to fund an expedition to Cyprus. He plundered the island, stripping it of anything gold. When the Greek clergy protested, he took the leading clerics, cut off their noses, and sent them to Manuel Comnenus as a present."

"The Hawk had, however, bitten off more than he could chew. In a rage, the emperor gathered up all the might of his empire and marched on Antioch. The Hawk saw he could not win this battle, so he quickly changed his tack and came alone before the emperor in sackcloth and ashes, prostrating himself before him, begging pardon. Manuel agreed to pardon the Hawk if he would make Antioch a vassal of the empire and swear fealty to Byzantium."

"The Hawk was more than happy to do so, as long as he kept his wife and his power. However, Baldwin III, the king of Outremer, had got wind of this by now, and he came storming into the negotiations. Baldwin was a mighty king, and he was not about to let Antioch slip out of his control. The Hawk was thrust to the side while the king and the emperor argued and bargained. In the end, they reached the compromise that Antioch would remain a Frankish city, but the Hawk himself would accept Manuel as his liege lord."

"When you get to Antioch, you will see the results of all this. The Hawk is chafing under his oath of fealty, but is afraid to break it lest Manuel Comnenus should come to oust him from his throne. Manuel has forced Reynald to endure Andronicus as his honored guest, both to keep Andronicus out of Constantinople, and to make the Hawk suffer for what he did. The Hawk gets bored when he isn't fighting, so he constantly raids the northern Arabic and Turkish cities, disregarding any truces made with them. The Arabs and Turks hate him, but the Hawk is under Byzantium's protection, and Antioch is under Outremer's protection, so they are unable to harm him without fighting both the kingdom and the empire."

"In other words," said Jacques, "it's a bloody mess up there."

William chuckled and caught his breath. "I wish you luck. You'll need it, thrust into the war between Andronicus Comnenus and Reynald de Chatillon."

Godfrey finished chewing the tough meat to a pulp, swallowed it, and stood up. Jacques was already packing the remaining pork into the saddlebags. He snorted at William's words.

"We'll manage, deacon. You do your part, and we will do ours."

William raised his eyebrows, but then turned and began to pack his saddlebags. Godfrey sighed and swung up into his saddle, followed by William, and the three horses rode on down the desert road towards Jaffa.

☩ ☩ ☩

By evening they had left the hills of Jerusalem behind them. The ground turned flat and green and fertile. They were approaching the coast. Little farms and villages lay on the roadside, but for some reason, William preferred to make camp in an open field. William and Jacques started arguing about that, but there were no farms in sight, and Godfrey was growing tired, so he threw in his weight with William. Jacques sullenly agreed to make camp. There was no talk that night.

By afternoon the next day, Jaffa was in sight. They had made better time than William thought they would, a fact which Jacques was quick to point out. The city was seated on a low rise overlooking the sea. Due to the flatness of the land, however, it could be seen for a long ways away, and it was still quite a ride before they actually reached the town. The shadows were just beginning to lengthen as the three horsemen rode up the rise to southern gate of Jaffa.

Godfrey looked up at the city. It was smaller than Jerusalem, and the walls were much lower—a little coastal city, nothing more. The citadel, standing tall against the horizon, was a different matter. It loomed high over the tallest city buildings, and the granite looked tough enough to resist even the heaviest of trebuchet bombardments.

Jacques glanced at the outer ramparts. He shook his head dismissively.

"Wouldn't like to have to defend the outer wall," he muttered. "Ramparts are too low, no slits for archers or boiling pitch. Might as well fight out in the open."

Godfrey nodded. "Well, God willing, we will never have to defend it."

William was no soldier. Ignoring their talk, he rode ahead. A small stream of workers were pouring back into the city. The three riders were soon engulfed in it, and they moved slowly the rest of the way. The sky was beginning to darken by the time they passed through the city gates.

They rode up the sloping streets, looking for an inn. Godfrey looked up toward the citadel, and caught a glimpse of the heavy doors swinging shut. He turned to look out towards the sea, quiet and calm. The setting sun lit up the waters in a brilliant display of gold. He paused a moment, letting Jacques and William ride on ahead. The gulls were crying their shrill, lonely calls, and the last ships were coming in. Something tugged at the end of Godfrey's mind, something about ships, about…

"Here's a good place," said William, stopping before an inn. Godfrey's train of thought flew away as his attention was jerked towards William's voice. What was it he had been thinking? Something about ships…

✠ ✠ ✠

That night, Godfrey slept on a matted pallet of hay, a much more comfortable bed than the ground he had slept on the night before. His belly was filled with bread, wine, and juicy meat, much better eating than the day before. He lay back, feeling spoiled, even decadent. Sleep eluded him a few minutes, though his thoughts were scattered and careless. At last he drifted off, and his dreams were troubled that night. For Godfrey dreamt not of imagined things, but of real things, past things, that had been ground into his memory.

He stood again on the wharves of Genoa in Italy, a boy of eight. He stumbled on the wooden planks, unused to a still platform after weeks at sea.

His uncle, William de Montferrat, stepped off the ship and led Godfrey towards the dirty, smelly harbors, with his children stumbling after him. Godfrey, Conrad and little Boniface had spent the voyage with rolling stomachs and green faces. Will, the eldest son, was untouched as always. And Adelaise...even then, at seven, Adelaise had proved more resilient than her brothers. She had loved the sea most of all.

The Lady Julitta, Godfrey's aunt, had come out with her household to greet her nephew, newly arrived from Jerusalem, to his new home. Julitta was tired and weakened, for she had just given birth to son, Renier. All the same, she folded the scrawny, bewildered child who was Godfrey in her slender arms and embraced him. From that moment on, she became a mother to Godfrey...

Then Godfrey was ten years of age, and he was in the practice yard of Montferrat Castle. The soldiers were away in the south, watching the Genoese, so the practice yard was empty. Godfrey, Conrad, Adelaise and Boniface had snuck down to hack at each other with the wooden practice swords. Will was already too mature to play games with them, and Renier was still a baby, but the four of them had danced about for hours, pretending to be the knights that Otto of Freising told them of in his histories. They laughed and squealed in delight and re-enacted the battles of crusaders like Godfrey de Bouillion and Bohemund and Tancred, and the legends of Lohengrin and Tristan and Roland.

In the end, though, Conrad had grown angry with Boniface when Boniface beat him at a mock duel. Then he had struck Boniface hard across the face with the wooden sword. Godfrey, always eager to share in his friend's adventures, began to beat Boniface with his own fake sword. Boniface had begun to cry, and Adelaise had joined his side, yelling angrily at Conrad and Godfrey and defending Boniface with her sword. When that happened, Godfrey tried to slink away, ashamed, while Conrad and Adelaise argued and Boniface sobbed.

The steward had found them like that, and dragged them before their father. William de Montferrat had scolded them all severely...all except Godfrey. There was always a distinction between Godfrey and the others, and Godfrey was never able to forget that he was a cousin and not a brother; a nephew and not a son. William and Julitta meant well of course; the distinction usually took the form of being more lenient or indulgent to Godfrey. Had Godfrey actually been a brother, his siblings would have envied and disliked him as a favorite child. But he was not a brother, and so instead his favored treatment served only as a reminder that he was not William de Montferrat's son. At first Godfrey had enjoyed being treated differently. But on this occasion, for the first time, he wished that William would have scolded him equally, for he was just beginning to understand why he was not being treated the way his cousins were...

Godfrey was fourteen, and they were at a feast. Conrad was whispering something to a new squire, a tall, well-built, straw-haired boy named Jacques de Maille, while Godfrey sipped at the wine his uncle had allowed him to have, sore and hurt that his beloved cousin was ignoring him.

Godfrey had arisen and left the table, not wanting to watch Conrad ignore him any more. And, as he slipped away, he was joined by his cousin Adelaise. She was thirteen then, already transforming into the beauty she would one day become. Her hair was brown, curling at the edges. She was beginning to round into womanhood, though her figure was still thin and girlish. She had followed Godfrey, and shyly, quietly, they began to talk. Godfrey was awkward at first— like the rest of his cousins, Godfrey had never seen Adelaise as a sibling, though he had been raised with her. His male cousins he treated like friends, but Godfrey was always awkward around girls, and didn't really know how to treat Adelaise.

But that night they fell to talking. They spoke first of the feast and the guests, of Conrad and Jacques, and of Godfrey himself. Their words turned to old Otto of Freising, William de Montferrat's brother-in-law, beloved by Godfrey and all of his cousins. Godfrey had begun to tell Adelaise of some of the tales he had learned from Otto, and Adelaise listened raptly. They spoke of the histories and the legends late into the night, and Godfrey had felt quite dizzy as he left for his bed that night...

Then he was nineteen, racing his palfrey against Jacques, who was now his closest friend, towards the gate of Montferrat Castle. They were returning from Aachen with his cousin Will and Otto of Freising. Jacques out-rode Godfrey, as he always did, but this day Godfrey was in high spirits and he did not mind.

The gates were opened for them, and Conrad and Adelaise were waiting on the walls for them. Conrad came bounding down, happy to see Godfrey. He greeted Jacques too, though he and Jacques had long since grown distant. It was Adelaise who surprised Godfrey, for she greeted them with a radiant smile such as Godfrey had rarely seen on her already beautiful face.

With a start, Godfrey had realized that the smile was directed at Jacques, and Jacques alone. The realization had stung him like a wound. Once, many years ago, he had fancied his cousin Adelaise, but he had realized ever since he was fifteen that she was his cousin and as such he could never marry her. He had long since been reconciled to the fact that she would marry another man. But this was too much for him: that her love should go to his best friend.

For Godfrey was going to leave in a week: he was taking ship to Jerusalem, where he would enter the Temple and swear a vow of celibacy. He was ready to become a monk; he wanted *to do it. Yet in his more selfish impulses, he wanted to be admired and even envied by his friends and cousins. He had thought* that for his last week in Montferrat he would have the undivided attention of Jacques and Conrad and Adelaise. The thought of Jacques gaining his cousin's love and marrying her awoke a hidden anguish in Godfrey, and the thought that for these last few days their attention and care would be given not to him but to each other was unbearable.

So Godfrey had spent the rest of the day in a vile mood, at times sullen and at times volatile. Conrad had noticed; they had all noticed. That evening, when Godfrey was able to speak to Jacques alone, he unleashed all his anguish and jealousy with bitter words and insults, and Jacques had struck back. He had called Godfrey a coward for becoming a monk: told him that he was too scared and too pathetic to marry and so he was running away to the Temple. They had cursed each other, and Godfrey had left with hate for Jacques filling his heart. And in the dream all fell into darkness…

Suddenly Godfrey left the past, and found himself walking strange paths. No longer was he dreaming about bygone memories, but about new and terrifying things.

He stood before the gate to Jaffa Keep. Before him lay a host of spectral figures which he could never get a clear view of. They did not dance or twist out of sight, but there seemed to be some power over them, so that his eyes simply rolled over them. He could be staring straight into the middle of a crowd, and yet not see a single figure. He knew they were there, though, sensing motion and color out of the corners of his vision. And down by the sea, something was coming. Something great and powerful and inexorable. He looked out towards the sea, unable to see it, but still it came, rolling up like a wave.

A face too; there was a face connected with that thing from the sea. Afterward, Godfrey was never sure where exactly in the dream he had seen it; he was sure there was never a moment when the face appeared, the picture simply seemed to bypass the normal mode by which images enter the brain; it skipped the stage in which Godfrey actually saw it, and went right to the stage where Godfrey already knew it. It was a long face, bearded, with blue eyes and dark hair; a face that gave the impression of strength, courage, and cruelty. It also gave the impression of height, for even though there was no body, the face seemed to belong on a man who would tower over all men, tower over buildings, tower over even the citadel of Jaffa…

The sea was gone, and he was in Egypt again. At least, he was in a place where all that could be seen for miles around was sand. No, there was something. It was something big, and he was standing next to it. It was the head of a giant statue, half buried in the sand. The trunk was nowhere to be seen. Looking at *the head, Godfrey saw it was not human. At least, not fully human. It had a beak, and feathers were carved delicately into the stone. The eyes, however, were human eyes; oval, with sharp corners, set in the front of the head rather than the sides, and at the base of the head was a very human chin.*

There were faces here, too, just as in Jaffa. First a woman's face, but a young woman, almost a girl. An Egyptian. No, there was something Arabic about her. Her face was pretty, with long black hair flowing freely. And a man's face, a Saracen this time, with brown hair and angry eyes. This face, however, Godfrey recognized, or thought he did. He had seen this man before…where?

He stood atop a giant golden dome, looking down on a great city, larger than any he had seen in his life. The dome stood high above the metropolis, but the buildings spread out for miles around, as far as he could see. Far off to his left, he caught a glimpse of the red rim of the sun sinking beneath the horizon. Strange—he couldn't recall ever seeing the sun in a dream before. Then again, here in this dream he couldn't recall any other dream, except for traces of sound and color just beyond the reach of his memory.

Something strange on the corner of his vision caught his eye. He turned to the right, and saw another sun rising. Now he noticed that far out on this side lay a wide channel of water, a large inlet, wider than most rivers. The city came right up to the shores of the inlet, and continued on the other side, stretching out towards the rising sun.

Suddenly Godfrey realized that he held a sword in his hand. He had not noticed the sword before, but knew that he had been holding it ever since the dream began. He could not feel pain, but he knew that the hilt of the sword was burning hot. Looking down at his hand, Godfrey saw that the skin was charring and burning. With a cry he flung the sword away. He did not hear it clatter against the roofs, but he saw it falling, sliding down the golden dome and plummeting far, far down into the city. A man appeared on the dome, appeared in mid-stride. He continued walking until he stood before Godfrey, and handed him a sword. The man had copper skin and golden hair. Godfrey took the sword, and the man's bright blue eyes flickered with a strange light. He smiled, but it was not a friendly smile. Godfrey started with alarm.

Then there were other dreams, scattered images coming thick and fast. He saw Gerard de Ridford, with the Temple in one hand and the Crown of Jerusalem in the other, trying to juggle the two like a court jester. He saw himself at Roncevals, like Roland in the ballad, with Jacques beside him and Turpin at his other side, with Moors rushing down at them. He shouted to Jacques to blow his horn, but Jacques didn't listen…

Then he was somewhere else, a place of brightness, but it was a cruel brightness that blinded his eyes. He was fighting someone, someone who looked vaguely familiar. A knight, in shining armor and a white cloak, with a blue and silver surcoat. The memory of this man was on the edge of Godfrey's memory... he was a hero, a hero out of legend... but what legend? The knight vanished...

He saw Raymond of Tripoli fighting with a skinny, sandy-haired man on the head of a giant bull, between the horns. The bull was bucking back and forth, trying to throw them off to their deaths, but they did not notice, so intent were they on killing each other.

Then he knelt before someone. No, something. It was a monster, with the shape of a man, but a hideous, mutilated face, without any nose, but merely two slits. The skin was rotting, and the bone showed through the lips. It smiled down at him, raised him to his feet, and the bony lips gave him the Kiss of Peace.

He was back in Jaffa, and the Thing was rushing up from the sea, sweeping about the town. And Godfrey was rushing towards it; riding towards it on a horse, riding through the spectral figures, trampling them, though he still could not see them. He plunged towards the Thing, unable to stop or to alter his course.

Godfrey twisted in anguish both at the old memories and the frightening new images, but the dream was not yet over—not yet. For just as Godfrey fell into darkness and thought he would awake, he found himself rising high above Jaffa. He found himself standing atop the Temple Rock, looking up at the sky, and the sky was black with clouds and illuminated by flashes of lightning. Godfrey could see the whole of the kingdom, from the Sea of Galilee to the Red Sea, to the point where Asia Minor jutted out into the Mediterranean.

He heard a low rumble, and looked out to the south and east to see storm clouds gathering, sweeping over Outremer. There was no rain, but lightning bolts streaked down, streaked across the sky, streaked down toward the kingdom. Then Godfrey saw another man facing him, up in the clouds. His face was shrouded in a black cloak, but he was riding the storm clouds, and striding towards him, a flashing sword in his hand. Godfrey stepped out to meet him, but his foe's sword swung, and he fell, plummeting toward the earth as lightning flashed...

Godfrey awoke with the sun shining across his face. His sides were heaving and beads of perspiration glistened on his face. *A storm is coming,* he thought. *A storm is coming.*

Chapter 14

ANTIOCH
Godfrey

When the three of them set out again, they continued to ride north along the sea-road. They remained out of sight of the shore, though just barely. Godfrey could feel the breezes and catch sight of gulls drifting overhead. But they caught no glimpse of the sea, and Godfrey had no more dreams—at least, none that he could remember. As the days passed the strange images slowly faded from Godfrey's mind, and he dwelt once again in the present, not in the past or the future.

William and Jacques argued less as they went on, but their peace was merely the uneasy peace of men who do not like each other, but know they will be stuck together for a while. As they rode north, William grew more at his ease, while Jacques grew less so, for the simple reason that they were coming closer to William's home and farther from Jacques's.

They rode on north for some days. They passed out of the Kingdom of Jerusalem proper, and into the principality of Tripoli—the domain of count Raymond, Godfrey and Jacques's recent acquaintance. None tried to stop them; two Templars and a priest could pass unharmed through most places in Christendom. Unless, of course, the ruler of that country was angry at the Temple or under excommunication. Raymond of Tripoli was neither.

Summer was in full force by the time they passed out of Tripoli into the principality of Antioch. They still had a couple more days to go before they could reach the city proper, but the relief showed on all their faces that the journey was almost over.

The day after leaving Tripoli, they came to the Orontes River: a great river, as wide as the Nile. But it flowed faster than the Nile and was much clearer, very deep in the middle. The current was strong as well as swift; a man could drown easily trying to ford the Orontes. Men *had* drowned trying to cross it.

With that memory, Godfrey looked at the river and Orontes Field beyond it in a new light. During the First Crusade, Godfrey de Bouillion, Raymond of Toulouse and Bohemund had fought a great battle here. *A hundred years ago,* thought Godfrey, *Kerboga's two hundred thousand men filled this very plain before us, Orontes Field, with Kerboga's black banners waving above every corner of the camp.*

"Keep riding, Godfrey," said William. "We have a ways to ride to the east before we come to Orontes Bridge."

The archdeacon turned his horse to the right and began cantering along, following the river. Jacques followed silently. Godfrey waited a moment longer, looking out across the plain. Far off he could see the City of Antioch outlined against the sky. Tiny against the walls, he could see the great gate opening, just as it might have opened a hundred years ago…

The Christian defenders of Antioch were starving and exhausted, while Kerboga's men were well-fed and well-rested. The gate opened, and a sorry little army came pouring out, led by Bohemund and Godfrey de Bouillion and Raymond of Toulouse. A few thousand crusaders, most without armor, almost all of them without horses. They rode on camels and donkeys, or walked on foot.

"How far," groused Jacques, "to the bridge?"

"Just a mile or so," murmured William.

Godfrey was still picturing the Battle of the Orontes in his mind. *Kerboga had been playing chess with one of his emirs. When he heard of a couple thousand unarmored, starving Christians sallying forth from Antioch, he laughed and told his captains to deal with it. Within half an hour of the first clash of arms, he had stopped laughing, for he could see his mighty army fleeing towards the river. Kerboga himself drew his sword and led his mamelukes to fight. He rallied his army and brought the full weight of two hundred thousand disciplined Saracens to bear on the ragged band of Christians. But the Saracen army…simply melted away.*

"There," said William, sounding relieved. "There lies Orontes Bridge."

Afterwards, the Christians said that St. George and an army of saints came to fight at the crusaders' side. A Cloud of Witnesses, surrounding the Warriors of the Cross. Whatever the cause, Kerboga's mighty army was torn asunder by the Christians. They came pouring back towards the river. Some tried to swim, but were swept away and drowned. The large mass of men pressed towards Orontes Bridge, and there the press of fleeing men and horses became clogged. Hundreds were trampled to death there by their own friends, trying to cross. Men rushed over Orontes Bridge, stepping knee-deep in the mangled remains of their comrades.

The three horses stepped onto the stone bridge. By some chance, at that particular moment, there were no other travelers crossing Orontes

Bridge, and so the two Templars and the deacon rode across with nothing but their own silence to disturb them.

Kerboga fought on bravely, trying to hold the bridgehead. But the Christians pressed forward, and his bodyguard was unable to hold. By midday, it had become hopeless. Kerboga would have stayed and died with his men, but his bodyguard insisted that he get to safety. The bridge was too clogged up, however, and in the end Kerboga's bodyguard had to cut a path through his own men to get him safely across Orontes Bridge. Kerboga escaped to Mosul, while the rest of his men were left to the Christians. Few survived.

"What happened to him after the battle?" asked Godfrey, only half aware that he had voiced his thoughts aloud.

Jacques and William turned to stare at him.

"Yes?" asked William. "Explain." The two of them were smiling at him. Godfrey scowled. He said nothing, and they rode on.

Small clusters of houses lined the road to the city itself. A few children peered at them from their hiding places, but most of the folk ignored them. All manner of knights and priests passed the road every day.

William looked out at the City outlined against the darkening sky. "By tomorrow morning, we will be in Antioch. Listen carefully now, so you understand what we're going to do inside the city. As soon as we enter, I will ask for an audience with Andronicus Comnenus. I will bring you two with me, and introduce you to him. He has already prepared lodgings for you. Neither of you need worry about money; Andronicus Comnenus will supply you with all your needs. Paid for from the Antioch treasury, of course—Reynald de Chatillon dares not refuse. From there, it will be up to Andronicus what to do next."

✠ ✠ ✠

The next morning the three of them passed through the great Orontes Gate of Antioch. Already laborers were streaming out of the city to work the fields, while workmen poured into the city to shops and forges.

Antioch was a large city, though not as large as Jerusalem. They rode through crowded streets and alleys, following William.

Godfrey had not realized it until now, but he was nervous, and had been for the last few weeks. He had no notion of how to assist in diplomatic matters. He was expected to meet a Byzantine, a nobleman, and then *what?*

His instructions had been very vague. He was merely supposed to be planted in Antioch to assist with negotiations...but what did that mean? *A go-between for the master's negotiators and Andronicus Comnenus.*

In all previous assignments, Godfrey had merely been an observer who scouted and then reported to Blanchefort. But now...*negotiations?* What could he do?

Very suddenly, William jerked his reins over to the right, pulling his horse to the side.

"Get out of the street!" he called to Godfrey and Jacques. Godfrey reined his horse in, following William.

All around them, people were clearing out of the middle of the street. A column of mounted lancers thundered by, and then another. Banners fluttered among the lances, and the people of Antioch began cheering. Godfrey frowned at William questioningly, but the archdeacon only shrugged.

More parties of horsemen galloped past, all coming from Orontes Gate. Godfrey counted thirteen bands of knights before a long row of Turkish captives were led down the street, chained to each other, hurried along under the watchful eyes of a dozen guards with horsewhips. The Turks screamed and ranted at the people, which only made them laugh and jeer even harder.

All three of them grimaced at the sight of the prisoners. Reynald de Chatillon, the Hawk of Antioch, was a brutal foe, and he would not treat his prisoners-of-war kindly. But there was little that could be done.

Suddenly William tensed. He touched Godfrey's shoulder and pointed behind the prisoners. A man was riding alone on a destrier. As he passed, the people's screams and cheers grew louder.

Godfrey watched as the man grew closer. He was a muscular man of average height. Curly brown locks lined his brows. He had a finely carved face, one that Godfrey supposed women would find attractive. Emblazoned on his breastplate was a hawk in flight against a scarlet field. A short axe with a cruel-looking half-moon for a blade was slung from the saddle, while strapped to his back was the biggest sword Godfrey had ever seen. It looked to be five or six feet long, wrought of thick iron, with leather wrapped around its long handle. Even the man's horse was big; the destrier was a giant, pitch black creature that snapped at any who drew too near.

"That," said William, "is Reynald de Chatillon, the Hawk of Antioch."

Reynald de Chatillon passed them by, and the people screamed out their cheers for the Hawk. Godfrey's ears rang with the sound long after he had passed.

After the Hawk had gone, more knights rode by.

"The Hawk," said Godfrey. "I thought he *lived* here. Why is he just entering the city now?"

"He is returning from a raid on the Turks of Iconium," said William. "He makes raids on all his neighbors occasionally."

At long last, the procession passed on. William rode back into the street.

"Come," he said. "This only makes it more important to get to the Greek quickly."

William galloped off down the street. Godfrey glanced at Jacques, then dug his heels in and followed.

A few streets down, William came to an abrupt halt before a huge stone structure. Godfrey looked up at in awe. It was very like a palace.

"This..." began Godfrey, questioningly.

"... is where Andronicus Comnenus lives," finished William. "Let's go inside."

Four men bearing swords were guarding the door. William of Tyre strode up to them confidently.

"I wish to speak to Andronicus Comnenus."

The guards, whom Godfrey guessed were strongarms hired by Andronicus to keep watch, frowned at him. One of them opened the door a crack and shouted something. A second later, a skinny little man with a beaked nose appeared in the doorway.

"Who are you?" he growled at them, glaring suspiciously.

William smiled. "I am the archdeacon of Tyre, sent by the archbishop of Tyre, and I have come to respectfully request an audience with Andronicus Comnenus."

The man frowned at him, then vanished again behind the door.

A few minutes later, he appeared again.

"Andronicus Comnenus has been expecting you. He will see you now."

William straightened and passed through the doorway. Jacques and Godfrey hesitated a moment outside.

"Come," said the archdeacon. "Andronicus Comnenus is waiting."

Chapter 15

ANDRONICUS COMNENUS
Godfrey

odfrey stepped over the threshold of Andronicus Comnenus's house. He found himself in a large room, as large as the Temple Court in Jerusalem. The floor was marble, inlaid with gold. A great marble staircase ascended to the second floor, while multiple hallways led off on all sides.

Godfrey heard a sharp intake of breath from Jacques beside him.

"This isn't a house. It's a bloody palace!"

William smiled, but said nothing and strode straight forward. Another servant came down the stairway. She was a young Syrian girl whose clothes covered far too little of her body. Godfrey wondered anxiously what kind of a man this Andronicus Comnenus was—the strongarms outside and the servants within gave him a strange impression. They would be dealing with this Greek for months…years, maybe.

"Sirs, follow me," said the servant, her eyes downcast. Andronicus Comnenus kept his servants humble. "I will take you to the Lord of the house."

Up stairways and through hallways they followed her, until at last they stood before two great doors. Two more guards stood before these doors, but they were not like the strongarms out in the street. Godfrey eyed them curiously. These were men like he had never seen before; big, brawny soldiers, young men, but with utterly white hair.

One of the men shifted his head slightly, and as the light reflected off it, Godfrey saw that his hair was not quite white, but a very pale blond. But it was still lighter than any natural hair Godfrey had yet seen; Jacques was French, but his hair was a golden yellow. These men must be Saxons. Strange; what would a Saxon be doing in Outremer, let alone in the service of a Byzantine? Their arms rippled with muscles, and the axes slung over their shoulders look heavy enough to smash the marble floor.

"Varangians," murmured William, but before Godfrey could begin to puzzle out what that meant, the Saxons threw the great doors open. The Syrian woman bowed and left, while William stepped forward.

Beyond the doors lay a great room, not quite as big as the first, again with marble floor and golden inlay. At the far end were a number of chairs, with one raised above the others.

Most of the chairs were empty, but the four in the middle were filled. Godfrey's eyes were drawn to the man on the raised chair, and he knew immediately, as much by the man's appearance as by the raised seat, that this man was Andronicus Comnenus.

Andronicus had blue eyes, golden hair and a fine Roman nose. He was not as muscular as Reynald de Chatillon had been, but there was instead a sort of elfin quality about him; the man radiated charm and eloquence, and his very manner seemed to draw all attention to himself.

It was some time before Godfrey became aware of the rest of the room. The guards had shut the doors behind them. William and Jacques had continued halfway across the room and stopped about ten paces before the chairs. Godfrey hurried to catch up to them. Andronicus Comnenus smiled disarmingly at the three of them.

"Archdeacon William," he said in a tone that somehow managed to convey comradeship, while at the same time retaining the distinction between a lord and a servant. "I am glad that you have returned so soon. Antioch has become quite boring after the battle."

"Battle?" asked William, frowning. "I thought the war was in Egypt."

Andronicus laughed. "No, there is always some fight going on here in the north. That's what comes from living too close to Turks. While Arabs and Egyptians only fight if they've got some reason to, the Turks fight for the fun of it. Lord, I think they derive sensual pleasure from it."

"My lord," interrupted William, still keeping his tone respectful. "The battle?"

"Yes," said Andronicus, laughing again. "Nur ad-Din made an attack on the castle of Harrenc, twenty miles to the north."

"Nur ad-Din himself?"

"No," said the Byzantine, dismissing the question with a wave of his hand. "The sultan is somewhere in the south, where the wine and women come freely. It would have been Maj ad-Din, or that black devil Ridhwan. Whoever it was, they started out by launching a head-on attack on the castle, but the knights repulsed it. The Turks broke and fled, and the Arabs had no choice but to follow. Our bold knights gave chase, but the infidel leader rallied his men and trapped the knights. Prince Bohemund himself barely escaped with his life, along with the regent, Reynald de Chatillon." A note of distaste entered Andronicus's voice at that last name.

William frowned. "Strange; I heard no news of any battle here in the north."

Andronicus shrugged. "I'm sure that the king and the master of the Temple know of it already."

There was a moment's silence before Andronicus Comnenus spoke again.

"Ah, but that is all over. Now we have the matter at hand. I assume that you have brought me my Templars."

Godfrey frowned. *His* Templars?

William nodded. "My lord Andronicus Comnenus, here are Jacques de Maille and Godfrey de Montferrat."

Godfrey and Jacques bowed deeply. Byzantine or no, he *was* a nobleman. Andronicus smiled benevolently down on them.

"It is a pleasure to meet you, Godfrey, Jacques. I have always wanted to meet a Templar. I have long wondered on why a man would choose your life of celibacy. Is it a penance for some grave sin, Sir Monk?" he asked to Godfrey.

"No, my lord," said Godfrey. "I came willingly to the Temple."

"Good," said Andronicus. "because you will not find life here very conducive to penance." He laughed. "Now let me introduce you to my companions."

Godfrey had half forgotten about the other three men sitting beside Andronicus Comnenus; they had remained silent throughout the meeting.

"This," said Andronicus, motioning towards the man on his right, "is Langosse Argyrus, a faithful officer of mine."

Langosse was a short man, with hair as golden as Andronicus. His face looked vaguely French, and indeed the name Langosse was Frankish, but there was also some similarity between his face and Andronicus. Perhaps he had some Greek blood in him. Langosse bowed his head formally in acknowledgement.

"This," said Andronicus, motioning to the man directly on his left, "is Basil Camateros, an officer of the Varangian Guard and captain of my personal bodyguard."

Basil Camateros was another Saxon, and he was even bigger than two men outside the doors. His arms were as thicker than other men's legs, and his hair was even whiter than the other Saxons'. He clapped his fist over his heart in a sort of salute, but there was a deep frown on his face.

"And this," continued Andronicus, "is Murzuphlus."

As his eyes fell on Murzuphlus, Godfrey wanted to laugh. The man had bushy black hair which stuck out in all directions. His eyebrows in particular were overgrown, hanging down over his eyes just as his hair fell over his face. His nose was not quite the right shape. There was something vaguely canine about his appearance; indeed his look was that of a badly-treated dog. In keeping with this impression, Murzuphlus growled something that might have been a greeting, but could just as easily have been a curse.

Andronicus laughed aloud. "Murzuphlus here doesn't like Latins. Do you, Murzuphlus?" Not waiting for a reply, Andronicus continued. "Murzuphlus's real name is Alexius Ducas, but we call him 'the bushy-eyebrowed': *murzuphlus.*"

Godfrey smiled. *Apparently,* he thought to himself, *not only does Murzuphlus look and act like a dog, but they treat him as one too.*

"Now," continued Andronicus, "I must have you two set up in your rooms. You shall stay right here and—"

Jacques had been waiting carefully for this. He quickly broke in.

"My lord Andronicus, with all due respect, as we are to be the Temple's agents, independent of any other party in these negotiations, I think we should stay somewhere else."

Andronicus smiled, smoothly and without hesitation. "Of course. It seems that you do have some small experience in negotiations, Master De Maille. Yes, it would give me a slight advantage to be your host. Well done, Templar."

Jacques frowned. "Experience? No, my lord. Just good common sense."

The Greek nodded agreeably. "Very well. I will have you installed in the palace. Prince Bohemund and the Hawk will not interfere with your work."

Jacques bowed respectfully. "My gratitude, lord Andronicus."

"And what about you, dear Archdeacon. Will you stay a few days in Antioch?"

William shook his head. "As much as I would like to, I am afraid that the archbishop of Tyre requires that I return immediately. I thank you for your hospitality, but I must go now."

"Oh, but you must eat before you go. Nuri!" Andronicus snapped his fingers and the Syrian woman appeared at the doors.

"No," said William quickly. "I apologize, but I have no time. I would like to cross the border into Tripoli by nightfall. Now I must go."

William inclined his head respectfully, and turned to leave. "*God be with you,*" he whispered to Godfrey and Jacques. "*You will need all the help you can get.*"

Andronicus nodded understandingly. "Nuri, please escort my friend here to the door. Farewell, Archdeacon."

William hurried out, following the Syrian girl.

"Now," said Andronicus Comnenus, turning to the Templars. "I will arrange with the Hawk for you to stay at the Palace. There will be a feast tonight in his honor; the Hawk always holds a feast in his own honor when he returns from any military adventure. I must go now, but I will speak to you tonight. My servants will fetch you when your apartments are ready."

Andronicus Comnenus rose and inclined his head slightly to the Templars. They bowed, and he left the room, leaving the two Templars with Langosse, Basil, and Murzuphlus.

For a long time an uncomfortable silence prevailed. The two Templars stood where they were, and the three Greeks made no move to offer them chairs. Murzuphlus glared at the Templars with a look of utter hatred, while Jacques, Godfrey, Langosse and Basil tried not to look at each other.

It was Langosse who at last broke the silence.

"You know that he isn't serious about this," he said conversationally.

Godfrey and Jacques frowned.

"About the negotiations," continued Langosse carelessly. There was a smirk on his face.

"Silence, Langosse," said Basil. "Lord Andronicus would not have you talk so."

Langosse laughed. "Lord Andronicus does not mind."

"Why," asked Godfrey, still bemused, "did he summon us here, then, if he does not mean to negotiate with the master of the Temple?"

Langosse laughed. "Lord Andronicus was getting bored here. Antioch's a fun city, but it's not easy to entertain our lord. Even Lady Phillipa is not enough to keep *him* occupied for long. Oh, I'm sure he thinks he's serious about the negotiations, for the moment, but soon enough he'll tire of diplomacy, and it will all degenerate into just one more game."

"Besides," growled Murzuphlus in a very dog-like voice, "Lord Andronicus would never seriously consider submitting to Rome." By the way Murzuphlus pronounced the name, he made very little distinction between the lord Andronicus and the Lord God.

"Hold your tongues, both of you!" snapped Basil Camateros, still ignoring the Templars. "Lord Andronicus does what he wills, and you will not interfere with it."

The other two did not seem inclined to obey the huge Varangian, despite his being a head taller than them. They continued taunting the Templars, so that Godfrey did not breathe freely until Nuri came to direct them to the Palace.

Chapter 16

The Hawk

The doors to the palace swung open as Reynald de Chatillon, the Hawk of Antioch, rode through them.

He was in a good mood; he always was after parading through the streets, being cheered by the crowds. It was refreshing, seeing that; it showed a man that his position was secure. Almost as good as the thrill of the charge, the thrill of smashing a dozen foes under the destrier's hooves and the two-hander's blade.

Reynald de Chatillon had risen up from a landless squire in France to become the Lord of Antioch, and he was of a mind to rise even higher. He lived for the thrill of the moment; he loved battle, and he loved fame. He might even have been content, but for that cursed Greek hovering about his court, flirting with the women, demanding anything he wanted and—worse yet—receiving it.

Inside the courtyard, his wife was waiting. Constance of Antioch was still young and pretty, and the Hawk loved her dearly, though many whispered sad stories as to what would happen when she grew old and wrinkled.

Constance ran up beside the Hawk's stirrup, holding up a cup of wine and looking up adoringly at her husband. Reynald de Chatillon had gotten quite used to women looking at him like that, and he took it all in stride. He took the cup, drank it down in one gulp, then tossed it over his shoulder where a servant caught it and carried it off to the kitchens.

The Hawk leapt down from the saddle. Three servants rushed out and began struggling with the big destrier. Reynald de Chatillon's war steed obeyed none but its master. The Hawk turned his back on them, leaving them to fight it out with the horse. He kissed his wife, and then looked around to see who else was there.

Sir Bruce L'Anguille, Reynald's seneschal, stood waiting a few paces back. To his left was Bohemund III, prince of Antioch. In name,

Bohemund was the ruler of Antioch, but so long as Reynald was Regent, he was unlikely to do much ruling, even when he came of age.

Constance, having greeted her husband, hurried off to the kitchens to oversee the preparations for the banquet. Sir Bruce took a step forward.

Bruce was a thin weasel of a man, with shaggy black hair that grew denser towards the back of his head. He had followed the Hawk on Crusade to Outremer, and had risen in rank with him. Sir Bruce was cold and calculating, and so while Reynald was called the Hawk, Bruce had earned the nickname Bruce *Saunce Pite*.

"My lord Reynald," said Sir Bruce, handing the Hawk a piece of parchment with a great seal stamped in red wax. "A messenger, while you were gone. Wearing the Greek imperial colors. The parchment bears the seal of Manuel Comnenus."

Reynald frowned darkly. He took the parchment and tore it open. His frown deepened as he read it, then he crumpled it up.

"Bloody Greek," growled the Hawk. He carefully stuffed the paper in his coat; it was worthless to him, but if he threw it on the ground it would end up in Bruce's pocket, and God alone knew what would happen then.

"Lord Reynald," said Prince Bohemund petulantly, his boyish voice taking on the whine of a nephew asking for money from a bad-tempered uncle. "You must do something about that Greek lurking about the palace."

"Andronicus Comnenus?" asked Reynald, frowning again. "What's he doing now?"

"It's my sister," said Bohemund, his voice still a whine. "Phillipa."

"God's bones," swore the Hawk, "is he trying to bed her?"

Bohemund nodded, his face that of a frightened deer.

Reynald let loose a long string of profane curses, some directed at the Almighty, some at Greeks in general, and the rest at Andronicus Comnenus himself. For a man who could charm any woman at will, the Hawk possessed a larger vocabulary of profanities than any other in Outremer.

"You know what he's trying to do, boy?" growled Reynald. "He's going to try to marry your sister and then raise his own claim to the city of Antioch against me." Bohemund started to stammer something. "And against you, of course," Reynald added, as an afterthought.

"Yes," said Bohemund. "Sir Bruce explained it all to me. He said I should tell you."

Prince Bohemund looked up at the Hawk, his eyes anxious, as though he feared the man's next move would be to take his head off. Bohemund was afraid of most men who were bigger than he.

Reynald gave a loud roar, and raised a muscular arm in the air. Bohemund whimpered and shut his eyes, not realizing that the roar was a roar of decision, rather than anger. The Hawk clapped Bohemund across the back with a force that nearly sent him sprawling. Bohemund let out a squeak of alarm, and went stiff. Sir Bruce L'Anguille had a mysterious coughing fit and turned his face away from Bohemund for a few moments, making noises that sounded suspiciously like laughter.

"Well then, boy," growled the Hawk. "Let's go prepare for the feast. And as we go, I will explain to you how we are going to cleanse our fair city of this Greek."

Chapter 17

THE TRAP
Godfrey

odfrey started to object when Andronicus Comnenus told him that he and Jacques would be sitting beside him at the High Table at Reynald's banquet, but he soon realized that Andronicus would not yield.

So it was that he and Jacques found themselves looking out over the hall, sitting in places of honor in a banquet attended by all the lords of Antioch.

Godfrey's mouth watered as the servants brought out platters of food: roasted boar and fowl, steaming loaves of bread, fruits that could only be found here in the east, tubs of beer from the west and wine from the south.

Godfrey was seated with Andronicus Comnenus on his right and Jacques on his left. All around them were the great knights and lords of Antioch. Many glanced askance at the two Templars. Godfrey felt a surge of anger against Andronicus Comnenus, realizing that the Greek had not put them here at the high table out of any desire to do them honor—rather, he had put them there just to spite the lords of Antioch and the Hawk himself, knowing full well that the Templars would take blame and the anger, instead of himself. Langosse was right: it was all a game to the Greek.

To Andronicus Comnenus's right was a lady, a few years older than Godfrey himself, whom the Greek introduced as Lady Phillipa, sister to Prince Bohemund himself. Phillipa was dressed all in white, with her long golden hair rippling down past her shoulders. She was well worth looking at, and for that reason Godfrey kept his gaze down in his wine cup. Sworn to celibacy, Templars were also sworn to avoid women. *Anyway,* Godfrey told himself, *I have no interest in hearing the Greek flirt for hours on end.* Godfrey took another sip of wine. His gaze moved slowly back towards the Lady Phillipa, and he wrenched it back to his cup. *Oh God, she really is worth looking at...but Adelaise was even more beautiful.*

No! God help me, no! Turn my thoughts from this, God, or I'll die! Save me, Christ! Blessed Mother, pray for me!

Seeking a distraction, Godfrey peered down into his cup and found that it was empty.

He refilled it, and before he knew it, it was empty again.

The feast was still going strong, and there was nothing to do but have another cup of wine.

And another.

For hours the feast continued. The lords of Antioch began to leave as the night grew dark. Close on midnight, the Hawk and Prince Bohemund left, and, an hour later, the Lady Phillipa. All this went by in a blur for Godfrey as he drained wine cups, interspersed with roasted meat and exotic fruits. There had never been this much wine at the meals in the Temple refectory.

Next to Godfrey, Jacques stood up and left for his quarters in the palace. Half an hour later, Langosse and Basil got up.

"Lord Andronicus, shall we leave?" asked Basil.

Andronicus had just discovered how good the wine was. "Go on back," he said. "I'll join you soon."

The big Saxon glared at Godfrey, then he and Langosse left. Murzuphlus looked around, seeing his two friends gone, and then got up himself.

"My lord Andronicus, will you need my assistance?"

"No," said Andronicus, his voice a little slurred. "Go on back."

Murzuphlus left. Godfrey glanced up for a second from his wine cup. The hall was mostly empty, except for a few others still drinking, and servants clearing away the food. Godfrey kept on drinking.

"You Templars," Andronicus spoke suddenly to Godfrey, ripping off the leg of a roasted bird. "You call yourselves knights."

Godfrey nodded, drinking deeply from his cup.

"In Byzantium," continued the Greek, "when we hear of knights, we think of the ballads that your troubadours in Europe sing. But you are nothing like that."

"The troubadours?" Godfrey laughed as he filled his cup with wine. "No, I hope not. You don't know much about the West."

Andronicus drained his cup and spread his arms wide. "Enlighten me, then."

Godfrey sighed and set down his wine cup. "You must have heard of the troubles in Languedoc."

Andronicus Comnenus laughed. "Yes, the Cathars. We in the East find it amusing. We have no heretics in Byzantium."

"Well," growled Godfrey, "I suppose there would be fewer heretics when the emperor controls the church and uses the state as a weapon."

"Leave it, Sir Templar," said Andronicus. "It was an idle boast, if boast it can be called."

Godfrey nodded, taking a deep draught of wine. "Most of the troubadours," continued Godfrey, "are Cathars. So I pray God I never become like one of *their* heroes."

"Yes," said Andronicus, "I'm sure Rome would never approve of much of what they sing. I guess that celibate men will always be prudish."

Godfrey sighed, ignoring the jibe. "Not all the ballads of the troubadours are so twisted, though," he said. "Have you ever heard of Roland?"

"Yes," said the Greek, "I have. The *Chanson de Roland*, the greatest ballad of the West. Roland, mightiest of Charlemagne's twelve Paladins. A fine legend."

Godfrey drained his cup and refilled it.

"In Greece we have legends of our own," continued Andronicus. "Older than the *Chanson*, older than Roland, older than the Christ himself. The Greeks were worshipping the old gods centuries before the Maccabees fought in the land which you now inhabit."

"Don't know much about them," said Godfrey. "There are few or perhaps none in the West who can read Greek. We hear but hints of ancient perversion and cruelty."

"Perversion and cruelty? Yes, the old gods were no strangers to those." He laughed mirthlessly. "They slew mortals in fits of jealousy and chose mortals as their lovers whether they willed it or not."

Godfrey frowned, and Andronicus laughed again. "But there was more than that. Perversion...well, we would consider it so now, but the Greeks of old did not. And beyond that, there was much good in the old world that is now lost to us. *Thou hast conquered, Galilean...*"

Godfrey glanced up from his wine. "Who said that?"

Andronicus smiled. "A great man. The pagan world was much merrier than ours, don't you agree? It is one of the...imperfections of our Christian world. And our esteemed Saracen foes, much as they hate us, like to join in that ecstasy of pessimism and frenzy of self-denial—the belief that this world is merely an unhappy preparation for the next." Andronicus's eyes narrowed, and his voice, which had been growing steadily more serious, hardened. "That belief," he said, "has done too much evil already."

"Evil?" asked Godfrey, a suspicious frown crossing his face. "You believe that the Church—both Greek and Latin—has brought more evil into the world?"

Andronicus hesitated now before speaking. "Sir Templar, there are many with whom I would not speak of this, but I deem you to be more… intelligent than many. You will understand the thread of my thoughts presently."

"Go on, then." The frown on Godfrey's face only deepened.

"The pagans, the old Greeks, did not worry so much about penance, unless it was to watch tragic heroes performing it on the stage. They did not worry so much about it because they saw that it was possible to truly enjoy life. You see, Sir Templar, they really *lived*. They tried both to do right and to be happy. The Christian world has forgotten what it means to be happy."

For a long moment, Godfrey was silent. He drained his wine cup empty, but he did not refill it this time. At last he had found something more interesting than the drink. Godfrey looked over at the Greek and spoke. His tongue was loosened by wine, and he paid no heed to how long he spoke or whether Andronicus was even listening.

"Yes, perhaps it is true that the pagans lived merrier lives than we did. They showed their joy for the world to see, and, as you put it, they *lived*. But…therein lies the problem. They wore their joy like a cloak, flaunting their bacchanalia before the world, as though trying to convince themselves that they were happy by convincing everyone else that they were happy. The Christian, on the other hand, wears his suffering as he would a cloak, for that is all the world can see.

"But," continued Godfrey, "they were scared—surely you have seen that. The pagans strove to *live*, but it was merely a game to try and forget, for a moment at least, the coming darkness. I know little enough of their dramas and their plays and their epics, but I know this much: the thing they strove after most was *immortality*. They were afraid, very afraid, for they saw clearly that after they were done living, all that was left was to slip into blackness and despair. A story that tried to portray a really lasting happiness could not satisfy in the pagan world; why do you think the death of Hector or the blinding of Oedipus were the most enduring of the heathen epics? They saw the good things of the world and loved them, but they knew that their joy could not last.

"With the Christian," said Godfrey, his voice growing louder with excitement, "the world sees only his suffering. But that is merely a covering, for underneath it lies his joy. And that joy is Christ, for there alone is any good thing eternal—there alone can we love any good thing and not despair. So, Andronicus Comnenus, I must disagree. I am glad, very glad, that the pagan world has faded. The gods of Olympus are dead, and thanks be to God for that."

Andronicus Comnenus was chortling into his wine.

"Well said, Sir Templar. You are a rare individual. I do not often hear Christians speak as you do." The Greek's tone was too carefree, too pleasant. "I will think about your words," he said in a voice that meant he would not. "But," he continued, "Sir Templar, I must say that I have never found this joy you say is buried in the Christian's heart."

"Perhaps," said Godfrey, peering down into his goblet, "you have never really looked for it." After the words were out of his mouth he wished he had looked the Greek in the eyes as he spoke. But now it was too late, and his thoughts were beginning to blur together, moving in confused and untraceable patterns.

The Greek snorted. "Sir Templar, you *are* an idealist."

"If that's so," said Godfrey, "I intend to live up to my ideal."

Andronicus grabbed some grapes from a platter. "For all that you scoff at the knight of the troubadour's ballad, you are rather like them yourself."

Godfrey choked on a mouthful of bread. He frowned at the Greek, who continued.

"Like any hero in a minstrel's song, you have your impossible ideal which you will follow to your death. From what little you have said to me already, you would be accounted a fool by any statesman or lord; you seem to know nothing of diplomacy or pragmatism. And yet, you treat the troubadour's ballads with scorn. You are a curious fellow, Sir Templar. Godfrey de Montferrat, the Knight of the Impossible Ideal."

Godfrey chewed slowly and said nothing. Smiling to himself, Andronicus looked down into his wine cup.

Suddenly, Godfrey laughed. "The Knight of the Impossible Ideal. I like it." Godfrey stood up, and finally noticed that the hall was nearly empty. He turned and bumped into a chair that shouldn't have been there.

Next to him, Andronicus Comnenus stood up also. He looked around at the vacant seats.

"Sir Templar," said the Greek, "it appears my companions have all departed. Come with me, and I will show you the fair city of Antioch."

Godfrey could not find it in him to sleep, so he nodded dizzily. He stumbled when he walked. He was drunk as he had never been before. He felt a guilty stab of conscience, but pushed it away. The master had given him dispensation as was necessary from the restrictions of the Order. Not that it had been necessary to drink himself into this state. But what else was there to do for two hours?

Godfrey was not very sure how long he walked the streets of Antioch with the Greek that night, but he remembered fuzzy glimpses of the citadel, the great gate, the palaces of the city, and some of Andronicus Comnenus's favorite brothels, which the Greek was prudent enough not to try to convince Godfrey to enter, even while drunk. They passed many others; tramps and workers, wealthy noblemen and friends of Andronicus on their way to taverns and brothels.

Godfrey never knew what time of night it was when they stumbled around a corner into a dead end. Not even a faint touch of light had shown itself in the horizon, though Godfrey was sure that he had been outside for hours. On the west side of the city, near the docks, they stepped into a cul-de-sac. In the dark they didn't see the men until too late.

Three men had emerged from an alley to block their way out. They were big men, taller than the Greek and as tall as the Templar, with arms twice as thick as either.

Godfrey took a step back at the sight of them, but Andronicus stood his ground. "What do you want, friend?" he asked.

The man in the center growled something to the other two, and they moved forward.

Andronicus took a careless step backwards. Godfrey looked over the men. The one in the center was wearing a torn ringmail shirt. The other men wore only tattered clothing, but they had cudgels and knives in their hands.

"We have no money on us, friend," continued Andronicus calmly, almost threateningly. "If there's anything else, you can ask for it, and we may be willing to part with it."

"Would you give up that sword?" came a growl from behind them. Godfrey whirled around to see three more men waiting in the alley behind them. Andronicus did not move, only glanced down at his sword, a beautiful, finely crafted one-hand blade.

"No," he said airily. "I will keep that."

The big man with the ringmail shirt drew a greatsword, nodded at the others, and they closed in fast.

Godfrey grabbed the hilt of his sword, but one of the men from behind grabbed him first, slamming his hand down on the hilt before Godfrey could draw it. Godfrey punched the man in the face. His assailant reeled from the blow, but swung around punched Godfrey back, smashing in his nose. Godfrey stepped back and tried to draw the sword again, but the man was on him, smashing his face again and again.

Andronicus, however, had been faster. Even as the footpads closed in, his light Greek sword was in his hand, flashing under the pale sliver of moonlight. He lunged forward as his foes drew forth their weapons. He rushed at a big man with a cudgel and closed with him, too close for his foe to swing. As he did, he drove his sword upward. For a moment the two stood an inch apart, staring at each other. One of Andronicus's hands was on the other's shoulder. The tip of the Greek's blade stuck out of the man's back, the blood black against the shining sword. The cudgel had dropped from the man's hand.

Andronicus shoved the body into the way of the others, using the force to brutally rip his sword out, spraying himself with blood and innards.

The rest tried to close in on the Greek, but Andronicus was already moving swiftly through the narrow space allowed him, slicing into one man's wrist, landing a hard blow upward into another's nose. Cudgels swung, knives stabbed, but the Greek slipped through unharmed. One man whom Andronicus had knocked down scrambled up behind him, raising a knife to stab. Catching a blur of movement from the corner of his eye, the Greek crouched and spun about, sticking the man in his stomach. This time the blade slid out of the dead footpad's body neatly as Andronicus danced away from another man's cudgel.

Finally recovering himself, Godfrey rolled away from his assailant's blows. He could feel slick, wet blood running down his face, but the adrenaline was flowing through him now. The man lunged in to finish him, but Godfrey caught him in the stomach with his foot. His foe doubled over, winded.

Godfrey stepped back, and now he finally had room to draw his sword. He glanced around quickly. Four of the assailants lay dead on the ground, and Andronicus was fighting the man with the greatsword.

The footpad with whom Godfrey had been fighting caught his breath and ripped a rusted morningstar from his belt. Whirling the spiked ball on its chain above his head, he came at Godfrey. Godfrey backed up, his sword held in front of him. He turned his head slightly and saw from the corner of his eye that he was backing into a wall.

The morningstar swung and wrapped about his blade, pulling his sword aside. Godfrey gripped the hilt tightly to prevent the sword from being ripped out of his hands. He pulled loose, struck again, and the morningstar swung in response, wrapping round the sword and pulling it out of line. The man wrenched the morningstar, again trying to pull the sword from Godfrey's hands. This time Godfrey was ready. He stepped forward, in the same direction as the man was pulling, stepping farther and wrenching forward. The morningstar was ripped from the footpad's hand and went flying off into the alley. In the same motion, Godfrey came swinging around full circle and opened the man's throat with his sword.

He turned to see Andronicus standing over the dead body of their last assailant. The Greek was smiling drunkenly, and when he saw Godfrey looking at him, he began to laugh.

"Well, Sir Templar, it's been years since I've had a fight like that."

Godfrey sheathed his bloody sword. "How?" he asked, dazed and confused. "You took on five of them, while I was struggling to fight one." Godfrey's head was spinning, and he was wondering how he had ever defeated Malik al-Harawi in Egypt.

Andronicus kept on laughing. "I have trained at this for years. You Templars, all that you do for practice is to hack at wooden stands for an hour every day. Perhaps that builds your strength, but it teaches you nothing of the use of a blade."

The Greek was walking among the slain, opening pouches and sacks. When he came to the leader, he found a large sack that jingled when he nudged it. With the point of his sword, he slit it open. Gold coins spilled out onto the street. Andronicus frowned.

"They had money to last them for weeks. Any petty pickpocket could see that we have little or no coin on us. Thieves might have been attracted by my rich clothes, but they weren't interested in clothes—or coin for that matter. They asked for my sword, but that was merely a jest. What did they *want*?"

"It was a well prepared ambush," said Godfrey. The Greek nodded, his frown deepening. Neither of them spoke, but the thought of assassination was in their minds.

Finally Andronicus shook himself, as though the physical action would shake off any mental anxiety. "Well, Sir Templar," he said, "since you seem to know nothing of swordplay, how would you like to learn?"

Godfrey frowned. "From you?"

"Of course. Your master has given you no specific assignment, and you could be here for months. Years. It would entertain me for quite a while."

"Swordplay," repeated Godfrey. "But what *use* is that? You don't need swordplay from the back of a horse; you just need to have strength enough to keep hacking at the men below you."

The Greek laughed. He seemed to do that frequently. "Look around you—five men could not take me down. That is what use swordplay is. You Franks are all alike; you never see past the end of your horse's arse. What happens when your horse is killed? Do you know how many bold knights have died because they didn't know one end of a blade from the other once they fell from their noble steed?"

Godfrey's mind did not register most of what the Greek was saying.

Instead, all that he saw was himself, fighting desperately against Malik al-Harawi in the Egyptian desert, being beaten back because he knew nothing of swordplay.

"Yes," he said. "I would be glad to learn."

✠ ✠ ✠

Late the next morning, Godfrey briefly related the last night's events to Jacques. Jacques listened, quiet, stroking his scraggly blond beard. When Godfrey was done, he just sat there, saying nothing. Finally, Jacques looked up at his friend.

"You know, Godfrey," he said, "if you insist on following your ideal to the end, you'll be a pain in the arse to everyone around you."

Godfrey grinned. "I know."

Jacques nodded expressionlessly. "Just making sure."

Two and a Half Years Later

Chapter 18

THE THWARTED LOVER
The Gatekeeper

Fall, AD 1166

Arnold de Torroga tried to lean back into the shadow of the wall. High noon in Jerusalem turned the Temple Court into an oven.

Arnold had been born of a noble family in Spain. As the youngest son of seven brothers, he had been promised to the Temple from a tender age. In former years, his noble birth would have guaranteed him a high position in the Temple. Bertrand de Blanchefort, however, was no respecter of persons. Arnold de Torroga had been assigned to duty as gatekeeper.

I suppose, he thought, *it's right and fair that a king should stand beside a peasant in the ranks of the Temple. It's the way it should be. All the same, I would not have complained if my birth had gotten me something better than this.*

For the most part, gate duty in the Temple at high noon involved two choices: he could bake inside the gatehouse, or burn outside in the Temple Court.

Inside the gatehouse, he was sheltered from the rays of the sun, but in the enclosed space, it seemed twice as hot as outside. In the Temple Court, it was a little cooler, but the sun's rays shone down on him cruelly.

Today, Arnold had chosen to burn rather than to bake.

God's bones, it's supposed to be autumn! Back in Navarre, there would have been snow. Instead, it's hotter than summer is in the Pyrenees.

There were rarely more than a couple visitors in a day, and that on a particularly busy day. When Arnold had complained to Blanchefort of the boredom, he had been told to pray rather than let his mind wander. He did pray…for about an hour. He could not spend longer than that just praying.

I'm naught but flesh and blood. I doubt that Blanchefort could pray for more than an hour straight, either. Only difference is, he's master and I'm not.

Arnold sighed and tried to settle back more into the shadow.

Maybe if I am patient enough, I will be master one day. But I doubt it.

Slowly, a noise began growing from the path beyond the Temple wall. Arnold was just beginning to doze when a sharp rap on the gate woke him. He scrambled to his feet and ran to the gatehouse, opening up the little shutter. Two priests waited outside, sitting on donkeys. Both they and their mounts looked tired, covered in dust and sweat. They had come a long way.

"Who is it?" called Arnold.

"The archbishop of Tyre and the bishop of Bethlehem wish to speak with the master of the Temple," called the younger of the two.

Arnold frowned.

So these two dusty priests riding on donkeys claim to be a bishop and an archbishop.

"Make haste, sir," said the priest. "We are on our way to Tyre, and we must be off in an hour."

I doubt they're really bishops. But if they aren't, I'll let the master take off their heads. Less trouble for me.

Arnold scurried down and unbarred the gate. He gave a shout, and two grooms came running up from the stables at the base of the hill. They snickered a little when they saw the donkeys, but Arnold gave them a stern look, and they took the donkeys off to the stables.

The two priests hurried on inside, eager to get out of the heat. Arnold sat back, glaring enviously at them as they made it inside the cool confines of the refectory.

Presently, Arnold heard the sounds of something else coming up the path. He cocked his ear and listened.

A horse, this time. And a big one. A destrier.

In his months of gatekeeping, with nothing better to do, Arnold had practiced at identifying different mounts by the sound of their hoofbeats. He had become quite talented at it. Slowly rising to his feet, he went to the gatehouse window where he peered out through the shutter.

And drew back in surprise when he did.

God's beard, that can't be him! Why would he be here? What is bloody well wrong with me today?

Arnold peered back out through the shutter. Before the wall stood a knight, knocking loudly on the gate. His hair was golden and curly, his face resembling that of an angel. His sigil was a red field with three black foxes.

Arnold took a deep breath, then shouted out to the knight.

"Gerard de Ridford, is that really you?"

The knight looked up in surprise at the sound of the voice. "Arnold de Torroga? You still praying your arse off with these bloody monks?"

"Yes," said Arnold. "I'm still here at the Temple. But what brings you here?"

"Open the bloody gate and I'll tell you." Arnold scurried back down and unbarred the gate.

Gerard de Ridford rode in, looking magnificent on his warhorse, despite the dust of his journey. He dismounted as Arnold shouted for the grooms. They came running, and there were no sniggers now. Bowing respectfully to the knight, they led the horse off, showing as much deference to it as to its rider.

"Well?" asked Arnold, once the grooms were gone. "Last I heard, you were courting some wench in Tripoli. You haven't gone monk on us, have you?"

Arnold stopped abruptly when he saw De Ridford's face. All merriment had left it, leaving only a mask of despair and rage.

Gerard de Ridford spoke in a cold, emotionless voice. "I have come to enter the Temple. I have come to be a Templar."

Arnold stared at Gerard blankly, until the golden-haired knight spoke again.

"It is as you said. I was courting a woman in Tripoli. She was…she was the fairest maiden ever to walk these barren sands in a thousand years. She was sweet and she was pious, her hair was golden as the sun, and her smile could set a man's pulse pounding like a drum. And she…loved me."

De Ridford paused, making a choking sound almost like a sob. Arnold frowned.

This is not the man I knew. What has happened to him? Gerard de Ridford might have made a speech like that, but only in flattery. He sounds as though he's been listening to the troubadour stories.

"She was a ward to that bastard, the count of Tripoli," continued De Ridford. "Tripoli had promised her in marriage to me, if I would serve him faithfully. But then, Amalric summoned the banners to war, and Tripoli was low on bezants. He needed money to fund this new expedition, so he started borrowing from the merchants. One merchant, some lecher who was as wide as he was tall, offered Tripoli my betrothed's weight in gold if he would give her to him."

Arnold felt pity welling up in him. He had never seen a man so distraught.

"And the promise he had made to you?" he asked, knowing the answer already.

"Tripoli...he forgot about his bloody promise as soon as he heard how much gold he would get. He even said..." De Ridford choked back another sob, "said that he wished she were twenty pounds fatter." His speech degenerated into profane curses.

Arnold sighed. "So you have come here—"

"I have come here," said De Ridford, "because there is no happiness left me on earth. All that is left is for me is to avenge myself on Tripoli."

De Ridford began to walk forward, but Arnold placed himself in the way of his old friend.

"Wait, Gerard," he said. De Ridford shoved him aside and walked on towards the Temple.

"Gerard!" called Arnold, towards his friend's back. Gerard de Ridford stopped, but did not turn around.

"Gerard! Do not enter the Temple out of hate!"

Gerard de Ridford turned his head to stare at Arnold de Torroga. There was nothing but a cold hate in those eyes. He turned forward and walked on.

The thwarted lover crossed the threshold of the Temple, and the fate of Jerusalem was changed forever.

Chapter 19

WHAT WAS LOST
Joscelin

oscelin de Courtenay looked out at the sea, watching the breakers roll across the remains of the great causeway that Alexander had built. He loved the city of Tyre, jutting out into the ocean so that it was nearly an island; he loved the way the sea rolled around it, loved the feel of the city, millennia old already. Hiram the Builder and Alexander of Macedon must have felt the same, looking out towards the mainland, with the cool calm of the sea all around them. He loved even the storms, watching the awesome power rage round the unyielding stone of the city.

Joscelin lay back, closing his eyes, trying for a moment to shut out the rest of the world. Next to him sat his sister, Agnes de Courtenay, muttering angrily about the king's latest blunders.

There came a knock at the door. Joscelin looked up.

"Come in," he said, tired. A servant poked his head in the door. "My lord," he said, an anxious look on his face, "the king himself is here. He wishes to speak to you."

Joscelin struggled to his feet. "By the Mass, what is this? Amalric here in Tyre?" He looked around the room.

"Agnes," he began, "if you want to—"

"I will stay," said Agnes, proud defiance in her eyes.

Agnes de Courtenay was Amalric's wife.

Or at least, she had been.

The Courtenays were second cousins to the royal family. Joscelin and Agnes had been close friends to Amalric and his older brother Baldwin as children. Baldwin, as the heir to the throne, married a Greek princess, but Amalric was a younger brother, and as such he married whom he pleased. And so he chose to wed Agnes. The Church forbade marriages between cousins of the second degree and closer, and so their marriage had been technically uncanonical. Yet Amalric loved Agnes dearly, and none had the heart, or the courage, to quibble with him over what seemed a minor issue.

Then the unexpected happened. Baldwin III had died childless, leaving Amalric the heir to the throne.

An unimportant relative of the king could have an uncanonical marriage and no man would gainsay him. The king of Jerusalem, however, could not.

So Amalric was forced to choose between the Crown and Agnes. And the man who had lived in his brother's shadow for so long chose the crown, and cast Agnes de Courtenay aside. Even the children that Agnes had borne him, Sybilla and Baldwin, were taken from her, and Agnes de Courtenay was left with nothing.

Joscelin had been torn also between his sister and his friend. In the end, though, he had decided that as a knight, his duty lay to the king of Jerusalem, even though that king had betrayed his sister. So he had stayed the king's man. But Joscelin had come to dread the man who wore the crown. King Amalric was not the same man as Joscelin's friend from six years before.

And so Joscelin almost jumped when the door swung open and Amalric stepped into the room.

"Your Grace," he said, bowing. "I did not expect a visit."

"Leave the titles, Joscelin. This is too important for that." Amalric strode across the room and collapsed into a small wooden chair, the beams straining under his weight. Then he noticed Agnes. She was still young, and beautiful in her azure dress. She raised her head, tossing golden curls, to fix the king with a cold stare.

"Milady," said Amalric, rising stiffly, an embarrassed look on his face.

"You," said Agnes simply.

The trace of a smile crossed Amalric's face. "You haven't changed, Agnes."

"You have," said Agnes coldly. "I would never have married Amalric the king."

Amalric laughed. "Well, if you wish, you may stay while I talk to Joscelin; they are your children as much as mine."

At that, any trace of defiance went out of Agnes, leaving only a face of despairing anguish.

"My children—Amalric, let me have my children!"

A frown crossed Amalric's face. "Would that I could, Agnes. But Baldwin—"

"Is my son!" said Agnes, her voice harsh and desperate.

"And the heir to the Crown of Jerusalem."

"Leave the crown out of it, Amalric! If our marriage is not valid, why must you keep the children? They cannot be the true-born heirs if I am not your wife."

"You know as well as I do, woman. I have no other male heir, and the barons will have to accept him if he is my son. Perhaps I can marry, if I find a suitable bride, and I will have another son, and then you can have Baldwin and Sybilla. Until then..." Amalric sank back into the chair.

Agnes's face had twisted at the mention of Amalric marrying again. She stood up as the king sat. "Another woman? You *would* try to comfort me by saying that, wouldn't you?" Her hands clutched at her dress, the knuckles white. Agnes de Courtenay swept from the room, her face a mask of cold fury.

For a few moments there was silence. Then Amalric breathed a sigh of relief.

"God's beard, Joscelin. I've come to dread seeing that woman. She would have made a fearsome queen, one to make that rabble of barons and knights tremble. If only it could have been so. Oh God, is the crown really worth it?"

Joscelin said nothing. He looked out at the sea, and wondered if when Alexander the Great had stood in this same city, looking over the men he had crucified, he too had asked if a crown was really worth it.

Finally Amalric spoke again.

"Joscelin, I have something I need to ask you."

"Your Grace, you are the king," said Joscelin. "You need not ask, only command."

"Yes," said Amalric. "But I will not always be king."

Amalric waited a second, his words hanging on the air. Joscelin frowned, confused as to Amalric's meaning.

"My children, Joscelin. Agnes had the truth of it when she said that if she were not my wife, they were not my true-born children. When I die, there will be others who will claim that Baldwin is not my valid successor, and make a grab for the throne. Raymond of Tripoli and Bohemund of Antioch and Barisan d'Ibelin will all try to wrest the crown from my son's head. The barons of the land follow only a strong man, and a child cannot be strong. So I will need you, Joscelin, to defend my son, to stand down the might of Ibelin and Tripoli and Antioch, and see my son to manhood."

Joscelin frowned. "Your Grace, why should you not live until your son is a man?"

Amalric sighed. "In an hour I must sit at council before the barons of Outremer. And I must tell them that I will be leading them to war, again."

Joscelin turned and looked Amalric full in the face. "War, Your Grace?"

Amalric went on grimly. "I have received a plea for help from the vizier of Cairo, asking us to liberate Egypt."

"Liberate Egypt?"

"You remember, Joscelin, how after the Battle of Tinnis we fled wildly across the desert, trying to make it back to Jerusalem before Shirkuh could?"

"Yes, Your Grace.. But Shirkuh never gave chase."

"No," said Amalric. "Instead of chasing us, Shirkuh and his Saracens turned towards Cairo. I have little doubt that when the sultan sent Shirkuh from Damascus, he gave him orders to annex Egypt if he could. So Shirkuh let us escape when we were beaten, and instead focused his attention on the Egyptians. But luckily for us, he couldn't simply seize Cairo by force—the outcry in the Muslim world would be too great. So instead he showed up at the Egyptian capital, demanding a hero's welcome for saving Egypt. And he has stayed there ever since."

Joscelin's heart sank as he heard the king speak, but he said nothing and listened in silence and fear as Amalric continued.

"It has been two years, and still the Saracens are there, solidifying their control. So the vizier of Cairo, Shawar, has sent a quiet plea for help. He promises tribute if we will drive Shirkuh from Egypt. And I accepted his offer. This time all the different factions must agree. It is a just cause: we are aiding the native people against an invader. Shawar has promised to make Egypt a vassal of Outremer if we come. We have no choice but to go."

"No choice?" asked Joscelin desperately. "Amalric, I speak as your old friend now. Leave the Ishmaelites to kill each other. We have no business going to war. We need to strengthen Outremer, not weaken it."

Amalric shook his head. "Don't be naive, Joscelin. The best way to strengthen the kingdom will be to add Egypt to it, or at least to stop the sultan from getting his hands on it. I would know, Joscelin. Before I was king, I was count of Ascalon, right on the Egyptian border. The sandpigs always came out of Egypt to attack us back then. Egypt is where the money is, for that is where the grain is. Egypt is dangerous."

"Accept it, Joscelin," continued Amalric. "When Godfrey de Bouillon and Baldwin set up Outremer, they began a war that has continued for a century. It is us or them; either the sandpigs lose their lands, or we lose ours. We have a chance now—a brief respite while the Muslims fight each other instead of us. If we take Egypt, if we make it our tributary state, then the sandpigs will fade back into the desert. If we do not take Egypt, the Kingdom of Jerusalem will die. It is as simple as that."

"Your Grace, whether we need land or no, we do not have the right to simply take it."

"Lord! Joscelin, that's the whole point. *We have a right now. We have a just cause*! An appeal from the natural lord of the land. The Templars would not go with us in the last fight because they said it was an unjust cause. They have no such excuse this time. What more do you want, Joscelin?"

"Peace."

Amalric rose. "That," he said, "is the one thing I cannot give you."

Joscelin nodded and looked to the sea.

"I will need your support in the council, Joscelin. If even you do not support the war, the other barons will seize the chance to check the king's authority. And I cannot turn back now: I have already negotiated with the Greek emperor. If we go to Egypt, his fleet will accompany us. Hard times are coming, Joscelin. The Mohammedans are beginning to recover from the shock of the First Crusade, and it will be a dangerous day for us when they unite again. We need unity, Joscelin. We must renew our friendship with the Greeks, or Outremer will die."

For a long moment Joscelin said nothing. Then he nodded.

"I will support you on the war, but only for unity's sake. Nothing more."

Amalric looked relieved. "And my children, Joscelin?"

Joscelin turned to face Amalric. "Yes," he said. "I swear to you, Amalric, that so long as I draw breath, your heir will be safe on the throne. And more than that, I swear that he will be a mighty king, greater than any Outremer has ever seen."

"Mightier than me?" asked Amalric. Then he laughed.

"Your Grace?" A servant had poked his head in the door. "You asked for the archbishop to be sent up here."

The servant vanished and a man in clerical robes entered, half-leaning on a bishop's staff. Amalric rose.

"Archbishop! I have not yet had a chance to congratulate you. A week ago you were an archdeacon, old Arnulf of Tyre's errand boy, and now you're the archbishop with your own deacons to do your work for you."

William of Tyre smiled. "Your Grace, you requested my presence. I must say Mass in an hour, so I cannot be here overlong."

Amalric strode over to where the archbishop stood.

"Father," he said, "I would speak with you."

"About the kingdom, Your Grace?"

"About the will of God."

Joscelin shifted uncomfortably. "Your Grace...Amalric...should I leave?"

Amalric glanced at him, then shook his head. "No, Joscelin, stay. Whatever may have come between us...I would value your company."

The king began to walk down the hallway, and William of Tyre kept pace. Joscelin looked uncertainly after them, then got up to follow.

I am no theologian. Why does Amalric want me here?

"I will warn you," William was saying to the king, "God does not answer men who come before him as kings. Before Him, you are no greater than the Moorish slave who cleans the privies of Damascus."

Amalric said nothing. They walked on down the hallway. William glanced out the arrow slits at the sea far below.

"Archbishop," said the king, "the stories tell of kings and warriors who are peaceful men at heart, men who fight their battles unwillingly, men who prefer peace, and who go back to their farms and their families when the fighting is done; men who are even happier at peace than at war. Scripture speaks much of it."

"They will beat their swords into ploughshares," said William quietly.

"You see, Father," said Amalric, "what troubles me is that I cannot be like these men."

No, thought Joscelin, *You cannot. They would never have traded a wife for a crown.*

William did not speak at first. He waited for the king to continue. But Amalric had stopped for the moment. He continued walking until they arrived at the chamber at the other end of the hallway. Here Amalric's cloak was slung over a chair, and his helmet, shield, sword and mace hung on the wall. Amalric reached up and took down his sword. It was a great hand-and-a-half sword, with an unusually thick blade. With one glance at it, Joscelin knew that it was heavier than most twohanders. Amalric hefted it easily with one thick, muscled arm. He sliced the air twice.

"You see this, Father? A fine blade. It belonged to my father, Fulk, and then my brother, Baldwin. Now it is mine. As a blade, it is priceless." He sliced the air again. "As a ploughshare, it would be useless to me. I would make a pathetic farmer." Amalric hung the blade back up. "Father, how can I be a Christian, how can I love my fellow men, if I live only to split their heads open? I could not be like Cincinnatus or Josiah, for I don't really desire peace. Life without battle would seem boring, senseless. And yet, Father, that is not the way it is supposed to be, is it?"

Amalric sat down in one of the wooden chairs that lined the room, his head resting against a tapestry of Roland blowing on his white ivory oliphant horn, with Saracens fleeing in all directions. William stood in the center of the room, leaning on his crozier. The archbishop's hair was not yet grey, but at that moment he looked old and forlorn. Finally he strode over to where the shield and mace hung next to each other, speaking as he went.

"Amalric—" he began.

"Your Grace," corrected Amalric automatically. William glanced at him.

"Are you speaking to me as the king or as the man? God does not answer kings."

Amalric sighed. "Continue."

This one thinks well of himself for a priest, thought Joscelin, but even as he thought it he did not really believe it. Whatever fault there was in William of Tyre, it was not pride.

William stopped below the shield. "Priests are forbidden to wield swords; did you know that? They are forbidden to spill blood, also. The Church does not want her priests fighting. They are supposed to be peacemakers." William closed his eyes and continued, almost as though he were speaking to himself. "Very good measures, very good, very prudent."

He leaned his staff against a chair, then reached up and took the mace down from the wall. "Now," he said, "all know that a priest who violates Ecclesiastical Law can be defrocked and excommunicated. So no priest would openly draw a sword and spill blood." William swung the mace around. He was a smaller man than Amalric, but strong, and he held the mace with ease. "So," he continued, "many of my brothers in Holy Orders go into battle wielding maces, so as to maul rather than cut."

Amalric laughed at that, his whole body shaking, making the tapestry of Roland wrinkle back and forth. William of Tyre put the mace back on the wall.

The archbishop picked up his staff again and walked to the center of the room.

"I do not claim to know," he said, "why it is that we men desire conflict and death. If you want to know why, perhaps you should look to the Fall for an answer. But what I can tell you is this: holiness is not in your emotions. It is in your deeds. A man who desires drink need not suppress that desire all the time; only when he is in danger of becoming drunk. A man who desires a woman need not suppress that desire if she is his wife. And just so, there are times that you *must* fight. I know already, from the patriarch of Jerusalem, of your plans to go to war again. Last time you went to Egypt, you went as an invader. It was an unholy war, one that the Church condemned. This time, you go as a liberator, to fight a just war. So give thanks to God that your desire has coincided with your duty."

Amalric bowed his head and stood. "Thank you, Father. I will keep your counsel in mind. I must go speak to the barons now. But first—will you give me your blessing?"

William bowed his head. "Kneel then, my son."

The king of Jerusalem knelt before the priest.

Perhaps, thought Joscelin, *The Amalric who married Agnes is not completely dead.*

Chapter 20

NEWS FROM AFAR
Godfrey

wo men were sparring, high on the roof of the mansion. Here in the high place, the wind whipped around them, slicing like a blade, but they did not feel it. Their wooden practice swords beat against each other in a steady rhythm.

The sweat rolled down Godfrey's face, only to be brushed away by the wind. CLACK! CLACK! CLACK! His practice sword slashed down on the Greek's, seeking to crack his defense.

Andronicus Comnenus was like no other teacher. The great warriors of the East trained to abandon their minds during the battle and trust only in their training. And many blademasters were taught not to think during combat at all, merely to flow from stance to stance until the battle was over. The Greek, however, could not and would not do this. He said that it was because in Outremer you were forced to fight against too many different weapons, too many different fighting styles. You had to think, and to adjust your style accordingly, or you would die. You could not expect to get into a swordfight with a Varangian Guard—they would simply club you down with a halberd unless you jumped and wove your way up close to them. You couldn't expect a mameluke to do you the favor of fighting you sword-to-sword—more likely he'd split your head open with an axe.

Godfrey had not cared to ask Andronicus Comnenus when he had fought a Varangian Guard. It might not be a subject he was inclined to share. But Godfrey had at least learned from Andronicus what the Varangians were. They were the Greek emperor's personal bodyguard, the descendants of Vikings and Rus who had long ago sworn allegiance to the imperial crown. Fanatically loyal and immensely strong, they stood in stark and simple contrast to the sophisticated, even decadent Greek culture, standing by their oaths and remaining loyal to the death.

But in the past few years Godfrey had learned more from Andronicus than mere curiosities about the Varangian Guard. Within three months of his arrival in Antioch, it had become apparent to Godfrey that the negotiations between Blanchefort and Andronicus Comnenus were little more than a fraud. Or rather not a fraud so much as a game. On the master's side, at least, he believed the effort was sincere. Andronicus, however, had no real interest in the reconciliation of the churches. In fact, he had little chance at becoming emperor, even if the negotiations succeeded. Murzuphlus and Langosse had spoken truly, the very first day in Antioch. Andronicus Comnenus had started negotiations because he was curious to meet some Templars.

For the first year, the master had continually sent messengers and messages, to which Andronicus would give witty but useless responses. After a year, the stream of messages began to slow, as Blanchefort realized that the Greek was not even seriously considering any of the proposals.

For a time, it seemed that Andronicus was growing bored of the Templars and was ready to close negotiations and send them back. Godfrey was doing poorly in his training, and Jacques avoided Andronicus as much as he could. But just when Godfrey was sure that he would at last be able to turn his back on Antioch, something had happened.

Throughout the negotiations, Andronicus had put far more effort into training Godfrey than into the negotiations themselves. Godfrey, however, had been a poor student, clumsy and slow. Langosse and Murzuphlus had sometimes come into the practice yard to train with them, but Godfrey was as helpless against them as against their master.

And then, just when Andronicus had given up and was on the verge of ending their stay, Godfrey had beaten Murzuphlus in the practice yard.

Murzuphlus fought with two dirks—weapons that would be useless on the battlefield. Murzuphlus, however, never planned to fight on a battlefield. He would merely take part in streetfights and maybe palace skirmishes should one of the common Byzantine civil wars break out. But he was quicker even than Andronicus, and he always left Godfrey covered with little bruises where the wooden sticks had jabbed him in the ribs. But Godfrey had at last beaten him, and beaten him again, and then again and again and again, until Murzuphlus admitted defeat with bad grace. He stopped entering the practice field after that, but instead watched from the side and insulted Godfrey.

A month later Godfrey beat Langosse, who took it with much better humor.

CLACK! CLACK! CRACK! Andronicus's sword smashed into Godfrey's ribs. Even under the mail Godfrey wore, he recoiled from the force of the blow. Andronicus Comnenus always insisted that Godfrey wear whatever gear he would wear into a real battle, so that he would be used to it weighing him down. The mail certainly weighed him down, but it never seemed to protect him from the sting of Andronicus's blows. The Greek said that this should give him an incentive not to get hit.

Godfrey nodded tiredly and pulled off his helmet, breathing heavily as he conceded defeat. The Greek was not even sweating.

"Good, good," said Andronicus happily. "You're getting better. Soon you'll be an opponent worth facing."

Soon after he began training, Godfrey realized just how poor and ineffectual a swordsman he was. Even after he had learned the stances, parries and attacks, he could not stand up to Andronicus. The Greek was very strong; his arms were knotted with muscles. But this obstacle could be overcome—Andronicus could defeat the giant Basil Camateros who was easily twice as strong as he. Andronicus was also quicker than Godfrey, for unlike many of the Frankish knights, Andronicus's muscle was not accompanied by fat. Though Godfrey learned stance after stance after parry after riposte, and used them all against Andronicus, he would always find his blows turned aside and his defenses beaten down, both because of the Greek's superior training, and simply because his opponent brought the same parries and attacks against him, only twice as fast.

So finally, Godfrey began to teach himself, after a fashion. He was too clumsy to be quick with his hands, and not strong enough to beat down his enemy's defenses. But he knew he would be facing stronger and quicker men in most battles, so he would have to teach himself not to rely on these advantages anyway. Instead he would focus on what strengths he had.

Godfrey was taller than Andronicus, but he knew that he could never count on that advantage either. He also had strong legs, unlike so many lords of his day who rode whenever they had to travel. So he had used these as best he could, jumping, running, mustering up enough speed on his feet to counter his opponents' speed with their arms.

Basil Camateros, the giant Varangian strode out onto the rooftop to slouch next to Murzuphlus, who was already standing by watching through his doglike eyebrows. Langosse was out in the city, wining and wenching, and Jacques was also out there somewhere, though Godfrey prayed he was not doing the same.

"Fight again," said Murzuphlus. "I want to see you crush the Latin. It's always good to watch."

Basil Camateros had not changed his manner towards the two Templars one bit in two years. He rarely spoke to them, and when he did it was always to voice his contempt for them. He was fanatically loyal to Andronicus Comnenus, but none was so loyal as Murzuphlus.

Two years had only confirmed Godfrey's impression of Murzuphlus as a lapdog. He followed at Andronicus's heels like a faithful hound, worshipping him and licking his boots. Unlike Basil, he spoke to the Templars constantly, gleefully telling them of the glories of Constantinople and Andronicus Comnenus, interspersed with tales of how evil and stupid the piglike Latins were. Basil Camateros was loyal to Byzantium, but he merely distrusted other peoples. Murzuphlus hated all peoples who were not Greek, and above all the Franks. He did his best to torment the two Templars, and had succeeded at least in making Jacques dread his presence.

Langosse Argyrus, however, seemed to harbor no ill will against them. He jested with the Templars, accompanied them, and drank with them— or more properly, with Jacques. After that first night, Godfrey decided not to abuse the dispensation granted him by Blanchefort, and spent more time fasting—a fact that amused Jacques, Langosse, and Murzuphlus to no end.

Godfrey stood straight again and pulled his helmet back on. Andronicus shifted back into fighting stance. Andronicus wore no mail, only boiled leather, so that he could move faster.

They strode to the center and began.

Andronicus opened the attack, slashing low at Godfrey's ribs, then again, higher, at his throat. Godfrey stepped back from his quicker opponent, keeping his distance, neither parrying nor attacking with his sword, only keeping it between the Greek and him.

Andronicus drove him back towards the waist-high wall that lined the roof, trying to trap him. Godfrey mentally gauged how much space he had, and then struck back.

His first blow was a wild slash, meant only to force Andronicus to cease his attack. The Greek stepped back quickly, dodging it easily, but before he could resume, Godfrey was spinning into a series of attacks, slashing and stabbing, these attacks more coordinated. Andronicus parried each blow with a lazy ease, but no sooner had he parried than Godfrey was hacking again.

The Greek began to grow impatient as Godfrey's flurry of blows continued. His eyes searched for an opening, and finally it came when Godfrey was a second slow on the backslash. Andronicus sidestepped Godfrey's wooden sword and lunged—just as Godfrey knew he would.

Godfrey did not bother waiting for Andronicus to start the lunge, for he knew that he would do it as soon as he let up the attack for a moment.

So even as Andronicus lunged, Godfrey stepped to the right, springing forward. Airborne for a second, he slashed down.

CRACK! The practice sword landed right at the spot where the shoulder met the neck. Godfrey held the sword there, panting like a dog, but otherwise unmoving.

There was a moment of silence. Basil's face had gone as hard as stone, and Murzuphlus's mouth hung open. Never before had they seen their master defeated, not in the practice ring, not in a brawl or on the field of battle.

There was a hollow rattle as Andronicus dropped his practice sword. Then he laughed, and the silence was broken. Godfrey let the sword fall from his hand.

"It must be ten years since anyone's done that," said Andronicus, clapping Godfrey on the shoulder.

"My lord Andronicus?" It was Nuri, the servant girl. "Someone to see you. It's the priest from Tyre. William."

Andronicus picked up the practice sword and placed it on the rack. "Send him in, then."

Nuri vanished and reappeared a second later with William of Tyre.

"Archdeacon!" said Andronicus, looking genuinely pleased, though Godfrey had learned long ago that Andronicus could have put on that sincere look for Satan himself. The Greek had a thespian flair—he was an actor and a dramatist at heart.

"My lord," said William, inclining his head.

"What news of Tyre?"

William cocked his head for a moment, as if thinking.

"There is little to speak of in Tyre," he said slowly. "Rather, I have a message from Jerusalem, from the master of the Temple."

"Good!" said Andronicus, once again sounding pleased, though Godfrey doubted it.

William sighed. "The master of the Temple regretfully informs you that, as negotiations seemed to have slowed to a halt, he wishes to break them off completely."

Godfrey had been expecting this for some time and now it was official. The negotiations were over, and none too soon. He needed to get back to Jerusalem—he had almost forgotten his vows, here in Antioch.

The smile on Andronicus's face did not fade, and for once Godfrey thought he really did not mind so much. The negotiations themselves had never meant anything to him, and the Templars...well, they were only a minor amusement.

143

"It is a pity," said the Greek pleasantly. He sighed. "Men will ever turn away from God and towards division and schism."

"Also," said William, ignoring Andronicus, "the master orders that Godfrey de Montferrat and Jacques de Maille return with all possible haste. He has urgent need of every Knight of the Temple."

"Why is that?" asked Andronicus. William's face was stony.

"It is not a matter I may reveal to a foreign noble."

That did not go off well with Andronicus—not well at all. His face did not change, but Godfrey could tell that he was angry, both at William and at Master Blanchefort.

William inclined his head again.

"I am sorry, my lord Andronicus, but I must go now. I have urgent duties."

He turned towards the stairs, then paused for a moment.

"Oh, and my lord, I forgot. You asked for news from Tyre, and there is one piece of news there. The archbishop has died. They have chosen a successor."

William walked towards the stairs. As he began to descend, he called out.

"They chose me."

Then he was gone.

Andronicus was frowning at the stairs. "A hard man, that one. I fear for Tyre, now, if he is archbishop."

Even as William of Tyre's footsteps receded, they heard more footsteps coming up the stairs. Jacques and Langosse came running up—running, and breathing hard.

"Andronicus," said Langosse, breathlessly. "They have taken the Hawk."

"Taken?" asked Andronicus, questioningly.

"Dead, or captured mayhap. By the Turks. There are a thousand rumors flying about the city, but it was most likely the Seljuqs. Although some say the sultan of Rum. Muhammad Ridhwan, the black devil, was involved somehow. Reynald de Chatillon went out on a raid, looking for booty and a good scrap. They say that Ridhwan laid some sort of trap up in the mountains. I don't know all that happened, but the Hawk is gone."

"Gone." Andronicus frowned. "You didn't need to run through the city just to tell me that."

"But it's Bohemund," said Jacques. "Bohemund's taken over. He started out by spreading the word that Antioch would never submit to any Greek rat in Constantinople, but they say that Felos, your ambassador, scurried down to the palace and spoke with him for an hour, and now he's changed his mind and is going to submit to Manuel, but only so long as he gets to stick your head on a spike."

Langosse cut in. "You should have kept your hands off that girl Phillipa, Andronicus. Bohemund wants you dead."

Chapter 21

TIME TO BE GONE
Godfrey

Andronicus rushed about the room, stuffing a few clothes and possessions into a pack. Godfrey and Murzuphlus stood by the door, keeping watch.

Nuri hurried up the hallway, with a bulging pack of food.

"My lord," she asked in a fearful voice. "How long will you be gone?"

Andronicus set down the pack and turned to look at her. After a moment, he reached into his chest and pulled out a heavy purse of gold, tossing it to Nuri.

"Nuri, you have served me faithfully and well. That should last you until you find new employment."

From the look on her face, it seemed that with that purse she could live in comfort for years without work.

"You should leave now, Nuri," said Andronicus. "If the other servants find you with that, they will try to take it from you, and they will not be gentle about it."

There were tears in the young Syrian's eyes. "My lord is gracious. I will never forget my lord's kindness." She curtsied, and was gone.

Andronicus grabbed a larger purse of gold from his chest and stuffed it into his pack. "If we can't get the horses out of the city," he muttered, "we'll need Basil to carry this. Too bloody heavy for me."

He turned to look at Godfrey. "Sir Templar," he said, "how will you and Jacques buy food on the way back?"

Godfrey shrugged. "My lord, we are monks. If necessary, we will beg."

Andronicus snorted. "I'm not leaving this gold to Bohemund." He grabbed another purse and threw it to Godfrey, who caught it clumsily, spilling a few coins.

"My lord," said Godfrey, "as Templars, we are not permitted to have possessions of our own. Everything must belong to the Temple."

147

Andronicus swore violently as he tied up his pack.

"Then consider that my donation to the bloody Temple. If there's any left, put it in your bloody treasury, or whatever the hell you have in there. God's blood, just take it!"

Godfrey smiled. "Yes, my lord."

Andronicus shouldered the pack.

"And Godfrey," he said. "You have my thanks. You do not need to help us escape."

Godfrey shook his head. "If I ever shrunk from aiding a friend, I would not be a knight."

"A friend?" Andronicus cocked his head. "A noble like me has no friends, only servants and enemies."

"Well," said Godfrey, "a knight has friends. Even a Templar."

"We shall see. When I first met you, I named you the Knight of the Impossible Ideal, and you have grown no more pragmatic since then. But even a servant deserves a reward for good service, and I have a token my esteem to give to you."

Godfrey frowned. "I just told you, we cannot have possessions."

Andronicus spat to show what he thought of that. "Then consider this next another donation to the Temple. When you get back, take it up with your bloody master. I'm giving it to you anyway."

Andronicus pulled one last thing out of his chest. It was a great horn of smooth, shining white ivory, with gold rims.

"You said once that Roland was one of the few acceptable troubadour ballads. If you know his Chanson, then you may know what this is."

Godfrey reached out fearfully, even reverently, his voice almost a whisper.

"*An oliphant.*" He could picture in his mind's eye a tapestry of the dying Roland standing about his fallen companions and blowing on his horn to summon the king.

"Yes," said Andronicus. "Made of an elephant's tusk. From India. Just as Roland blew at Roncevals. It was given me by the Empress Maria, shortly after she arrived in Byzantium, as a sign of her favor. As it seems I am no longer in her favor, it is only fitting that I pass it on."

Godfrey buckled it on, still staring at it with awe. Andronicus laughed.

"Don't forget; it's not yours: it's the Temple's."

Godfrey nodded. "I will not forget."

"My lord," barked Murzuphlus, peering up and down the hallway, "Basil and Langosse and the Frank should have gotten the horses by now.

We cannot waste time." The look he gave to Godfrey seemed to add, *and especially not on Franks.*

"Yes," said Andronicus, "we should go."

They hurried down the hallways, down flights of stairs, through the mansion that Godfrey had come to know well in his two years in Antioch. *It will be strange to return to the Temple,* he thought. *Two years. Thank God I fasted for much of that, else it would be hard, coming back to Jerusalem and resuming life as a monk.* All the same, he and Jacques had been far too lenient with Rule of the Temple, dispensation or no. Godfrey was not even sure that Blanchefort had the power to grant such a dispensation. It would be very like Blanchefort to give one anyway. And then there was the matter of the gold—and the oliphant. But those could wait.

Then they rushed through the doors to the stables. It was dark inside, with only a thin crack of light shining in from between the double doors. Jacques, Langosse, and Basil stood with five horses, saddled and bridled.

"My lord," said Basil, "we must hurry, before soldiers come."

Langosse had his eye up against the slit of the stable doors. Then he jerked back and started swearing.

Basil frowned at the doors. "Everyone mount! What is it, Langosse?"

Langosse stepped back from the doors. "There are soldiers in the street."

Andronicus mounted up. "Are they making for the main door?"

Langosse nodded. Even as he did, they heard a pounding at the main door of the building.

"Then," said Andronicus, "let's get out of here. Langosse, open the doors, then mount up quick. We'll ride down anyone who gets in our way. Keep moving, make for the gates. There are many gates in Antioch. If Fortune smiles on us, the guards at our gate will not be ready."

Andronicus drew his sword. "Weapons out," he said. He laughed, and looked at Godfrey. "Like in a troubadour's ballad."

Godfrey grunted noncommittally as he mounted his horse. But as he did, he could feel his pulse pounding faster. They were going to cut a path out. He felt as he had before the Battle on the Nile. He did not, however, draw his sword—he was trying to escape, not to cut a path through his fellow Christians.

Langosse silently lifted the bar on the stable doors. From inside the mansion, they could hear the main door bursting open and Bohemund's soldiers pouring in. Langosse looked back at Andronicus, who nodded.

Then he threw the doors open and jumped to the side, grabbing onto his horse as the other five came galloping out.

For a second, Godfrey was blinking in the sudden light. Then he saw the street, saw soldiers in hauberks with swords crowding around the main door. They saw the men riding out, and rushed over to meet them, but the six rode on. One man almost got in front of Andronicus's horse, but dived out of the way at the last moment, lest he be trampled by the Greek's palfrey.

In a few moments, they had left the mansion behind them and were galloping through the streets. People rushed to get out of their way. As of yet, none tried to stop them.

"My lord!" shouted Basil. "More soldiers behind us!"

Godfrey glanced back to see a patrol of mounted Antiochenes riding after them. Not knights. *Thank God for that.* But there were still twenty Antiochenes, and only six of them.

"Just ahead," said Andronicus. "A gate is coming up!"

They put spurs to their horses, making for the gate. They turned a corner, following Andronicus, and there it was. For a moment Godfrey's heart leapt to see that there were only three guards, and these lounging about, weapons lying on the ground.

But then he saw that the gate was closed and barred. There would be no time to open it before their pursuers caught them. Andronicus was already wheeling his horse about and trying to make it out of the street before their pursuers closed off their escape. The other five wheeled and followed, riding hard.

They made it back into the main street still ahead of their pursuers, but precious seconds had been lost.

"Make right!" shouted Godfrey.

Andronicus did not question him, but veered sharply down a street to the right, the others following. This was the blacksmiths' street. On both sides they could hear the ring of hammers and the hiss of molten metal plunging into barrels of water.

"There's a big gate up ahead," Godfrey shouted. "I don't think they've closed all the gates. We might be able to make—"

"Not enough time," yelled Andronicus, glancing back. "Everyone separate. Into the shops. We'll meet outside the gate." Then Andronicus sprang from the moving horse, landing deftly like a cat on all fours. Godfrey's stomach reeled at the thought of doing the same. He pulled hard on the reins, bringing the horse almost to a stop, before he leapt off. Andronicus had already vanished into a shop, and Jacques, Langosse, and Basil were scattering out of the street. The Antiochenes were fifty yards away now, riding hard.

Godfrey was just about to dart into a shop, when he saw Murzuphlus. The bushy-eyebrowed Greek had tried to leap from the saddle, as

Andronicus had done. Instead his foot had caught in the stirrup. Luckily for him, the stirrup had been loosely attached and tore off, else he would have been dragged down the street by his running horse, and by the time it stopped his head would have been a bloody pulp.

But now Murzuphlus lay in the street, trying to untangle himself, while the horsemen rode down on him.

Godfrey had no time to think. Instead he grabbed Murzuphlus by the hand and dragged him into a blacksmith's shop a few seconds before the cavalry thundered over the spot where Murzuphlus had lain.

Godfrey glanced out the window as Murzuphlus scrambled to his feet, glaring angrily at Godfrey. The Antiochenes were bringing their horses to a stop farther up, to dismount and search the shops.

"Have you come to buy, or do you need something mended?" came a voice from behind.

Godfrey had completely forgotten that in a blacksmith's shop, there were likely to be blacksmiths. He turned to look around.

The shop was dark, though there was a roaring fire at the other end of the room, next to the anvil. The blacksmith was resting at the moment, wiping off his hands on a dirty apron while his apprentice was wiping soot off his face from the water in the already sooty water barrel.

The smith was a big man, though short, with arms that looked as thick as Godfrey's neck. Murzuphlus was still scowling, saying nothing, so Godfrey had to act.

He reached into the purse Andronicus had given him, and pulled out two gold bezants. He glanced back at the street, where the troopers were dismounting and entering the shops. He placed the gold pieces on the anvil and looked down at the smith.

"Is there a back entrance to this place, Master Smith?"

The smith looked suspiciously at the bezants, then at the troopers searching the houses. Suddenly, from the house across the street, there came a shout, followed by the ring of steel. They had found someone.

The smith reached for the bezants quickly, but Murzuphlus snatched them up first, even as he and Godfrey turned to rush out into the street, ignoring the blacksmith's curses. As quickly as the gold vanished into Murzuphlus's coat, his two daggers were out. Godfrey had his sword out now; if need be, he would fight to protect a friend.

Even as they rushed across the street to this shop, more soldiers were pouring out of the other shops, running in the direction of the shouting.

Godfrey rushed into the shop a step ahead of Murzuphlus. The building was on fire and the blaze was spreading, creeping across the floor, smoke covering the chaotic scene. The blacksmith was wrestling with one of the soldiers—Godfrey did not know how that had come about, nor did he have time to find out. Glowing embers were scattered about the room and flames licked at the wall. Another soldier lay dead while Andronicus fought with a third and fourth

Quick as a mouse, Murzuphlus leapt at one of the soldiers, ducking beneath a flailing sword to plant a knife in his throat. Andronicus cut down the man he was fighting while Godfrey dragged the last soldier off the blacksmith, who dealt the man a hefty blow to the head that left him unconscious.

Two more soldiers entered the shop, and Andronicus and Murzuphlus leapt in their way. The blacksmith, a short but hefty man, was looking about, realizing that his shop was destroyed. Godfrey hurried to him.

"The soldiers won't be in a forgiving mood. You'd best be out of here."

The smith looked around, dazed. "My... shop..."

Godfrey hesitated, then pulled out the purse of gold and handed it to the smith.

"This is the best I can do to repay you. For now, you'll need to get out of Antioch. Come with us."

More soldiers were coming, and Andronicus and Murzuphlus were turning to run. Godfrey half dragged the heavy smith to the window in the back, which was barred and shuttered.

"Hold them!" he shouted to Andronicus, who attacked the men rushing in the doorway. Godfrey swung his sword, splintering the rotting wood. He gave a push and the shutters collapsed, leaving an open window. The smith, finally recovering, scrambled out, followed by Godfrey and Murzuphlus, and last of all Andronicus.

The soldiers came rushing to the window, but even as they did, there came a crash. The roof had caught fire and was coming down on their heads. Most of the soldiers turned to run out the door, but one man leapt out the window. He landed before Andronicus, weaponless, sooty, and dazed. He stared up with wild, confused eyes.

They left him there and ran.

Sure enough, this gate was open. The guards glanced up, looking suspiciously at the four men's dirty clothes, but surprisingly, miraculously, they did not seem to be looking for anyone in particular, and they let them out without questions or challenge.

Half an hour later, they were in the green fields beside the Orontes, the sun shining down brightly. Godfrey was giddy with relief that they had made it.

"What do we do now?" asked Murzuphlus, looking sullen. Basil, Langosse, and Jacques were still somewhere within the walls of Antioch.

Andronicus shrugged and sat down behind a little hillock that would hide them from the city. "We wait."

Chapter 22

BREAD UPON THE WATER
Godfrey

ome time later, Godfrey's pulse had stopped pounding and the ringing in his ears was nearly gone. He heaved a deep sigh, and was able to think and to turn his attention to his surroundings. Godfrey had almost forgotten the blacksmith's presence, but now, as they sat behind the hillock, out of sight of the city, he looked down at the stocky man whose life they had so dramatically changed in the space of half an hour. His skin was more dark than fair—he looked at least half Syrian, like Godfrey himself. The Templar could not help feeling sorry for the man.

"What's your name, Master Smith?"

The smith looked up at him, a half blank look on his face.

"Landuin Erail."

Godfrey sank down to the grass next to him.

"Do you have a family in Antioch, Landuin?"

The smith shook his head. "No, sire. Just me."

They sat in silence for a moment, then Landuin glanced sideways at Godfrey.

"You are a strange fellow, you. What's your name, anyway?"

Godfrey looked over at him. "Godfrey," he said. "Godfrey de Montferrat. Knight of the Temple."

Landuin stared at him, his face inscrutable. "Godfrey de Montferrat. You bust into a man's shop, being chased by a dozen soldiers, set fire to it, and then offer to pay me for it and take me along with you. Did you ever think I might be angry? It might have been wiser to leave me there in the shop. I could slit your throat as you sleep, and perhaps I should. I worked hard in that shop for years, and now it's all gone, just like that. Do you think any amount of gold can make up for it?"

Godfrey shrugged. "A man must risk his life sooner or later. It was the right thing to do."

Landuin frowned. "The right thing, Templar?" he chuckled. "Would you do the right thing, even if it brought suffering to all those around you? For this thing well might. If I murdered you all in your sleep, it wouldn't do me any good; I'd starve sooner or later, and you and your friends would be dead. But I think I just might do it anyway. I have nothing better to do, for you've left me nothing to live for."

"*Cast your bread upon the waters*," said Godfrey. "I will do the right thing, and if men choose to reject it and bring more suffering, then so be it. If I die because of it, it will only benefit me more than we here on earth can imagine."

"So," said Landuin, chuckling, "I would be doing you a service by murdering you?"

Godfrey shrugged again. "You would be doing yourself a disservice."

Landuin laughed, but mirthlessly. "I'll think on it, Templar. But you should know: you're an arrogant fool of a whoreson, and one day it's going to get to you." He glanced over at Andronicus and Murzuphlus, who were talking quietly at the other side of the hillock. "Why are we waiting here, anyway. What if a patrol of soldiers come looking for you? But don't tell me why they're hunting you, I'd rather not know."

Godfrey sighed. "There were three others whom the soldiers were hunting. We were separated from them within the city, so now we wait for them to come out. If a patrol of soldiers comes out, then we die fighting."

Landuin squinted at him. "You are a strange man, Templar. And dangerous. Maybe I *will* murder you in your sleep. It would prevent a good deal of suffering if I did."

Godfrey smiled. "You're assuming that we live until sunset. If we do, then I'll die happily."

"*Quiet*," hissed Murzuphlus. "Horsemen coming out of the city."

Godfrey and Landuin turned around, pressing flat against the hillock, and slowly climbing up to peer over the top.

From a distance, Godfrey could make out six or seven horsemen. That was good—if they were soldiers, there likely would have been more. Then again, this might be just a search patrol that would raise the alarm and bring more men if they found Andronicus Comnenus. And six or seven were too many to be their friends.

The horsemen drew nearer, clearly shaping into six horses. Six horses... but only three riders.

"It's them," said Murzuphlus, sighing with relief.

Jacques, Langosse, and Basil rode down the road, leading three riderless horses behind them.

Andronicus stood up and began walking towards the road, followed by Landuin, Godfrey, and Murzuphlus.

The riders brought their horses to a halt before the four walkers.

"What kept you?" said Andronicus, looking up at Langosse.

Langosse laughed. "When all the soldiers came running after you, they left the street empty. The three of us walked out and met by the gate. We saw no sign of you, but seeing as we had lost our horses, I thought we might need new ones." Langosse held up a half-empty purse. "I spent most of my gold buying them, but I know well enough that gold is never in short supply when you are there, my lord."

"Who's this one?" growled Basil, frowning down at Landuin, who pulled himself up to his full height. The top of his head barely reached Godfrey's chin.

"This," said Andronicus, "is one of our hangers-on. We caused him a little trouble, so Sir Templar here saw fit to bring him along and try to make reparations."

Jacques snorted. "You had to make more trouble, Godfrey?"

"My lord," said Langosse to Andronicus, "it would seem that men everywhere are drawn to follow you."

Andronicus shook his head. "This one came with Godfrey. Perhaps you have the makings of a great captain in you, Sir Templar."

Landuin had not yet said anything, but now he spoke.

"So," he said, "what do you plan on doing with me? It seems that there will be no horse for me. It also seems that it will be dangerous to return to Antioch." His hands were clenched into fists. Godfrey had seen the blow he dealt the soldier in the shop, so he took a step back. Landuin would fight, and with his bare hands if he felt he needed to.

Basil frowned down at him. "If he will not serve any purpose, I say we slit his throat and hide his body in that hollow there."

Godfrey's sword was out in a second. "If you mean to murder an innocent man before my eyes, I will not stand by and see it done."

Both Landuin and Basil glared at him fiercely, until he lowered his sword a few inches.

Jacques's face was buried in his hand—Godfrey thought he was laughing. Murzuphlus was scowling at no one in particular. Langosse looked from man to man, a worried half-smile on his face.

Andronicus broke the silence. "No need to kill him. We will find some other use for him."

Godfrey spoke now. "Landuin, you could come with me to Jerusalem. There would be work for you there."

Landuin cocked his head at him, as though thinking.

"I could," he said. "But," he added, "you are a dangerous man to be around, Templar. Is it worth the risk?" He ground his giant fists together. "Yes, I will come with you, if only so that I can kill you when I find no work."

Godfrey nodded. "Come then, you are welcome, whether you slit my throat or not."

Jacques was frowning, his face seeming to say that Godfrey could get his throat cut on his own if he wished, but that he wanted no part of it.

"There is," objected Jacques, "the problem of horses. There are only six—we have no steed for him."

"There will be no more going into the city," said Basil. "We have risked enough this day."

For a long moment there was silence. Then Godfrey spoke.

"Landuin and I will take turns walking; that way we can make it to Tripoli in two days, where Landuin can buy himself a horse. I am sure that he now has ample money to do so."

Andronicus frowned at that, but did not speak. None of the others knew that Godfrey's had given his money to Landuin, and Godfrey doubted that Andronicus would be happy if he found out.

"Very well then," said Landuin. "I have gone to places farther than Tripoli on foot. I will survive."

Andronicus mounted his horse. "Then," he said, "let us be gone before Bohemund begins searching Orontes Plain. "Godspeed, Templars."

Murzuphlus mounted beside him. The Greeks began turning their horses around.

"Where do you ride?" shouted Godfrey. Andronicus glanced back.

"Cilicia," he said. "Perhaps my noble cousin the emperor will grant me sanctuary once I reach his territory. Constantinople calls me—it is my home! I have been gone too long. You may head south, to your Holy City, but I ride for home."

Jacques frowned. "And if your cousin tries to kill you?"

Andronicus shrugged, and began to ride off. A moment later, he looked back again.

"Godfrey," he said. Godfrey turned back to look at the Greek. "Two years ago, I named you the Knight of the Impossible Ideal."

Godfrey nodded.

"You have not changed since then," said Andronicus.

Godfrey smiled.

"Frank!" It was Murzuphlus this time. He tossed something in the air, and the two bezants he had snatched from the blacksmith's shop landed at Godfrey's feet. "I would not dirty myself with gold that belonged to you."

Godfrey smiled again. "My thanks, Murzuphlus."

Andronicus then spurred forward, sending his horse galloping over Orontes Plain, with Murzuphlus and Langosse and Basil beside him.

"Cilicia," said Godfrey, to no one in particular. "Strange. He cannot really believe that Manuel will accept him with open arms." He gazed north, holding the bridle of his horse. "In stories, men may ride home, even knowing that death awaits them there, but that is not like Andronicus."

Landuin spat onto the gravel. "If I'm walking halfway to Tripoli, best start now."

Jacques nodded. "You'll have hours to puzzle it out, Godfrey. We should move now, before Bohemund widens the search for Andronicus and catches us instead."

Godfrey knelt down to pick up the two bezants. Jacques snorted. "Leave them there. They were meant as an insult, not as a gift."

Godfrey picked them up anyway. "They were given as a gift, and I will take them as such, no matter what words accompanied them."

Landuin climbed up onto Godfrey's horse. "Speaking of gifts," he said, "I'd be happy to accept the gift of taking the first turn to ride."

✠ ✠ ✠

The progress was slow, but not much slower than if Landuin had not been there. Godfrey and Jacques would have had to stop often to rest their horses and walk them for a ways, and one extra rider on one of the horses did not slow them much.

That evening, they made camp some miles south of the Orontes River.

Godfrey sat on a log that night before the smoking embers. Jacques was trying to make a bed of leaves, while Landuin whittled. They had brought no packs, had brought nothing but food and drink to last a few days. There was much that they would have to buy in Tripoli.

Strange, thought Godfrey, *this morning I awoke in Antioch, thinking that I would be there for months to come. Where will I be in a day? A week? A month?*

That night Godfrey dreamed something he had dreamed before; he stood once again in the clouds above Outremer, watched the dark storm roll in, and fought with the man who rode the storm clouds. He could not remember how it ended, only that something or someone fell, fell long and far, and the lightning flashed and the thunder roared. *A storm is coming.* The words pressed into his brain, and unlike the rest of the dream, did not fade with waking. *A storm is coming.*

✠ ✠ ✠

The weather was grey and wet from there on. Winter was upon Outremer, and though it was never quite cold, it was chilly. All through the next morning, Jacques looked anxious. Finally, as afternoon rolled in, Landuin went off to fill a canteen with water. With the blacksmith gone, Jacques seized the chance to speak to Godfrey quietly.

"Godfrey," he said, "do you know just what you have done in bringing this tramp along?"

Godfrey shrugged. "An act of charity?"

Jacques snorted. "He talks casually and constantly of murdering you, and you assume that it is all in jest. Did you ever think that he means it seriously?"

Godfrey shrugged again. "He may. I don't know."

Jacques glared at him. "You fell asleep early last night. But *he* didn't. He just sat there whittling with a knife—God knows whether he brought it or stole it from you. I lay down and pretended to sleep, but I was watching him. For an hour or more he whittled and whittled, until finally he took the stick, snapped it, and threw it away. Then he just sat there, still holding the knife, and his eyes were going back and forth between the knife and you, the knife and you." Jacques shuddered. "It was...unnerving. Then, he got up, and walked over to you. I was starting to shift, ready to get up and shout, but he just stood there, looking at you, holding the cursed knife, before he moved away and lay down to sleep."

Godfrey did not say anything, but he was shaken, and badly. Jacques could see it—for Jacques knew his friend well. Mentally, Godfrey had accepted the possibility that Landuin might murder him. Emotionally, however, it had not hit home...until now.

"He was struggling," continued Jacques, pressing his friend's indecision. "Struggling in his mind. Going back and forth. His conscience won over his frustration this past night, but what about the next? What about all the nights until we reach Jerusalem?"

Godfrey shuddered, then slowly cleared his face. He still said nothing.

"We could leave him here," continued Jacques. "Just ride off while he's getting his water. He's close enough to Tripoli that he can make it there safely. And of course you had to give him your gold, so he'll be able to support himself until he finds work. God's blood; with all that gold, he could go half a year without work, and live like a prince."

Godfrey was wavering, visibly now. Jacques pressed harder.

"Prudence is a virtue, Godfrey. No sane man would think that honor or duty or love binds him to stay with that man. You have made proper reparation, nothing more is required. There's no good reason to. No logical reason, no moral reason. What is it that you see in him that makes you think he *won't* slit your throat tonight?"

It was there that Jacques failed; for he had gone too far.

"The Image of Christ," said Godfrey. "The same Image I see in all men. The Image of Christ."

Jacques sighed. Godfrey was shaking his head now.

"No," he said, "I told him he could ride with us to Jerusalem, and I will not lie." Godfrey's face had resumed its normal pose, the same confident and, in Jacques's opinion, self-righteous look it always had. Then it slipped again.

"But," he said, "you have no such obligation, Jacques. If you think Landuin will turn on us, you may leave, ride ahead to Tripoli, buy food there, and then straight on to Jerusalem. I won't hold it against you, Jacques. I mean it."

Jacques spat, to show what he thought of it. "I should," he said, ruefully. "As I just said, prudence *is* a virtue. But...no. We both chose to give our lives to the Temple, and one day we may have to pay for it with our friendship. But not yet. Not unless we must. I'll stay." He chuckled. "Perhaps I truly had a vocation for it, but the mere fact that you went to the Temple was one of the reasons I entered the Temple. You aren't rid of me that easily, Godfrey."

I know, thought Godfrey. *I know all too well. And I will always be grateful to you, Jacques. Always grateful for what you did...even though I don't understand it.*

Godfrey breathed a sigh of relief, and then Landuin returned, and they moved on toward Tripoli. By night, Godfrey had put it all from his mind, and he slept soundly. Jacques did too, and so none but God knew what Landuin the smith did that night.

The next morning they reached the city of Tripoli. A light drizzle was soaking the land, and the chill had increased, making the weather miserable.

As they rode through the gate, Jacques saw a familiar sigil waving from the lance of the knight who had charge of the gate. It was an argent hawk on an azure field. The knight sat in full armor on his horse, his helmeted head slumped over as though he were asleep.

"Humphrey!" he shouted. "Humphrey de Vinsauf!"

The knight looked up, shaking his head through the helmet as though he were waking up. He looked again, then ripped off his helmet, splashing them with water.

"God's beard! What are you two monks doing here in the north?"

Jacques laughed as the rain ran down his face. "We came to watch you soak your arse off in a metal tin, what do you think?"

Humphrey spat out a gob of dirt and spittle. "Guard duty," he grumbled. "Unfitting for a knight. But soon I'll get a break from that, once the army gets on the move."

"On the move?" asked Godfrey. "Has Amalric called the banners again? Or has Tripoli?"

Humphrey shook out his soggy hair. "I don't know what kind of sorry rat-hole you two've been hiding in, if you haven't heard. The kingdom's going to war! We're heading back to Egypt."

Chapter 23

Montgisor Plain
Godfrey

"Careful ahead! There's a wadi that cuts across the path; we're crossing it one at a time. Slow down!"

Odo de Sant'Amand went riding back along the column of Templars, shouting out for them to slow down as he went.

Godfrey glanced up as the marshal rode past him. He quickly lowered his head again, coughing up the dust that Odo's horse kicked up behind him.

They were riding across Montgisor Plain, a broad expanse of dust and flat ground that lay just south of Montgisor Castle and east of Ramleh. The plain stretched out for miles, broken only by a long ridge to the east and another to the south.

The wadi, a deep dried-up streambed, cut straight through the plain like a long, sinuous snake. It ran roughly northwest to southeast, but it zigzagged back and forth at odd angles. It was fairly deep, and would take a while to cross.

Godfrey sighed as the column of Templars slowed to a halt. He glanced ahead to see if he could make out the wadi. It was there, twenty feet ahead of him—a steeply cut trench slicing through the dirt and brownish grass of Montgisor Plain. At the moment, Arnold de Torroga was leading his horse up over the opposite bank.

Odo and Phillip rode by, each leading another column of Templars to cross the wadi at different points.

Godfrey sighed again and consigned himself to wait. He slumped forward in the saddle and closed his eyes. Sleeping in the saddle was an art that every Templar learned early on, otherwise they could spend days without sleep.

It was a matter of relief to Godfrey that silence was required on the march. The week or so since his return to Jerusalem had put Godfrey on edge.

They had ridden to Jerusalem with Humphrey and the knights of Tripoli. Landuin rode with them, rarely speaking. When they reached Jerusalem he left without a word and vanished, leaving no hint of where in the city he had gone.

Godfrey and Jacques had returned to the Temple. It had been two years since they left it. Godfrey had felt strange riding into the Temple Court and calling for the gatekeeper to open the door. But Arnold de Torroga came running in answer to their shouts, just as he always had. It had felt comforting to know that some things never changed; Arnold still watched the gate as he had two years before.

However, within an hour of their return, Godfrey had realized that Arnold was perhaps the only thing that remained unchanged.

He had expected that, on his return, he would be showered with questions about Antioch by his brother Templars. He had expected to be embarrassed and annoyed because he would not have a free moment for a week.

So it came as a blow to his pride when his return was not even noticed. Oh, Bertrand de Blanchefort had questioned him for hours without end on what happened in Antioch, but no one else seemed to notice he was there. The reason for this soon became plain: there was a new arrival in the Temple. To Godfrey's dismay, he recognized him.

Gerard de Ridford had become a Templar.

Godfrey knew that he still did not have a good reason to dislike De Ridford. Though De Ridford made no more jibes at Templars, the man was now too polite and too friendly. But such behavior could come close to qualifying as a reason to dislike him. He seemed to have a quiet contempt for religion and for all things intellectual—scarcely good things to Godfrey's mind—but so did two dozen other men in the Temple with whom Godfrey got along passably well.

Godfrey was fairly sure that the dislike was mutual; De Ridford seemed to have a quiet scorn for him. He could not decide whether his dislike was in response to De Ridford's scorn, or De Ridford's dislike was a response to his own, or whether both were instinctive. De Ridford, however, seemed to have the power to draw all the attention in a room to himself, while Godfrey seemed merely to make others ignore him.

Biting down bile, Godfrey told himself that, as a Templar, he was not supposed to hold petty jealousies like this, or yearn so much for human esteem. But every time he looked at De Ridford, the bitterness and anger would get hold of him.

Ahead of Godfrey, the line of Templars began moving forward at a rapid rate now. Godfrey jerked himself out of his thoughts. He looked ahead to see that part of the wadi bank had collapsed, creating a sloping bridge. The Templars now surged across the wadi, riding quickly to make up for lost time.

Peering far ahead, Godfrey caught sight of the tail end of the knights of Tyre. He did not look back, but he knew that the knights of Tripoli were riding behind the Templars.

On the ride back from Antioch, he had been concerned that they would be left behind if the knights of the Temple rode to war before they reached Jerusalem, but he need not have feared. Blanchefort had previously dispatched Templars to every corner of Outremer, and it took time for the whole Temple to assemble in Jerusalem. They had left at the same time as the forces of the northern principalities. No soldiers had come from Antioch—they were afraid of the Turks there. Ridhwan had done his work well in capturing the Hawk.

Godfrey rode over the wadi. He glanced to either side, and saw the empty stream bed winding its way until it turned and vanished from sight. Then he crossed the wadi, riding along the old road to Ascalon.

When the sun reached its midday peak, Odo came riding down the line, telling them to halt. They were to stop for half an hour to eat.

Godfrey sat in his saddle for a few moments as the men all around him leapt down, leading their horses away from the road. He was tired, too tired for all this. He had long since grown used to riding, and he rarely got saddle-sore, but life in Antioch had made him soft. It had been two years since he had spent a whole day riding.

Somewhere to the left, a large group of men started laughing. He glanced that way, then grimaced: as usual, it was some joke of De Ridford's.

Sometimes Godfrey would go over and sit with the men who congregated about De Ridford, but it always felt uncomfortable, and he rarely had anything to say. So, as often as not, he sat off on his own.

Godfrey, he thought, *you are pathetic. You could not make any woman love you, so you became a monk. Even here you have no true friends, so you sit off on the side and brood. You imagine yourself to be holy, to be a knight of God, but you are as subject to the jealousies of the flesh as any of those whom you hold in contempt. You have lost any real love, and all that is left is self-righteousness. And now you are going to go hide away from the others because of your grudge against De Ridford.*

And that was exactly what Godfrey did. He led his horse to a palm tree a little ways away from the other Templars, and sat down with his back against the tree. He tried to deny the accusations his conscience made against him, but it nagged at him.

I did not become a monk because no woman would love me! I became a monk because it was my calling! It was God's will!

You know better than that. You were scared. Scared of women. Scared of life. It was your will, not God's.

Godfrey sighed, trying to close his mind, maybe to sleep. He could not bring himself to eat anything in his saddlebags. He tried to assure himself that he was human, and so subject to the jealousies of the flesh, and that there was nothing self-righteous about battling those temptations. But fighting his doubts was like fighting shadows. When he faced them head on, they vanished, only to return as soon as he let his guard down.

Godfrey glanced over at the other Templars, gathering in groups along the roadside, breaking out food.

"Godfrey," came a voice from behind him.

He started, then turned to see Jacques leaning against another palm tree. "Oh," said Godfrey sourly. "You. I haven't seen much of you since we got back to the Temple."

Jacques smiled. "Get up, Godfrey. I don't know why it is you hate De Ridford so much, but you can't spend the whole day grousing and griping about it."

"I don't *hate* anyone," growled Godfrey as he stood up. "De Ridford is just..." he went on grumbling under his breath.

Jacques laughed. "Best get you away from him, for the moment at least." Jacques turned and began walking east, towards where the men of Tripoli were stopped to eat. "Come on," he said, "I want to show you something."

Still grumbling, Godfrey followed. Jacques passed out of the sparse grove of palm trees until he stood on the edge of Montgisor Plain.

It was a barren plain, with very little grass, very little life. For miles around nothing but brownish-grey dirt and rock covered the ground. There were a few little hills, but for the most part it was flat. Far to the east a long, high ridge rose up, and another to the south. Beyond that, all that could be seen was the brownish-grey stretching out to the north and west, broken only by the wadi.

Godfrey came to stand beside Jacques, following his gaze to the northeast.

"Godfrey," said Jacques, "did I ever tell you where I lived before I came to William de Montferrat's estate?"

Godfrey thought back to the days of his childhood, but he could remember nothing of where Jacques had come *from*.

"Outremer, of course. From this side of the sea."

Jacques had become a page at Montferrat five years after Godfrey came there. Godfrey had first resented Jacques, who seemed to steal Conrad's attention, but Jacques and Conrad became estranged, while Godfrey and Jacques soon became firm friends. But then Adelaise had fallen in love with Jacques even as Godfrey prepared to enter the Temple. There was little doubt that William de Montferrat would grant his daughter permission to marry Jacques, whom he loved almost as a son. Godfrey had thought never to see Jacques again after he left for Jerusalem. But a week before the departure they had had their violent argument. Godfrey remembered the quarrel all too well...remembered the anger on Jacques's face, and remembered the hate in his own heart. When he left Montferrat, he had been struggling in his heart with his hate, trying to find the strength to forgive. The nights aboard the ship as he sailed to Jerusalem were engraved in Godfrey's memory: the nights that he lay on the hard board, trying to root the malice out of his heart, praying for the ability to forgive, but always slipping back into hate.

It had proved impossible, for Godfrey de Montferrat soon realized that the fault, and the offense, had truly been his and not Jacques's. To forgive Jacques might have been possible, but to repent of his actions, actions fueled by bitterness and jealousy at his friend, was something he could not do. He prayed, but God had seemed silent, and the hate remained in his heart. He had gone to the Jerusalem cursing God. He prepared to enter the Temple, for there was nothing else to do. But the Temple had ceased to have any meaning for him.

A week later, against all hope or expectation, Jacques de Maille appeared in Jerusalem.

Jacques had taken the next ship after Godfrey, and now he had come to enter the Temple with him. Jacques' appearance had left Godfrey awestruck—and at last repentant. It had changed Godfrey indelibly, for though he had repudiated his hate, he had never forgotten it, never forgotten the misery. And he never forgot that just when he, utterly possessed by bitterness and resentment, was unable to love, God and Jacques had reached out and given him a miraculous gift which had seemed impossible.

Godfrey now loved Jacques as his closest friend, though he did not understand why Jacques had chosen as he did. He had longed to ask Jacques why he did what he did, longed to ask him what had happened with Adelaise and with William de Montferrat. But...he did not ask. Godfrey was never sure whether it was charity or fear that held him back, but whatever the reason, he did not ask. He only accepted that Jacques had followed him to the Temple. That had been six years ago, and throughout those six years, he had hoped that Jacques would tell him the reason—but Jacques never did. He never even mentioned it.

Now Jacques looked out across the plain. "Yes, I am from Outremer. I came from right here—Montgisor." Jacques pointed to the northeast. "Just out of sight is Montgisor Castle. My father was a knight there, serving the lord of the castle—that is, until he died, leaving my mother a widow and me an orphan. My father had gone on Crusade with William de Montferrat, and so when William heard of my father's death, he offered to take me on as a squire. My mother seized the opportunity to send me to Montferrat. She died a few years later—I never saw her again."

Godfrey glanced sidelong at Jacques. He did not appear to be sad, merely wistful.

"What was Montgisor Castle like?"

Jacques shrugged. "Like any other minor castle. Cold and damp, cramped and smelly. I was not sad to leave the castle. This was what I loved. The plain."

Godfrey glanced at the barren plain and nodded, understanding Jacques's love for it, despite its ugliness.

"This," said Jacques, "was where I learned to ride a horse. You see that ridge to the east? I would ride up and down there, once I really learned to control my steed. Sometimes I would bring my little wooden practice sword and pretend to be knight; I would ride up and down the hill shouting 'Deus le vult! Deus le vult!'"

Jacques smiled a little to himself. "You know old Blanchefort's psalm? The one that starts, 'I will lift up mine eyes to the hills'? I always thought of this ridge at Montgisor when I heard it. Still do."

Godfrey's gaze traveled over the plain and up the ridge. *I will lift up mine eyes to the hills...*

"I always thought," said Jacques, "that Montgisor Plain has the look of a battleground. It's barren and rocky, useless for building on or for pastureland or farming. It's useless for anything, except, of course, for a great battle. Whenever I rode my horse up and down that ridge, I would always imagine that the plain below was filled with armies clashing with each other." Jacques smiled again and laughed to himself.

Godfrey nodded, looking again over the plain. It truly was useless, except for a sort of wild beauty that lay in its sheer size and emptiness.

"A great battle," he said, quite seriously. "Perhaps."

Jacques turned back to the road. "Let's go," he said. "We should get something to eat before Odo comes back."

Chapter 24

HORNS IN THE WEST
Joscelin

One Week Later

With a quiet hiss, the torch came alight, casting long shadows over the men standing around it. Tristan de Monglane, his squire, held the torch aloft, while Joscelin and Sir Hugh Grenier bent down to inspect the map they had spread out in the sand.

Joscelin glanced out across the sand and dried brush, illuminated only by the sliver of a crescent moon. Somewhere out there in the darkness lay the Egyptian host, their allies, with whom they were supposed to meet. The two armies were supposed to join at the Nile crossings south of Bubastis. If the reports were correct, they were only a few hours' march from the crossings now, so Amalric had given the order for the Christian host to press on through the night.

Examining the map in the flickering firelight, Joscelin saw that the crossings were marked some ten miles south of Bubastis, which they had passed in the lazy hours of the afternoon. If the map were not far wrong, they should hold their course to the south and west and they would come directly to the crossings—and, if fortune held, to the Egyptian camp.

But there was a trace of unease and fear in his movements as Joscelin folded up the map. For Shirkuh, with his entire Saracen army, had vanished.

Shortly after the vizier Shawar had sent his plea north for aid from the Christians, Shirkuh seemed to have gotten wind of the plot, for he had pulled all his troops in and assembled the army. Shawar had barred the gates of Cairo and prepared the Egyptians for a siege, but instead of marching on Cairo, Shirkuh and his army had disappeared.

Now all the Franks were on edge. The possibility of facing a general like Shirkuh was frightening enough when you knew where he was. Now, when he could be anywhere, the fear was trebled. Many years ago, when Joscelin was just a boy, his father had ridden off with the flower of Frankish chivalry to try and retake their lost county of Edessa. Shirkuh had met him there with Nur ad-Din's army, and in the green fields of Edessa, the bravest knights of Outremer had fallen, outmaneuvered and entrapped by Shirkuh. Joscelin's father had been taken prisoner—he was blinded and thrown into a dungeon where he rotted for nine years before his death.

Joscelin suppressed his fear as he carefully placed the map in his saddlebags. If nothing else, he would not allow himself to be taken prisoner; he would not rot in a dungeon as his father had. Joscelin would go down fighting.

Tristan, his squire, helped him to mount before climbing onto his own horse. Tristan de Monglane had changed much since the first invasion of Egypt, when he had been a scrawny little boy. He was sixteen now, no longer scrawny or clumsy. His arms had thickened and were now knotted with muscles. He moved with an easy grace, and his horsemanship was unequaled. He could already unhorse most knights in the lists. There was no question now; Tristan would be a knight like none other since the First Crusade.

Joscelin's only worry now was that Tristan would let it go to his head. In two years, his dark hair had curled, and his face alone had won the love of half the girls in the court. Still, Tristan had not changed entirely. Though he was not shy as he had been, he did not speak a word more than he needed to.

But suddenly, Tristan did speak.

"My lord Joscelin?"

Joscelin glanced over at him. "What is it, Tristan?" he asked quietly. Sir Hugh Grenier had mounted his horse and was preparing to ride back.

"Southron horns, blowing to the west. Did you hear them?"

Joscelin frowned. "I heard nothing. By southron, do you mean—"

"Arabic horns," said Tristan. "Not Egyptian."

Hugh Grenier frowned too. "I heard nothing. My outriders would have reported by now if Shirkuh were anywhere near."

Joscelin felt a shiver of fear run down his spine.

Due to lack of supplies, Shirkuh had been forced to send most of his troops back to Arabia during his two years in Egypt. The Saracen army was little more than six thousand men. The Egyptian host was five thousand, the Frankish host was seven thousand. Combined, their strength doubled the Saracens. Even Shirkuh could not fight against those odds.

But the image of his father, chained to the wall of a dank dungeon cell still haunted Joscelin.

Tristan's face was tense but unafraid. "I heard Saracen horns. I am sure of it."

Hugh Grenier snorted dismissively, and Joscelin wanted to agree with Hugh, wanted to assure himself that Shirkuh was miles away. But then he looked at Tristan.

"Sir Hugh," said Joscelin, "Tristan does not give false alarms. If he heard southron horns, we have cause to worry."

Tristan glanced gratefully at Joscelin for a moment, and then began to turn his horse to the west.

"My lord," he said, "they were coming from the west. Should I ride out that way and have a look?"

"I have outriders scouring the west. If they—"

Just then they heard the loud, low, mournful sound of an Arabic horn blowing from the west.

No sooner had it died away than they heard the sound of hoofbeats coming across the sand. A horseman came galloping at full speed towards the three of them, bearing Grenier's colors on his tunic.

"My lord Hugh," he said, "Shirkuh is here! Five or six miles to the west. He's sacking the Egyptian camp. The Egyptians are fleeing before him!"

"God's bones," said Joscelin. He did not feel panic now, however, but only the excitement that always pounded through his veins before a battle. The wait, the tension, the fear were all over. Now was the time for action.

"Tristan," he said. "Find the king. Tell him that battle has begun."

Chapter 25

BLOOD AND STEEL AGAIN
Godfrey

AHOOOOOOOOOOOOOOOOOO!

Godfrey jerked up in his saddle at the sound of a horn echoing in the south. He glanced around wildly at the Templars riding next to him, but they too looked just as shocked.

The column of Templars was riding south along the river road. The only light over them was a shining crescent moon. The stars were dark this night, and a cool breeze whipped around the Templars.

aHOOOOOOOOOOOOOOOOOOOOOOoooooooooooooooo!

The horns called again, many of them now. Godfrey began to grow alarmed. He glanced at Jacques next to him.

"How close do you think we are to those horns?"

Jacques's face was pale. "A mile, not more."

Godfrey looked to the south. "Those are southron horns."

"Maybe it's just the Egyptians," said Jacques, but neither of them believed it. Godfrey reached back and unhooked his helmet from where it hung. Reluctantly, he pulled it on. It was a rounded metal cask with a flat top. The only openings were an eyeslit and a few breathing holes by his mouth.

No more scratching or clearing my nose until the battle's over.

Next Godfrey unhooked his shield. It was kite-shaped, made of thick oak, and painted white. It slid neatly onto his left arm.

Philip de Milly came riding to the head of the column.

"Halt!" he shouted. The column stopped in the road. De Milly turned his horse about to face the Templars. "Outriders have just come back with word that there is a battle going on ahead. It appears that the Saracens have caught our allies by surprise. The Egyptian camp is on fire."

"The Greek boats have got themselves lost somewhere in the mouths of the Nile," continued Philip contemptuously. "So we will be without naval support. The king has given orders for the host to draw up into battle formation. The Templars have been given the far right flank, on the Nile. We must keep the line anchored against the river, so that Shirkuh will not be able to outflank us."

From behind, Godfrey heard the pounding of hooves as Odo de Sant'Amand came leading another column of Templars. De Milly looked up expectantly at him.

"Blanchefort's coming," said Odo.

Godfrey could feel his pulse pounding faster.

Another battle.

More Templars came riding down the road, led by Blanchefort. The old master of the Temple rode up to the head of the columns of Templars, where Phillip de Milly and Odo de Sant'Amand waited.

Blanchefort led them to the west. As they rode, Godfrey could hear the sounds of battle coming from the south. Somewhere down there, something was burning. He could see the plumes of smoke rising into the sky.

Somewhere ahead, Godfrey caught sight of the dark river, flowing ever so slowly to the sea. Blanchefort called a halt, and the Templars began forming their double line, facing the south.

The master rode along the line, looking over his knights. He paused when he reached Godfrey.

"Godfrey," he said, "do you have that oliphant the Greek gave you?"

Godfrey nodded.

"Then be ready to sound it."

Godfrey's pulse was pounding even harder. He took a breath, trying to calm himself. Now and again, the sounds of battle drifted towards them on the wind. He took the horn from his side and held it, feeling the smooth ivory and the gold inlay.

Somewhere to the east, a trumpet called.

DA-DAA! DA-DAA!

Further to the east, more trumpets answered the call. Then there came another blast very close to them. Blanchefort turned and nodded to Godfrey.

Godfrey put the oliphant to his lips and blew.

HAROOOOOOOOOOOOOOOOOOOOOOOOOOOOOOOOO! The ivory horn called louder than any horn Godfrey had heard before, a call that hurt his ears.

No wonder Roland killed himself blowing on an oliphant, Godfrey thought.

Blanchefort was already moving, spurring to the lead.

"Knights of the Temple, advance!"

Godfrey hooked the horn at his belt and dug his spurs in. The line of Templars began riding forward slowly, following Blanchefort. Godfrey could not see, but he knew that out to the east, the whole Christian host was moving towards the battle.

They were riding up a ridge now, eyes straining to see what lay beyond.

"Draw your swords!" shouted Blanchefort.

Godfrey reached to his side and drew out his blade. As soon as he felt the steel in his hand, he could feel strength running through him, and he began to sense the wild battle-fever. But besides the excitement, he felt a slight apprehension. Though he had fought in one battle before, he had never actually killed a man. Now, if the Templars charged headfirst into battle, he would have little choice else...

Then the line of Templars was at the top of the ridge, and below them lay the battle.

The Egyptian camp was a fiery blaze, smoke and flame leaping up from the tents. They had set up a few perfunctory defenses facing east, but the Saracens had come from the west. The camp was full of disordered knots of men struggling in bloody hand-to-hand combat. Down at the ford, Saracens were pouring across the river into the camp.

Bertrand de Blanchefort began to ride faster, and the Templars picked up their speed to keep up. They rode over the crest and began to ride down the ridge.

"*Deus le vult!*" roared the master.

"Deus le vult!" roared the Templars. Godfrey shouted along with the rest, letting the battle fury take him. They were going even faster down the hill.

"Full speed!" roared Blanchefort, digging his heels his.

Godfrey gave a wild yell, waved his sword in the air, and dug his spurs in. The line of Templars moved with him, thundering down the hill.

"*Christus regnat!*" roared the master, and the Templars echoed his battle-cry.

All around the camp, the Frankish trumpets were sounding, and all around the camp the columns of knights were charging down. Godfrey had no time to notice any of this, though. The world was quickly shrinking down to what lay just before him.

What was before him was a company of mamelukes, on foot, with their great axes and swords. The line of Templars was turning to meet them, to charge them head-on.

The mamelukes rushed fearlessly into the oncoming storm of steel and hooves, and the Templars trampled them down. Godfrey found himself hacking to his right at a shining helmet. He split it open and felt the skull break under his blade. To his left a mameluke rose up to strike at him, and Godfrey moved his shield to block, but he needn't have, for the Templar next to him struck the mameluke down.

They rode on over the mamelukes, heading towards the river.

"Right wheel!" bellowed the master, and Godfrey pulled on the reins, turning with the rest of the line. Saracen horsemen were charging out of the camp, trying to hit them on the flank, but the Templar line turned too quickly.

"Charge!"

The Templars went thundering forward again. Godfrey saw an Arab lancer aiming his lance at him, and he drove straight towards him. As the lance point came at his chest, he caught it on his shield. The lance splintered harmlessly against the shield, and Godfrey's destrier bowled over the smaller Arab mount, leaving both horse and rider to be trampled by the second rank of Templars.

Arrows began falling among them, but they could not pierce the Templars' armor. Godfrey felt an arrow clatter off his back, and another stuck harmlessly into his clothing at his shoulder and stayed there without piercing the chain mail.

"Full right wheel!" roared Blanchefort.

Godfrey turned hard to the left, as did the whole line. The line swung about until it faced the archers directly behind them, crouching amidst the reeds in the river.

"Charge!"

Godfrey dug his spurs in and charged, waving his sword above his head. It was spattered with blood and brains, and sent specks flying about, but Godfrey didn't care. Once the battle-fever had him, no amount of blood or gore could give him pause.

The Templar line rode into the shallows, trampling down the archers. Godfrey split open a man's face and trampled down more. Suddenly Blanchefort was shouting again.

"Left wheel!" he roared. "Left wheel!"

From both sides, Saracen horsemen were charging down into the ford. Godfrey could see at a glance that the trap had been deliberate. They were about to be hit from behind.

The Templars tried to turn, but the Saracens were on them first. About half the line managed to turn about, but by then there was no room to charge. The Saracens pressed in around them, hemming them in. Godfrey fought desperately, beating away lances and scimitars with sword and shield.

Suddenly Godfrey felt his horse rear up. He had half a second in which to realize that a Saracen spearman had slipped beneath his horse and stabbed it through the belly. Then the horse threw him.

Godfrey landed on his back in knee-deep water. For a moment he felt the surface of the water slap his back, then he was beneath the water, struggling for breath. His helmet fell off, his shield slid from his arm, and his sword slipped from his hand.

His feet pushed against the muddy bank. He slipped, then caught himself and his head resurfaced.

My sword!

Godfrey felt frantically about the river bed, and luckily the first thing his hand encountered was the blade. He gripped it tightly, then pushed himself to his feet.

Godfrey went immediately into the fighting stance Andronicus had taught him, and looked around. The river was full of fighting men from all sides: white-cloaked Templars, golden-armored mamelukes, silver-armored knights, archers and spearmen, both Saracen and Egyptian.

A Saracen spearman caught sight of him and struck, trying to put his spear through Godfrey's belly. And Godfrey reacted, just as Andronicus Comnenus had taught him.

No different than the practice yard in Antioch.

He spun around the spear and opened the man's throat with a two-handed blow.

The Saracen's spear clattered from his hands, and he collapsed as Godfrey pulled his sword out of him. Then, as Godfrey saw the light go out of the man's eyes and the blood spurt from his mouth, he realized that it was *very* different from the practice yard in Antioch. Now, Godfrey was shaken, for he had just slain a man. He watched the man's body fall into the water, watched the blood mix with the water and flow away.

Oh God! It was half a thought, half a prayer. *Oh God, do not let it be like that! Do not condemn this man whom I have killed. Have mercy on his soul, pagan though he be...*

Godfrey's head jerked up as another Saracen tried to gut him with a spear.

Instinctively, Godfrey moved as he had been taught. It was harder this time, for he needed to fight down his revulsion. He knew all too well now that he was about to kill another man. But the man struck again, trying to put six inches of iron through Godfrey's ribs, and now Godfrey felt the anger and the fighting instinct rise in him.

The wooden spear haft splintered at a blow from Godfrey's sword, and the spearman fell with a blow to his ribs. Godfrey turned his face away, but there was no time now to think or to pray.

Forty yards away, an archer caught sight of him and tried to put an arrow through Godfrey's unprotected head. Godfrey ducked down and then charged the archer, sending up splashes as he sprinted through the water. The archer tried to back up as he fitted a second arrow to his bow, but Godfrey was too fast. He caught up and struck, cutting halfway through the man's neck.

A Saracen lancer came riding down on him. Godfrey assumed the fighting stance, waiting until the last moment to step to the lancer's left side. The lancepoint missed him by a foot, the horse missed him by a few inches, and Godfrey cut open the horse's neck. The lancer leapt from his dying mount, but Godfrey cut him down as he tried to catch his balance in the river.

Soon it fell into a pattern—a bloody, awful sequence. Godfrey, who was normally clumsy and awkward, now moved about calmly and gracefully through the middle of a battle, cutting down any who challenged him. Andronicus Comnenus had taught him well. He always turned his face away from the men he killed and murmured a brief prayer, but his arm remained steady despite the revulsion that gripped his mind.

A dance, Andronicus Comnenus called it. And a dance it is. I need not feel in a dance. I need only move.

Godfrey was never sure how long he fought there. He had no sense of time; there was nothing in the world but his sword and the enemy who happened to be in front of him. But some time later, he glanced about, and his heart sank.

The handful of Templars in the ford was being overwhelmed. From both sides of the river, more and more Saracens were streaming into the battle.

Somewhere far off to the east, he heard the Frankish trumpets calling. DA-DAA! DA-DAA!

It was a forlorn call, for it was sounding the retreat.

That's not possible! We were supposed to outnumber the Saracens two to one!

"Godfrey! Godfrey!"

Godfrey heard his name shouted over the clamor of battle. He turned to look, and saw Humphrey de Vinsauf riding through the shallows towards him. He halted in front of him.

"Let's get out of here," he said, looking around hurriedly. Godfrey climbed up behind him.

"You got me out last time," said Humphrey. "Now the score's even."

The trumpets were calling again, still sounding the retreat. Humphrey turned his horse about and galloped away. Already a press of knights was riding away from the river, riding breakneck out of the camp. The Egyptians were fleeing too, away from the river, to the north and the east.

They were out of the river now, leaving the battle behind them. Godfrey glanced back one more time. The last thing he saw before they rode out of sight was the flames rising up to touch the crescent moon.

Chapter 26

CAIRO
Joscelin

A Few Days Later

"*Subhanaka Allah humma wa bihamdika, wa tabaraka ismuka, wa ta'ala jadduka, wa la ilaha ghairuk.*"

Joscelin de Courtenay watched in fascination from the outer door of the mosque as the long line of white-robed Egyptians stood, folding their hands in front of them, and recited the fajr.

"*Audu bi Allah i mina ashaitan i errajeem.*"

Joscelin had a sketchy knowledge of Arabic, but this bit he knew well. *I seek God's shelter from Satan, the condemned.*

The line of the faithful went on with the litany, scores of voices praying in unison. There was more of the prayer, but after a few more sentences they bent the top half of their bodies forward, in a bow of sorts.

"*Allah hu akbar!*"

"My lord Courtenay!"

Joscelin heard someone calling him. Tristan, standing beside him, turned to see who it was, but Joscelin's gaze lingered on a moment in fascination. It was a fascination somewhat mingled with horror, a horror at the strange and the alien, but it was fascination nonetheless. Tristan had told him of the strange manner in which the Muslims prayed, and so he had come to see for himself.

"My lord?"

Joscelin tore his gaze away, and he turned and found himself facing Abu Rashid, the steward of Cairo Palace.

God's bones, this man is annoying!

Two days in Cairo, and Abu Rashid was always there, scurrying about, watching every one of the Christian commanders with a suspicious eye.

"Yes?" he snapped impatiently.

"Lord de Courtenay, your king commands your presence in the Palace."

Joscelin sighed. "Take me to him, then."

A few guards were waiting outside. Abu Rashid always seemed to have armed men to defend him wherever he went. Joscelin and Tristan strode down the steps, and the guards formed up around them.

Cautious little Ishmaelite, this one, thought Joscelin.

They walked through the streets of Cairo, the guards clearing a path for them. Joscelin sighed, wondering what he was doing here. The Christians and Egyptians had fled south from the fords of Bubastis, flinching at every hint of an alarm, but for the second time, Shirkuh's army had not pursued them. Now the Frankish and Egyptian armies were cowering in Cairo while the Lords of Outremer argued with the Egyptian nobles, and the tension slowly grew.

God's beard, this is *a poor city*, thought Joscelin as he looked about him. The streets of Jerusalem were filled with the poor, Franks, Syrians, and Jews, but nothing like this. In Jerusalem, it seemed that even the poorest had *something* to do, something to sell, some labor. Even the beggars had some gleam of hope in their eyes. In Cairo there was a sense of listlessness. The poor did not try to move, to struggle. In Jerusalem the beggars would call out for alms and try to catch the attention of richer men. Here in Cairo the beggars sat immobile, leaning against the walls, bowls sitting on their laps with a few sorry coins lying in them, or just hands cupped in the hope that someone would give them bread. *Maybe we're just going through an especially bad part of the city.*

Joscelin dropped a few coins into one of the beggar's cupped hands. The beggar did not even stir. He did not so much as blink. His eyes had a glazed look to them.

"Is he alive?" Joscelin asked Abu Rashid.

The steward glanced worriedly at the beggar.

"Yes, he is alive...if you can call his existence life. Move on quickly, my lord. Do not waste your time on this filth."

The guards fingered cudgels at their belts as they passed by the beggars. The ones behind Joscelin hurried him along the next time he tried to reach one of the men sitting against the walls of the alley.

But further on, Joscelin tried again. He slipped away from Rashid's guards and leaned down in front of one of the paupers. He dropped a coin into the bowl on the man's lap, and then waited, staring into his eyes for some sort of reaction.

None came. With his seemingly lidless eyes, the shriveled old man stared back at Joscelin.

"Do you have a name, man?" asked Joscelin desperately, feeling the hackles rise on his back.

The man said nothing.

Angrily, Joscelin seized the man's shoulder and was about to shake. As he grabbed him, however, a part of the beggar seemed to come to life. While his face remained lifeless as ever, his hands suddenly seized Joscelin's neck, tightening with a freakish strength that did not seem to come from the man's emaciated muscles.

Joscelin wrenched back in shock, but the hands gripped him tightly, squeezing the very life out of him. The bowl fell over, and the coins spilled across the cobblestones.

Just as suddenly as the man had grabbed him, he seemed to forget that Joscelin was even there. His hands slid off Joscelin's neck and fell to his sides.

All this had happened in a split second, too fast for anyone to reach the beggar. Tristan was at Joscelin's side already. He grabbed Joscelin and pulled him back, while the guards looked on, still shocked. Two Templars who had raced up to help came to halt, glancing about strangely at the listless beggars.

"My lord!" shouted Abu Rashid. "Please, my lord. Do not waste your time on them! Did I not tell you to hurry? Come, let us be gone."

They hurried away from the alley.

Chapter 27

AMONG THE FORGOTTEN
Godfrey

Thirty feet from behind, Godfrey watched as Joscelin rushed away, his hands feeling his neck. He glanced at Jacques. "Interesting little episode, that."

Jacques frowned. "All the more reason to get out of here, Godfrey."

Godfrey laughed. "What is it you're afraid of?"

He walked down the street, carrying a huge sack of bread. He would stop before each beggar, break of a piece from a loaf, and place it in the pauper's bowl.

Jacques glanced around anxiously. "Well, let me see...we're walking through the poorest part of the city with more food than most of these people get in three months, flaunting it for every man to see. You aren't in the least bit frightened we might be robbed?"

Godfrey shrugged. "Not here, no. None of these people seem to have the energy to rob a broken old woman hobbling on a stick, let alone two men with swords. Anyway, we're giving the food away, every man can see that."

Jacques grumbled to himself, keeping a hand on his sword hilt as Godfrey walked down the alley.

"Godfrey," he said finally. "Does it ever occur to you that you're not really doing any good? These men will get a bite to eat for a day, their stomachs will swell up, so then they can die a few days later with pains racking their bellies. It would be more of a mercy to kill them here straight off."

"Do you think?" asked Godfrey as he dropped half a loaf into the cupped hands of an ancient looking woman. Her eyes followed Godfrey as he moved on, but she did not move in any other way. Godfrey murmured a quick blessing on her, and then turned back to Jacques. "I am sure that there are thousands here in this city who would agree with you. These beggars will die, and more poor, starving children who have lost hope will come to take their place. So there will always be the poor, for all eternity, always in the same state, never better, never worse."

"It reminds me," continued Godfrey, "of something I heard, once when I was very young, in the streets of Jerusalem, I heard a man from the Far East, from Persia, who was preaching some strange faith from even Farther East. He said that time turns like a wheel, repeating itself over and over again. He said that men and earthly things die but they are reborn and so they continue on in this illusion from which death is no escape.

"It scared me when I heard it, for it seemed to me that men now preached despair as a religion. If all things on this earth, the bad as well as the good, are too old to die, then nothing really matters. *But it is not that way in Christendom*: in Christendom things do change. Sometimes for good, sometimes for evil. But things *matter*."

"And because things matter, Jacques, these beggars matter. I know that nine out of ten, that ninety-nine out of a hundred, will never even notice the difference, but I am doing this in the hope that one *will* notice. If nothing else, I hope merely to shake up this world of illusion, to bring the hope of change to a few."

Jacques listened silently as Godfrey spoke, but he frowned at the look of desperation that was coming over Godfrey's face.

"What is it, Godfrey?" he asked finally.

"What is what?"

"You've been acting...desperate...for the last few days. What is it?"

Godfrey halted in the middle of the street.

"Desperate?" he said, quietly. "Yes, that might be it."

"What is it, then?"

Godfrey closed his eyes. "Well, you may have guessed. When I start... preaching...like I just was, it's because I'm preaching to myself as much as to you. More, I think. It's just that... these last few days, these last few weeks, even months, I...it...I don't know. It was something that hit me especially hard in the last days at Antioch. Just a sense of purposelessness."

"It's not a question of *knowing* what is right. I've never had any trouble with the knowing. It's just that everything seems so useless. I know that at the end of this life I will pass into a better, but the knowing doesn't help. If I'm just waiting for something better, what is the point here? I think, Jacques...I think I was not meant to be a monk. I want a *woman*, Jacques, a wife."

"Ever since the last battle I've been praying every night that I die in the next one, so I can end this thing. It's a twisted thing to do, I know, but I can't help it. I should never have joined the Temple, but now it's too late to go back, all because of that damned vow. What kind of a God would put anyone through this?"

Jacques stared at Godfrey, shocked at what he saw, and Godfrey knew why. He had always been so careful never to let any of it show. Not he, not Godfrey the bloody saint. He must have been the last person Jacques had expected to be saying this.

Godfrey sank to his knees, dropping the sack of bread. In Jerusalem, the beggars would have made a mad dash for it, trying to get away with as much food as they could carry. In this haunted alleyway, the beggars sat there without noticing.

It came as a final shock to Jacques to see the tears in Godfrey's eyes, and Godfrey could see what Jacques's reaction was: fear.

"Godfrey," he said slowly, "I do not know whether you chose right or wrong, but I know this much: you have helped me, Godfrey, more than you can know. You still do. I think I draw strength from your strength, Godfrey. I have been truly happy as a Templar, truly happy giving myself completely to God, and I think it is because you lead the way."

"Happiness," said Godfrey, bitterly. "That is what I told Andronicus, two years ago. I told him of how Christians are truly happy. How those words ring hollow in my ears now. *Happiness*. I have not known that since I entered the Temple."

"We discussed," said Jacques, "what you told Andronicus. But you speak wrongly: you did not even use the word happiness with him. You said joy. There is a difference, Godfrey, and you know it. Happiness is a mood, just as is your despair. All these things will pass. Joy does not. You still have that, Godfrey. Do not lose it. Now get up—we still have to give out the rest of this bread. Let's make it quick. I don't like being on this street, with so many people staring out into empty space."

Godfrey knelt there on the cobblestones for a long while before he slowly turned to look up at Jacques. A smile crossed his face. "Jacques," he said, "I am glad you entered the Temple with me."

Godfrey picked up the sack again and they went on down the street, giving bread to the poor.

Chapter 28

The Council
Joscelin

$\mathcal{A}$ll the way to the palace, Joscelin could not push from his mind the image of the old man, his eyes focused on nothing, his hands squeezing the life out of Joscelin's throat.

How did that happen? I am five times stronger than him, I should have been able to pull free in an instant. Where did that terrifying strength come from?

Joscelin shuddered.

Abruptly he realized that he was inside the palace now, following Abu Rashid down the corridors. They were heading towards one of the upper rooms, for they had already gone up several flights of stairs.

Rashid stopped before a doorway overhung by strings of glass beads. Two guards stood outside the entrance, leaning on their spears.

"The count of Edessa," said Rashid to the guards. They nodded, and Joscelin passed through the entrance.

The first thing that hit Joscelin as he entered the room was the noise. A dozen people were all yelling at each other, creating a cacophony from which Joscelin could not pick out any individual voices.

He walked down a little hallway, and there was the source of the noise.

Every man of importance in either Egypt or Jerusalem was in that room, bellowing at someone else. Amalric was there, arguing with the Greek *sebastos*, Alexius Vranas. Barisan d'Ibelin and Bertrand de Blanchefort and Gilbert d'Aissailly were there too, arguing with the Egyptian vizier, Shawar, and his captain of the guard, Fahad Adham. A few Egyptian nobles were in one of the corners, watching nervously.

Suddenly, Amalric noticed Joscelin. He turned his back on the red-faced Greek and smiled at Joscelin.

"Ah, Count Edessa. We have been waiting for you."

Slowly, the others noticed him too, and stopped arguing.

Joscelin looked grimly about the room. "I wasn't interrupting anything, Your Grace?"

"No," said Amalric, firmly. "I was just…chastising this Greek. Do you know where the Greek navy was when Shirkuh attacked? We thought they were lost somewhere in the delta, but it turns out they had *gone on ahead!* If they had merely taken the trouble to keep in contact with the army, they could have been there to blunt Shirkuh's drive across the river! But the *sebastos* thought that he could take Cairo on his own, so he went rushing on ahead. Damned Greeks."

Amalric went back to glaring at Alexius Vranas. Shawar smoothed his copper Egyptian face of any expression and spoke up.

"Your Grace," he said respectfully to Amalric. "We should present the problem at hand to the count of Edessa."

"Yes," said Amalric, darting an annoyed look at the vizier.

God's beard, thought Joscelin, *These men will be at each others' throats if the least provocation arises. God send that it does not happen! If Shirkuh can defeat an army twice his size, how ill will it go if this alliance crumbles?*

"You see, Joscelin," said Amalric, "I wanted you to hear our latest piece of intelligence. We know now for sure that Shirkuh did not even try to chase us. Instead, he turned north and is now marching on Alexandria."

"Alexandria?" It was not what Joscelin had expected.

"Alexandria," said Blanchefort, angrily. "We allowed the old fox to trick us again!"

"It's not all that bad," said Amalric. "Let him have Alexandria. It is a useless city, and far off from anything of importance."

"Useless, my lord?" asked Shawar, and there was a dangerous gleam in his eyes. "Not useless. It is vital to our economy, and holds great storehouses of grain—undoubtedly the reason that Shirkuh wants it. We cannot leave it long in the possession of an enemy. And there is worse news yet: the caliph is in Alexandria! I sent him there, thinking that it would be safe. It would seem that it is not."

"Then let them have your stinking caliph, and accept the true Faith!" said Barisan d'Ibelin, taking in all the Muslims in the room with a disgusted look.

This was too much. Joscelin broke in. "Quiet, Ibelin," he said. "We already signed the treaty and said there was to be no talk of conversion, on either side. The king has signed, and his word stands for all Outremer."

Barisan spat. "I obey God, not pieces of paper."

"You obey the king," growled Joscelin.

"*I* do not obey the king!" shouted Gilbert d'Aissailly, the Master of the Hospital. Blanchefort looked as though he had been about to say the same thing, but he could not bring himself to agree on anything with a Hospitaller, so instead he shouted an insult at d'Aissailly.

The whole room erupted in shouting again. The Egyptian nobles huddled in the corner looked as though they were going to try to escape. Every man was red in the face, and some had their hands straying towards their knives when Fahad Adham, a giant, heavily muscled man with a shaved bald head, who had remained silent until now, broke in.

"My lords," he shouted over the din. "My lords, silence, if you will! My lords, I have a proposal!"

Slowly, the din quieted again as men turned to look suspiciously at the Egyptian captain of the guard.

"My lords," he said, "I have a design which, if we move swiftly, may foil even Lord Shirkuh."

"Then speak it, Egyptian!" said Barisan d'Ibelin.

"My lords," said Adham, "may we safely presume that Shirkuh is moving towards Alexandria because he needs grain?"

"Yes," snapped Shawar. "That is why *we* must hold Alexandria."

"If you please, Vizier," said Adham, respectfully. Shawar glared at his captain of the guard, but he said no more.

"My lords," continued Adham, "based on this, may we assume that Shirkuh does not have any good supply of food at the moment?"

There was a ripple of nods from the lords.

"Then," said Adham, "this I propose: Shirkuh seeks to outwit us through sheer audacity and unpredictability. He thinks that we will do him the favor of responding in predictable ways to his unpredictable moves. I suggest that we do just the opposite. Shirkuh thinks that we cannot afford to lose the grain, and so will hold Alexandria at all costs. Instead, we will send messages to the garrison through pigeon post: they must burn all the grain in Alexandria."

"What!" exclaimed Shawar. "Never! You have gone mad, Captain!"

"My lord Vizier, please," said Adham, still firmly.

Shawar eyed his captain for a moment, and then nodded. "Continue."

"We will burn all the grain there," said Adham. "Then, we will have much of the garrison leave quickly, leaving no trace that they were there. When Shirkuh arrives, he will find only a tiny garrison defending the great city. They will put up a fight, just long enough to make it believable, but because they are so few, Shirkuh will not think it strange when they surrender quickly."

"In the meantime," continued the captain, "our armies will board the Greek fleet and sail up quickly behind Shirkuh, giving him as little warning as possible. Shirkuh will take possession of Alexandria and find the granaries empty. He will then want to move on to look for more grain, but it will be too late, because our army will be outside the walls of Alexandria. Shirkuh will find himself trapped in a city without food, besieged by an army that has fully recovered from the battle on the Nile."

"And what of the food?" asked Amalric. "Leaving the enemy without food is all very well, but what of us? We must eat too."

"For this," said Adham, "we will also use the Greek ships. Once they deposit the army outside of Alexandria, they can sail back up and down the Nile, bringing grain from upriver to the army. I have a system organized whereby we can keep a steady flow of food coming to the army."

"And the caliph?" asked Shawar. "We cannot let harm come to him!"

"The caliph," said Adham, "has the great advantage that Shirkuh does not know he is in Alexandria. He will think him safe in Cairo. Let him think so. When the larger part of the garrison leaves Alexandria, they will take the caliph with them, and bring him to safety. The Lady Maryam, too. They will make their way quietly down to Cairo and to safety. Even if Shirkuh were to learn about them, he would be unable to pursue, for by that time our army will be camped outside his walls."

"Captain," said Shawar, "you are remembering the reports coming from the north: the sultan is assembling an army in Damascus to send to Shirkuh's aid; it may be as many as ten thousand men."

Fahad Adham shook his head. "But it is all infantry, and it will take long to assemble. Shirkuh has almost six thousand men—they can't last long with the granaries burnt. Shirkuh will have surrendered long before any relief army can reach us, and an army that is only infantry cannot stand on its own against our combined forces."

Adham finished, and looked up expectantly.

"It is...a daring plan," said Joscelin slowly. "But it is well thought out. It may work."

"Or it may leave us without food on the edge of the sea," growled Barisan d'Ibelin.

"No," said Amalric, "the Egyptian has thought of everything. There are always the ships to bring us food. The Saracens have no navy here on the Nile, no way to cut off the river. The river will keep us supplied."

Amalric nodded. "It is a good plan. I approve of it."

Blanchefort was nodding too. "I agree. It's more than just a good plan, it's brilliant. I think we will outfox the fox this time."

"I like it," said Alexius Vranas. "It is a sound plan. There are not many infantry commanders who understand how to use ships effectively. It appears you are one of them, Captain Adham."

"No," said Gilbert d'Aissailly. "It is folly. We cannot abandon Cairo! Let the Saracens have the bloody city and your cursed heathen pope. They mean nothing to me."

That last comment seemed to push Shawar over the edge. "Yes," he said, "you have done well, Captain. I approve."

Adham smiled.

Gilbert d'Aissailly and Barisan d'Ibelin were moving towards each other, stepping away from the king.

"Your Grace," protested Ibelin, "you cannot do this!"

"Yes, Your Grace," said d'Aissailly. "The Hospital is not behind you in this."

Amalric smiled. "I am going with all of my knights. Let any who fear the infidel flee or cower as he will. The brave go with me to Alexandria. But if either of you stay back now, I will never forgive nor forget your cowardice."

Ibelin and d'Aissailly glanced at each other. Finally they nodded.

"We will go," said d'Aissailly. Barisan d'Ibelin just glared at everyone.

"Good," said Amalric. "Then let us go and ready the army. Shirkuh will be caught like a rabbit in its warren."

At that, everyone made for the door at once. Two of the Egyptian nobles managed to slip out first. Joscelin was close behind them. He did not breathe easily until he was outside and well away from anyone who had been in that room.

Chapter 29

To Alexandria
Joscelin

Two Weeks Later

he boat rocked about gently as Joscelin came to the prow. He leaned against it, gazing down at the slow-moving river.

The sun was shining down on them, making the world seem lazy and slow. For once, Joscelin felt comfortable and content even his full armor. He had wrapped a light sheet of silk about his halfhelm, Egyptian-style, to keep it from absorbing the heat of the sun. His green surcoat kept his armor from growing too hot. The weight did not bother him—he had grown used to that years ago.

Joscelin did not like sailing, not before this, but all his earlier voyages had been at sea. He did not mind the rocking and swaying, but the sight of the waves stretching away until the met the horizon with no land in sight troubled him to no end. Here on the river, however, it was different. He had enjoyed the journey downstream. They had been sailing fast, very fast, but on the river, even that seemed lazy and slow.

"My lord Joscelin?" It was Tristan, attired in a green surcoat that bore the Courtenay sigil. Joscelin glanced at the boy, who was looking more and more like a man every day—he was already taller than Joscelin himself.

"What is it, Tristan?"

"The captain wanted me to tell you that we will be at Alexandria in half an hour."

Joscelin nodded and looked downriver, towards the mouth of the Nile. The boat began to veer to the left. Joscelin glanced to the right and saw a few hippopotami wading through the shallows. The captain was steering away from them. The creatures looked harmless and sluggish enough, but Joscelin had been told that they could smash holes in boats that came too near.

"Are you ready for a battle, Tristan?"

Joscelin had allowed Tristan to fight alongside him in the battle on the Nile. Tristan had slain a mameluke and two Saracen lancers, and come out of the fight completely unscathed. He had refused to wear a helmet, saying that it limited his vision too much, and he had worn only half a hauberk for greater speed. He had performed better than any squire Joscelin had ever seen, better than any knight. No one else was that quick or that graceful, not in the middle of battle.

"Of course, my lord," said Tristan. He fingered his sword hilt impatiently.

Tristan had grown wroth beyond measure in that battle when the trumpets began sounding the retreat. He had cursed the king for a coward and a false knight to retreat in the face of the infidel.

Joscelin glanced at the shore on the left side. He frowned.

"Tell me, Tristan, do you think the boat's getting too close to the shore?"

Tristan came over to the rail to look down, but someone else answered the question first.

"My lord De Courtenay," said the Greek captain, coming to the prow. "Your king wants the army to disembark here. He does not want to present Shirkuh with the opportunity to attack as the army gets off the ships."

Joscelin shrugged. "Very well."

The boat banked against the sandy shore, and the Greek crew hurried along the side, lowering ramps to the ground.

Joscelin straightened. "Come on, Tristan, let's go."

They made for the nearest ramp, climbing slowly over in their armor and onto firm ground. Joscelin glanced back upriver, and saw that all along the shore, the boats were pulling up against the sand, spilling out Frankish and Egyptian soldiery.

The Greeks were running down to open up the lower compartments, and grooms came to lead out the horses for the knights. Tristan got there first, bringing out Joscelin's warhorse. Joscelin mounted as Tristan produced his shield from the pack. He helped Joscelin get the shield on, then went and got his own horse.

Tristan mounted up nimbly and rode to join Joscelin. Joscelin looked out over the mass of soldiers crowding off the boats and caught sight of the Banner of the kingdom flying over it all. That banner would not be far from the king. Joscelin made for it, followed by Tristan.

The usual crowd of sycophants and barons was gathered about Amalric. D'Aissailly and D'Ibelin were there too, both red in the face as though they had just made a last attempt to dissuade Amalric from this attack.

None of the barons got too close to Joscelin; he was always a source of embarrassment to them: a baron, but without lands or money, with only a handful of knights to follow him. Joscelin would have avoided them altogether if Amalric had not needed his help.

Of course, Amalric might beg for his help in private, but he could not be seen being too friendly to Joscelin de Courtenay in front of the barons. So the king passed him by with a scornful look when Joscelin joined the group.

The beach was filling up fast. The Franks and Egyptians were trying to sort themselves out into their separate companies, but it was nearly impossible in the narrow space they were given.

Taking note of this, Amalric began shouting orders for the army to advance. He spurred forward, riding west, away from the river. Joscelin and Tristan followed with the rest of the barons.

When they caught up, the king was roundly cursing the Egyptians, blaming them for slowing down the advance. Joscelin didn't bother listening. He slumped forward in his saddle, feeling drowsy.

Amalric broke off his tirade when they saw Fahad Adham riding towards them on his monstrous camel, his ridiculously large axe strung to the saddle. The captain was called Greataxe by many in Cairo, and seeing the length and weight of his weapon, Joscelin conceded that the title was deserved. The Egyptian vizier had chosen to remain safely back in Cairo, sending Fahad in his stead. It was, as far as Joscelin could see, an unfortunate choice for the king. Shawar was cunning and shrewd, but it was possible to cow him. Nothing seemed to frighten this man, except perhaps the vizier himself.

"Your Grace," said the Egyptian, bowing his shining and hairless head. "We must move quickly. It may be that Shirkuh is trying to flee already."

Amalric's face purpled, but he bit his tongue and nodded dumbly.

The knights of the king's household were assembled by now. Amalric turned deliberately away from the Egyptian and began shouting orders to advance farther. Joscelin sighed. Any hope of catching Shirkuh by surprise was out of the question.

✢ ✚ ✢

Three hours later, the armies of Jerusalem and Cairo began to march the last few miles to Alexandria. They sent outriders far ahead, searching to see if Shirkuh had fled or remained in the city. Joscelin stayed close by the king, hating every moment of it. Half the barons fawned over the king, praising him and laughing at his every jest, while the other half remained on the outside of the group, muttering treasons and curses against the king.

There is not a loyal man among them, thought Joscelin. *Perhaps if a few of them lost their lands, they would come to appreciate true loyalty.*

Blanchefort alone seemed to remain aloof, but Blanchefort had always steered his own course. Blanchefort was a Templar, and Templars were dangerous.

Soon the walls of Alexandria loomed up before them. The outriders began to return, reporting that there was no sign of Shirkuh outside the walls, but Alexandria was defended by a garrison of at least several thousand men.

"Ha!" crowed Amalric. "He has stepped right into the trap! We have caught Shirkuh the Lion at last!"

Fahad Greataxe frowned. "Do not be so sure, Frank. Shirkuh is not blind. Do you think he might have found some store of grain, or that the vizier's orders were not carried out?"

Amalric snorted. "You think too highly of this Saracen. Even men such as he can make blunders."

"He defeated you easily enough both times you fought him. Why do you think he will fail the third time?"

Amalric carefully ignored that question. "This was your stratagem, Egyptian. Do you doubt even your own counsels?"

Joscelin groaned. The king of Jerusalem was squabbling like a child.

So it went as they approached the city, with the king arguing with the Egyptian captain. Had Amalric been a more masterful king, he would not have deigned to argue with an inferior, but Amalric was nothing if not fractious.

God be good, let this quibbling end soon.

God was good, this day at least. The rest of the outriders returned soon, with the unanimous verdict that Shirkuh was inside the walls of Alexandria. There were several thousand men inside the city, which at this point must be the whole of Shirkuh's army.

Amalric was jubilant.

"We'll starve him out. It won't take long, not with that many men in a city without grain. We've won!"

Fahad Adham was not so sure, but he agreed to cooperate. The great Egyptian and Frankish armies began the final march to Alexandria itself, and soldiers began unloading siege weapons from the boats. So the long Siege of Alexandria began amidst squabbling and folly.

Chapter 30

A Minor Disturbance
Joscelin

One Month Later

For a month they besieged Alexandria. For a month they held Shirkuh bottled up with several thousand men, while the Frankish trebuchets pounded the walls relentlessly. The pitiful supply of grain left in the city should have given out within two weeks. Shirkuh should have come slinking out of his hole by the third week, a shrunken, hungry wreck begging for surrender. But instead the garrison held strong for a month.

Halfway through the month, the vizier Shawar arrived. He bided his time until he was sure that the besieging army was in no danger. Then he arrived at Alexandria with several boats loaded with mangonels. The Egyptian siege engines added their fire to the Frankish ones and Shawar rode daily in front of the walls of Alexandria, close enough to be seen but well out of bowshot. He was taunting Shirkuh.

In the fifth week of the siege, the engines opened a breach in the wall. Joscelin was about to lead a band of knights through the breach when Amalric sent a messenger to calling him back for special instructions.

In a black fury, Joscelin pulled the helmet over his head. It was only a half-helm with a nasal, leaving his face mostly unprotected. He was in no mood to bottle himself up in a metal can. If a Saracen arrow took him through the mouth, so be it.

His destrier pawed the earth restlessly, but Joscelin had a tight hold on the reins. He secured the shoulder strap on his shield, and then reached out for Tristan to hand him the lance. It was ten feet of oak and three feet of steel, with the green and white of House Courtenay painted on the wood. At the moment, Joscelin wanted to spear something. Anything or anyone would do.

There was a hole in the walls—an opening in the cursed stone barrier Joscelin had stared at for a month—and suddenly Amalric was ordering him and two thousand men off on some fool's errand to the south. *He cannot really believe that there is another army come to relieve the city. There is no army within a hundred miles that could challenge us.*

The soldiers were assembling a mile south of the city. Joscelin could still hear the sounds of fighting coming from the breach in the wall. His knights were gathered near a grey thicket, their squires rushing about to help them arm.

Having finished assisting Joscelin, Tristan mounted his own palfrey and pulled up next to his lord. Tristan was very lightly armed—his hauberk only went down to his thighs, his shield was small and light, and he wore no helm at all. Yet Joscelin knew that Tristan would prove more deadly in battle than most fully armored knights. It was less than conventional for a squire to fight beside his master, but Tristan was no ordinary squire, and Joscelin had permitted him this much.

Joscelin raised his lance, resting it against his hip. He waited a few minutes for the knights to finish arming, then he spurred forward and they rode after him.

Five minutes later, the whole of Joscelin's force was moving out to the south. There were many trees and thickets here, but none dense enough to hinder the knights' progress.

Half an hour ago, the scouts had begun reporting a body of armed men sweeping up from the south. Amalric had lost his nerve, and pulled two thousand men out of the assault to meet this new threat, giving Joscelin the command. Joscelin had no doubt that the reports were false—it would turn out to be a few scattered Saracen deserters, or some other false alarm. Where would an army come from?

Joscelin had his battle-host spread out over a great distance, so as to sweep out any armed bands trying to hide in the thickets. As soon as there was a sign of battle, the line would fold in on that point, enveloping any audacious fools who thought they could sneak up on twelve thousand soldiers besieging a city.

Twelve thousand men truly was a great host, greater than had been seen in decades. The chroniclers of the First Crusade told of greater numbers, but Joscelin doubted some of them. If a hundred thousand men had really come from Europe in the first place, they were not here now. The armies of Outremer had been fighting battles with armies of two or three thousand for as long as Joscelin could remember. *If only we had more capable commanders, we could work wonders with this army.*

But Amalric and Shawar were hopeless as commanders. The Egyptian, Fahad Greataxe, was competent enough, but his genius showed only in rare bursts. Joscelin had no delusions of his own brilliance. None of them could come close to matching Shirkuh.

"My lord!" shouted Tristan. "Look out!"

In the thicket before them, two Saracens sprang up, horn bows in their hands. They drew them back to fire, aiming straight at Joscelin's face.

Joscelin was not fast enough to react, but Tristan moved before the archers, spurring forward and raising his shield.

The two arrows thudded into the oaken shield. The Saracens turned to run. Now Joscelin found his voice.

"Ride them down!" he bellowed. The knights went charging after them. The Saracens tried to run faster, but the horses were about to trample them down.

The Saracens stumbled and vanished into a ditch that rose up suddenly in the underbrush. Joscelin leveled his lance. His blood was up now, and he was seeing red.

Then a line of mamelukes stood up from where they had been crouching in the ditch. They leveled long steel spears at the charging horsemen.

Joscelin did not hesitate for a moment. He aimed his lance at one of the mamelukes and let go of the reins, pulling a few strides ahead of the line.

His lance took the mameluke through the chest. Joscelin heard a sickening crunch as the steel tip pierced through metal and bone. He felt the familiar snap as the lance broke. Joscelin cast aside the lance-butt and drew his sword.

The Frankish knights swept aside the line of mamelukes with ease. Joscelin reined in and called a halt. The horses cantered to a stop. On those knights with half-helms, Joscelin could see foolish grins on unshaven faces. The battle had barely begun, and they were already giddy with victory.

Joscelin turned his horse sideways to look about the line.

aHOOOOOOOOOOOOOOOOoooooooooooooooo!

No sooner did the line of knights come to a stop than the southron horns began blowing and the thickets to right and left were swarming with more Saracens. They were a disorganized rabble, all on foot, but the ambush had been planned perfectly.

Joscelin looked about desperately. They would have to wheel, and that would take too much time. He glanced back and forth, but could see no advantage in attacking either side.

Indecision is death.

"Right wheel!" he roared, picking at random.

The line of knights wheeled, but already the Saracens were on them, dragging knights off their horses and butchering them.

What was left of the line wheeled and charged. Joscelin went trampling into the midst of the Saracens, leaving spilled blood and torn flesh behind him. A dozen spears were thrust up at him, but they rattled off his chainmail, leaving him unscathed.

Then Joscelin saw a long hook on a pole lifted up towards him. He hacked it off with his sword, but another catchpole came from the other side, hooking onto his belt. Joscelin pulled desperately in the other direction, but the catchpole was stuck fast. There was a sharp tug, and Joscelin was ripped from the saddle.

He landed flat on his back amidst brambles. His half-helm had come off in the fall. He lay there, dazed, expecting to feel a Saracen spear thrust into his stomach at any moment.

All around him, he could hear the ring of steel, but the Saracens seemed not to have noticed him. He leaned his head over and saw a pair of leather-clad feet stepping about from side to side. Dizzily, he sat up, and saw why he was still alive.

Tristan was standing over him, on foot, his sword red with blood. The Saracens pressed in, but he held them back. His shield had splintered, but he fought on with his broadsword, wielding it as though it were as light as a stick.

Joscelin pushed himself up, groaning under the weight of his mail. He struggled to his feet, put his back to Tristan, and raised his sword. A Saracen tried to split open Tristan's back, and instead Joscelin opened up his skull. But even that blow was clumsy and ill-aimed. Joscelin had fought all his battles from horseback; he could not fight like this.

"Run, my lord!" shouted Tristan. "Run! The king needs you!"

And Joscelin did, throwing honor to the winds. He ran through the brambles, though his legs ached already.

Two of the Saracens tried to break away and follow, but Tristan was in the way first, cutting them down and spinning on to face the next man.

Everywhere Joscelin looked, he could see only swarms of Saracens surrounding little groups of Franks. He had led them into a disaster.

This is Shirkuh's work.

Joscelin was hard of breath already. *I am too fat for this.* He stumbled, caught himself, and went on running at a slower pace. *Oh God, I am too fat for this!*

From behind him he heard a cry. He glanced back and saw a Saracen horseman, the first mounted foe he had seen among that crowd. The

Saracen spurred forward, raising a long scimitar.

Joscelin did not want to try to outrun a horse. He wanted nothing more than to collapse on the ground and die. Instead he stood and held his sword ready.

I am the last count of Edessa. I will not be taken prisoner. I will not rot in a dungeon.

Joscelin braced himself to fight, and to keep on fighting until they killed him. He did not let himself think that he would die leading two thousand others to their deaths.

The Saracen came riding down, ready to sweep Joscelin's head off with that scimitar. Joscelin held his sword in readiness, waiting....waiting...

There was an explosion of pain in the back of his head as something heavy slammed down on it. For five seconds Joscelin's skull screamed in agony, then blackness overtook him.

Chapter 31

THE KING
Amalric

The sun was setting as a grizzled but smiling Saracen mameluke stepped aboard the ship, bearing the white flag of truce. Four Kurdish lancers waited for him on the shore as the ship rocked gently in the Nile, held fast by its anchor.

Placing his fist over his heart, the mameluke bowed respectfully to the king of Jerusalem.

"Your Grace," said the Saracen in broken Frankish, "I am Ali Nu'man, the captain of mamelukes. Lord Shirkuh has sent me to negotiate the peace."

Amalric felt anger rising in him that Shirkuh, who had done nothing more than get trapped inside the city and hide like a rat for four weeks, would demand his surrender. All his honor, all his chivalric pride, shouted their protest.

"I will not surrender to Shirkuh. I will surrender to the man who commanded this new army, the man who *defeated* me."

Just as the wall was breached, just as Alexandria was within their grasp, a mighty Saracen host had attacked from the south, unheralded and unexpected. It had swept away Joscelin and the Frankish rear, crushing the Christian and Egyptian forces even as they poured into the city. The plain between the siegeworks and the river was littered with bodies from the great battle that had raged about Alexandria. But the battle was over now. The Franks had fled to their ships while the Egyptians scattered.

Ali Nu'man smiled again. "Your Grace," he said in his thick Syrian accent, "Shirkuh *is* the man who commanded the relief army."

Amalric scowled. "Shirkuh was penned up in Alexandria, cowering behind crumbling stone walls for the last month."

The mameluke shook his head. "Your Grace, I fear you were deceived. When Lord Shirkuh found that there was no grain in Alexandria, he left with most of his army. They filtered across Egypt in small groups, making their way to Damascus. There Shirkuh took command of the relief army that the sultan was assembling, and returned to save the garrison he had left in Alexandria."

Amalric gaped. "But when we first arrived, the walls were packed with soldiers. Shirkuh had but four thousand men. How...?"

"Your Grace," said Ali, "Lord Shirkuh left but a thousand men in Alexandria, which is why the food was able to last them so long. For the rest...wooden figures dressed in clothing, townsmen paid to stand on the walls, and the like. Perhaps you should have taken a closer look a the soldiers you saw on the ramparts."

"God's blood, your Shirkuh is no man. He's a conjurer...a devil."

Ali merely smiled again. "Can you make peace with a devil? Or would you like him to finish you all? This I swear to you: none of you will leave Egypt alive if you choose to continue the war."

The threat made Amalric's blood rise again, but he glanced back across the corpse-littered plain, and knew it was not an idle one.

"Hold your tongue, sandpig—you have no right to speak to a king so. Return to your master. Tell him...tell him that we will have peace."

✠ ✠ ✠

It was raining the day they returned to Jerusalem.

The whole army was miserable. The roads turned to mud. The food was soaked, hair was soaked, clothes were soaked.

"God does not answer men who come before him as kings," William of Tyre had told him half a year ago. *"Before Him, you are no greater than the Moorish slave who cleans the privies of Damascus."*

Before the rain, thought Amalric grimly, *we are all the same too. I am just as wet as the lowest footman marching in the rear.* He could not remember a worse moment in his life. *Not even when I found that Agnes hated me.*

Amalric was about to send for Joscelin, but then he remembered that Joscelin was not there. Joscelin had been captured, taken by the Saracens in that last battle outside Alexandria. Amalric had tried to arrange for the ransom of prisoners with Shirkuh, but Shirkuh had flatly refused. His captives would go with him to Damascus. And it was no wonder—with all the riches of Egypt at Shirkuh's disposal, he had no need for ransom money. So Amalric had left his friend to the infidels. Joscelin would rot in some Saracen dungeon, just as his father had.

Joscelin was gone. There was no one left who he could trust. Amalric had paid a high price for the crown.

Who can take his place? Amalric asked himself. *Bohemund of Antioch is still a boy, Barisan d'Ibelin is too ambitious, Gilbert d'Aissailly corrupt, Bertrand de Blanchefort serves only the interests of the Temple. Joscelin wanted nothing more than his lost county of Edessa. The others all want something of mine.*

But with a rush of panic, Amalric realized he had lost even more than that in Joscelin, for Joscelin was the one he had entrusted his children to if anything should happen to him. Amalric needed some assurance that his children would be safe—Sybilla, his oldest, nine years old, with her dark curly hair. She was going to be a beauty such as had never been seen in the Holy Land. And Baldwin, seven, already showing the mark of a warrior. He loved them more than any other. They were the last piece of Joscelin and Agnes left to him: Agnes's children and Joscelin's nephew and niece.

Even if I make a miserable king, Amalric told himself, *they will make up for it. I will have a son and daughter so strong and so beautiful that everyone will love them.*

While Joscelin was there, Amalric had not feared for them. Joscelin would hold to his word; Joscelin would protect them. Now, though, Joscelin was gone, and Amalric was afraid.

The gates of Jerusalem loomed up before him. The rain still poured down. Amalric rode through the gate, his head bent, his shoulders sagging.

Scarcely anyone was there to greet them. Word had traveled before them of the defeat Shirkuh had inflicted on them. No one came out this day to cheer a conquered king.

Already, most of the knights had left for their own cities. At Ascalon, Amalric's column had broken off from the rest of the army, going back to Jerusalem with only the Hospitallers and Templars to accompany them. The knights of Ibelin and Ascalon and Jaffa and the Northern Principalities had ridden on along the sea road to their homes.

As Amalric looked at the tired, beaten knights riding through the gates with him, he knew that more than even Joscelin had been lost. Egypt had been lost—lost to the Arabic sultan, Nur ad-Din. And once Egypt was under the sultan's control, Jerusalem would follow soon. With a feeling of despair, the king of Jerusalem realized that besides leaving his only loyal friend behind in Egypt, he had left behind any hope of saving the kingdom. He had sacrificed Agnes for nothing.

✠ ✠ ✠

Inside the palace, Amalric went to the banquet hall. The tables were empty and forlorn; the tapestries looked withered and old. There were no fires burning in the pits, and the spring chill hung heavy in the air.

Amalric sat down on one of the long benches and waited. He had sent servants out with his orders, and it would not be long.

It took half an hour. The chill was just beginning to settle in when a servant announced the Archbishop William of Tyre.

Amalric rose.

"Your holiness, it is good to see you."

William of Tyre said nothing, merely walked in and stood there, on a level with Amalric.

"What have you heard, Archbishop?"

"Many things. You were defeated and badly. That much I know."

Amalric nodded. "Twice Shirkuh smashed our armies. Once on the banks of the Nile, and again before the walls of Alexandria. In the second battle, he captured Joscelin de Courtenay."

"The count of Edessa?" William looked surprised. "Will they ransom him?"

Amalric shook his head. William sighed.

"Just like his father. They say that they tortured Joscelin the Second before the end, to try to force him to renounce Christianity. Do you think they will do the same with the son?"

Amalric shrugged. "I do not know. I am going to be very blunt, Archbishop. Whatever they do to Joscelin, he is beyond my help. He was the only one of my barons I trusted. In fact, he was one of two living men whom I trust. The other is you."

William inclined his head. "I am honored, Your Grace."

"Don't waste your breath, Archbishop. I have no stomach for flattery. You are a godly man, that is enough. I need to know this: is there any warrior whom I can trust beyond doubt to protect my son?"

William raised his eyebrows. "Is he in danger, Your Grace?"

"Any prince is always in danger. Leave it at this, Archbishop. I want him to live. Who can I trust to protect him?"

William of Tyre thought for a moment. "There is one I know, Your Grace. I will have to speak to Blanchefort first…"

"The Templars?" Amalric grimaced. "I do not trust Blanchefort."

"You need not, Your Grace. Blanchefort will not be guarding your son. There is a Templar I know, though, whom I would trust with my life. He is very good with a sword; trained by some Greek blademaster. Make him the captain of your son's bodyguard, Your Grace, and Baldwin will be safe."

Amalric frowned. "And if Blanchefort tries to use this Templar as an agent?"

William shook his head. "The man I am thinking of would not allow it. He would defy any human power before he broke faith with one to whom he owed it. You may find him...annoyingly virtuous...but that is his worst fault."

Amalric nodded. "I trust your word, Archbishop. You cannot guess what it means to me... my daughter, and especially my son."

The archbishop raised his brows. "Are you playing favorites with your children, Your Grace?"

The king sighed. "No, Archbishop, but Baldwin is my heir."

William of Tyre nodded in reluctant agreement.

"I am fast realizing that I have failed. In the past, there has always been some hero who barely saves the Kingdom of Jerusalem when it is threatened. Well," said Amalric, "I tried to be that hero, and instead I have put Jerusalem into greater danger. My only hope now of accomplishing anything is to raise a son who will be so great that he can save the Holy City. I *must* see my son grow up, Archbishop. Can you understand that?"

William inclined his head. "Yes, Your Grace, I can understand that."

Amalric breathed a sigh of relief. He had not realized until that moment just how anxious he had been about the archbishop's response. But William of Tyre understood. Everything would come out right.

"I should also tell you," said William to the king, "you are wanted at court. The upper halls of the palace are flooded with Greeks. There's Heraclius Felos, the emperor's ambassador, and the *sebastos* Vranas. He arrived in Tyre with his fleet long before you made it to Ascalon. He sent the fleet on to Constantinople and came here instead, I think he merely wants to complain and to quarrel. Then there's your brother's widow, Theodora—she has come to see you. And one more: a renegade cousin of the emperor, called Andronicus Comnenus."

Chapter 32

THE CHILD
Baldwin

Sir Balian d'Ibelin was showing him how to joust when the Templars arrived.

Baldwin liked being taught by Balian—Balian could ride like no one else in the kingdom could. But much as he liked it, it didn't quite feel right. His uncle Joscelin had always taught him before.

His uncle was not as good a rider as Balian, but Baldwin liked him much better. Joscelin was very fat, and always happy, at least while in Baldwin's presence. Baldwin had seen him, sometimes, when Joscelin thought he was alone with the king. Then Joscelin would grow angry, or glum. Sometimes Baldwin thought that Joscelin hated his father. But as long as Joscelin knew Baldwin was there, he would be happy.

All that was unimportant now, for Joscelin was gone. Baldwin had cried when his father the king had first told him that Joscelin was not coming back. His father had looked sad also, though his mother had only looked unhappy. Baldwin didn't know quite why, but there was a difference between his father's sorrow and his mother's unhappiness.

Baldwin had not cried for long, however. He was seven now, and he was a king's son. A prince, he knew, did not cry. A prince learned to fight, so he could ride to war and rescue his dear fat uncle.

They had given him a pony to ride—he was not yet big enough even for a palfrey. Before going to Egypt a second time, the king had ordered a small hauberk fitted for Baldwin. The chainmail had proved too heavy for him, but Baldwin had taken a small buckler from the rack to use as a shield, and he had the blunted lance that his uncle Joscelin had shorn down to the right length for him.

Uncle Joscelin had been a better teacher than Sir Balian. Joscelin had always shown Baldwin how to *fight*. He would demonstrate how to ride down an enemy who was on foot, how to spear an enemy horseman, how to use a sword. Sir Balian only seemed concerned with the niceties of jousting.

Baldwin's uncle had taught him long ago that jousting was a dandy's sport, a sport that true warriors avoided. When Baldwin told that to Balian, Balian had laughed and told him that Joscelin only said it because he had never been good at the joust—he was too fat. Baldwin didn't believe a word Balian said, though. He knew that his uncle could have unhorsed Balian if he had wanted to.

Balian had also laughed when Baldwin told him the reason he wanted to learn more about fighting was so that he could go rescue his uncle Joscelin from prison. That was the annoying thing about Balian. He was a valiant knight, and was always kind to Baldwin, but he seemed to laugh at everything Baldwin said. Uncle Joscelin had never done that. Balian had said that if the prince wanted to free his uncle, he had better start opening some books and learning to lead an army—his personal prowess would not help against the whole Saracen army.

Baldwin knew better than that, though. He had heard the histories of Godfrey de Bouillion and Bohemund, and Charlemagne and Roland. He knew that a great knight could scatter an enemy army if his prowess was great and his heart was pure. It did not happen often, that was certain, but if a knight devoted himself to attaining such a goal and did not falter, Baldwin had no doubt that he would attain it. Baldwin would do anything to save his uncle.

He had tried to imagine his fat uncle in some dirty Saracen prison, being tortured by dreadful Paynims, but he could never quite picture it. Joscelin was always happy underneath, even when he grew angry with the barons or with the king. Baldwin simply could not imagine him lying in a cell with no light and little food. Joscelin deserved to be happy, and God would not deny him that.

So every day after he heard that Joscelin was captured, Baldwin had dragged Balian from his duties to the practice field, to teach him to fight. It was not as good as learning from Joscelin, but it had a real purpose now.

Balian was just showing him how to set his lance in rest when the Templars came into the practice yard. There were four of them, young men, but they sported thick beards, as all Templars did.

Balian reined in his horse and gestured for Baldwin to do the same. With some difficulty, Baldwin pulled in the reins until his pony came to a halt. He followed Balian's lead and got his pony to trot around and face the Templars.

One of them stepped forward and inclined his head respectfully. "My lord prince," he said. "Your father has assigned us to be your guard." The

Templar looked younger even than Balian. He had black hair, and his skin was darker than most.... *What was that word father used? A poulain.*

Baldwin looked curiously at them. His father had told him about the Templar guards, but Baldwin had not thought much of it until now. He was not used to having guards about him.

"All of you at once?" inquired Balian. "Won't you get in the prince's way?"

"Only one at a time, sir knight," said the Templar.

Balian frowned. "Why does the king think his son needs a bodyguard?"

The Templar shrugged. "Ask his Grace." Then he turned to Baldwin and bowed. "My lord prince, my name is Godfrey de Montferrat. My sword is at your service."

Baldwin inclined his head and replied graciously as he had been taught. "I accept your service, Sir Godfrey."

Godfrey smiled. "Thank you, my lord. My companions are Jacques de Maille," he pointed to a knight with blond hair and beard, "Arnold de Torroga," he pointed to a Spanish knight with a scraggly dark beard that bordered on a goatee, "and Robert de Ais," he pointed to a big man with thick arms and a tawny golden beard.

The Templars bowed, and Baldwin inclined his head. He turned to Balian. "Thank you for your training, Sir Balian," he said gravely. "I give you leave to return to your duties, if you wish."

Balian appeared to stifle a laugh, and nodded. "Thank you, my lord." He saluted the prince, and then rode off. As he rode by Godfrey, he frowned for a moment, then his face lit up.

"Godfrey de Montferrat? I remember you...back in Egypt. Not this time, but the one before. I talked to you when we got back to Jerusalem. Do you remember?"

Godfrey's face had brightened too at that. "Yes," he said, "I do. Sir Balian d'Ibelin."

Balian smiled. "The king has chosen well in his choice of a bodyguard." He nodded again, and then rode out of the practice yard.

Godfrey then came forward and bowed again before the prince. "My lord," he said, "we will take turns guarding you—we will divide the day into three parts, with one of us remaining awake every night. I am to take the first shift guarding you. You may act as you always do—just pretend that we're not here. We will not disturb you, nor speak unless you wish us to." Godfrey nodded to the other three Templars, who bowed and left the yard.

Baldwin looked curiously at the Templar. "Have you fought before, Sir Godfrey?"

Godfrey smiled. "I have. Twice. In Egypt."

Baldwin nodded. "Have you ever jousted in a tournament?"

Godfrey's face wrinkled in dislike. "No, my lord. I am a passable swordsman, but I have never enjoyed the joust. I am not even sure that my vows would allow it. But even before I entered the Temple, I was not much of a tilter."

Baldwin smiled, glad to have found someone else besides Joscelin who looked down on jousting. "I agree, Sir Godfrey. I don't like jousting either. Will you show me how to fight?"

Godfrey glanced at Baldwin's pony. "Shall I get a horse from the stables?" he asked.

"Teach me to use a sword," said Baldwin eagerly. "On foot."

Godfrey's face lit up a second time. "As my lord commands."

The Templar helped Baldwin down from the saddle, and together they led the pony back to the stables. Leaving it in the care of a groom, the two of them went into another section of the practice yard.

Here the yard was full of baskets with wooden swords. There were a handful of knights hacking away at each other with their false weapons. Those who noticed the little prince all paused and saluted when they saw him, then returned to thrust and parry.

Baldwin hurried over to a basket where his own wooden sword was—it had been made just for him, also by his uncle Joscelin. It was hacked down to just the right length for his arm.

Godfrey was getting a sword for himself out of the basket. He chose a one-handed sword, and a short one at that. Baldwin frowned.

"Take a bigger sword," he said. "I want you to fight just like you would fight the infidel. That's what uncle Joscelin always did."

Godfrey blinked. "I always use a sword like this, my lord. A longsword is no good in the hack and return of close combat—you don't have enough room." The Templar unfastened the real sword that hung at his side and held it out for Baldwin to examine. Sure enough, it was similar in length.

The Templar shrugged. "But, if my lord wishes…" he began to search for a longer sword.

"No!" said Baldwin quickly. "If that's the sword you would use to fight the infidel, use it when you fight me."

Godfrey smiled. "Yes, my lord."

Godfrey proved to be a good teacher. Not as good as Joscelin, that was certain, but much better than Balian. Godfrey spoke to Baldwin as he seemed to speak to everyone else: frankly, and a little distantly, as though half his mind was somewhere else. Balian had talked down to Baldwin, and Baldwin hated that. Godfrey still wasn't the same as Uncle Joscelin, but he would do. When Balian had laughed, it had always seemed like some sort of private joke at Baldwin's expense. When Godfrey laughed, though, he seemed to be laughing at himself as well as the rest of the world. Baldwin usually didn't understand *why* Godfrey was laughing, but he knew instinctively that whatever the joke, it was one in which he was included, so he laughed with Godfrey.

Baldwin learned much more about parrying and striking, than he had ever learned with Joscelin or Balian. Joscelin had taught him all the necessary attacks and defenses, but he was a slow fighter, and Baldwin had had no trouble parrying most of his blows. Baldwin had asked once how his uncle managed to survive battles, and Joscelin had told him that in a real battle, strength mattered more than speed. Baldwin believed him—his Uncle Joscelin was accounted a mighty warrior, and he could pick Baldwin up with one arm.

Godfrey was not strong, but he was *fast*. He lacked the grace of movement that most knights had, but he made up for it with sheer audacity and an uncanny sense of where to strike. True to his word, he fought just as he would against an infidel, and Baldwin found himself being rapped over the arms and chest with astonishing speed.

Eventually, he began to catch on. If they had fought with real swords, of course, he would have been dead on the first blow. With wooden swords, however, he let himself die a few times, and watched the ways that Godfrey killed him. After a few more tries, he managed to parry some of Godfrey's attacks. He was sweating now, sweating hard, but Godfrey smiled in admiration as his blows were warded off.

"Bati!" came a voice to Baldwin's left. Godfrey lowered his sword and turned to look. Baldwin leapt in, stabbing upwards, jabbing the wood into Godfrey's stomach. Godfrey doubled over, the breath going out of him. He gasped for a few moments, then he started laughing.

"Well struck, my lord."

Baldwin smiled back at Godfrey and turned to face the newcomer, though he already knew who it was.

"Bati!" His sister Sybilla was running across the practice yard, her dark curls bouncing in the wind. She was two years older than him—nine. Balian always warned Baldwin that one day he would have to stop playing with her since she was, after all, a girl. But none of that mattered to Baldwin. To him she was just Bili, no more, no less. She was always his first friend and teacher, though he knew that he would soon outstrip her in riding, the pastime they shared constantly.

"I came to ride with you!" she said as she came to a halt before him, breathless. "But Balian said you had sent him away. Why'd you do that? And who's this?" She frowned up at Godfrey.

Baldwin smiled proudly. "This is my bodyguard, Godfrey. He's teaching me to fight. I just killed him."

Sybilla smiled back. "No one can beat a prince. Except a princess." She grabbed a wooden sword from the rack and began hacking at him. Baldwin was quick to defend himself—after Godfrey, Bili's blows seemed slow and clumsy. Godfrey laughed as the two went at it, and Baldwin laughed with him for the sheer joy of it.

"My prince!"

Both Baldwin and Sybilla fought on a few moments longer, and then dropped their swords by unspoken consent and turned to see who was addressing Baldwin.

A youth was standing there. He looked nearly a man to Baldwin, but he could not guess his age. He had curly black hair, and looked just a little effeminate. At closer glance, though, Baldwin saw that his arms rippled with muscles.

"My prince," he said. "Do you wish to learn the art of swordplay?"

Baldwin frowned at the youth, wondering if he were stupid. "That's what I'm *doing*, can't you see? Sir Godfrey is teaching me." He nodded at the Templar.

Smiling, the other replied, "My prince, the Templars know little of swordplay. Their training consists of spending an hour a day hacking at a wooden block. I can teach you, if you wish."

Godfrey's face twisted in irritation, but he remained silent. Baldwin saw it, though.

"My prince," continued the youth, "this Templar can show you how to hack and bash, but I can show you how to *dance*."

Baldwin made a face. "I don't want to dance. I want to *fight*. Who are you, anyway? Are you a knight?"

"No, my prince, I am only a squire, though I could carve up any knight who challenged me to combat. My name is Tristan de Monglane. I was—I *am*—squire to Joscelin de Courtenay, count of Edessa."

"Yes!" said Sybilla, smiling up at him. "I remember you. Uncle Joscelin said that you were the best swordsman he knew."

Baldwin frowned. "You knew Uncle Joscelin?"

Tristan nodded. "Yes, my prince. I am his squire. I have not given up on him. I will rescue him, my prince, if he cannot be ransomed."

Sybilla seemed to have made up her mind already.

216

"Let *him* teach you, Baldwin. He can make up for Uncle Joscelin, if anyone can."

Baldwin shook his head, peering suspiciously at Tristan. "He can't make up for Uncle Joscelin...he's not *big* enough." Baldwin turned desperately to Godfrey. "What do you think, Sir Godfrey?"

The hint of a smile crossed Godfrey's face. He turned to Tristan.

"Perhaps, Tristan de Monglane, you would care to prove your claims?" Godfrey stepped forward, hefting his false sword.

Tristan smiled. "Very well," he said, taking a wooden longsword from the rack. "You may find another knight to help you. I will take on any two challengers." This offer was made without malice, or even condescension. Tristan de Monglane knew what he could do, and could speak of it without boasting.

Godfrey took it as an insult anyway. He spat as he began walking across the sand of the practice yard. "One Templar will be enough to take on the likes of you."

Then Tristan began to move. He sped forward, cutting across the sand, making a fast stroke that was clearly intended to cleave Godfrey in two.

But Godfrey was no longer there. He twisted swiftly and struck downward, trying to take off Tristan's arm as he stabbed.

Tristan drew his arm back just in time, so Godfrey's sword struck his with a CLACK, driving it down into the ground. Tristan tried to disengage and stumbled backwards clumsily. No longer did he seem graceful or powerful.

A moment later, though, he recovered his poise and, angered at his mistake, renewed the attack. Now Tristan truly began to dance, driving Godfrey back across the sand.

Baldwin watched eagerly as the wooden swords CLACKED against each other. Godfrey had none of Tristan's grace or agility, or even his strength. It would have seemed an uneven match, but Godfrey seemed to make up for all else that he lacked with a sort of raw speed, and a sort of common sense that many men left behind when they entered the practice yard or the battlefield. Godfrey did not bother parrying blows that would not otherwise score a solid hit. Instead he merely stepped back and let them fall short, then would strike back before his foe could bring his blade into line.

The sun rose higher in the sky, and still the two of them fought. Sweat was rolling down their faces, and they were beginning to slow just a little. Baldwin watched hopefully each time Godfrey struck, wanting each blow to strike Tristan's neck. They never did. Godfrey was constantly moving, jumping forward and back, but Tristan only stood there, parrying each blow with ease, sometimes spinning, always riposting.

It all ended very abruptly. Tristan had had enough of it, and was ready to end it. He lunged forward, sword stabbing outward, putting his whole body into it. It was fast and it was accurate. The sword drove home towards Godfrey's chest.

Godfrey reacted almost contemptuously. He spun aside slowly, fully aware that Tristan was unable to stop his attack. He spun around completely and brought his sword hard into Tristan's ribs even as Tristan tried to turn and face him.

Tristan dropped his sword and stood there, panting. Godfrey lowered his weapon and faced him, expressionless, squinting to keep the sweat out of his eyes.

Then Tristan laughed. "You're good, Templar. Better than most. I was accounted the best at swordplay among the king's knights before this day." He reached out a hand, and Godfrey took it, dropping his sword and smiling. Their sweaty hands clasped hard, and then Tristan released him to wipe the sweat from his brow.

Sybilla scowled, but Baldwin was already running as soon as Tristan had laughed. He stopped a few feet in front of Godfrey, beaming up at him. "Sir Godfrey! You won!"

Chapter 33

MEMORY FROM BEYOND THE SEA
Godfrey

S ome hours later, Jacques arrived to relieve Godfrey. The prince gave a fond farewell—in Godfrey he had found a new hero. Godfrey's head spun in confusion as he left the Palace. There was elation in his mind: elation at his triumph and elation at the admiration of the prince of Jerusalem. But there was also sadness—sadness and longing.

Put it all aside, Godfrey. You must seek after the glory of God, not after earthly things. You know this all too well. Turn it all to God's purpose, not your own. That is the only way to find joy.

He left the palace and strode out into the streets. Dusk had fallen over Jerusalem, and the sunset left the sky awash with glorious autumnal colors. The longing in Godfrey's heart was stirred up all the stronger at the sight. It was a strange longing that tugged at his heart, a longing for something he could not quite place; something...

A youth was waiting in the corner of a street, watching Godfrey pensively as he left the palace. Godfrey glanced over at him, and realized with a start that it was Joscelin's squire, the young man whom he had just fought at the sparring yard.

"Sir Godfrey," he said, stepping forward.

"Tristan," said Godfrey in greeting. A sudden thought struck him. "Tristan, with your master gone, are you fed? And lodged? Do you need food or a place to stay?"

Tristan's face darkened. "I have taken care of it myself, Sir Godfrey. For now, I came to tell you...tell you how important the prince is."

"Well," said Godfrey, "he *is* the prince."

"But more than that," said Tristan. "You must see how much more important he is than other princes. My master, Lord Joscelin, loved Jerusalem, loved Outremer. Do you love Jerusalem, Godfrey?"

"Yes," breathed Godfrey. "That is why I came here from across the sea."

"Then," said Tristan, "you must feel the danger she is in—know how precariously she has always been perched here on the coast, surrounded by her enemies."

"I do feel her peril," said Godfrey. "I came to defend her, to stave that peril back if I could."

"Well," said Tristan, "you must have seen by now that Amalric has failed as king. But Joscelin always knew he would fail: he told me so years ago. That is why Amalric's son is so important. His son must be a hero; his son must be greater than an ordinary man, greater than an ordinary king. I wish to God that I had been chosen for your position, to guard him with my life. For you will do more than keep him safe, you and the other guards. With Joscelin gone, and the king busy with his duties, it will be those who are placed around the prince that will form him. So you must form him into a hero, Godfrey."

Godfrey frowned. "Why are you telling me this?"

"Because," said Tristan, "it is what Lord Joscelin would want me to do. Joscelin loved Jerusalem, and Joscelin loved Baldwin."

Godfrey looked Tristan in the face, meeting his sad, dark eyes. Very suddenly, he was conscious that this boy had grown up too fast—he was trying to be the peer of all the knights and lords of Jerusalem at the age of sixteen. *Poor lad*, thought Godfrey, pity welling up in his heart. And at that thought Godfrey felt very old, though he was only twenty-four.

"I will do it," said Godfrey firmly.

"You will make him into a hero?"

"Insofar as it lies in my power, Baldwin will become a king who will make the nations tremble. He will be greater than Roland and Charlemagne, greater than Constantine and the Caesars, greater than David himself, if that is what is needed to save Jerusalem."

Tristan nodded wearily. "Thank you, Sir Godfrey." He turned to leave.

"Tristan," said Godfrey, "the Temple can offer you food and lodging for a night, and can help you—"

"I have taken care of it already," snapped Tristan. He turned and vanished down an alley. Godfrey paused a moment, pondering whether or not to follow him, but he was needed back at the Temple, and Godfrey knew he would not be able to help Tristan short of dragging him unwilling to food and shelter. So he turned wearily and made his way towards the Temple.

The elusive longing still tugged at his heart as he trudged through the streets. Godfrey pondered this new task he had taken upon himself. For years his dream was to be the hero who saved Jerusalem. But perhaps if he could not be that hero, he could form that hero. Perhaps he could give everything for Baldwin, and make him into the hero Godfrey himself had wanted to be. Already the prince showed spirit and promise surprising for a seven year old.

Godfrey remembered Baldwin and Sybilla dancing about with their wooden swords, and as he did so he once again remembered Conrad and Adelaise dancing about with wooden swords, in the practice yard of Montferrat Castle, Adelaise laughing and Conrad yelling.

Godfrey's head spun and his heart thumped loudly as he remembered that day, and the days after it...the nights when he and Adelaise would sit in their corner and talk of the stories that Otto of Freising told, talk of their brothers and cousins, talk of the future.

At the age of thirteen, Godfrey had dreamed of going to the pope and getting a dispensation to marry his cousin—it had happened before, and could happen again. But this, he had soon realized, was folly, and he had given up any hope of marrying Adelaise. The realization had left him confused and uncertain, but his teacher, Otto, had helped him through, and told him to read the lives of the saints.

Godfrey, who loved the old churchman dearly, had obeyed. He had read Augustine and Bernard of Clairvaux, Anthony and Athanasius. Reading these had awoken in him an even older desire: the desire to be a hero—a desire first planted years ago when his aunt Julitta had read the great histories and myths to the scrawny, forlorn child who came from the Land Beyond the Sea.

At that time, all of Godfrey's heroes fell into two categories: warriors and saints. So it was that somewhere in his head, the two kinds fused together in his mind, and so Godfrey de Montferrat had conceived the idea of becoming a Templar, a warrior monk.

He had wanted badly to become a Templar. And yet, at the same time, he hated the idea and feared it. He feared giving up marriage, feared the giving up everything. For a time, Godfrey tried to put off the decision. He tried to savor those years in Montferrat Castle, but he found that he could not enjoy the time spent when he was *trying* to savor it. At last, he had gone to his uncle and aunt and told them he had decided to enter the Temple.

The weeks that followed this announcement had been weeks of joy and anguish, weeks of comfort and torment. They had been paradoxical and confused, but one memory stood out in Godfrey's mind. It was a memory that had returned to his mind when he dueled Tristan...

✟ ✟ ✟

He was eighteen, standing in the practice yard of Montferrat Castle, only this time Conrad was not there. Instead he and Jacques faced each other, wielding their practice swords. And Adelaise was watching.

Adelaise was at her most beautiful then, her hair long, brown, curled; her bosom full, her hips smooth and rounded, and her face lovely enough to set most men's hearts pounding. Godfrey had unconsciously walked a narrow line, pulled towards Adelaise even as he tried to flee from her. He knew the only safety would be to forget her. But that he could not do while he lived at Montferrat Castle.

In the days after his announcement, Godfrey had tried to find solace with his friends, Conrad and Jacques. He had gone often to the practice yard with them, and tried to forget Adelaise in the midst of their mock duels.

On this particular day, however, Adelaise came to watch. And that had changed everything. For when she came and began talking with Jacques, an insane jealousy stirred within Godfrey, so that when he and Jacques began to spar, it was no longer a practice, but a duel.

As they fought, Godfrey became aware of a great many things. Jacques was taller than he; Jacques was stronger. Godfrey's arms were thin and scrawny while Jacques's whole body rippled with youthful strength. Jacques's face was pleasant and handsome, while Godfrey was ill-favored. Jacques moved, if not with grace, with an air of strength and confidence, while Godfrey was clumsy. All this became apparent to Godfrey under Adelaise's gaze as he and Jacques fought. Godfrey struck hard and bitterly, and Jacques fought back viciously in self-defense. When Jacques at last defeated Godfrey and clapped him on the shoulder, smiling, Godfrey felt hate in his heart for perhaps the first time...

✠ ✠ ✠

As the days went by after that, Godfrey and Jacques grew farther apart, and Jacques began seeing more of Adelaise. Godfrey became sullen and twisted with envy. He was jealous of Jacques simply because Jacques was not Adelaise's cousin. In those days, he had come dangerously close to forgetting his dream of being a hero. At times, the mere goal of hurting Jacques or Adelaise seemed a noble enough purpose to which to devote his life.

Ordinarily, Adelaise of Montferrat would have been well out of Jacques's reach. She was the eldest daughter of a powerful baron, related to the pope and the German emperor. She was a match for a king. However, William de Montferrat seemed to have picked up a curious affection for Jacques, an affection that became love. Godfrey's jealousy only increased at this, for it seemed that now William de Montferrat loved Jacques as a son, loved him as he had *never loved Godfrey. Such was William's love for Jacques that Godfrey was sure he would give Jacques his daughter the moment Jacques asked.*

By then Jacques and Adelaise were openly sweethearts. The sight of either made Godfrey burn with anguish. He began looking eagerly towards the day that he could leave Montferrat and Jacques and William and Adelaise behind. Then, the week before Godfrey left for Jerusalem, he had unleashed all his anger and jealousy at Jacques. They had cursed each other, and Godfrey had left with his heart full of hate.

And so it had remained…until Jacques had appeared in Jerusalem a week after Godfrey, declaring his intention to enter the Temple.

✠ ✠ ✠

Godfrey's thoughts returned to the present. He still did not know why Jacques had followed him, but whatever the reason, he was grateful. Whatever might happen, however much Jacques might annoy him or insult him, he would always be grateful to him.

Oh God, he thought quietly, *Thank you for everything. Thank you for making it bearable. Thank you for Jacques.*

Chapter 34

An Old Friend
Godfrey

Andronicus Comnenus was in Jerusalem!

Godfrey had only learned it a day ago. Baldwin had been chattering on about his adventures at court, as was his way, while Godfrey listened, silent except for the occasional grunt of assent when Baldwin asked a question.

The prince had been talking about some of the visitors to the court: about how beautiful his aunt, the widow Theodora, was; and how fat the Greek ambassador Felos was. Baldwin seemed to take enjoyment from teasing the obese Byzantine.

"But today," Baldwin had said, "there was some other Greek who tried to chase me away. He was even skinnier than you, Godfrey. He told me, 'A Latin should respect his betters,' whatever that means. I asked him what his name was, and he told me some nonsense, so I kicked him. He got even madder, then, and he grabbed for me, but I got away. He didn't try to chase me. Too lazy, I guess."

Godfrey had frowned and reprimanded Baldwin, which made the prince sullen for a while, as it always did. But Baldwin accepted Godfrey's rebuke. Godfrey had had to repress a smile all the way through. Afterward, he asked Baldwin, "Has it ever occurred to you, my lord, that maybe this Greek didn't chase you because if he had laid hands on you, your father would have had his head?"

Baldwin shrugged. "Maybe. But I don't think that was why. It was because all Greeks are lazy."

Godfrey had thought a moment, then asked, "What he did he tell you when you asked his name?"

Baldwin thought. "It was something long and garbled... Marsofal... ...Marsafalp...."

"Murzuphlus?"

225

Baldwin had nodded vigorously. "Close enough."

Godfrey said nothing more about it, but he asked around at the Temple when he returned. Most of the knights had no idea what was going on in the palace, but Arnold de Torroga did. Godfrey did not inquire into *how* he knew; that was a question he suspected Arnold would be loathe to answer.

Sure enough, according to Arnold, a man named Andronicus Comnenus had arrived in Jerusalem shortly before the Frankish armies returned from Egypt. He had brought with him a small entourage (which Godfrey surmised to mean Langosse, Basil, and Murzuphlus) and a large bag of bezants. Andronicus and his men were guests in the palace. They were reportedly trying to avoid Heraclius Felos. On the other hand, Andronicus Comnenus was paying more attention than was proper to Theodora, the widow of the previous king of Jerusalem. The palace was full of rumors of this liaison.

It all sounded very like Andronicus. Godfrey did not doubt that Arnold's information was correct: Andronicus was here.

At the next opportunity, Godfrey found Jacques and told him.

"Andronicus Comnenus?" asked Jacques incredulously. "He said he was going back to Constantinople."

Godfrey shrugged. "Well he's here now, or so Arnold says. We should try to find him."

Jacques snorted. "I'd rather avoid him."

Godfrey frowned, not understanding Jacques's reluctance. "Why?"

"Oh, I don't know. Why *should* I look for him?"

That was no answer, but Godfrey could not argue with it either.

"Will you come for my sake, then?"

Jacques sighed. "I told you, Godfrey, I don't want to find him. And I wouldn't trust Arnold de Torroga. He's good for nothing."

Godfrey had left sadly, unable to shake the feeling that Andronicus himself had little to do with Jacques's refusal. Jacques and Godfrey had become distant ever since they returned from Egypt. It was nothing tangible, nothing definite. But Jacques was trying to rise high in the Temple now, and Godfrey could not shake the feeling that Jacques had come to regard his idealistic and stubborn friend as a nuisance, an obstacle to advancement. Though Godfrey saw it, he could not prevent it. So instead he simmered with resentment.

The long and the short of it, though, was that Jacques had refused outright to make any contact with Andronicus Comnenus. Blanchefort would not allow it, he said.

So Godfrey found himself going on his own to the palace to search out the Greek. Blanchefort had not given him permission to go, but that was probably because Godfrey had not asked in the first place. As long as Blanchefort did not forbid it, and, more importantly, so long as he never found out, Godfrey was not going to worry about that.

Godfrey nodded respectfully to the palace guards as they opened the gates for him. They had long since grown used to the four Templars and let them in without question.

How the king trusts William of Tyre! What if I were a traitor bought over to kill the prince? Who would be there to stop me?

Such worries filled Godfrey's head as he made his way into the palace. He didn't realize that he had no plan for finding Andronicus. As it happened, though, the problem was solved for him.

Godfrey was wrapped up in his own thoughts as he walked down the hallway, and was dimly aware of a large hulk of a man walking towards him. It was a narrow hallway, but Godfrey was skinny enough that he tried to brush past him. Instead the man stopped in his tracks, blocking Godfrey's path squarely.

That made Godfrey look up. Basil Camateros towered over him, glaring down. Godfrey sighed.

Of all the Greeks he could have met, Basil was the one he wanted to see least. Langosse would have been friendly, and would have told him what he needed to know. Murzuphlus would have heckled him, but would have told him where Andronicus was, if only out of spite. Basil, though, would only tower over him and say nothing.

For a moment they stared at each other. Godfrey broke the silence.

"Well met, Basil Camateros."

Basil stared back at him without answering. Godfrey ground his teeth together, trying to think of something to say next.

"I… I didn't know that you were in Jerusalem," he lied through his teeth. "Are the others here? Andronicus and Langosse…and Murzuphlus?"

Basil grunted in assent, and then stepped past Godfrey and began to walk on. Godfrey called after him.

"Where are they?"

Basil turned and glared at him. "In the jousting yard. They're *tilting*."

That gave Godfrey pause. Basil strode on down the hallway, as Godfrey tried to picture Andronicus Comnenus accoutered as a knight, with a lance and shield, trying to knock a Frankish knight off his horse. Next he tried to picture Murzuphlus doing the same. The thought made Godfrey laugh.

✠ ✠ ✠

Ten minutes later he found himself at the jousting yard, which was really just a practice yard. When a tourney was held, the lists were set up in an open field. The jousting yard was little more than a flat piece of ground over which the knights rode with blunted lances.

Godfrey had never been much of a jouster. As a boy, his closest friends, Jacques and Conrad, had been so much better than him that he had simply given it up to look for areas in which he could surpass them. Jousting took coordination and strength. Godfrey had little of either.

He knew the rudiments of it—you had to knock the enemy off his horse without getting knocked off yours. The way to do this, of course, was to hit him with your lance before he could hit you.

If you wanted to get the greatest range, you extended your lance straight out to hit the other knight on his helmet, or failing that, his shield, with the point of the lance. If you hit, it would almost certainly unhorse him. However, going for a point hit was difficult and risky. A slight waver or slip and your point would miss him completely, or only nick him. A more reliable way was to slash across with the lance and sweep the opponent off his horse. You were more likely to score a hit, but you cut your range in half, so that if your opponent successfully hit you point-on, you would never get a chance to hit him.

That was as much as Godfrey had learned. His interest had waned quickly as he realized just how little jousting had to do with real battles. Godfrey's imagination as a child had always been captivated by battles and great deeds done for some greater good, and these dreams left no room for something as mundane as jousting for sport.

The picture that he saw in the Jerusalem tilting yard, however, did capture his imagination, for a moment at least. Though the grass was not as green as it should have been, and there were no brightly colored pavilions, the knights themselves made up for the lack of scenery. When knights practiced on foot, they wore as little formal gear—in fact as little clothing—as they possibly could. On the jousting field, however, they had to wear full armor anyway, so each knight wore his full heraldry and colors. The field was aswirl with the colors of chivalry.

For a few moments, Godfrey was content to sit and watch, picking out individual knights and watching them tilt. On the far end of the field, a knight whose shield bore a red field with three black foxes was doing quite well, unhorsing every opponent who came against him.

Closer in, another horseman caught Godfrey's eye. The man wore a gaudy surcoat that glittered with gold and silver inlay flashing in the sun. A scarlet serpent was the only device his shield bore.

As Godfrey watched, the knight dismounted and two men came onto the field to assist him. To Godfrey's surprise, he recognized the men as Langosse and Murzuphlus. Upon seeing them, it was not hard to guess whose face was behind the helmet grill.

Langosse and Murzuphlus pulled off the helmet. Andronicus Comnenus shook his head vigorously, and stumbled off the field, looking a little dizzy. By the time Godfrey approached the three of them, however, Andronicus had recovered his poise.

Godfrey smiled at his old companions. He approached them, a warm greeting on his lips. But a singularly unpleasant and annoyed smile crossed Andronicus's face when he saw Godfrey. Godfrey hesitated a moment, but the Greek was his friend, and so he went forward to greet him.

"My lord Andronicus," he said.

"Sir Templar," came the reply. Andronicus's voice had lost the friendly, careless tone it had always had in Antioch. Now it only sounded unctuous. "Have you come to tilt?"

"No," said Godfrey, simply and earnestly. "I heard you were in Jerusalem, so I came to see you."

The Greek shrugged. "Yes, I am in Jerusalem. Very kind of you." Andronicus began walking forward, with Langosse and Murzuphlus following obediently as ever. Godfrey fell into step beside him. Andronicus's coldness bewildered him. Their last parting had been friendly. But at the back of his mind, Godfrey remembered that Langosse had once said that life was all a game to Andronicus Comnenus.

Was that all our friendship was? wondered Godfrey, irritation and worry rising in his gut. *A game? A passing fancy?*

"I thought you were going to Cilicia," he said to Andronicus, beginning to be annoyed himself.

"I did go," said Andronicus. "But I did not wish to stay long."

"I thought," said Godfrey, "that you were longing to return home."

"I was," said the Greek, shrugging. "But my dear cousin the emperor was none too happy that I had escaped Antioch. I think he was hoping I would spend a few years languishing in an Antiochene prison while he pretended to be scraping up a ransom. I disappointed his plans by escaping, but the emperor is the emperor, and it is hard to avoid his displeasure when you are in his empire. So I ransacked the treasury in Cilicia and sailed for Jerusalem. The king here has become fond of me—and the princess Theodora Comnena has become very fond of me too."

Godfrey thought for a moment. "The former king's widow? She's also a cousin of yours, isn't she?"

Andronicus nodded. "And a very beautiful woman."

Godfrey looked at him sideways. "She's your cousin," he repeated.

The Greek only shrugged. They had reached the entrance to the palace building now. Andronicus stopped and cleared his throat.

"Sir Templar," he said, more unctuous than ever, "I am pleased to see you again. However, I am on my way to visit the lovely Theodora. She is not...fond...of monks."

Godfrey halted and nodded. Andronicus smiled thinly and went on into the palace, leaving Godfrey standing there. Murzuphlus sneered as he passed him by, while Langosse smiled pleasantly.

For some time Godfrey stared after them, bewildered and downcast. *Perhaps*, he told himself hopefully, *it is only a passing mood.* But he didn't believe it himself.

Godfrey sighed and glanced back at the tilting-yard. The knight of the three foxes had just unhorsed another opponent.

Chapter 35

THE GREAT TOURNEY
Baldwin

Summer, 1167

T ime seemed to slow as the day of the great tourney grew closer. Baldwin had been angry at first when his father, the king, had told him he was to marry again. A beautiful Greek princess named Maria Comnena was coming from the city of Constantinople to be the queen of Jerusalem, his father had said. Their marriage would seal the alliance between the Greeks and the Franks. Amalric was going to marry her in Tyre in a month.

Baldwin did not want an alliance between the Greeks and the Franks, not if it meant his father marrying a woman who was not his mother. Baldwin loved his mother—she was still young, and to him she was the most beautiful woman in the world. No Greek princess could replace her, any more than another knight could replace his Uncle Joscelin; not Sir Balian nor Sir Tristan nor even Sir Godfrey. Uncle Joscelin had never liked the Greeks. Sir Godfrey tried to be kind to them, but Baldwin could tell that he didn't like them either. As far as Baldwin was concerned, if his mother and Uncle Joscelin agreed on something, and Sir Godfrey agreed on top of it all, they were right and his father was wrong, even if his father was king.

But the anger had slowly worn away as Baldwin began to think about the tourney that was being held to celebrate the marriage. He had never seen a full tourney in his life, but he had heard so much about them from Balian and Tristan and Uncle Joscelin, and above all from his father. His father had loved the joust, once, before he grew too fat to be good at it. But Amalric still talked of it often, and Baldwin had soaked it all in eagerly.

✟ ✟ ✟

Baldwin got very little sleep the night before the tournament. He awoke as the first grey light was filtering in through the window on the east. Sir Arnold de Torroga was sitting on a chair, looking half asleep. Baldwin knew from experience, however, that he was alert as ever. Sir Arnold had once been the gatekeeper at the Temple, and he knew how to stay alert for long hours at a stretch even as he appeared to relax.

Arnold helped Baldwin to dress. Baldwin had grown used to having the Templars with him at all times: they were just another part of life to him by now. He had been told that Templars were rough, violent men, and he supposed that many were, but these four were kind and gentle, at least to him. Sir Arnold was undoubtedly the strangest of the four. Many of the knights seemed to treat him with scorn, but Sir Arnold didn't seem to notice. Godfrey said that Arnold's greatest virtue was patience. Arnold often seemed to be ignoring Baldwin, but Baldwin could see now that he seemed to ignore everyone. The Templar had acquired an air of perpetual drowsiness from his long hours watching the Temple Gate, but it did not mean that he was bored or tired. If he did not talk much to Baldwin, it was only because he did not talk much to anyone.

Baldwin had watched the four Templars closely ever since they first became his bodyguard. He still liked Godfrey the best of the four, but he was now beginning to think that he liked Arnold the next best. He liked Godfrey because Godfrey always acted like a warder should. His first attention was on Baldwin, and he never made a show of body-guarding when others were around. Jacques and Robert always seemed to be paying more attention to what the other adults were doing or saying, and half the time seemed to be ignoring Baldwin. Sometimes they even seemed embarrassed to be following a child of seven around—even if that child were the heir-apparent of Jerusalem. Arnold, on the other hand, was always listening, even when it seemed he was not.

Sir Arnold de Torroga helped the heir-apparent get himself ready for the tournament with half-closed eyes and unmoving lips, but Baldwin did not mind. Soon he was daydreaming that he would win his first tournament as soon as he was old enough to joust.

✟ ✟ ✟

An hour later, he made his way through the streets towards the great jousting field that had been set up outside the city. Sir Godfrey had relieved Sir Arnold, who went back to the Temple. A whole retinue of knights accompanied Baldwin when he rode through the city, so Godfrey was only one of thirty. He stood out discordantly from the other knights, who tried to keep a bit of distance from the white surcoat and red cross, but Baldwin could not help feeling safer for Godfrey's one sword than for the other twenty-nine.

The streets were filled with people making their way to the tourney. They cheered as their prince went by. Sometimes, when food was scarce or plague troubled the city, the people would only stare at him sullenly, but on the day of a tourney, every man, woman, and child was ready to die for their prince.

Sir Balian d'Ibelin was riding near by Baldwin, so Baldwin called him over.

"Are you jousting today, Sir Balian?"

Balian smiled. "Of course, my lord. Do you think I would miss a chance like this?"

"Do you think you'll win?" asked Baldwin.

Balian laughed. "I hope so, my lord," he said, but his words showed that he did not think he would.

"Who do you *think* is going to win?"

"Well," said Balian, thinking, "there's a Templar out there—one Gerard de Ridford. Keep an eye out for him; his shield bears three black foxes on a red field."

"A Templar!" cut in Godfrey, who had been riding just behind them. "Has Blanchefort permitted De Ridford to joust? Are Templars even *allowed* to joust?"

Balian shrugged, looking a little irritated. "You would know better than I, Sir Monk."

Godfrey pulled back, muttering something to himself. Balian continued.

"This Sir Gerard is good, Templar or no. He stands a good chance of winning—as long as he doesn't go up against John de Arsuf. Sir John is a big fellow—biggest I've ever seen ride a horse. He must be something close on seven feet tall, and weighs more than his horse, for all I know. Half the knights couldn't move him even if they got a solid hit on him, and no one does that to him—not before he gets a solid hit on them: the man's a master of the lance. You'd have to be very fast and very accurate to unhorse him. Sir John is a silver badger on a green field—but just look for the biggest knight on the field and that'll be him."

"Sir Brastias is good too—English crusader; too damned fast to hit. He's three golden martlets on a red field. My brother Baldwin is good, better than I am, but I don't know if he can stand up to Brastias or John or Gerard. And there's one other. He's a newcomer, but I've seen him unhorse men who've been jousting for decades. He's a Greek, a cousin of the emperor's named Andronicus Comnenus. Look for the crimson serpent with gold and silver and white gleaming about his surcoat—that'll be him."

"Andronicus Comnenus is not a knight!" Godfrey broke in again. "Why is he being permitted to take part in the tourney?"

Balian sighed. "Go complain to the king, Sir Monk. I don't really care. If I meet him in the lists and he unhorses me, I'll accept it. A better horseman is a better horseman, knight or no."

"Is that all knighthood is about? Horsemanship?" Godfrey was growing audibly angry.

Balian cocked his head and shrugged. "Perhaps it is. Now, we are almost to the tourney field, and we cannot have the king's retinue arguing amongst themselves as we pass through the gates; so I must ask you, Sir Godfrey, to return to your place."

Godfrey gritted his teeth and grimaced, but he said no more. Baldwin glanced back and forth curiously between Balian and Godfrey, puzzled by the exchange.

✠ ✠ ✠

Baldwin entered the raised stand where the royal family sat. It rose above the benches where the people crowded, and even above the platforms where the nobles sat. His seat was next to Sybilla's. The two of them were on the left side of their father, Amalric I, by the Grace of God, king of Jerusalem.

At the king's right side, *she* was sitting: Maria Comnena, princess of Constantinople and grandniece of Emperor Manuel Comnenus. For the first time in his life, Baldwin laid eyes on the woman who was supposed to supplant his mother.

The king and his betrothed were already sitting when Baldwin arrived in the stand. The first thing he noticed was that the princess was short. *That's just because all Greeks are short.*

Then he looked again, and he blinked. The princess of Byzantium was a girl—she couldn't be older than thirteen or fourteen!

Baldwin had been told that she was beautiful, and so she was, but the only thing he could register was her youth—with the mad disregard to age that was so common in arranged royal marriages, she might just as easily have been betrothed to him as to his father.

The princess, soon to be the queen, had long, dark hair and black eyes. For a moment, Baldwin believed that she might one day be more beautiful than his mother—but this was heresy, so he quickly changed his mind.

Amalric greeted them kindly and courteously, as a king should. He even rose at their entrance, but Baldwin looked up into his face and saw shame and anxiety behind the smiles. Baldwin only glared at him stubbornly, and then glared across at Maria Comnena. She was looking uncertainly between the man to whom she was to be a wife and the children to whom she was to be a mother. She was scared, in the way that only a girl of thirteen can be, and she was clearly trying to decide whether to stand with Amalric, or to remain sitting. She compromised by rising a little off her seat and smiling anxiously. Baldwin only scowled back at her.

Sybilla was hurrying over to her seat, and Baldwin followed, a little confused. Sir Godfrey took up his place behind Baldwin's seat. Baldwin glanced around at the royal stand. It sloped up, as did all the stands, so that the rows in the back could see over the rows in front. In front of the royal family sat the courtiers and guests who had been granted the privilege of sitting so close to the king. Baldwin recognized a handful of them, but many of them were strangers: Greeks who had come in the princess's retinue. Heraclius Felos, the fat Greek ambassador, was there, chewing greedily on a leg of mutton. Around the edges were a handful of knights of the king's household, guarding their sovereign, as well as a handful of Greek soldiers guarding their princess.

Then Baldwin's attention was pulled away by a noise.

The great tourney opened just as Baldwin had imagined any storybook tourney opening: with a flourish of trumpets. Within a moment, he forgot about Maria Comnena and the Greeks, for all other thoughts were swept away with the excitement of the first joust. The sun was bright and the grass was green.

The stands below and around them were filled with people. Most were from Jerusalem, but Baldwin was told that many had come from the far reaches of the kingdom. Baldwin could hear from them the familiar dull roar that any crowd makes, now tinged with anticipation as the tourney was about to begin.

Far below, the heralds were calling out the first knights to the joust. Baldwin clenched the arms of his chair tightly as he fixed his eyes on the field far below. The people in the stands were roaring out their approval. He leaned forward eagerly and asked old Barisan d'Ibelin, sitting in the row before him, who the first two jousters were to be.

"John of Montgisor, I think," said the Lord of Ibelin. "An old greybeard who should be in the stands with me. He's tilting with Reginald of Sidon. No question really as to the victory—if Reginald can't knock old Montgisor off his horse, *I'll* go down there to knock him off it."

"What's Reginald's charge?"

"Oh, a lion, my lord. Or three of them...I wouldn't remember. I've seen far too many tourneys in my day to keep track."

A moment after Lord Barisan was done speaking, the trumpets blew again, and the tilters rode out. As it happened, Reginald of Sidon's shield bore a golden lion on a green field.

A long, low wooden wall was erected across the field, with each tilter riding so that the wall, and his opponent, was on his left side. John of Montgisor looked sturdy enough in full mail armor and a helmet, but Baldwin reasoned that even Heraclius Felos would look knightly in that. The old knight's sigil was three black crosses on a scarlet field—or at least, the field should have been scarlet. The shield itself looked old, and the red had faded until it was nearly as dull as the black.

The trumpet blew again, and the two knights spurred forward to a gallop, riding across the lists. Baldwin watched intently as Sir Reginald fixed his lance on his opponent's helmet, while Sir John kept his lance in the crook of his armpit.

Reginald's grip was not steady enough, and Baldwin could see the lance wavering as he rode. When the two actually passed, Reginald's lance swung wide of the helmet. John of Montgisor brought his lance across, but apparently he really was too old for tilting—his blow glanced harmlessly across the shield.

The crowd jeered as the two knights rode to the end of the lists and turned about to face each other. They had not so much as broken a lance, let alone unhorsed an opponent. Baldwin could not see through the metal cage surrounding the knight's head, but he could imagine the angry, frustrated face that must be hidden by Reginald's helmet.

The two knights thundered forward again across the lists. Baldwin heard a crunch as one of the lances shattered, but when the two horses reached the ends of the lists, both knights were still seated firmly on their horses. Reginald of Sidon had thrown away his broken lance and was seizing a new one from his squire.

Then they wheeled about a third time and charged. There was an eager buzzing in the crowd—if an old greybeard such as John of Montgisor managed to unhorse Reginald of Sidon, he would win the crowd's sympathy for the rest of the day, if nothing else.

It was not to be, though. At the third pass, Reginald knocked his foe soundly off his horse, shattering his lance on his shield. Baldwin smiled. The shattering of a lance was a satisfying sound. He could not wait until he was old enough to joust.

For the rest of the day, Baldwin was swept away in the glory of the tilt. He followed Sir Balian hopefully—even if Balian were annoying at times, Baldwin still liked him better than most other knights—and rejoiced when he unhorsed first Sir Hugh Grenier, and then Sir Humphrey de Vinsauf. At his third joust, though, he came up against the self-same Sir Brastias that he had warned against, and was unhorsed at the second pass of arms.

The crowd grew excited when the heralds announced that the next knight to joust would not give a name, but that he would joust as a mystery knight. The knight who rode out onto the field was very tall. His face, of course, was hidden by his helmet, but his shield bore a silver swan on a blue field. Baldwin thought immediately of Lohengrin, the Knight of the Swan, from whom Godfrey de Bouillion was said to be descended. Baldwin grimaced. He did not like Lohengrin half so much as his descendant. He was relieved to hear that this knight's opponent was to be Sir John of Arsuf.

John of Arsuf was every bit as big as Balian had described him. The Knight of the Swan was tall, but John de Arsuf, Knight of the Badger, was taller. He was bigger too, and obviously so, even through the armor. The crowd knew him well, apparently, for they cheered even more for him than they had for the mystery knight.

The crowd went wild when the Knight of the Swan unhorsed John of Arsuf at the first tilt, hitting him squarely on the helmet and throwing him hard off his horse. There was no contest, no question. John of Arsuf had barely pulled his lance into line when he was hit. The Knight of the Swan galloped on, throwing aside his shattered lance and waving at the crowd. Sir John of Arsuf had to be carried off the field by his squires.

The two others whom Balian had pointed out, however, fared better. Baldwin noted the Knight of the Three Foxes—Sir Gerard de Ridford, and the Knight of the Serpent—Andronicus Comnenus, the Greek. Both of them swept aside their opponents and advanced quickly.

By midafternoon, the tournament was coming to a close. Four competitors remained: Sir Gerard and Andronicus Comnenus, Sir Brastias the English crusader, and the Knight of the Swan.

Baldwin, who always took sides in any sort of competition, was praying earnestly for Sir Brastias's victory. He had hoped at first for his defeat, since he was the one who unhorsed Sir Balian, but as the competition began thinning out, he realized that he didn't dislike Sir Brastias as much as he did the others, and his lack of dislike soon turned into positive affection. He decided that he had liked Sir Brastias best all along.

With four knights left, there were only three matches remaining. The first one was to be Sir Gerard against Andronicus Comnenus. Baldwin ground his teeth as he watched, waiting impatiently for his champion Sir Brastias to come on again.

In the first pass, both the Knight of the Three Foxes and the Knight of the Serpent broke their lances against each other's shield, but neither came close to unhorsing the other. The two rode angrily to the end, seized new lances, and wheeled about to charge again.

This time, Andronicus Comnenus tried something new. As his opponent bore down on him, he swung his body suddenly to the side, trying to swing away from Sir Gerard's lance while he struck his foe down from the side.

It was ingenious, but it didn't work. Gerard de Ridford merely followed the Greek's body with his lance and thrust him soundly off his horse.

The lists were cleared, and it was time for Sir Brastias to joust with the Knight of the Swan. Now Baldwin leaned forward eagerly, watching the left side of the field where Sir Brastias was to emerge.

Sir Brastias rode out to scattered cheering from the crowd. Then the Knight of the Swan appeared, and an earsplitting roar arose from the people in the stands. They had taken the Knight of the Swan to heart, and they would be most upset with Sir Brastias if he unhorsed their knight.

But Brastias never stood a chance. The Knight of the Swan unhorsed him as easily as he had unhorsed John of Arsuf. Baldwin shut his ears to the sound of the cheering crowd and scowled.

The last tilt went by in a daze for Baldwin. With Sir Brastias unhorsed, he could not decide whether he wanted the Knight of the Swan to lose to Sir Gerard, thereby getting his just deserts, or whether he wanted him to win, so that Sir Gerard would not be proved better than Sir Brastias.

As it happened, Gerard de Ridford was unhorsed as easily as all the others, and the Knight of the Swan was victorious.

The knight rode across the lists to the thunderous applause of the crowed, and stopped before the royal stand. Baldwin glared his disapproval down at him, but the champion didn't seem to notice. He dismounted and knelt before the king of Jerusalem, who stood up, smiling broadly. The people were happy, and so Amalric was happy. Baldwin glared up at him, unable to understand how his father could have so little spine.

"Sir knight," said Amalric, "will you remove your helmet, now, and tell us your name? Or are you like the Knight of the Swan, in which case we should never ask what your name be?"

The nobles all laughed at the king's joke, some in earnest, some dutifully. Baldwin sighed. The story of Lohengrin was a boring story anyway, about the knight who came in a boat pulled by a swan, who saved his lady in distress and married her, but told her she must never ask his name, or he would have to depart.

The Knight of the Swan knelt before the king, bowed his head, and removed his helmet. "No, your Grace, I am not Lohengrin. I am free to share my name and title, however low it may be."

But Baldwin recognized him even before he spoke his name. He was Uncle Joscelin's old squire, Tristan de Monglane, whom Godfrey had trounced so soundly back at the practice yard.

Tristan de Monglane...the Knight of the Swan. Bah!

"Your Grace," said Tristan, "I am Tristan de Monglane, squire to the noble Lord Joscelin de Courtenay, count of Edessa. Your Grace, it is my wish to rescue my master from the infidel. I beg of you two boons: that I be knighted by your hand, for I am still a squire, and that I be given my spurs by the noble lady Sybilla, who will be the fairest lady in the world."

Sybilla blushed at the honor. Baldwin wanted to yell at her, but he held off. *She's only nine,* he reasoned.

All he could do was to grimace at Tristan's courtly drivel. *Tristan can't be the one to rescue Uncle Joscelin—I have to do that! And anyway, he's not supposed to be in a tournament if he's not a knight.*

The king, however, seemed ready to overlook this fact. His smile only widened.

"I grant the first willingly, but the second will have to be up to my daughter."

Sybilla got up quickly. "Of course, father."

Baldwin was left sitting with the Greek princess, who was still looking embarrassed. He glared fiercely at everyone and everything around him.

"You could have beaten him if you hadn't been guarding me, Sir Godfrey," he said to the Templar behind him. Godfrey sighed.

"No, my lord. I can fight, but I cannot joust."

Baldwin glared at him too. Finally he fixed his glare on the hateful swan emblazoned on Tristan's surcoat. Sir Tristan de Monglane, Knight of the Swan, indeed.

✠ ✠ ✠

"Godfrey," Baldwin said that evening, as he walked through the little palace garden with Sybilla. "Do you like the story of Lohengrin?"

Godfrey smiled to himself, remembering the hours he spent sequestered away in Otto of Freising's library, reading old stories and tales, and the even more pleasant hours spent sitting at Otto's feet, listening to the old scholar tell stories of knights and mythical heroes.

"Not particularly, my lord," he said. "I liked the Song of Roland far better." *There wasn't enough fighting in the Lohengrin tale.*

Baldwin nodded, looking relieved. "Why would Tristan pick someone like that to name himself after? The Knight of the Swan is so *boring*."

This time Godfrey smiled down at the prince. "Well, my lord, some people come to love the story as they get older. I never did, but some do."

"I never will," said Baldwin obstinately.

Godfrey laughed. "I believe it, my lord."

Sybilla had gone on ahead, following a songbird that was flitting from tree to tree. Baldwin walked slowly behind, deep in thought.

"Godfrey," he asked again. "What is the *graal*?"

"The *graal*," repeated Godfrey. "Have you been listening to some troubadour's tale, my lord?"

"Balian was making fun of the *graal* stories yesterday."

"Ah," said Godfrey, feeling a little annoyed at Balian. "The Grail stories. The French like to tell of them—though the English do as well. Percival and Lancelot and Ywain, and many other valiant knights. And of course their king, Arturus. They are good stories. I always liked them as much as Roland."

"The king," said Baldwin. "Tell me about him. Tell me about Arthur."

"King Arthur," repeated Godfrey. And he began to tell the tale. He spoke of Arthur and his Round Table, of his brave knights and his mighty friends. He told of the kingdom they built, and of the brief, shining moment when Caerleon and the Round Table held back the foes of Christendom. He told of Medraut—of Mordred—the vile traitor, bastard son of the king, who broke the Round Table and brought down Caerleon.

Baldwin listened intently, interrupting every now and then to ask questions, but following the stories closely. Soon Sybilla stopped chasing the bird and joined them, listening just as intently as her brother. Godfrey forgot about everything else and immersed himself in the story he was telling, adding in all the twists that Otto and Aunt Julitta had given the tales, making them as good as he could.

When Arnold came to relieve Godfrey, Baldwin's talk was of Arthur and nothing else. He and Sybilla ran off, grabbing sticks and playing at

Arthur and Mordred. Godfrey was content that day as he walked through the twilight back to the Temple.

✠ ✠ ✠

The next day, Baldwin wanted more stories. And Godfrey told him willingly. They talked long and earnestly about the tales. The young boy bewildered Godfrey, for he could see so much of himself in the child, and yet so much that was better than himself. Every now and then he felt a tinge of jealousy, but it was never as strong as his devotion to the child. So Godfrey told on, weaving his stories with all the skill he possessed.

The days stretched into weeks, the weeks into months. Godfrey looked forward more and more to each day spent with the prince. He told him stories of Arthur, but did not stop there. He wove together stories based on the little tidbits he knew from Homer—of swift-footed Achilleus and cunning Odysseus and Hector, tamer of horses. Another day he described the conflict of David and Jonathan and Saul, and when he had exhausted the stories of the kings of Israel, he related the wars of the Maccabees. Other days he told Baldwin of the classical heroes, of Caesar and Alexander the Great, of Hannibal and Scipio.

Sometimes Sybilla would listen. Once, seeing her eager and intent look, Godfrey remembered the time so long ago when he had told these same stories to Adelaise, but that memory brought too much pain, and he suppressed it. Usually it was just Baldwin listening, though. The prince drank in every word, every tale that Godfrey told him.

Bewilderment was soon replaced by wonder. The child had all the qualities Godfrey was proud of in himself, but none of the faults. He was bright, cheerful, and attentive, not morose and self-absorbed as Godfrey had been. Godfrey could not help but smile every time he saw the boy.

So the months passed. Godfrey told stories, he trained Baldwin to fight, taught him to pray, watched him and guarded him day and night. Once he had loved Baldwin as a teacher loves a student, but as he grew closer to the boy, he began to love him like a younger brother. And as Godfrey, in spite of himself, became more of a man, and Baldwin admired him the more for it, Godfrey came to love the prince as a father loves his only son.

Chapter 36

THE APOSTATE
Godfrey

AD 1169

One day as Godfrey entered the *Templum Domini*, the sense of despair struck him more strongly than ever before.

Gilbert Erail was watching the gate, since Arnold de Torroga was guarding the prince. Godfrey passed through the gate unchallenged, and entered the Temple Court.

Once his heart would have lifted to see the familiar stones and rubble baking in the sun. Now, though, it only made his heart more anguished.

Godfrey had entered the Temple at the age of twenty, six years ago. Then, with Jacques at his side and his cousins and old life behind him, Godfrey could not have imagined that he would be anything less than satisfied to be a Templar—a white knight, a hero who gave his life in defense of the kingdom.

But of late, he was beginning to hate it. Glory and courage seemed empty and cold. He had no doubt now that he should have married, should have become a knight in the service of his uncle, William de Montferrat. He had learned much as a Templar—enough to know that he was not meant to be a monk, or a hero. Six years ago, he had thought that it would be enough to know he had God's love, even if he were forsaken by all human love. Now he began to believe that it was not enough.

That was the worst of it: the loneliness. When he had decided to become a Templar, back in Montferrat, Jacques had been there. Conrad, who was both cousin and friend, had never understood the decision to become a monk, but he had remained a friend. William de Montferrat was never quite able to be a father to Godfrey, but never unkind or cruel either. Even once Godfrey came to Jerusalem, Jacques had still been there, and William of Tyre had become a close friend too.

Now, though, Jacques had become estranged—he had moved on, trying to advance in the Temple. Godfrey, because of his idealism, had refused to consider political ambition of any sort, so during the years since the return from Antioch, the two had grown apart. Jacques was still was the closest friend Godfrey had, and so Godfrey had not hesitated to choose him as a part of the prince's bodyguard. Yet Jacques continued to become more and more of a stranger.

But the rest were all gone now. William de Montferrat and his household were far across the sea, making war on the German emperor, or on the pope. It was five years since Godfrey had seen any of them.

William of Tyre was busy with his episcopal duties. Godfrey saw him sometimes as he came to tutor Prince Baldwin, but they had little chance to speak.

And Adelaise...Adelaise too was gone beyond recall.

So all of Godfrey's loves and friends were gone. He had sworn away a wife, sworn away all other human attachments, and now he was alone except for God. And God did not answer. God was silent.

Godfrey's last hope and love were given to the prince of Jerusalem. One day, Baldwin would be king, and Godfrey was determined to see to it that he would be as great a king as Jerusalem had never seen before.

Already, the prince was beginning to astonish those around him. He was brilliant. He understood and amassed knowledge at age nine that many full-grown men did not possess. He was brave and he was athletic, and his dream was to be a knight-errant.

Soon enough Baldwin would realize that he must be king instead of a knight-errant, and then Godfrey knew he would set himself wholeheartedly to that task. So Godfrey guarded him and taught him when he could, trying to make him into the hero that Godfrey himself had once dreamed of being, and more.

The other knights all tried now and again to teach the young prince some of their cynicism—Balian of Ibelin and Hugh Grenier and John of Arsuf, and even De Ridford. But Godfrey fought them with his words and with his actions, to protect the prince from their mentality. Andronicus Comnenus hovered about the Palace, but he seemed to be avoiding Godfrey now, which was just as well. If Godfrey had his way, Baldwin of Jerusalem would never speak to Andronicus Comnenus.

It occurred to Godfrey that he was becoming jealous of the prince's admiration, just as he had been jealous of Jacques and Adelaise. He had no right to be, nor had he the right to direct the prince as he wished. But he put such thoughts from his mind. Baldwin was all he had to love and to hope for. If he gave up on him, he would have no reason to live.

"Godfrey?" A voice cut into Godfrey's thoughts. He realized that he had been standing motionless in the center of the Temple Court.

Jacques de Maille was standing in front of him, his chin covered by his fair beard.

Godfrey's first reaction was antagonistic, and he realized that any estrangement between himself and Jacques was not entirely Jacques's fault.

"Yes, Jacques?" he sighed.

"Have you heard?" asked Jacques, sounding anxious, almost frightened.

Godfrey shook his head. "Heard what?"

"About the master?"

"No, nothing about Blanchefort. What?"

"He collapsed at the midday meal. They carried him out, and brought a leech in to see to him."

Godfrey frowned. "Is he dying, then?"

"Well, the leech said he would live this time, but all around the Temple, they're saying…saying the master doesn't have long to live."

"Blanchefort…dead," said Godfrey. "It seems impossible; he's been a natural part of life, these six years."

"Godfrey," said Jacques, still anxious, "I spoke to Philip de Milly. He has a large following, and he thinks he can get elected grand master when Blanchefort dies."

Godfrey raised his eyebrows. "You don't think he can beat Odo de Sant'Amand, do you?"

Jacques shrugged. "Maybe, maybe not. But you see, he's marshal of the Temple right now, so if he gets elected, they'll need a new marshal."

That made Godfrey stare. "And…*you?*"

Jacques nodded, smiling, half-proud, half-anxious. "Yes. Me."

Godfrey didn't know what to say to that. He began pacing about, hands behind his back. "Who else do you think will put their name forward?"

"I don't know yet—not everyone knows that De Milly is even going to try to run. Gilbert Erail is going to try for election as seneschal if Odo gets elected, but no one else has lined up for marshal."

Godfrey nodded breathlessly. "And you think you have enough support?"

"Well," said Jacques, a little abashed, "De Milly has promised…gold…"

"So he can buy votes for you?" Godfrey said, and suddenly he could feel anger and contempt rising up in him.

Jacques sighed. "Godfrey, I know it's not your way, but I couldn't win the election without it."

"I didn't protest, did I? It's your choice, Jacques." But there was bitterness in Godfrey's voice, and he felt old jealousies rising now—old emotions from before either of them had entered the Temple—joining with his frustration over their estrangement.

"There's some talk of De Ridford running against Erail for seneschal," Jacques said. "I think I have become something of a friend to De Ridford; if I speak to him…"

That was too much for Godfrey. He pushed past Jacques and made for the refectory. "Go win your election, Jacques. I'm going to the training butts."

"Godfrey," Jacques called after him. Godfrey turned and glanced back. Jacques was struggling for words. Finally his face twisted in anger. "Go to hell."

"I will." Godfrey marched on towards the refectory. A few steps later he stopped and looked back again. Jacques was just standing there, staring after him.

"Jacques," he said. "I will vote for you, no matter who is against you." Jacques did not reply. Instead he turned away.

Now, thought Godfrey, *I have lost a friend indeed.*

✛ ✛ ✛

Early the next morning, Godfrey returned to the Palace. He made straight for the prince's bedchambers, but paused a moment as he passed by a room where a great crucifix hung on the wall, the dawn's first light filtering through a window to illuminate it. Some pious lord or lady, no doubt, resided there. But the crucifix was beautiful, and Godfrey halted to gaze at it, gaze on the agonized face of the man hanging on the cross.

"It's beautiful," came a voice from behind him. Godfrey glanced back, and to his utter shock, he saw Andronicus Comnenus admiring the crucifix behind him. Godfrey turned to face him fully, unsure how to react.

"Yes," he answered. "It is beautiful. *He* is beautiful."

Andronicus's eyes did not move from the crucifix. "That face…it has the fullness of human tragedy written across it. The crucifixion captures that deep, profound sorrow that the Iliad and Oedipus Rex possess. That final cry of the innocent man, forsaken by man and god to die there on the cross…"

Godfrey did not know what to make of this sudden change in Andronicus's point of view. "Yes," he said quietly. "It is the deepest human tragedy of all. But it also has the fullness of joy, and that is what the human dramas do not have, for they do not have the Resurrection."

Something flickered across Andronicus's face. "The resurrection," he murmured quietly, and suddenly his voice grew sharp and angry. "The resurrection," he said, "is the reason that the Gospels do not rank with Oedipus Rex or the Iliad. It is a cheap ending, a pitiful attempt to combine comedy with tragedy. It demeans tragedy itself; the pagans would never have done such a thing."

Godfrey looked up, surprised. "Can't a story have both the fullness of joy and tragedy?"

"No," snapped Andronicus. "Life is precious because it has a definite end—we can value it most when we know we will lose it. That is why the Resurrection destroys the perfect tragedy."

Godfrey wasn't sure whether or not to laugh. "The Resurrection ruins the story?"

"Yes," said Andronicus. "Christianity has cheapened tragedy. The world is grown grey with the breath of Christ. Christianity is trying to kill drama." He stared at the crucifix again, and this time there was malice on his face. "*Vicisti, Galilae!* How I hate you, *Christos*—and I hate you all the more because you would abolish hate. How can there be love without hate? How can there be good without evil? I hate many men, and so I am able to love those worth loving, few though they be."

Godfrey was still shaking his head in wonderment. "I will not argue philosophy with you, Andronicus, but can you truly tell me that it is better for life and love itself to die than for them to live forever?"

Andronicus turned and looked Godfrey in the eyes, his own blue eyes burning with a cold fire.

"Yes."

Godfrey heaved a deep sigh, but to his surprise he felt not anger but sorrow for the Greek who stared at the cross with a look of anguished hate.

"I pity you, Andronicus," said Godfrey. Suddenly he remembered his original purpose, and turned swiftly on his heel. "I must go. God be with you."

Andronicus was no longer looking at Godfrey, however. He was staring at the crucifix, with that hate-filled look imprinted on his face.

✠ ✠ ✠

Robert de Ais was waiting just inside the doorway, sitting on a chair, looking tired, as well he might after spending a night awake in chain mail. It was exhausting for all four Templars, spending every fourth night awake guarding the prince, even when Blanchefort allowed them to sleep during the day to make up for it.

Godfrey relieved Robert at his place by the door. The prince was still sleeping. Robert hurried off to the Temple, while Godfrey settled down into the chair, thinking over what had happened the day before with Jacques. He was torn between trying to reconcile and letting go forever.

In some ways, Godfrey wanted desperately to have Jacques's friendship again, while on the other hand there was an element of indignation: Jacques had chosen to turn against him, it was not his place to try to turn him again. He could not tell whether the former was selfishness or the latter was pride.

"Sir Robert?"

Godfrey jerked his head up to see Baldwin rolling out of his bed. "Oh," said Baldwin, smiling drowsily. "Sir Godfrey. Have you heard what's happening today?"

Godfrey shook his head wearily. "What is it, my lord?"

Baldwin spoke in a hushed, conspiratorial voice. "Lady Maria says that they're going to arrest the Greek tonight."

Godfrey almost jumped up, but stopped himself at the last moment. "Who are they arresting, my lord?"

"The emperor's cousin, the man with the three soldiers who follow him about everywhere."

"Andronicus Comnenus?"

"I think so. Yes. Lady Maria said that Andronicus is in love with the lady Theodora. She says that he shouldn't be, since they're cousins. Now the Greek emperor wants his head—he thinks Andronicus is getting too dangerous to live. Lady Maria says that my father is only too happy to ship him off to Constantinople for execution."

Godfrey sank down into the chair. It was an open secret in the Palace that Andronicus had become Theodora Comnena's lover.

What have you gotten yourself into now, Andronicus?

✛ ✛ ✛

The next six hours, Godfrey wrestled with a new problem: whether to warn Andronicus Comnenus.

He had no doubt that Andronicus was unaware of these developments. It must be a closely kept secret, else Murzuphlus or Langosse would have ferreted it out. In fact it was probably something only the royal family was supposed to know about. 'Lady Maria' was what Baldwin called Maria Comnena, the queen of Jerusalem, Amalric's new wife. Godfrey knew that this was a secret he was not supposed to have heard.

But it was a secret upon which Andronicus's very life depended. Andronicus had studiously ignored Godfrey ever since his return to Jerusalem, but Godfrey could not forget that Andronicus had taught him to fight, and once he had been a friend. The two years at Antioch, the oliphant that Andronicus had given Godfrey: these things were all fresh in Godfrey's memory. He could not sit back and let an old friend die, not when it was in his power to save him. And then Godfrey thought of the outburst Andronicus had made that morning. The outburst against Christ should have made him fear the Greek, but instead filled him with pity. He did not want Andronicus to die in a state like that.

To warn Andronicus, though, would be treason. It was not so much the danger that worried Godfrey as the breach of trust. He had only gained this information because the king had trusted him to guard Baldwin. Amalric had placed his son's very life in Godfrey's hands, and if Godfrey used that position to commit treason, he would be proving himself unworthy of that trust.

All that day, as Godfrey stood guard over the prince, as he watched him eat, as he trained him to use a sword, he tried to find an answer. But a solution eluded him; either course of action seemed to be wrong.

He was never sure afterwards whether he made the right decision or not. It was something that troubled him for years to come, but he could see no other way.

After Jacques relieved him at his post, Godfrey made his way to the practice yard, where he knew he would find Andronicus Comnenus.

He did not, however, expect to find him sparring with Tristan de Monglane.

A little circle of soldiers had formed around the swordsmen, watching them as they fenced. Godfrey could hear the clatter of the wooden swords before he even entered the yard.

The fight must have been going for a while, because both Andronicus and Tristan's brows were covered in sweat. Godfrey watched, fascinated, as they danced about in a blur of motion.

Now this is worth seeing...

There was a wooden clatter as the sword fell from Tristan's hand. Andronicus swung about to bring his sword down on Tristan's neck, but Tristan turned with amazing speed, turning just enough that the sword passed in front of him. Then Tristan struck out with his fist, catching Andronicus squarely in the face.

Andronicus staggered backwards, throwing up his sword in a disoriented defensive position. By the time he had recovered himself, Tristan's wooden sword was at his throat.

The look on Andronicus Comnenus's face was murderous as he dropped his sword.

The crowd began to break up, murmuring. Godfrey watched as Tristan and Andronicus stepped away from each other.

"Sir Godfrey!" Tristan called, catching sight of him. "Have you come to spar?"

Andronicus looked up in surprise. His expression became uncertain as he surveyed Godfrey.

Godfrey nodded.

"Some of the knights want to see us fight again," said Tristan. "They were very surprised when I told them of your skill."

In this respect, Godfrey had to admit that Sir Tristan de Monglane had acted utterly unselfishly, however much the Knight of the Swan irritated him otherwise. Tristan never hesitated to tell the other knights that Godfrey had bested him at a sparring match.

"I would like to spar again as well," said Godfrey. "But not now. You're worn out. It wouldn't be a fair fight."

Tristan laughed as he wiped his brow. "True enough, Sir Templar. I must go, then." He turned to nod at Andronicus. "Well fought, my lord." Andronicus had recovered his composure by now, and he nodded courteously.

Sir Tristan de Monglane left the yard as the other spectators scattered to do their own combats. Godfrey was left facing Andronicus and his three perpetual comrades.

"What do you want here, Latin?" asked Murzuphlus.

"I came to spar with my lord Andronicus."

Andronicus raised his eyebrows.

"Oh," sneered Murzuphlus. "So it is unknightly to fight with Tristan de Monglane when he is tired, but you may spar with the Greek whenever you wish?"

"Shut up, Murzuphlus,' said Andronicus wearily. "I will fight him."

Godfrey took a wooden sword from the basket and stepped forward, slipping easily into the stance that Andronicus himself had taught him. He flowed forward into the combat, and as his sword clacked against the Greek's, their eyes met.

"You must leave before nightfall, Andronicus," said Godfrey.

Andronicus spun away and they continued to spar.

"And why is that, Sir Templar?" he asked as their blades met again.

"The king is going to arrest you tonight. Your cousin, the emperor, wants your head. He has demanded that Amalric turn you over, and

Amalric is only too happy to comply. He is tired of your adulteries with his brother's widow."

The Greek smiled as he spun away again. "If this is true," he murmured, "I am in debt to you, Sir Templar."

Godfrey shrugged. "We will find out."

Andronicus began pressing the attack harder, and Godfrey had to retreat. He had no desire to prolong this fight. If Andronicus wished to win, he would let him. Godfrey lowered his guard for a moment, and Andronicus struck him hard in the chest.

The satisfied smile on Andronicus's face was almost too much to bear. "You have improved since I last fought you," Andronicus said smugly.

"Thank you, my lord," Godfrey managed. In stories, a blademaster such as Andronicus would have realized that Godfrey had let him win, and would have acknowledged it somehow. He was not in the stories, though, so Andronicus really believed that he had beaten Godfrey, and now Andronicus's gratitude was mingled with scorn.

Godfrey turned bluntly, dropping the sword into the basket, and left to the sound of Murzuphlus laughing hysterically.

Chapter 37

KNIGHT OF THE SWAN
Tristan

The Next Day

The bread was fresh and warm. Tristan bit into it hungrily, savoring the warmth and the taste. But there was not enough. A minute later he was licking the crumbs off his fingers, and longing for more. But his pouch was empty of coins.

Any other pauper might have waited in front of the street vendors, staring hungrily at the breads and meats until someone took pity on him and gave him a crust or a coin. But Tristan was not a pauper; he was the Knight of the Swan. A knight did not beg.

While Joscelin had been his master, Tristan never worried about food or lodging. Though Edessa and its splendor were lost, the king had given Joscelin a small fief. The lands provided money to support a squire and a few knights. Now, however, Tristan was cut loose. His only possessions were his sword and armor. He had borrowed a horse and lances with which he had won that first tournament, and won his knighthood from the king himself. But that accolade had proved a difficult burden for Tristan. A knight was expected to support himself—was expected to have lands. Tristan had none. In time of war he might have found a lord who needed warriors, but Outremer was at peace now, and might be for some time.

Tristan scrambled to his feet and emerged from the alleyway in which he had sat down to eat his bread. He made for the lower levels of the city. There would be work there of some sort; there always was. He would work the rest of the day and earn a few coins which would feed him for another day. He could sleep amidst the hovels of the lower city, and work some more tomorrow, waiting for the next tournament, where he could prove himself again. Maybe the day after that he could go to the practice yards again, and fight Balian d'Ibelin. And maybe that day he would find a way to free

Joscelin. And if not that day, maybe the next, or the next, or the next...

Tristan rounded a corner and started in surprise when he saw Langosse Argyrus leaning carelessly against the wall. The Byzantine smiled at Tristan, but said nothing.

"Hasn't your master left Jerusalem?" asked Tristan. "He vanished last night. I assumed you left with him."

"You sound disappointed, bird-knight," came a voice from behind him. Tristan glanced back to see Murzuphlus coming around the corner after him. Tristan frowned and stepped away from both of them.

"Sir Tristan," came the clear, likeable voice of Andronicus Comnenus from behind him. "You must forgive me; I have a flair for the theatrical."

"Yes," said Tristan irritably as he turned to see Andronicus and the hulking Varangian, Basil Camateros, waiting behind him. "You do."

"To answer your question, Sir Knight: we spent the night in the slums of the Lower City. We went completely unnoticed—no one would expect to find a noble in the slums. But then again, no one would expect to find the Knight of the Swan there either."

Tristan frowned. "Why did you leave the palace in the first place? Do you prefer the slums?"

"The Court of Jerusalem has become a dangerous place, Sir Knight. There are some lords who have been conspiring against me, and my life is in jeopardy."

"If that is so," said Tristan, "even the Lower City will not be safe for long. Leave Jerusalem. Leave the kingdom if you must."

"I will," said Andronicus. "Tomorrow morning I make for my homeland, for Byzantium." A look of longing came into Andronicus's eyes. "Constantinople calls me. I have been gone too long."

"Well," said Tristan. The harshness in his voice vanished. He could feel some trace of pity in his heart now for the wandering Greek. "I wish you Godspeed. I enjoyed our matches in the practice yard."

"As did I," said Andronicus. "If I did not long for Byzantium so much, there would be many things I would miss about Jerusalem. But I wish you Godspeed as well, Knight of the Swan, in whatever endeavors you face."

Tristan bowed his thanks, and then turned to leave. He wished Andronicus well; the Greek had been a pleasant enough fellow. Perhaps he could even be of aid when Tristan rode to rescue his master. If the rumors were true and Joscelin was really being held in the north—in Aleppo or Mosul—then Greek aid would be of great worth.

Just as Tristan was about to turn onto another street and make for the slums, Andronicus called out to him.

"Are you hard pressed for food, Sir Tristan?"

Tristan did not even turn to look. "That is my own affair," he said coldly.

"I have no desire to pry into your affairs," said Andronicus affably. "But we do have gold to spare."

Tristan hesitated. He glanced back now, and saw Langosse opening a large, heavy pouch which jingled softly. Tristan's stomach rumbled quietly. He began to think how much he would give just to get a mouthful of roasted meat. But then he steeled his resolve.

"I do not accept charity, Greek," said Tristan firmly. He turned to leave.

"And I was not speaking of charity," rejoined Andronicus. "Nay, Sir Knight, there is a service you can render me, for which I would pay you. There is nothing unchivalrous or vulgar about that. I'll hazard a guess that you're looking for work now. I can give you work, and pay much better than anyone in the Lower City."

A second time Tristan hesitated. He vacillated, grinding his teeth and clenching his fists in indecision. Another vision of a steaming haunch of meat appeared before him. Tristan sighed and turned about to face the Greeks. When he did, he noticed just how big the pouch of gold was—that much coin would get him more than a haunch of meat. He could live well for weeks, maybe months, with that. And if he could stop worrying about money, he could start spending more time at court seeking support for Joscelin's rescue. Perhaps best of all, more time at court meant less time working like a dog in the slums...

"How much gold are you offering?" demanded Tristan.

"Three bags of this weight," said Andronicus. "It's imperial coin, but it holds good in Jerusalem. I don't ask much of you, but one of the conspirators from whom I am fleeing stole something from me. It is an oliphant, a finely carved ivory horn. That horn is of immense value on its own, but it is all the more important because it was given me by the empress. She gave it to me as a token of her favor, many years ago. I don't want to return to Constantinople without it."

All the while, Tristan listened, stony-faced and troubled in heart. "Why do you need me?" he demanded.

Andronicus smiled graciously. "You lived in the palace for many years with your lord, Joscelin de Courtenay. It occurred to me: perhaps in your days there you learned how to leave and to enter the palace...*discreetly?*"

Tristan frowned. "Discreetly?"

"If anyone discovered us," said Murzuphlus harshly, "blood would be spilled. It must be *very* discreet, Latin."

Tristan nodded. There would be nothing unchivalrous or treacherous about helping Andronicus to regain his stolen horn. "Very well, Greek. If discretion is what you need, I can give you discretion."

☩ ☩ ☩

The night was full of memories.

Tristan dropped lightly from the oak tree onto the palace wall. He glanced about to make sure no guards were within sight, but it was merely a precaution. Tristan knew that this section of the wall would be unwatched at this time of the night; no sentries would come for several hours.

Fighting down a wave of nostalgia at all the old familiar sights, Tristan padded softly to the stairs that led down from the ramparts. At the top of the stairwell, he peered around the corner to check for guards, but once again it was only a precaution. There would be no guards at this particular stair.

Tristan had come this way countless times in past years, when Joscelin dwelt in the palace. As squire, Tristan had lived in the antechamber to his lord's apartments, so that he would be ready for any task Joscelin required of him. But every so often, Tristan had snuck out at night to go into the city, to look, to search, to seek for...

He scowled, suppressing the memory of those long nights wandering about the city beneath the moonlight. He glanced up at the sky, but tonight the moon was only a thin sliver in the clear sky. He breathed a sigh of relief. Tonight was a good night to move about discreetly.

And tonight was so different from those other nights. The innocence of those days was lost forever, and though he was only eighteen, Tristan felt worn with age. So much responsibility, so much guilt.

Tristan began to creep down the stairs, knowing that he should not feel guilt. The stairwell was dark, and a stranger would have stumbled and fallen easily. But Tristan moved swiftly and softly. He knew these stairs by heart, had traversed them a thousand times in the dark.

At the bottom of the stairs was a small but heavy door with two great bars across it. It could not be seen in the dark, but Tristan knew it was there. He approached the door slowly but surely, without a hint of indecision.

The Greek had explained—sincerely, Tristan thought—that Miles of Plancy, the royal seneschal, had gotten his hands on the ivory oliphant that belonged to Andronicus. And now that Andronicus was returning to Constantinople, he wanted to have the oliphant with him to show the empress he had not lost the token of her favor. Miles of Plancy was now residing in the chambers that had once been Joscelin's, the chambers where Tristan had lived before Joscelin was captured. So, Andronicus had said, if Tristan could get them into his old rooms to find the oliphant, he would receive the gold. And this very night Miles of Plancy had left to settle a dispute in Ascalon. The way would be clear.

There was no hesitation either in his movements or in his thought as Tristan threw open the bolts and pulled the door inward. It was wood on the inside, but on the outside it was stone to match the walls—a postern gate which could barely be seen, much less broken in, from without.

Tristan peered through the opening, blinking in the starlight after the pitch black of the winding stairwell. He could hear his own breathing in the dark. No one was outside.

For five seconds Tristan stared blankly into the night.

They're not coming, he thought to himself. And suddenly a wave of relief swept over him. He had not realized till that moment how much he dreaded the task at hand.

Then Murzuphlus's head appeared from around the crack, grinning that vile grin of his. The relief dissipated, and with a silent groan, Tristan stepped back. Murzuphlus slipped in, followed by Andronicus. Langosse stepped in behind his master, and Basil brought up the rear, bowing his head so he could fit into the narrow passage.

The giant Varangian guard shut the door behind him, and darkness swallowed up the chamber again.

"Now," said Andronicus, "lead us to Joscelin's old chambers."

✛ ✛ ✛

Tristan knew all the ways through the palace by night; as a boy, he had eluded the guards many a time in his nocturnal wanderings. Now he just had to elude them one more time, with four others following him.

It was not easy, but somehow Tristan managed it. They passed through empty stone hallways and climbed wooden stairways, until at last they reached the wing of the Palace where Joscelin's chambers were. Tristan knew they would be safe now; this wing of the Palace was set back from the rest, out of earshot of most of the guards. For this was where the prince's chambers were. Amalric, trusting Joscelin alone, had placed his chambers closest to Baldwin's. The guards had watched the single way leading to Joscelin's chamber carefully, but none save Joscelin watched the single stair leading to the prince's room.

"Up these stairs," Tristan whispered. He climbed them softly. To his surprise, all four of the Greeks moved just as quietly—they must have had experience. Tristan did not want to know how they acquired it.

The stair was steep, and the climb seemed to last an eternity. A third of the way up, Tristan stumbled on a loose cobblestone. He fell to his knee and reached up to catch something, but there was only stone wall. He glanced back and found Andronicus staring at him curiously out of those bright blue eyes. A shiver ran down Tristan's spine as he scrambled to his feet.

At the top of the stair was a wide antechamber. Tristan walked slowly to the center of the room. The four Greeks paused at the top of the stairs and glanced about. To the left was a small room for a servant. To the right were Miles of Plancy's chambers, and before them was the lone stairway leading to Baldwin's room. Tristan nodded to the right.

"There are the Steward's rooms. I can help you no further from—"

He broke off mid-sentence when the door on the left opened, and a young maidservant walked out. She froze at the sight of the strangers, and then gave a scream. Tristan started to say something to hush her, to comfort her. But he never had the chance.

Swift as a cat, Murzuphlus slipped behind the girl and drove his dirk into her back. Tristan's comforting words died on his tongue and instead a shout of rage rose in his throat. His hand went to his sword hilt, but even as it did he heard the clanging of metal on metal as the Byzantines began to draw their weapons. The guards were long out of earshot now, and Tristan was alone in a room full of enemies. With hope fading but anger rising, Tristan drew his sword.

Chapter 38

KNIGHT OF THE IMPOSSIBLE IDEAL
Godfrey

It was another one of those nights.

Godfrey leaned back in the stiff wooden chair, half an eye on the sleeping prince, the other half on the doorway to the room. But his mind and heart were not on his duty. Inwardly he was writhing in agonized indecision, a thousand worries and fears playing about his conscience. Guilt still pricked at his mind when he thought of Andronicus, as he wondered whether he had done right in warning him. But to make matters worse, underlying these anxieties there was the older fear that he did not really belong in the Temple, that he should have married, should have found a wife...

Yet as often as Godfrey looked at the child sleeping on the bed, the prince whom he had come to love as a son, he could feel some comfort.

At some point in the middle of the night, Godfrey tried to turn himself to prayer. He began to mutter the words of the *paternoster*, though his attention was not really on the words.

"... *sed libera nos a malo*," Godfrey finished with a sigh. Even as he did, a cry from the bottom of the stairs cut into the silence.

"Murderer!"

Godfrey sprang to his feet and made for the doorway, where a spiral stairway led down from the prince's room. His heart pounded furiously in his chest as confusion and panic gripped his thoughts. He began to clatter swiftly and heedlessly down the stone steps, but caught himself a little ways down. He slowed his pace and padded cautiously onward.

"Guard!" came another shout. "Guard!"

"There's no one to hear you," came the clear, pleasant voice of Andronicus Comnenus. Godfrey frowned in confusion, as Andronicus continued to speak. "We left the guards far below. Remember?"

Godfrey rounded the last curve of the stairway, and the scene unfolded before him.

There was a wide antechamber at the bottom of the stairs, with other entrances and exits. At the doorway to the right of Godfrey, a woman—a servant—lay on the ground. A scarlet blot was staining the linen that covered her left breast, and a pool of scarlet was spreading below her.

Standing over her, Murzuphlus was sheathing his dirk. Next to Murzuphlus stood a man whose head was shadowed under a dark hood, but Godfrey could clearly see the bronzed face and bright blue eyes of Andronicus Comnenus. In the middle of the room stood Basil and Langosse, looking about nervously.

Facing them was Tristan, staring at Murzuphlus with a look of bewilderment and anger.

"Why would you murder an innocent—and a woman, no less—over your bloody oliphant? What sort of villains are you?"

Godfrey froze in shock, unable to comprehend the scene. Had Murzuphlus just murdered a woman? Murdered her in cold blood? And was Andronicus standing there and doing nothing?

Andronicus smiled. "You are mistaken, Sir Tristan," he said sincerely, "I would never see a woman killed over a lifeless piece of ivory. But you see, we aren't really here for the oliphant."

Unable to believe what he was hearing, Godfrey drew his sword as he stepped out of the stairwell. All the eyes in the room turned towards him.

"Whatever you came here for," said Godfrey, "it's over now." He raised his sword, pointing it at the four Greeks. Godfrey's mind was as bewildered and lost as Tristan's face looked. Was it really possible that murder had just been done? He could believe it of Murzuphlus, but Godfrey could not accept that Andronicus would simply stand by and watch the slaughter of an innocent. Yet there Andronicus stood, with a calm, even smug look on his face, while the woman lay in a pool of red on the ground.

"Sir Godfrey de Montferrat," said Andronicus warmly. "It's good to see you."

Tristan stepped forward, brandishing his drawn sword. "You're murderers, all of you, if you just stand by and let that villain wash his knife in an innocent maid's blood. And you," he said, turning his gaze to Andronicus. "You're the worst of them, with your smug smile and your damned mocking eyes."

"It is for a higher good," said Andronicus simply, and Godfrey's blood chilled at the sound of it. "She had to be sacrificed for a higher cause." Andronicus's eyes met Tristan's, and they held each other's gaze for a moment.

Then Tristan lunged.

He slid past Langosse and Basil even as Langosse brandished his sword and Basil a cruel curved axe. Murzuphlus dropped his blade in surprise when Tristan charged, and now he was scrabbling on the floor to pick it up. Godfrey still hesitated, unable to concede that Andronicus was here with evil intent.

But the Knight of the Swan was faster than them all. He did not slow as he approached Andronicus, did not pause as he raised his sword for a downward slash to sever the sinews of his neck.

Andronicus Comnenus did not flinch. Instead his left hand shot out and caught Tristan's wrist just as he was about to strike. He twisted Tristan's sword arm downward and outward, so that the sword clattered from his hand.

Tristan made to punch Andronicus, but the Greek was faster. Andronicus struck Tristan hard and fast in the face, coming up into his nose from below—an ugly blow that made a loud crunch.

Andronicus let go of Tristan as he staggered backwards. Then the backblow from Basil's axe struck Tristan in the base of his skull. The wooden axehaft smashed Tristan's head, and with a loud CRACK the Knight of the Swan crumpled to the floor. His nose and mouth were covered in blood.

Numb with shock, Godfrey realized that his last chance of facing the four Greeks was gone.

"Shall I finish him, my lord?" asked Basil, raising his axe and glancing at Tristan's limp body.

Andronicus gave a nod.

"NO!" cried Godfrey. He stepped forward, raising his sword and preparing to fight. Andronicus glanced over at him, and raised his hand for Basil to stop. He looked amused.

"I'm sorry, Sir Godfrey, but you must follow him soon. I told him, and I will tell you as well—it is for a higher cause."

And Godfrey realized with a sinking feeling that all this was in deadly earnest. Andronicus had consented to murder, and he was ready to murder again.

"What cause is great enough," asked Godfrey in a desperate, broken voice. "What cause is so high that you would murder innocents for it, murder the man who saved your life?"

"Love," said Andronicus simply.

"Love?" asked Godfrey, letting his sword arm drop to his side and staring bewildered at the Greek. "Love of slaughter? Love of villainy?"

"Love of a woman," said Andronicus, and there was a sort of pain in his face as he spoke. "They have taken her, Godfrey," he said softly. "They have taken my love. They have locked her away in some distant reach of the kingdom—I do not know where. I have to find her, have to be with her. And if a few must die in order that we may be reunited, so be it.

A thought struck Godfrey, and he began to grow angry.

"You are speaking of the lady Theodora!"

"Yes," whispered Andronicus.

"But she is your cousin. It is against the Church, against nature..."

Andronicus's face wrinkled in irritation and surprise. But he quickly regained his composure. "You cling to your rules and restrictions, Godfrey. They mean nothing to me. You do not know what it is to be caught up in wild, consuming passion. You have known nothing but a monkish life. Come, Sir Knight, I will make you a new offer: throw aside your clerk's robes and become my vassal. Travel with me like a knight errant—you always wanted to be a knight errant, didn't you? You will have all the adventure you sought after, and none of the misery that afflicts you now." Andronicus stared piercingly at Godfrey and added, "And you *are* miserable, Godfrey. I can see it."

"Silence," said Godfrey, harshly. Whatever misery ate away at his heart, the offer did not even tempt him. To betray Baldwin would rend his heart in twain. "You know I will not join you."

The Greek sighed. "Then you too must die." Hearing the words brought no sadness to Godfrey's heart, only wrath. He knew he was going to die—knew he could not defeat all four Greeks—but his fighting instinct was on the rise, and now Godfrey only wanted to take Andronicus down with him. He raised his sword and slipped into a fighting stance.

"Believe me," said the Greek in that comforting, earnest voice of his, as Basil and Langosse and Murzuphlus began to advance, "I am very sorry for all those who must die tonight. And I am especially sorry about you, Godfrey—I wish that it had been another Templar on guard this night. But you are standing between me and the stairway that I must climb."

Then Godfrey realized what Andronicus had come for. In his lovesick rage, the Greek was trying to capture something so valuable that the king would have to exchange Theodora for it. Andronicus did not want the oliphant—he wanted to kidnap Baldwin.

And that made everything change for Godfrey. A desperate stand, a noble death fighting intruders, were no longer options. Biting down his anger, Godfrey suppressed the urge to charge, to hack and slash and kill—to die with his sword in Andronicus's gut. It would be a satisfying way to die. He wanted to go down swinging, sticking his sword into a villain's innards. But if he did it, Baldwin would be unguarded. If Baldwin was in danger, there could be no heroic failure: Godfrey must succeed.

O Lord, he prayed, *make haste to help me.*

Even as he finished the plea, Godfrey knew what he must do. Still holding his sword in his right hand, he reached down with his left, and drew out from his belt the oliphant which Andronicus had given him so long ago. He lowered his sword and raised the oliphant to his lips, backing up towards the stairs.

"The guards cannot hear our shouts," he said defiantly. "But they will hear *this.*"

Andronicus stiffened. Basil, Murzuphlus and Langosse prepared to rush Godfrey, but Godfrey cried out confidently, "Halt where you are. If you take another step, the sound of this horn will be louder than Roland's last blast of the oliphant. *Halt where you are, I say!*"

And they halted.

It was Andronicus who spoke at last. "Godfrey," he said softly, "if you blow the horn, we will kill you, and we will get to the prince before the guards come."

"Perhaps," said Godfrey. "Or perhaps I will stand on the stairway so that you come at me one at a time. And then perhaps I will hold you off until the guards come, and then you would all die, while I would live and the prince would be safe."

And none of them could give any response to that.

Godfrey smiled, possessed by a confidence he had never felt before. "Enough speech. I am giving you this one chance: leave now. I will give you ten minutes to escape before I blow the horn and summon the guards. I don't want to risk the prince's life if I can help it, so I give you this chance to flee."

Godfrey and Andronicus's gazes locked, and for a moment, Godfrey saw a flicker of doubt in those sparkling blue eyes.

But when Andronicus spoke, the doubt vanished, and only a quiet, diabolical certainty remained.

"And what will happen after that?" he asked. "What will you do, Godfrey? You will go on with your monkish life, never knowing passion, never knowing happiness. I can see the misery in your eyes, Godfrey. Don't try to hide it. Don't try to lie. It is an empty life you lead."

"That's my own affair," said Godfrey sharply, though he felt a pang of despair as he said it; Andronicus was nearer the mark now. "Choose quickly, or I'll blow the horn."

"Ah, but Godfrey," said Andronicus in a tone that was almost compassionate. "I think I can help you after all. I misjudged you just now when I asked you to join us. You are not the sort who would enjoy our adventures, and you would undoubtedly be more miserable than you are now. You don't want to be a scoundrel—you want to be a knight. You want to be a hero."

"But," continued Andronicus, "you are frustrated, for none of your comrades thinks of you as a hero. And so I can help you. I can give you a noble death."

Andronicus raised a pacifying hand as he took a step forward. "Put down the horn, Godfrey. Put down the horn, take up the sword, and fight us. Fight bravely—make a last stand worth remembering. You will die heroically—a death every knight dreams of. Maybe you will even kill some of us. And when you are dead men will speak of you with reverence—they will tell of the unexpected valor that you showed in your last moments."

The Greek paused a moment, letting the words sink in.

And this time, Godfrey was tempted.

For this was exactly what he did wish for—to be a hero, even at the cost of death. He felt so tired, so wretched, so miserable; it would feel so free, so liberating, to throw it all away in one last noble battle. Slowly, he began to lower the horn.

Andronicus saw that his words had an effect. "Surely," he said soothingly, "your God will not condemn such an action. You believe that He is gentle and kind. How could he send you to Hell for laying down your life like that? No, you will die valiantly, and then...then I am sure you will hear the words, 'Well done, my good and faithful servant. Enter into the—'"

"NO!" shouted Godfrey, and with a violent motion, he raised the horn again to his lips. "NO! I will not abandon Baldwin. I will not betray God. I am going to blow this horn!"

Andronicus stared at him pityingly. "Do you really believe, Godfrey, that your Christ would send you to Hell for dying like that? How could anyone reasonably think—"

"Reason has nothing to do with it," said Godfrey, his voice shaking. "I know not where my soul would go, *but I know this*: in the end it is love, and not reason, that is the measure of all things. Your talk of love and devotion is nothing. You can not know those things until you are ready to suffer for the ones you love."

And as he spoke those words, a strange, wild joy filled him—a joy that surpassed all happiness.

O God, he prayed, *I want to come to you, but only by the path You choose. Let the Greek come, and I will fight him. I will fight them all!*

For once in his life, Andronicus Comnenus was at a loss for words. He stared back at Godfrey, and Godfrey saw the doubt and confusion in the Greek's eyes.

Then Godfrey de Montferrat stepped back into the stairway, put the horn to his lips, and blew.

HAROOOOOOOOOOOOOOOOOOOOOOOOOOOOOOOOOOO!

The blast of the oliphant echoed about the walls of the antechamber, echoed down the stairways, echoed throughout the palace. Far behind him in the bedchamber, Godfrey heard the startled prince come awake.

Basil, Murzuphlus and Langosse lunged for the stairs. Godfrey stood squarely in the narrow corridor. There was no chance to clip the oliphant to his belt again, so he dropped it to the floor and gripped his sword in both hands. The horn clattered down the stairs even as the Greeks climbed them. On the last step, it made a sickening sound as the precious ivory cracked.

Murzuphlus was first up the stairs, a shortsword in one hand and a dirk in the other. He struck, hard and fast, distracting Godfrey with the sword and stabbing with the dirk. But Godfrey parried the sword and spun away from the dirk, kicking Murzuphlus down the stairs as he did. Murzuphlus fell, dropping his dirk and tripping up Basil as he slid to the bottom of the stairwell.

Then there came a sound to warm Godfrey's heart—answering horns. The alarums were being sounded throughout the hallways, and the palace was coming awake. Soon guards would be coming this way to see that the prince was safe.

Langosse sprang over his fallen friend and ran up the stone steps. Godfrey crouched into a fighting stance, sword upraised. With a ring of steel their blades met, and they began to fight—no longer sparring as they had in Antioch, but seeking in deadly earnest to kill each other.

Godfrey pressed the attack, plying all his ferocity, all his skill, and all his experience. Langosse fought back, and for a minute or two they clashed on the stairs. But that night Godfrey was filled with a sureness and grace that Langosse could not contest. The Greek began to retreat down the stairs, inch by inch, step by step...until without warning Langosse backed up into the antechamber, and Basil's axe came swinging down on Godfrey's head.

Dodging the blow, Godfrey stumbled on the step and fell painfully. Basil struck again before he could rise, and though Godfrey parried, this blow knocked the sword from his hand. As Basil raised the axe to strike again, Godfrey grabbed the dirk Murzuphlus had dropped. He rolled to the side as the axe came down and stabbed upward, driving the dirk hard into Basil's underarm.

The Varangian gave a muffled cry of pain and dropped his axe. Godfrey seized his sword and scrambled to his feet, advancing as Basil stumbled back into the antechamber.

And Godfrey found himself facing Andronicus Comnenus.

A gleam of moonlight glinted off the bright Greek blade in Andronicus's hand, and his blue eyes sparkled enigmatically. Godfrey did not advance—one step further would carry him out of the stairwell, where all four of them could attack him.

The Greek took a step forward, but Godfrey did not move, did not hesitate. For a moment their gazes locked. Godfrey remembered the flicker of doubt he had seen in Andronicus's face earlier, and was seized with the desire to say *something*. He could again feel pity for the Greek: in a flash he remembered the way Andronicus had looked at the crucifix that morning, and he was able to feel sorrow for the tortured soul that stood before him.

"Andronicus," he said, not knowing what else to say. "You were my friend, once. I will never forget that."

Andronicus raised his sword.

Then there came another horn from within, closer now, and with it the sound of feet hurrying towards them. The guards were on the way.

Something suddenly smoothed itself out on Andronicus's face. He lowered his sword and straightened.

"The drama will continue a little longer, Knight of the Impossible Ideal." Andronicus nodded to Langosse, Basil, and Murzuphlus as he sheathed his sword. "Put up your weapons. We're leaving."

Godfrey's face did not change, but relief flooded into his heart.

Then Andronicus shot Godfrey a look of pure malice. "You are not my friend," he said. "Nor were you ever."

Summoning all the power his will could command, Godfrey kept his face unmoving. He did not reply, but only stared back. The Greek's three servants had gathered about him, Basil biting back his pain and clasping the arm from which the knife still protruded. Andronicus turned to go. He called over his shoulder as he did,

"This drama has not ended, Godfrey de Montferrat. I am the hero of it, and you are only a despicable supporting character, a thorn in my side. I will be glad to be done with you."

Andronicus vanished through the doorway, followed by Langosse and Basil. Murzuphlus paused a moment in the doorway. Godfrey's fists clenched as his gaze met the Byzantine's dark eyes. He was letting a murderer walk away, and there was nothing he could do about it.

"One day," snarled Murzuphlus, "I'm going to kill you, Latin. I'm going to take pleasure in killing you."

Godfrey gave him no answer, and Murzuphlus too vanished down the passageway.

For a moment Godfrey stood there in the silent room, alone with the thoughts of his heart.

"Godfrey?" came a cry from the top of the stairs, and Godfrey realized that Baldwin must have been awake since he blew the oliphant, must have heard and perhaps seen the battle.

"My lord," Godfrey called back. "Do not leave your room—I will come there in a moment."

Godfrey turned and hurried over to Tristan. He knelt beside the Knight of the Swan and felt for a pulse. To his relief, it was there. Tristan de Monglane was alive but unconscious.

Then Godfrey made his way over to the servant girl. The blood stain had spread both on the floor and on her dress. She was, as Tristan had said, simply an innocent maid. And now she had been stabbed through the heart because Godfrey had warned an old friend in peril. Godfrey knew her state already from her still, glassy eyes, but he felt for a pulse anyway.

Godfrey did not weep or shout or rail. He closed the girl's eyelids, unable to think, unable to hope. Something was dead inside him. But Godfrey could pray, and he did.

"*Requiem aeternam dona eae, Domine*," he murmured. "*Et lux perpetua luceat eae...*"

Chapter 39

The Changing of the Guard

Two Weeks Later

Godfrey stood behind the prince's chair as Baldwin sat up, listening intently to a conversation which he only partly understood.

"Do not trust this *Salah ad-Din*, Your Grace," said Gilbert D'Aissailly, Master of the Hospital. "Have you not learned that you cannot trust any heathen?"

"Your Grace," said Barisan d'Ibelin, "you can trust him more than his master, Nur ad-Din. We have heard that there is friction between them. If we could make alliance with him against—"

"No," said Amalric. "This Saladin is a traitor and a murderer. He has come to power through the murder of our ally. He is no friend of ours."

"My lord," said Barisan, "the Egyptian vizier was not our ally any more when he died. This Saladin must needs be a friend of ours. He is the master of Egypt now. The caliph is his puppet. You know better than any man how important Egypt is."

"And I know better than any man the cost of trying to take it. What would you have me do? Invade Egypt yet again?"

"*No*," said Barisan. "I would have you ally with Saladin."

"Do not discard the idea of invasion so easily, Your Grace," said D'Aissailly. "Egypt will be at its weakest—"

"No," said Amalric. "It will be at its strongest. Now I want silence from all of you. I have to think. Where have all my sensible councilors gone? Even Blanchefort would be welcome now. He has a good head on his shoulders."

"Blanchefort," said D'Aissailly icily, "is dying."

"God's beard, I know that already," said Amalric. "And who's to replace him? De Milly? Sant'Amand? God's bones, D'Aissailly, I'd rather have *you* than either of them."

D'Aissailly glared hatefully at the king. "Your Grace honors me."

Amalric ignored him. "*All* of my best councilors are gone. Blanchefort dying, and Joscelin rotting in some Saracen prison. Even that Hawk of Antioch might have been of use, but he's been taken by the sandpigs as well. And the emperor has been cold towards us ever since we let that cousin of his escape."

Godfrey winced. His conscience still plagued him because of his breach of trust, and all the more so because the servant girl might still be alive if he had let Andronicus die.

What should I have done? O Jesus, what should I have done? I did not will any of the evil that happened, did I?

Amalric pounded his fist down on the table angrily. "Council dismissed," he growled. The barons began to scatter. Only one man remained besides Godfrey and Baldwin. Tristan de Monglane stood at the foot of the table, waiting patiently, his eyes downcast.

The king looked up and groaned when he saw him.

"Not you again, boy. I have told you already."

Tristan went down on one knee.

"Your Grace, I have come to ask a boon of you."

"God's blood, you have asked it before, now get out."

"Your Grace," Tristan continued unperturbed. "I beg of you leave to raise a party to rescue Joscelin de Courtenay. I will take only free knights who can pay their own way—it will not cost you one bezant."

"We are at peace with Nur ad-Din, and I'm not going to let you go start a bloody war."

"Your Grace, you can disavow any actions on my part. Tell them I went against your will."

Amalric snorted. "Nur ad-Din won't believe it, and rightly so. You want it done against my will? Try it. I will hunt you down, boy, and throw you into prison."

"Your Grace," said Tristan, looking up at last, "how can you let Joscelin de Courtenay perish a captive? His father died in prison. I would know—my father went with Joscelin the Second on that last fatal attempt. My father died fighting beside Joscelin's father. Do not let the same as happened to the father happen to his son."

Amalric stood. "Do not speak to me of that, *boy*. Joscelin was a dearer friend than any other I have had. I remember too, Knight of the Swan. I still love Joscelin de Courtenay dearer than any other living man beside my son. He is like a brother to me, but I will not destroy the kingdom for his sake."

Tristan stood too, now. "He is like a brother to you, Your Grace? Well then, he has been like a father to me. You are a king, you have your duties to your kingdom. I have only a son's duty to his father. I bid you fare well, king of Jerusalem."

Then Tristan turned on his heel and stalked out of the room.

A few hours later, Robert de Ais relieved Godfrey at his post. Godfrey returned wearily to the Temple, and was greeted with the news that Bertrand de Blanchefort was dead.

✟　✟　✟

All the knights of the Temple stood by as they said the prayers for the dead. Godfrey grieved in his heart for the steadfast old grand master, but he grieved still more for the friends that he had lost.

As they shoveled the hardened dirt over the master's cold body, Godfrey remembered the words of the hymn that Blanchefort had so loved.

I will lift up my eyes to the hills...

After Blanchefort was buried, they held the election for a new master.

It soon became clear that the only two candidates that stood a chance were Phillip de Milly and Odo de Sant'Amand. The Templars stood in formation and cast their votes one by one while Gilbert Erail the seneschal kept count.

Arnold de Torroga cast his vote for Odo, while Jacques cast his for Phillip. Godfrey watched as the votes were cast, trying to guess at who was ahead.

It was not hard. Phillip had a good two thirds of the Templars in his hand, some convinced through words, others convinced by gold.

Godfrey cast his vote for Odo, simply because Odo had probably used less bribery. He didn't believe for a moment it would make a difference, and it didn't. Phillip de Milly was elected master of the Temple.

As his first act as master, Phillip called an election for the marshal of the Temple, since the post was now vacant. He put forward his candidate, Jacques de Maille, and asked if there were any other who wished to contest the position.

For a long moment there was silence. Godfrey looked around and nodded, unsure whether to be pleased or dismayed. Phillip had bribed them well—none would contest Jacques today.

Just as Phillip was about to call a vote, someone in the back raised his voice.

"I wish to contest your candidate, Master de Milly."

Every head in the Temple Court turned to stare as Gerard de Ridford stepped forward. Phillip's mouth moved wordlessly, while Jacques turned pale.

At last the new master found his voice and called for a vote. There was no chance for Jacques. Even Phillip's gold was not enough to overcome De Ridford's overwhelming popularity. Godfrey cast his vote for Jacques, as he had promised, but less than a quarter of the Templars sided with him.

De Ridford, the new marshal of the Temple, stepped up to stand beside De Milly, while Odo, as seneschal, stood on his other side. Odo was grinning outrageously. Gerard de Ridford had voted for him, and De Ridford was Odo's man through and through. Phillip had won the election, but his moment of triumph had been spoiled.

When it was over, Godfrey caught up to Jacques and tried to speak to him. Jacques ignored him and went to speak to the new master of the Temple.

With Robert de Ais guarding Baldwin, and Phillip, Odo, and Gerard too busy consolidating their power, Godfrey had a few hours of freedom. He strode off down the street, his heart twisting in anguish.

✠ ✠ ✠

In a darkened room, Amalric stared glumly at a tapestry which showed the dying Roland sounding his ivory oliphant. Behind lay a table full of letters and dispatches, accounts of taxes and vassal's pledges, untouched and ignored. A servant had just arrived from the Temple, informing him of Bertrand de Blanchefort's death.

Old Blanchefort, gone for good. I wouldn't have thought it possible. The man was too alive, to vigorous. He gave me no end of grief, but at least the man knew how to fight, knew how to lead. This new master does not, and Odo is little better.

Amalric's thought turned to his little son.

He must learn how to fight and how to lead, for none of us old men can do it any more.

Somewhere outside, a horn blew. Out on the walls of Jerusalem the sentries were filing out, while new men came to replace them. It was the time of the changing of the guard.

I have failed, thought Amalric. *I have lost two wars for the kingdom, two wars which I never should have begun. I lost the woman I loved, and I lost the best friend I ever had.*

A phrase that had been floating around in Amalric's memory came suddenly to mind. It was something Joscelin had said, years ago, as they sat by a campfire in Egypt speaking quietly.

"Baldwin is the king who should have been." Amalric murmured the words to himself. "Baldwin is the king who should have been." When Joscelin had said it, he was speaking of Amalric's brother, Baldwin III. "But," said Amalric to himself, "there is another Baldwin now."

Amalric went slowly back to the table. "My son," he said quietly. "Do not fail me. Do not fail Jerusalem."

✣ ✣ ✣

Sir Humphrey de Vinsauf was sitting on a stool, sharpening his axeblade, when Tristan de Monglane entered the weapon shed. Humphrey did not look up at first. Tristan watched him a minute or two, his eyes following the grating movement of the whetstone.

At last Tristan spoke the knight's name. Slowly Humphrey set down the axe and looked up. Tristan was accoutered in a shining coat of mail, topped by his self-styled surcoat—the silver swan on the blue field. Couched under his arm was a helmet.

Humphrey raised his eyes to Tristan's face.

"Sir Humprey," repeated Tristan, "I am sorry to hear that you have been discharged from Raymond of Tripoli's service."

"Aye," said Humphrey, frowning up at him. "I am sorry too. Many of us have been cast out."

"What do you plan to do now?" asked Tristan.

Humphrey shrugged. "I don't know. Tripoli has no need for us any more, and neither do the other lords. Half of us will end up as highwaymen, half go back to France or Italy, and another half will starve because they're too proud to do common work. I'm not sure which half I'm going to choose; they all look equally appealing."

"I have need of you," said Tristan. "I have need of brave men who have fought in battle before."

"And what need have you for such men?" asked Humphrey.

"I am going on an adventure," said Tristan. "I will start by sacking the citadel at Homs, where the sultan has stored much of his treasure. And that is only the start of it. With the money and supplies I gain there, I will start a new expedition. I will go north and rout that black devil Ridhwan out of his hole. Then, when he can no longer threaten our rear, I march east, towards Aleppo and Mosul, to rescue Joscelin de Courtenay from the Saracen dungeons."

"You are an ambitious man, Knight of the Swan," said Humphrey.

"More ambitious than you may guess," said Tristan. "The king has forbidden such a venture. Any who come with me will be outlaws, hunted by Muslim sultan and Christian king. And like as not we'll have the Greek emperor and the Turkish emirs after us before long. I must travel in haste, and cannot take more than threescore with me, even if I find threescore desperate enough to make this journey. It is a mad venture. Will you come with me?"

Humphrey rose, hefting his axe lightly. He ran his finger along the blade, feeling the sharp edge.

"Aye," he said. "I'll come with you. The world has turned miserably sane of late—I want some madness. Where you lead, Knight of the Swan, I will follow." He rose, slowly, hefting his axe. "But tell me, Knight of the Swan: do you ever plan to return?"

"I will never come back," said Tristan gravely, "while that fat fool Amalric sits on the throne. But the day that Prince Baldwin becomes king, I will return and pledge my troth to him. Lord Joscelin believed in the boy, so I believe in him also." Tristan turned. "Gather your gear," he said. "There is much work to be done, and little time to do it in."

✠ ✠ ✠

The inside of the church was quiet and dark, lit only by a few candles. Far up at the head of the church, a priest moved past the altar bearing the Sacrament. Otherwise, the church seemed empty. Godfrey de Montferrat knelt at the back and poured out all his troubles and sorrows to the Host, seeking for some measure of comfort. Andronicus had spoken truly: Godfrey was wretched and miserable. *Perhaps,* he thought, *God has called me to this sacrifice. I will not be the hero I longed to be. But Baldwin may be that hero. If I can only help him on his way, God will have given me more than enough.* When Godfrey looked up again, William of Tyre was sitting next to him. Surprise stopped Godfrey's tongue, but he gave a bewildered look.

William smiled. "Even an archbishop needs to pray sometimes, Godfrey. It has been a long time since I have seen you, save at Baldwin's lessons."

William was tutoring the prince, and Godfrey saw him often enough while he was guarding him, but he rarely was able to speak during that time, for Amalric often sat in on his son's lessons.

Godfrey's eyes went to the crucifix above the altar. He had been thinking of Adelaise and of Conrad, of Jacques and of Baldwin, even as he prayed. *It should not be like that.* He sank back into the pew, feeling forlorn beyond all measure. "Your Excellency," he said, "you are a priest, as well as an archbishop. Shrive me."

Godfrey knelt down right before him to confess. He spread his hand before his face to cover it.

"Father," he murmured, "I have sinned often since I was last shriven. I have lingered on lustful thoughts too many times to count, and I have taken God's holy name in vain. I have lied and been deliberately fractious. Also, I betrayed a sacred trust, justifying it because I was trying to save a friend. But the sin that presses me most now, father, is one that is a state rather than an action. I have been living in a state of pride, Father, for many years."

William's face did not change expression.

"And how have you been proud, my son?"

Godfrey closed his eyes. "I have demanded something of God that I had no right to ask, and should have known I would never attain. I wanted to be a hero, wanted to be a great man—one of God's heroes—when I am only a selfish, proud, weak, sinful little man. Like Simon Magus, I wanted to buy spiritual power for myself, and I could not even offer the gold that he did."

William smiled a little. "It is true, my son," he said. "That just as he who would keep his life will lose it, and he who loses his life for Christ's sake will keep it, so you will only become a hero by ceasing to demand it of God, and accepting His will. You must never seek after fame, but desire only to be unknown. However, I ask you, Godfrey de Montferrat: was your desire really prideful at its core? The mere desire to be heroic, if detached from the hunger for fame and glory—from the desire to be recognized as a hero—is not a sin. Every Christian must desire to do great things for Christ. So I ask you, Godfrey de Montferrat, was your desire then pride, or is your desire now despair? Do not forget that despair is another form of pride, more subtle by far. It was despair that dragged Judas Iscariot down to his perdition. Do not let it drag you down too."

Godfrey said nothing. He looked up slightly over his hand to stare at William.

"Of your other sins," said William, "of your lust and your cursing and your breach of faith, *ego te absolvo, in nomine Patris, et Filii, et Spiritui Sancti.* But as for pride, I want you to answer me: have you truly committed the sin of pride?"

Godfrey continued to stare up at him, uncertainty on his face. At last he answered.

"No Father, I have not—not in wishing to be a hero. But I have been proud in my despair, and of that, now, I repent."

William nodded, his smile broadening. "Of that sin as well as the others I absolve you. For your penance, Godfrey de Montferrat, I want you to fast for these next thirty days." Godfrey started to rise. "And there is one more thing I am giving you as a penance. For the rest of your life, you must never give up your desire to be heroic, to do great deeds for God. *Never,* Knight of the Temple. Now go. Go forth and be a saint." William said the blessing. Godfrey bowed before the Sacred Host, and walked out into the bright sunlight.

Chapter 40

Homo Factus Est

AD 1174

Godfrey paused on the walls of Jerusalem as he made his way back to the Temple. He was relieved to find that he could look on the sunset and smile.

Phillip de Milly had abdicated as grand master after only two years and Odo de Sant'Amand had succeeded him. Somewhere in the years since Odo's election as master, Godfrey had found a balance of sorts. Life was bearable again. It was hard, of course, but he had never imagined being a Templar would be any thing else.

The sinking sun set the sky afire with oranges and purples, and Godfrey was content just to look at them for a few moments.

Godfrey was thirty years of age now, though he still thought of himself as a boy barely come into manhood. Maturity did not seem to touch him as the years went on. In his heart, Godfrey was still chasing after the stories of the paladins and heroes, however vehemently he denied it. He had found balance in the realization that he would never become a famed and admired hero but he found comfort in the knowledge that the prince, whom he continued to guard and unofficially to teach, could and would become a hero.

He felt truly content there, standing upright, looking at the sky, with his hands folded behind his back. His beard and hair were black and slightly curly, his darkish skin shone, and his white robe was clean, outlined by the sunset. Godfrey looked truly resplendent, though he would never have believed it had he been told.

There it was that Baldwin found him.

Godfrey started suddenly when he heard the boyish voice behind him, choked with a frantic desperation.

"Sir Godfrey?"

Godfrey turned swiftly, looking in surprise at the boy who stood before him.

"Baldwin? What are you doing? Where is your guard? Where is Jacques?"

Baldwin the prince was thirteen years of age now. He too had not changed significantly since he was a boy of eight. He had matured, but his dreams had stayed the same. He had come to love Godfrey, almost as a second father, but he had never forgotten his Uncle Joscelin, and he loved his own father more than either. The Perfect Prince, he was called, and most of those who called him so meant it in earnest, not in jest or in scorn.

"Godfrey," said Baldwin, and Godfrey could hear tears behind his voice. Then Baldwin started to sink down to the stones. Godfrey caught him quickly, and the tears burst forth.

"Sir Godfrey," he cried, "I...sent Jacques away...I...because..."

"Easy," said Godfrey, bewildered. Baldwin had considered himself too manly to cry since he was age nine. Godfrey began to worry in earnest, though he kept it out of his voice.

"Forget about Jacques," he said. "What has happened?"

"I...I'm...dying," whispered Baldwin.

Godfrey stopped and held the prince out at arm's length. "You don't look it," he said, feeling a tinge of relief. Whatever it was, it couldn't be that serious.

"No," said Baldwin, the tears almost breaking forth again. "I'm *dying*, Godfrey!" He began talking very quickly, barely intelligible. "We were playing in the garden, Hugh and Roger and I. We were wrestling, trying to throw down each other. I was...I was winning. I was doing so well. I could beat the both of them at once...I was so happy...and then Archbishop William called me in. He showed me my right arm, and I saw it had gotten torn badly—we were wrestling on rough ground. But I hadn't...hadn't even felt it."

Then Godfrey began to grow worried.

"The archbishop took me inside, and he...he...he tested me several times, and he said...he said I had..."

Baldwin burst into tears again, and Godfrey took him in his arms, comforting him as best he could.

Suddenly Baldwin broke free. "No!" he shouted violently. "No! I'm a leper, Godfrey! A leper! You cannot touch me, or you'll become a leper too. No!"

Godfrey caught him by the arm as he tried to run, and this time he held fast.

"Hold still, my Lord," he said. *"Hold still!* The first thing a Templar learns is that he is expendable. How did you get here? Did the archbishop and Jacques simply let you run loose through the streets of Jerusalem?"

Baldwin looked up at him with frightened, angry eyes. At last he stopped struggling and looked at the ground.

"No...I escaped."

Godfrey smiled a little, despite the horror of it all. "You escaped them all? William, Jacques, the guards...?"

Baldwin nodded sullenly.

It was then that the full tragedy sunk in, and Godfrey understood. At the moment, he could be proud of the prince who could escape from a palace full of guards, but the leprosy would take that away from him in time. And it was hard enough for Godfrey to be celibate when he had chosen to be. Baldwin, though, would have it thrust upon him, for he could not marry now.

Grimly he asked the boy, "Has your father been told?"

Baldwin shook his head. "He is gone...to Jaffa. He will be back on the morrow..."

Godfrey's head was spinning, but he knew that he had to act quickly. "Come with me, Baldwin."

He stood up, letting go of the prince, but ready to grab him again if he tried to run. Then he began to walk down the stairs. Slowly and unsteadily, Baldwin followed.

✠ ✠ ✠

It was with relief that the guards let them back into the palace. Miles of Plancy, the seneschal and steward, had been fuming and threatening them with what would happen if the prince were not found.

Godfrey and a handful of guards guided Baldwin to his chambers, where William of Tyre and Miles of Plancy were waiting. The steward had brought a handful of leeches to examine the boy, but they all knew that there was little the doctors could do about leprosy.

While the doctors began examining the frightened boy, Godfrey rounded on William.

"Where is Jacques?" he asked fiercely. "He should be here; it was his shift to guard."

William sank down tiredly into a chair. "I don't know, Godfrey. He disappeared somewhere in the chaos..."

The archbishop looked haggard, and Godfrey repented of his irrational impatience. He sank down next to William and looked on at the pitiful figure of the golden-haired prince being plied at by the doctors.

"What does it mean, William? Leprosy...I have always feared it, but I don't know much about it. What will happen to him?"

William sighed, and spoke very quietly so that a stray word would not reach Baldwin's ears.

"He has not long to live. If he is unlucky he will live another ten years; if he is lucky he will die before then."

Godfrey looked at him, alarmed. William continued.

"The sickness will take his sense of feeling first. Already he cannot feel heat or cold or pain, except when any one of those is exerted with extreme force. As the disease rots his skin he will soon feel nothing at all. His sight will begin to dim, until he can see only blackness with his waking eyes. Then his limbs will rot away so that he can barely move. Last of all, it will take his hearing, so that he will be plunged into a black void, unable to see, hear, or feel. Eventually it will take his life."

Godfrey shuddered.

One by one the leeches departed, shaking their heads or casting down their eyes. Miles of Plancy left, trying to hide the fear in his eyes. Only Godfrey and William remained.

Baldwin sat on the bed, facing them.

"My lord," said William hesitantly. "You should...should get some sleep."

Baldwin stared at him a moment, then he nodded. "I will. If I can."

To Godfrey's surprise, the prince's voice was calm. No longer did Baldwin waver, no longer did he sound on the brink of tears.

"My lord," he said, "are you...have you..." Godfrey trailed off, not knowing how to ask the question.

Baldwin glanced back and forth between the two of them, and then, taking a deep breath, asked his own question.

"Am I...dying...then?"

Godfrey's mouth moved wordlessly; he knew not what to say. William did, though.

"Yes, my lord."

Baldwin gulped, started to say something, then stopped. Finally he nodded.

"How long?"

William hesitated. "Ten years at most... five at the least."

Baldwin nodded again. For a moment he looked helpless and hopeless—for a moment he looked exactly what he was: a dying child.

Then his face changed, and set into a grim determination.

"Then," he said, "I will have to be a great warrior in the time that is left me."

Godfrey stared. "My lord...Baldwin?"

Baldwin tried to smile but abandoned the attempt. "Archbishop, you have told my father often that this life is but a vale of tears, and at the end, the curtain will draw back, and we will enter into Life Eternal."

"I have," said William weakly. "But that does not mean..." William too trailed off, not knowing any more than Godfrey what to say.

Baldwin tried again, and this time succeeded in smiling. "Then I need fear nothing."

One last time, Baldwin's face wavered, and Godfrey thought he might cry again, but he did not. Instead the prince of Jerusalem lay down on his bed to go to sleep.

As easily as that, thought Godfrey, *He has found his comfort. For the moment, at least. But I shall not be satisfied so easily...*

Godfrey could feel anger and frustration welling up in him. For years he had loved this boy, devoted himself to training him, to shaping him into a hero. Now Baldwin was dying, rotting away piece by piece. Godfrey thought of William's description of what was to come, and he grew even angrier.

Godfrey stood up abruptly and walked out of the room. William, wrapped in his own thoughts, did not try to stop him.

✠ ✠ ✠

The chapel of the Temple was lit by a small candle that burned through the night. Its flickering light could illuminate only a few feet of space, just enough to show the tabernacle.

The door flew open as Godfrey stormed in. No longer did he wear his white robes; now he was in black for mourning.

"Why?" he shouted at the tabernacle. His eyes were red, with tears at the edges. His face looked tired and forlorn, but angry.

"*Why,* damn it?" Godfrey swore in the presence of that which he held most sacred, but such was his anger that he did not care. "You have taken everything from me when I gave it to You. Why take everything from him without even letting him choose? You Who said that everything created was good, why do You destroy it and corrupt it, why do You allow it to rot? He has done nothing to deserve this! What has he ever done, save be born into a race tainted by sin? Was it he who ate the fruit of the Tree? *Why?*" Godfrey was shouting.

"Godfrey?" came a hoarse, quiet voice from the back of the chapel.

Godfrey turned angrily to look. If it was the marshal, or one of the officers, he was ready to argue, ready to fight.

It was Jacques.

He was sitting huddled in the back of the chapel, his face disfigured as though he too had been weeping.

"Godfrey," whispered Jacques hoarsely, "I…I ran."

"What the hell are you talking about?"

"I ran. Ran away. From the prince."

Godfrey stared blankly.

"I was supposed to guard him, Godfrey, guard him with my life! Yet when I learned that he was rotting, I was scared. I ran."

"It doesn't matter," said Godfrey. "None of it matters. Not when He Who Created Us strikes children with such a malady." Godfrey had glanced up at the tabernacle as he spoke.

"Godfrey," murmured Jacques, "I have fought in battles and never felt fear. But I was scared today. I was terrified of the leprosy. It wasn't the death I was afraid of…it was the suffering."

"Yes," said Godfrey. "The suffering. If God had struck him dead, then there might be peace for him. Instead he will rot for years." Godfrey's voice rose up to a fevered pitch. "And as he rots, God will watch serenely from above, and I think that He will laugh as He watches."

Godfrey turned back to the tabernacle. "*Why?* You save some, and leave others to burn. Where is Your justice? Where is Your vaunted mercy?"

Then Godfrey's eyes fell on a little cloth the chaplain had left on the altar. It was folded up, but there were three words on it, barely illuminated by the flickers of the candle.

Homo factus est.

Godfrey raised his eyes to look up at the tabernacle, and then at the crucifix above it. His eyes met with those of they suffering, dying man on the cross, and those three words, the words from the Creed, echoed in his mind.

Homo factus est.

He was made man.

Godfrey turned back to face Jacques. The words impressed themselves in to his head. *Homo factus est.* Not a logical solution, but it was an answer, however strange or insufficient it seemed at a time like this.

The candle flickered on into the night as the two friends thought and struggled and groped for an answer. But Godfrey did not feel overwhelmed any more. He was still angry, still confused, but it seemed to have shrunk down to human proportions. No longer was he raging against the cosmos and against the Eternal, now he was only frustrated and tired.

Godfrey sat down next to Jacques, and for the first time that night, he was able to yawn and to acknowledge that he was tired.

"Jacques," he said, "I too am a coward. I am honored to be in such good company."

Then he sat back, lost in the vastness of the Tabernacle.

Homo factus est. He was made man.

Explicit Liber Primus Coronae Mundi

Here ends *Knight of the Temple*, the Tale of Godfrey de Montferrat—the first book of the trilogy, *Crown of the World*. The story continues in the second book—the Tale of Malik al-Harawi, and also of the Lady Maryam, the soldier Yusef ibn-Ayyub, the assassin Farooq al-Salih, and many others.

If you enjoyed this book, you might also be interested in these other high-quality works from Arx Publishing...

Angels in Iron by Nicholas C. Prata
"The novel's principal strength is its attention to historical detail and the unrelenting realism with which the battle scenes—and there are many—are described....In addition to being an exciting action/adventure yarn and quite a page-turner, *Angels in Iron* is valuable as a miniature history lesson....This is a book that belongs on the bookshelf of every Catholic man, should be read by every Catholic boy (11 or older, I would say), and stocked by every Catholic school library."

—Latin Mass Magazine

Belisarius—Book I: The First Shall Be Last by Paolo A. Belzoni
"The book strikes one as a conservative rallying cry to the 'Christian West' today...It presents and argues for, in an understated way, a Christian way of war, to be waged by manly men who value purity and patriotism for the sake of preserving Christian civilization. *Nobiscum Deus*, they cry in battle. So does this book. Not that the book deliberately carries a political message. On its own terms, it is an ambitious tale, filled with action, spectacle, and intrigues of all kinds."

—CatholicFiction.net

Dream of Fire by Nicholas C. Prata
"A powerful epic fantasy that sweeps the reader along with its exciting story line and two fabulous lead characters. Redeeming Kerebos seems almost like converting Hitler....The doubting Antiphon is sort of like Moses feeling he is too inadequate to do the task....The battle scenes that are vividly described and action-packed pale next to the hook that keeps the audience wanting to finish this work in one sitting." Five stars out of five.

—Harriet Klausner, #1 Reviewer on Amazon.com

Niamh and the Hermit by Emily C. A. Snyder
"When I first saw this book, I feared that it might be just another effort to hook on to the Tolkien wagon. It is not. Very far from that. It is wholly original, and all I can say is that it is beautiful, beautiful, beautiful. The author is entirely in control of her narrative, and, drawing on the tradition of ancient Celtic tales, gives us something genuinely new. What we have here is a very noble achievement."

—Thomas Howard, author of *C. S. Lewis: Man of Letters*

The Laviniad: An Epic Poem by Claudio R. Salvucci
"The author successfully writes in the style of the ancient epic in modern English. Lovers of classic tales will really appreciate the poetry and the plot. The poem reads easily and naturally with the flow and flavor of the ancient epics. A complete glossary in the back will help anyone who has not read the *Aeneid* or the *Iliad* to understand the relationship of the characters and the various names of the Greeks, Trojans, and Latins."

—Favorite Resources for Catholic Homeschoolers

For further information on these titles, or to order, visit:
www.arxpub.com

Printed in the United States
218459BV00001B/1/P

9 781889 758923